THE SOCRATIC CONTRACT

D C Russell

Copyright © 2015 D C Russell
All rights reserved.
ISBN-13:9781512378887
ISBN-10:1512378887

"Not life, but good life, is to be chiefly valued."
Socrates (469 – 399 BC)

PROLOGUE

Arlington, Virginia
October, eight years ago

"Careful, Sarah." Melancholy eyes followed her skipping through the fallen maple leaves.

A crisp breeze played with the yellow slicker as she scampered among the turning trees and manicured lawns. "Daddy, look," she squealed as a large white duck on the pond's edge complained vigorously about this little girl intrusion in such a quiet place.

He turned back to his wife's marker and whispered to the etched marble, "She has your smile." His chin bowed to his sweater, a nagging hurt buoyed only by the knowledge her illness could have lasted unmercifully for years. He breathed deeply, the sigh nudging a splinter in his heart.

Looking over his shoulder he found his daughter stalking the wary duck. He knelt, brushing leaves from the marble – the leaves wet with morning dew, the stone damp and cold. The chill climbed his arm and filled his chest. "We talked about this. I just hoped we'd never need it." He looked again at the headstone and managed a weak smile: "Yes, I'll take good care of our little one."

Sarah only knew that "Mommy is sick" and that "she needs to rest." Sarah spent much of that last month watching TV and playing with the kids next door. He insisted on taking care of his wife at home. "We are a family, and I want her to be here, with us, not in a cancer ward."

The oncologists had warned she would become increasingly debilitated, that radiation and chemotherapy would be of little value, that morphine would become a necessity, and that the illness would become more virile and increasingly sap her strength. Yet, in the end, she went quickly.

She had been a powerful presence in the courtroom. Her partnership two years earlier at the prestigious Baker and Jensen law firm had riled a few of the chauvinistic set. But her promotion at the age of 37 was well deserved.

The relationships, expertise and position she had forged made her announcement to the firm that she had a rare stomach cancer all the more tragic. She had turned over her caseload and left the firm to be with her family. He had been there for her announcement, to support her, to hold her hand, to help wipe away her tears.

Earlier on the day she died several of her female colleagues and the managing partner at the firm had briefly stopped by the house to bring flowers and talk a little about cases and clients. She lay in bed. While her young colleagues had given her hugs and stroked her hair, the managing partner, Nathan Jensen, had uncovered her foot and tickled her toes. She managed a laugh. He squeezed her foot and said, "Just want you to know you're one of my favorite people, sweetie. God bless you."

Parked a block away in a nondescript gray van, Erwin, a bespectacled, hunched over little man in his mid fifties, watched Sarah and her dad through high-powered binoculars. His colleague, HB, listened to what little conversation there was using a sensitive unidirectional microphone mounted on the van's roof. HB simultaneously made short work of a cold cheese burrito and a couple of messy soft tacos.

"HB, you spilled all over the console," Erwin barked, now on his PC and looking up briefly from the work he took so seriously.

"Relax, old man, I'll tidy up," returned the marginally competent but fun loving HB. "What're they up to?"

Erwin fretted over HB's lax attitude but tried to keep his emotions under control. "He's standing over the grave, arms folded. The little girl is playing in the leaves. The file says the missus has been gone six months. Our job is to determine his 'state of mind.'" Irritated by the vague nature of his assignment, Erwin muttered, "Cryptic crap." Then he motioned to HB, "I'll enter in the log that he is 'reflective and appropriately subdued in demeanor and that the girl appears to be adjusting well.'"

"Thank you, Sherlock," HB said grinning. "Man, you should lighten up. Not like I get this 'state of mind' surveillance stuff either – not like the guy has done anything wrong. We do like three of these a week? Guess we should just have a little fun with this easy stuff." HB shifted in his seat. "Uh oh."

"What? You didn't. Dammit, HB! You *promised* you wouldn't do that in the van. For chrissake!"

"Hey, man. It's the burrito!" HB laughed until he cried while inhaling with appreciation another virtuoso fogging up of the van. Still slapping his thighs HB roared, "Decent, very decent."

"I can't work with you," Erwin screamed. "You're a pig. You promised! Open the fucking windows. No, don't, he may see us. God *dammit*, HB!"

⇌⇋

"Come on, Sarah. It's time to go. Leave the duck alone. He doesn't want to play."

"Oh, all right," Sarah said, whining just a little. "I like it here. Can we come back again to talk to Mommy and visit Mr. Duck?"

"Sure, honey." Her dad held her hand as they walked back to the car.

Sarah looked up. "It's okay, Daddy," she said holding his hand tightly with both of hers. "Mommy's in heaven now." Her eyes looked for affirmation.

He swept little Sarah up and kissed her cheek.

As they drove away, the gray van stayed behind. The 'state of mind' report was sent via encrypted email to Erwin and HB's boss in Washington, D.C.

CHAPTER ONE

Rockville, Maryland
Offices of the Department of Health and Human Services
Friday, October 9, present day

The reception started at seven. Merritt left the Rockville office at 3:30pm to beat the traffic and have enough time to shower and change into something other than conservative government blues. Maybe even something fabulous. Suits were fine but the expected female government uniform got old – some sort of plain blouse, dark two-piece suit, and low heels. But she refused to wear pantyhose. She had nice legs, one of her several attractive features, and she wasn't about to cover them up with those bulletproof leggings. The Rockville, Maryland actuarial staff of the Department of Health and Human Services had assumed their boss would return to the downtown Washington office and, as usual, work until seven. Not on this Friday. This was her birthday.

No one had said much at work; she did get a handful of cards and lots of emails – but not a big production. Merritt liked it that way.

Her mom had called early in the morning, mostly to wish her happy birthday, but she knew the conversation would soon take its customary turn to either 'the boyfriend dialogue' or 'all work and no play makes for a dull Merritt.' "Now honey, you know if your father were still alive he would want you to be happy and not work so hard." Lana tried to get it right, and certainly had the best of intentions, but had nearly always missed something in the translation from her husband to daughter, at least as far as Merritt was concerned. Nevertheless Merritt was tolerant of the well-intended guidance.

"Oh Mom, I think what Dad felt" ... she was having a tough time staying focused on the conversation ... "was that stress from too many hours at work and not enough outside interests were ..." Merritt sighed and then smiled "... a recipe for meatless lasagna."

Lana took a moment to respond. "I thought you liked my vegetarian lasagna?"

Merritt detected a hint of hurt feelings but needed to go. "Mom, I have a meeting. I'll call you later. And 'yes' I love your lasagna. Love you..."

"Okay, honey. Love you, too, and happy birthday. Bye."

She had been close to her father. His steady, common sense tutelage had guided Merritt, and she strove to please him. While her mom had taken care of little sister Amy, her dad had taken Merritt to ball games, to the club to ride with him on the golf cart, to church, and to his office where he had served as a commissioner, and later as chairman, of the Federal Trade Commission. She had chosen government and public policy as her vocation, following his path.

The drive to Merritt's townhouse in Georgetown took about 20 minutes this time of day. Her place high on the hill overlooking the Potomac River was exquisite. From her river view balcony just east of the Georgetown University campus, she could see the Kennedy Center where the reception would be tonight. When her dad had died two years earlier, her mom gave each daughter half the insurance money from a very large policy. Lana had told Merritt and Amy that she was already well taken care of. Merritt put nearly all her share into buying the 2.7 million dollar townhouse.

As she clicked the opener and drove into the small garage on the lower level she sighed with approval. *What a beautiful place; you don't need vacations when you can come home to a gorgeous home like this.*

Merritt Royce, assistant deputy secretary of the Department of Health and Human Services, didn't take vacations. She put in 70-hour weeks. Just 34 years old, she had earned her spot in the Administration as one of the principal analysts of America's health care policies. She had a staff of 2,700 people and a big league government budget.

She opened the door from the garage to the house and was greeted by professional feline indifference. Meatball was his neutered name. This brown tabby was always at the door as she arrived but immediately feigned disinterest. 'Oh, it's you. How 'bout some food?' She loved him and, of course, he adored her.

She took the stairs to the main level quickly, looking forward to her birthday night out. Meatball was now sliding across the oak plank floor in a sloppy gallop to the kitchen. Up on the granite counter he went, awaiting his 'snacks' – a few treat things to hold him while she flipped through the mail and kicked off those plain shoes. Merritt really liked shoes. Tonight she could wear those stiletto Manolo Blahniks.

"Bills, bills, junk. Shove it, Publishers Clearing House." She shoveled unopened envelopes into the trashcan below the counter. *Why couldn't I get a letter from a fabulous man in Barcelona?* Meatball guessed what was next – three spritzes of water on the tall fern and flowers in the bright modern kitchen, and then off to the second floor master bedroom. He hated that 'spritzer' and beat her up the stairs only to recline in the hallway fatigued at all this earlier than usual activity.

As Merritt took off her clothes she took a few moments to gaze out the glassed rear of the house. The trees along the Potomac exploded with color this time of year – a cacophony of yellows, reds, and oranges basking in the reflected streaming of a setting Washington sun.

The shower refreshed her, and Merritt pampered herself with lots of that expensive body lotion Amy had gotten her for Christmas last year. "Meatball! ... Where are you?" He didn't like shower stuff and remained in the hall, now on his back, feet in the air. "What do you think I should wear, Meaty?" she queried, already knowing she would wear the clingy black Gucci dress. Cut low in back and angled in length from the knee to mid thigh she would show off a little tonight. Oh yes, and the 'Manolos.'

In college Merritt's girlfriends would often try setting her up with dates. But she was picky, very picky. She thought most of the fraternity types were "beer swilling bozos," and not very sophisticated. Besides, there was studying, part-time work, then the masters program and thesis. There wasn't much time, and she told herself she wasn't really looking. *It just wasn't meant to be, not now, not while I'm in school,* she had thought to herself. Now, when her old college friends would call they would hint that the biological clock was ticking. "That clock never started for me," she would say rather bluntly.

Meatball was still in the hallway, offended by the roaring blow drier. He seemed content to stare at the Picasso pencil drawing of a voluptuous nude woman. Merritt had received the elaborately framed piece from her dad on her graduation from Vassar College. She emerged from the bedroom holding the black crepe dress in front of her. "Hey brat, what do you think?" Meatball rolled over but not before Merritt saw his big green eyes set on the drawing. "Meaty, it's a good thing you're fixed."

She returned to her dressing area and tossed the Gucci over a large stuffed armchair. She slipped on black thong panties and went back to the mirror to finish her makeup. Running through her mind was the likely list of attendees at the reception. A veritable 'who's who' in the insurance industry and dozens of Congressmen would be there, not to mention scores of lobbyists and other hangers on. Merritt was comfortable with this upper crust socializing and looked forward to the opportunity to mingle. *Not quite like a birthday party, but a party anyway.*

Happy with the eye shadow, maybe a little more dramatic than she wore on most occasions, she shimmied into the beautiful black dress. Hazel eyes, thick auburn hair and high cheekbones complemented Merritt's great figure, a product of her running three days a week. Her trainer, also known as "the bitch" a day or two after a particularly gruesome workout, made it a personal goal to keep her star pupil fit and buffed. The dress didn't allow for a bra, but then a black crepe knit with ruching on the short side served to mute the overt sexiness of the outfit. She had allowed herself the perfect breasts that come from implants at the age of 23. From A to C cup between grad school and her first job as a GS-5 in government, Merritt had fixed her one physical attribute she didn't like, 'tiny boobs,' or as sister Amy put it, "we graduated from the tiny titty committee."

Next, sitting on the arm of the overstuffed chair, she put on the sandals. *This is fun – barely there, flirty, strappy shoes.*

Merritt looked up and gazed out the back of the house at the trees along the river. *Too bad work is so stiff,* she thought to herself. *I wonder if I make it that way. No, no, it is dull.*

Her dad had warned her of the pitfalls of government service: "Bureaucrats are not rewarded for risk taking; their natural motivation is to say 'no.'" He had also told her that if she chose to work in the federal government, she must constantly fight complacency. She remembered him saying: "At times it will seem impossible, but there is great reward in serving your country, in helping make a difference."

Merritt was determined to make a difference.

She grabbed the star-shaped Judith Leiber evening bag and headed downstairs. The handbags had been a gift from her mom to both Amy and Merritt the Thanksgiving after September 11, 2001. Lana didn't know how to help the hurt felt by the terrorist acts, but that handbag was her way of showing she cared. The bags were covered in red, white and blue crystals in a U.S. flag design and always brought rave reviews.

She stood in the living room in front of the gold-gilded full length mirror, fingers running through her shoulder length hair, viewing with favor the finished work, her girl-next-door beauty fitted with couture to kill. Meatball viewed with approval the new Merritt. "So, what do you think, you little monster?" Keys, bag, long black leather coat and one last look in the hall mirror to check her face and hair. She was off to the National Association of Insurance Companies' annual gala at the Kennedy Center.

CHAPTER TWO

Kennedy Center for the Performing Arts
Washington, D.C.
Friday evening, October 9

The young valet opened the door on the midnight green 750i BMW and grinned as Merritt's long legs led her exit. The next car in line was a white limo, and Merritt looked over her shoulder to see who it was but didn't recognize the three men and two women.

Beautiful people, she thought to herself as she entered the huge doors of brass and glass. *Hmm, men look* so *good in a tux.*

"Ms. Royce?" It was Congressman Joel Suben of Florida, ranking member of the House Subcommittee on Health and a frequent critic of the Administration's hands off oversight of the U.S. insurance industry. "Yes, it *is* you, and a lovely you this evening it is." Merritt turned to greet the short but meticulously dressed Congressman and couldn't help but grin at his speaking style. *An interesting blend of Jerry Stiller and Yoda.*

"Nice to see you Congressman. And this must be Mrs. Suben. Hi, I'm Merritt Royce."

The slender and petite Mrs. Suben, her blue gray hair coiffed to 1980s perfection, took Merritt's hand and held it as the Congressman gushed about Merritt and the job she was doing at the Department. "Yes, helping us she is and with such knowledge and dedication. Testified before the committee last week. Showed us how our seniors in Miami compare to other cities. Excited about it, yes, yes." Merritt liked his energy level and the sincerity in his voice, even if he was a little peculiar.

"Well, Merritt, I'm pleased to meet you. And isn't this a wonderful place for a reception? I just love the bust of President Kennedy here in the grand hallway. And these magnificent high ceilings and the red carpet." Mrs. Suben leaned over to Merritt as they walked to the coat check-in, "You know, Joel takes his work for the older people so seriously."

Merritt's eyes met Mrs. Suben's, "Yes, he's universally respected for his concern for seniors."

"Oh, I'm glad you see that, honey." Mrs. Suben liked hearing about the work of her husband.

"Anything we can do to help keep people happy in their golden years is very important to the Administration ... and to me," said Merritt.

Mrs. Suben touched Merritt's hair as she left with the Congressman to mingle with the other guests. "Such a *nice* girl," she whispered to the Congressman as they walked away. "So smart and pretty. And here by herself? Joel, you should help find her a nice young man."

"Cupid, my dear, I'm not, but a good worker she is. And more helpful certainly than her boss."

Guests were now streaming into the immense ballroom. Sparkling chandeliers glowed from above and balanced the softness of candle light on the elaborately dressed round tables graced by fresh autumn arrangements. The orchestra had begun and mellifluous strains of Gershwin filled the space.

Merritt found her table but walked past it to the bar, in part to avoid sitting down beside two rather dreary looking women. She guessed their husbands had ditched them and were probably bird watching at one of the eight bars.

Apparently, assigned tables and fancy buffet were the guest scheme this year. Last year it had been somewhat chaotic with open seating and no program. The incoming chairman of the National Association of Insurance Companies, she heard, had asked for a more formal approach. Merritt thought these fancy buffets were fine: they facilitated mingling, obviously something the association staff wanted, and people could select the food they preferred and in the quantity they desired. "Geez," she said out loud, "I hope I don't leave government someday to a lobbyist job where the big deal is whether or not to assign tables to guests."

"Excuse me?" The rumbling, deep voice came from behind her.

She turned to find a quizzical look on a bushy red-haired man in his fifties. "I'm sorry, what?" Merritt blurted.

"Oh, I thought you were talkin' to me," he said. He smirked, reached over several men he was talking with and offered her a glass of champagne from the bar.

Slightly off guard at having been caught talking to herself Merritt took the champagne. She noticed he was checking out her dress. "Thank you. Actually, I don't do that very often," she said, "although if you saw me around the house you'd probably think I do. I talk to my cat a lot."

"Well, I've never had a cat, the indoor kind anyway, but I have two teenage daughters and I guaran-damn-tee you talking to your cat is more productive than talking to them." The smirk on the barrel-chested man transformed to a broad smile, "Name is Dave Johnson, but everybody calls me Red."

Merritt shook Red's offered hand and met his friends, names she recognized from the National Association of Insurance Companies' list of board members. Red was chairman and chief executive officer at Republic in Oklahoma City, one of the country's top 10 underwriters. Red's face tensed up when he found out she worked for Secretary Vickers at HHS.

"Listen, Merritt. You know this business has been hell the last decade. Personal property aside – we've always done pretty well there. Thank Christ we stayed out of New York and New Orleans. And most any numb-nuts can make money in life insurance, but we're getting our butts handed to us in the health insurance side of things."

"Yes, I see the numbers on health insurance profits. Most firms are near breakeven." Merritt needed another champagne but saw more venting on the way from Red. *Two to one he mentions exchange products and the rules of Obamacare,* she thought to herself.

"We hoped for some help from y'all on getting rid of some red tape: too many reimbursement hassles," Red continued, "way too many rules. Hell, that's why we put you Republicans in the White House. And your Secretary Vickers is just this side of useless." He eyed up Merritt.

One of Red's colleagues tried to edge his way in by offering him another scotch. "Yeah, I'll take another Johnny Blue. Oh, and get Miss Royce here another Taittinger."

"Hell, I'm Republican, too, even know the President," Red continued, turning back to Merritt, "well enough to call him if I need to; we sure helped him in the Midwest when he was running for office. Ah, I don't want to call him on this stuff, though."

"Red, we want you to be successful in health care – *especially* in health care," Merritt said, trying to keep it light but stand her ground. All those baby boomers out there are depending on the industry." Out of the corner of her eye Merritt saw association staffer Cliff Wiles bolting for the scene. Evidently Red's reputation as a hard-ass bureaucrat basher preceded him.

Red wound down a little realizing Merritt wasn't his target. "Well, so much for a little arm wrestlin'. I'll have to get a hold of Secretary Vickers here and rattle his cage some. We're supposed to have some fun here tonight, right? Merritt, maybe we can get together later for another drink? I kinda like your style. You probably don't know as much about the insurance business as you know about how government shakes. Let me know if I can help you figure out my side of the business. Oh shit, here comes that little suck-up from the staff. What's his name?"

Merritt said goodbye to Red and his group just before Cliff showed up. Red turned his back on Cliff leaving Cliff to walk away with Merritt.

"What was *that* all about?" asked Cliff excitedly.

"Mr. Johnson wanted to make sure I understood the economics of health care insurance," Merritt explained. "Don't worry about it. He makes good sense even if it's slathered in testosterone. I'll catch you later, Cliff."

Cliff tried to think of something important to offer to Merritt but found himself alone before he could think of anything.

"Red, who was that fine, young hard body?" a colleague asked, admiring Merritt's backside as she walked away. "I *love* redheads. Think the cuffs match the collar?"

"That, my friend, is trouble for you if you don't keep it zipped. She's Vickers' industry watchdog, one of 'em anyway. Where is that Vickers? I want to chew on him for awhile."

"Aw who cares, but Red, just imagine those long, young white thighs wrapped around your old ugly face." Red's mustached friend slapped him on the back and looked over at Merritt again. "Damn, and I always thought women who worked in government were about ten thousand back of book. Lordy, double my Viagra."

"Claudia, hi! It's *so* good to see you." Merritt was happy to find a friendly face and escape the 'boys,' for a while anyway. Claudia Kelly, an attractive blond in her mid 40s, was Senator Tidwell's administrative assistant and his right hand.

"Merritt, what *have* you been up to, girl? I'm glad we're sitting together. The senator and his wife will be with us."

"Great, I haven't had a chance to talk to him since he asked me to work at HHS."

After graduate school Merritt had worked her way up from a GS-5 to a 13 at Health and Human Services as fast as civil service rules allowed before scouting out a job on Capitol Hill. Working on the 'Hill' and then coming back to a government department was one way to get to the top and she had set her goals high. After four years as a U.S. Senate staffer for two committees, Senator Tidwell, chairman of the President-Elect's Transition Team, had asked her to work in the Administration. She accepted immediately and was on board at HHS before former U.S. Senator, now Secretary, Donald Vickers knew the Department of Health and Human Services would become his political adieu.

"Did you bring a date?" asked Merritt.

"No, and you appear to be without one, too?"

"Oh, please. I haven't had a pedicure-worthy date in six months. No, actually it's been longer than that. In fact, not since I went out with that cute guy from the Majority Leader's office, Billy."

"God, Merritt, that's nearly a year ago! By the way, I think Billy's gay," Claudia giggled.

Merritt felt herself fade from surprise to resignation.

The evening was turning out as promised, a gala affair with all the ruffles and flourishes of parade dress. The immense Kennedy Center ballroom shone with white marble and huge brass and glass chandeliers. A Marine color guard presented the flag and a tenor from the Marine Band led singing of the Star Spangled Banner.

The buffet was sumptuous looking and aromas of broiled lobster and prime rib stirred the appetites.

With the 600 guests as settled as could be expected given the cocktail priming, the president of the National Association of Insurance Companies rose from the head table to give the chairman a brief but salubrious introduction. The president, an M.D. by profession, was one of the 110 full time staff of the association and, like all of the staff, deferential to those who paid the bills, the senior executives of the 300 member insurance companies.

It was the first time Merritt had seen the chairman and she was anxious to hear him speak. NAI Chairman Delbert Lee Burroughs was also chairman of the board of Delaware General, the country's largest, and arguably most successful, privately held insurance company. Fit for his 60 years, although a little broad around the middle, tanned, and with an air of confidence that moved in a wide envelope around him, Delbert Burroughs stepped forward to the podium.

Attired in classic black label Georgio Armani tuxedo, Burroughs spoke easily to the receptive audience with a broad smile, no notes, arms spread with hands firmly grasping the podium: "Good evening ladies and gentlemen, honored guests…" His crew cut gray hair fit his square jaw and six foot frame. "First, thank you to the United States Marine Corps for their presentation of the colors tonight, a splendid rendition of the National Anthem by Corporal Pendley, and to the Marine Band. *Semper Fi*. A special welcome to Members of Congress and their spouses for making time from their busy schedules to attend…"

Merritt listened intently as Burroughs spoke. She noticed Claudia watching her as she listened. Merritt liked Claudia but viewed her as a lifer on the Hill, tethered to her Senator, almost like an extra wife. Something about that bothered Merritt, but of course she would never mention it.

Claudia probably thinks I'm too much of a political climber, Merritt thought to herself. *No, it's just that working on Capital Hill is not the end; it's means to an end. This man Delbert Burroughs is a perfect example of a gifted executive who has accomplished a great deal in life – directing a successful company, wealthy, well respected.* Merritt acknowledged Claudia's attention and turned her focus back to the podium.

Burroughs had talked just a few minutes and seemed to be wrapping up: "Recent years have challenged us as a society. Morality, economic trials, social mores, life with our families – each continues to evolve. Our insurance businesses are keeping pace with this change and, where we can, anticipating the change." Burroughs raised his right arm in a wave and then a salute to the group, "Please enjoy yourselves this evening, and thank you, thank you so much, for being supportive of our collective efforts to care for America's people and property. God bless."

A little more than an hour later with the gala at its peak, Congressman Suben came over to the table. "Miss Royce, the honor of a dance if you will, please? Mrs. Suben has suggested it. She thinks once the young men here see your loveliness, they will run to ask you themselves."

Merritt joined the Congressman on the dance floor and he rather stiffly led her through an indecipherable waltz step to an upbeat Beyonce tune. Merritt could tell the Congressman was having a great time motioning to his wife and others as he twirled her. She felt fortunate that the Congressman was satisfied with only one dance.

As he escorted Merritt back to her table he said, "A wonderful dancer you are, Miss Royce. You kept me on my feet and off yours. A tribute to your balance, young lady."

"Congressman Suben, you are a delightful dancer. Thank you for asking me." Merritt sat down with Suben now leaning over Senator Tidwell. Claudia motioned that she needed to stay and hear what was going on, more difficult now with the music getting louder, so Merritt said she would get drinks for the ladies.

"Well, look who's back," Red bellowed as Merritt approached the bar.

"Nice to hear I'm popular, at least for a night," she mumbled to herself.

Red turned, "Say, Del, before you head back to your beautiful wife, let me introduce you to Merritt Royce. She's with Vickers down at the department. Merritt, this is Del Burroughs, this year's chairman."

Burroughs turned to meet Merritt. She hadn't seen Burroughs with the midwestern clique of executives. She didn't know why, but she flushed just a little. Maybe it was the surprise.

Merritt's firm handshake and a sweeping of her auburn hair from her face brought a generous smile to Burroughs. "A pleasure, Miss Royce. I've known Don Vickers for 30 years. Good man. Hope you can help us get some things done this year."

"We'll certainly do what we can," Merritt said as Burroughs headed back to his table. "Red, that was nice of you to introduce me."

"Sure thing. So, was that your first billionaire?" Red got a big belly laugh at that.

Merritt playfully slapped Red on the chest, "The first, but probably not the last – *gentlemen*." She took a tall Latin waiter in tow with drinks and sauntered back to her table, looking back over her shoulder at the insurance men whooping it up.

Merritt had seen Burroughs with his arm on Secretary Vickers' shoulder earlier having what looked like a lively discussion between old friends. As she sat down at the table again, she looked back at Burroughs now vigorously shaking hands with a congressman. *I wonder how close Burroughs and Vickers really are.*

As Merritt continued to look in Burroughs' direction, an older man with a cane helped by a young woman approached Burroughs and waited for him to finish his conversation with the congressman. When Burroughs saw them, the man with the cane extended his hand and said something to Burroughs. The handshake, it seemed, was more than a greeting. The young woman, taking Burroughs by surprise, Merritt thought, reached and gave Burroughs a hug. She looked like she was upset as she took the older man's arm and they walked back to their table. Merritt saw that Burroughs appeared quiet for a few moments before returning to his conversation with the congressman. *What* is *the effect this man has on others?*

The Taittinger was icy cold and the tiny bubbles were perfect. Sitting by herself, listening to the orchestra play the theme song from *Shaft*, Merritt felt a light bump against her chair.

From the table behind her and backing his chair next to hers forming an old fashioned love seat he said, "I like the way you handled the CEOs. That's a tough crowd."

Merritt turned a little to her right. He was one of the three young men she had seen get out of the limo. His voice was soft. *Very handsome*, she thought, *lots of dark hair but cleanly cut*. And there was a hint of a scent that she liked. "Oh," she said, "they're having a good time." *Who is this guy?* she wondered.

"Hey, finally they're playing something I like. Michael Bolton. How 'bout it?" He stood and held out his hand.

Merritt looked around and lots of people were dancing. "Okay," she said and took his hand as they walked a few steps on to the marble floor. It was neither a slow dance nor a fast one. He turned and let her hand slip out of his and moved to the music, all the time looking into her eyes.

Nice eyes, she thought, *and he seems relaxed, with big, warm hands – maybe a little too cocky?*

About half way through the song he moved closer to Merritt and said, "My name's Grant, what's yours?"

Hmm, interesting, she thought. *Something about him is catching my eye here. But thank God he didn't say 'Biff' or 'Lance' or 'Chad'*. "Merritt," she said.

They danced, at first without talking. Merritt admired the fit of his tux, his small waist and broad shoulders. They moved easily to the music, in harmony.

"You like music?" Grant asked.

Merritt nodded and said, "Yeah, mostly rock, loud rock, but some classical and jazz, too." *Hmm, I guess we're still dancing.*

"Okay, who wrote this one?"

"I think the name of it is 'Color My World' but I don't know who wrote it."

"Chicago," he said. "I always liked their trombone player. Really animated."

"Do you play trombone?" Merritt didn't really care if he played an instrument but wanted to learn more about this guy with the intoxicating brown eyes.

"No, no." He smiled. "I used to play sax – baritone saxophone."

"Is that the kind Clinton used to play?" she asked coyly.

Grant moved a little closer, close enough so his cheek touched hers and laughed a little, "No, he plays tenor – it's smaller." He stayed close to her and said, "Now, a real test. Who is this?"

Merritt didn't recognize the song but knew it was a slow dance. The organ played soulfully as Merritt felt Grant put his hands on her sides. She moved her hair from her face and gazed up at Grant hoping her blushing cheeks were disguised by the soft lighting. She felt herself move nearer.

"It's 'A Whiter Shade of Pale' by Procol Harum, really a classic." Grant took Merritt's right hand and brought it to his left lapel. They turned slowly and moved together, their thighs now touching, overlapping.

Merritt could feel him as the song ended. Her hand lingered on his chest, her heart racing.

"I knew something good was going to happen tonight," he said softly. Grant saw one of his friends motioning from his table. "It looks like my ride is about to bolt. I'm sorry, I need to go."

They walked back to the table. Merritt felt cut off from knowing more about this man. *Maybe this could be something,* she thought.

"Merritt, can we give you a lift home?" Grant offered.

"Thanks, but I drove. Nice limo, though."

He held Merritt's chair as she sat down and said quietly, "Listen, I know we just met but I'd love to have lunch sometime so we can talk. I work downtown at Baker and Jensen."

Yes, yes, she thought to herself. "Sure, that would be nice. I live in Georgetown and split my time working in Rockville and downtown. And it's Merritt Royce."

"Grant Launder. I'll call you." He touched her bared back and neck warmly with one hand and brushed his face against her hair whispering, "And I *love* your shoes." As he walked with the others toward the door, one of the two women put her hand on his shoulder and said something. He turned back in Merritt's direction and nodded.

Claudia hopped her chair closer to Merritt. "Damn, do you two look good together. Who *was* that hottie? Had you ever met him? Were his eyes *gorgeous*? And his tush! Merritt, Merritt."

Merritt beamed at Claudia, "Now that's what I call a birthday present."

CHAPTER THREE

Melbourne Beach, Florida
Home of a Gatwick Research sales executive
Monday, October 12

From her ocean front condo, she again scanned the large wall-mounted flat screen monitor displaying the Delaware General case file of Mr. Albert Thompson of Clearwater, Florida. She was ready for the call. Hopefully he would be in his office. The first three policyholders on her list today had been out or busy and, of course, she didn't leave messages. Her customized iPhone had an ear set so she could walk around, and it helped keep her focused on the call. No need to worry about intercepted calls as they were encrypted with the triple DES security algorithm. Caller ID at Albert Thompson's office would show the caller as 'Delaware General' and a local Clearwater number. The central switch of Gatwick Research would record the phone call. This remote computer and several networked PC servers managed voice analyzers and hot links to Gatwick's online database. With this hardware, it would be possible to access online Thompson's policy files and health records of his family. The software allowed comparison of Thompson's voice with future discussions to validate the incoming call as Thompson.

"Hello, Mr. Thompson. I'm glad I caught you. My name is Tracy Madson. I'm with the Office of the Chairman at Delaware General Insurance Company."

"Yes?" said Thompson.

"Mr. Thompson, you are a good customer of Delaware General and the chairman would like you to buy one more policy. It's one thousand dollars a year for five years or four thousand dollars paid up front." Tracy waited for his response.

"What? The chairman? Look, I have all the insurance I need. Thanks but..." Thompson was a manager at Walmart and didn't have time for telemarketers.

"Al, I know you need this. For the sake of Wally and Rebecca, certainly for your wife, Cathy." Again, Tracy waited.

"How do you know...? Who *are* you?" Thompson was irritated at the intrusive caller.

"Al, bear with me for just a minute and I'll explain." Tracy's voice was calming and professional, her style easy going.

Tracy sold on average three Contract policies a day and still had time for tennis, shopping with girlfriends and an active nightlife. She was a consistent, if not stellar, performer for Gatwick. Her only contact at the company was a man she had met three times in her four years with the company, and two of those occasions in the first two weeks.

The first introduction was the day she was hired, the second five days later to set up the technology for her work and provide intensive and strict guidance on how to approach calls, including a long list of particulars on what *not* to say. Her training had lasted six long, grueling days at her apartment. At first, she just listened on a connected cell phone as her supervisor made the calls. Then there was training on the technology and security procedures. Then more calls, first by Tracy to other sales agents acting as policyholders, then to real policyholders with her supervisor listening in. Tracy had caught on quickly.

The third contact with her supervisor occurred when Tracy had advised him, via email as required, that she was moving to her present ocean front condo. He came, moved the equipment personally, and installed it, along with hardware upgrades, at her new place. Since that move nearly three years ago there had been no need to talk to her supervisor. Every nine months or so she received hardware in the mail with explicit installation instructions and testing procedures, but no human connection. Gatwick recorded all her calls, monitored all her PC traffic. Tracy understood the arrangement.

What Tracy didn't know was that Gatwick also tapped her home and cell phones and used digital scanning technology to search for certain words. Should the scanning software detect words or phrases on her personal lines or PC email that potentially compromised Gatwick's security, Gatwick 'human resources' staff would begin to listen in on all her conversations. In the ten years of Gatwick history, there had only been a handful of occasions for the human resources staff to become involved, and in only one of those had the Gatwick CEO concluded he needed to act. A 'member' had helped him on that special assignment.

But Tracy was a no risk employee. For her it was the perfect job. She believed; it was easy work for her; she took eight weeks of vacation; and she liked the 160 thousand dollars she made last year – not bad for a 24-year old with less than two years of college and a license in cosmetology.

CHAPTER FOUR

Aspen, Colorado
Wednesday, October 14

"Del, why do you want to be here when everyone else left? The leaves have already turned. Most of the restaurants are closed. It's dead." Angela Burroughs tried to sound miffed.

"That's why I like it. The L.A. phonies are gone, the snobs from New England are home sucking clams, and the money grubbing locals are behaving themselves. Ideal." Delbert Burroughs was enjoying the loyal companionship of his golden retriever, Chuck, and the massive redwood deck on their 9,000 square foot mountain 'cottage' on the east end of town. The Roaring Fork River, more like a babbling brook this time of year, served as their property boundary about 50 yards from the rough hewn deck. He turned around from his big hand-carved rocking chair and smiled at his tall, beautiful brunette bride as she walked barefoot toward him from the large double doors leading from the great room. "Besides you and I can play some golf tomorrow at Maroon Creek. I hear it's going to be a wonderful afternoon."

Burroughs knew that would tug at Angela's heartstring. He had asked her to marry him eight years ago tomorrow on the tee box high above the eighth hole at Maroon Creek Country Club. On that late afternoon as the warm sun played in her brown eyes he took in a deep breath of the crisp mountain air, told her he loved her with all his heart and asked her to be his wife.

"Sweetheart, you remembered," Angela cooed as she sat down on his lap and gave him a long wet kiss.

"You are the best, Angela. Thanks for making me the happiest guy in the world. Hmm, thanks also for being so cute and sexy. Those short shorts show off those incredible legs of yours."

Still on his lap with her arms around him she said, "Delbert Burroughs, you are the sweetest man. How about coming inside with me so I can show you … more." She slid off his lap and moved her hand over him as she motioned to the door.

"Sweetie, that sounds wonderful. I'll be right in. Let me just call the pilots and tell them we'll be here through Sunday."

"Okay, honey." She leaned over and planted another long kiss on him. "I'll slip on something I know you'll like and open some champagne. Don't be too long."

I just love to look at that woman, Burroughs thought to himself. *Great body, and such a sweetheart. Okay, so she's 21 years younger than I am. Big deal.*

Burroughs pressed his speed dial. "Lyle? Yeah, say, we're going to stay a few more days. We probably won't leave for Dover until Sunday afternoon. Take the plane to Denver Friday morning and pick up Marc Friedersdorf. I was going to meet him in Denver but we're having a good time here. And, don't put his name on the flight log. Have Anita make the arrangements. I'll meet with him day after tomorrow for lunch at the The Nell – say, 11:30 am – then you fly him where he needs to go."

"Yes, sir, Mr. Burroughs. Consider it done," snapped Burroughs' pilot.

"And Lyle, take Tom over to the club and get in a couple rounds before you leave. Great time of year for hitting the ball. The caddy master will set you up with clubs and whatever you need."

"Many thanks, Mr. Burroughs. We appreciate it. By the way, sir, Tom really does know this jet. You made an excellent choice, sir."

Burroughs was breaking in a new copilot along with his new plane, a $27 million Challenger 350.

Burroughs clicked the phone off and instantaneously became a smiling teddy bear. *Now for some lovin'*, he thought to himself. "Angela, where's that champagne? Chuck, you big dog. Good boy. You stay here – you're too young to see this." Burroughs walked through the open doors into the log pillar great room and headed to the master bedroom suite past the floor to ceiling stone fireplace. "There you are. Wow... black stockings and heels. Come here, girl, you're in trouble."

"No, honey, I think *you* are." Angela swiveled her topless hourglass figure up to him and handed him his champagne. "Here, have a sip and I'll get you started," she said softly as she undid his jeans.

CHAPTER FIVE

Washington, D.C.
Headquarters, Department of Health and Human Services
Wednesday, October 14

"Good morning, Merritt. I hope you had a great birthday weekend. I had so much fun in Blacksburg on Saturday and my days off." Merritt's executive secretary, LaGretta, brought in the *Wall Street Journal, Washington Post* and *USA Today.*

"I had a great time at the association party on Friday and just laid back the rest of the weekend. How did Mo do at the big football game?" Merritt asked. "It wasn't on TV here." LaGretta's son was a star football player at Virginia Tech.

"Merritt, he did so good. An interception and a bunch of tackles. That boy makes my heart big." LaGretta beamed.

"He plays like he has a huge heart, and we know that his Mom is the biggest reason for his success."

"Oh, thank you, Merritt."

"And I think it was smart of the coach to move Mo to outside linebacker from tight end. It shows the scouts he has the speed and hands for both sides of the line." Merritt liked football. Her dad had taught her the game, and she appreciated the nuances of positioning.

"Well I do know that he was plenty upset having to play defense. But he seems to have warmed up to it a bit. But enough of that big son of mine. You have staff meeting with the Secretary in three minutes."

Merritt headed off down the hall to the Secretary's suite. Secretary Vickers' Wednesday morning staff meetings were always entertaining if not informative. Three dozen top managers attended representing 80,000 HHS employees and more than a trillion dollars in budget authority. Vickers usually gave a short view of hot topics from his perspective, including a few snippets from cabinet meetings, if there were any, and any significant repercussions from Congressional hearings from the prior week.

"Morning everyone," Vickers opened the meeting. "Lots going on this week. Thanks to those of you who attended the event Friday night at the Kennedy Center. It's good for us to show the flag and support the industry. These companies are still having a tough time making a go of it in health care and we owe it to them to listen and be as responsive as we can to their concerns, whether it's red tape and bureaucracy or Medicare or whatever."

Merritt realized Secretary Vickers had genuine concerns for a number of the industry executives and their companies.

"I had the honor of attending another cabinet meeting Monday," Vickers continued with his brand of Pennsylvania cynicism creeping in. "What I can tell you with every confidence is that nothing of value to society will ever be decided in a cabinet meeting as everyone there has risen to their level of incompetence – except the President, of course." Vickers raised his right index finger. "I may also have to make an exception for that young Vice President, Bobby Rolls. And, ladies, he's single. Now let's go around the room and see if we have some inspired commentary for this Wednesday morning."

Had the Deputy Secretary been present, Vickers would have begun with him. Former Congressman Marlin Houghton had been on medical leave for two months so his duties as Vickers' number two had been pushed down to a handful of the other senior political appointees, including Merritt. Houghton had suffered a heart attack and was expected back at the Department within the month. Merritt thought of him as over the hill in attitude, competent but not suited to the rigors of the chief operating officer role of Deputy Secretary. Houghton had served 26 years in the House before his constituency found the need for more youthful representation.

Merritt knew Vickers was comfortable talking about nearly anything in the weekly staff meetings, as his 'Wednesday morning team' would keep comments made in the room confidential. They were all loyal political appointees. The *Washington Post* had no access to the discussions of this group.

On the way out Merritt thought to herself, *That was certainly better than most staff meetings. I'll have to try to do as well myself with my staff here and in Rockville.*

When Merritt returned to her office the first of four half hour meetings were waiting with LaGretta managing traffic. Escorting the 8:30 am appointment in LaGretta reminded Merritt, "You have 10:30 to 1:00 to work on your testimony for next Tuesday. Ben from Congressional Affairs will ride with you to Rockville so he can brief you on the hearing."

"Terrific," Merritt scowled. "See if you can get truck shocks installed on my Beemer before he gets in the car." Merritt's appointment seemed oblivious to the comment and took a seat on the long leather couch where LaGretta directed him.

As LaGretta passed Merritt on the way out of the office she whispered in a devilish tone, "So did Grant, the hottie, call you yet?"

Shocked, mouth gaping open, Merritt stared speechless at LaGretta and at the same time shook the visitor's hand.

LaGretta walked faster but turned around just long enough to chortle, "Oh, and Claudia called and set up lunch for Friday. She said she had a wonderful time at the Kennedy Center, *too*." Merritt could almost feel the heat generated by LaGretta's pantyhose-created friction as she made her quick exit.

About noon as Merritt toyed with a tuna salad sandwich and marked up her testimony for the House Subcommittee on Health, LaGretta popped her head in Merritt's office, "Sorry, but this girl from the National Association of Insurance Commissioners would like to talk with you and it sounds like something you'd like to handle – line 2. By the way, if I was you, next time I saw that Claudia I'd kick her ass." The door shut and Merritt was sure you could hear LaGretta's laugh all the way to the White House.

"Miss Royce, my name is Amy Dennis and I'm director of the Financial Reporting and Analysis Division of the National Association of Insurance Commissioners."

"My sister's name is Amy and, please, it's Merritt."

"Oh that's nice and, uh, sure – Merritt. Yes, well, my division performs financial analysis of insurance companies designated as 'nationally significant.'"

"Yes, Amy. In fact we rely on NAIC's peer review process as input to our own assessment of the insurance industry."

"Oh good. Maybe I've finally found the right person to talk to. I was about to give up. I've tried at least ten offices over the last couple days and…"

"So what's the problem?" Merritt interrupted.

"No, no, there's no problem. It's the opposite. I mean, well…"

"That's okay, I have some time." Merritt sensed excitement from her caller and, from an analyst, that could lead to valuable information.

"Thank you. Well, we have a team reviewing ratios from IRIS, um, it's the Insurance Regulatory Information System. Sorry, we have a lot of acronyms."

"Hey Amy, remember you're talking to a Fed here. I think we invented them. Go ahead, I know a little about your Financial Analysis Solvency Tools. That's FAST, right?"

"You catch on ... fast. Sorry."

Geez, Merritt thought to herself. *What a nerd.*

"Oh, anyway, so these ratios from IRIS give the state insurance commissioners an integrated approach to screening the financial condition of insurance companies. It's all automated. I wrote a lot of the program myself. Well, me and... Sorry, I got off track. So, 11 percent of companies fall outside the range on four or more ratios..."

"Okay Amy, where are we going with this?" Merritt's patience was ebbing as she flipped through the thick briefing book she needed to study for the next day's hearing. Merritt was now thinking maybe big Ben could tell her what was important out of that three inches of paper on their nice little ride to the Rockville office together.

"So, ratio 5 shows the prior two years profitability. Since you read our stuff you know profits have declined sequentially in the health insurance sector over the last 5 years."

"And?"

"And Delaware General's profits have gone up every year for 8 out of the last 10 years. All the others are down. Delaware General is the only one that is up. Up significantly, although some of the data is in aggregate form because they're a privately held company and don't report earnings data like a publicly traded..."

"Delaware General?" Merritt said. "I wonder how they did that?"

"*That,* Merritt, is why I called."

Merritt could hear the relief in Amy Dennis' voice. "Amy, any ideas on how they are managing to show such profits? Demographics, pricing, targeted…"

"But that's what makes this interesting. Delaware General has a profile like scores of other multi-product insurance carriers with more than a million policyholders."

"Hmm, so what are you thinking, Amy?" asked Merritt, open to suggestions but already forming an opinion about what she was going to do.

"Well, we only look at companies that are having trouble and we're stretched pretty thin here. But we think it would be great if other companies could benefit from whatever the management techniques are at Delaware General that are allowing them to do so well in a complex, highly regulated industry."

Merritt was beginning to like this girl. The stuttering, nervous Amy Dennis had, over the phone, blossomed into a treasure of data. "Amy, I'll get some people from the actuarial staff on this right away. This may be something very helpful." Of course, it could also be high profits from exorbitant pricing, but Merritt didn't want to burst Amy's bubble and besides Merritt needed to get back to preparing for the hearing. "Thank you so much for sticking with it and taking the time to share this data with us."

"Oh, you're so welcome. Would you mind keeping us informed of whatever your staff comes up with?"

"I promise I'll keep you in the loop."

"And I'll email you the data from IRIS."

"Amy, next time you're in DC, look me up. I owe you lunch."

Before Merritt loaded up Ben for the drive to the Rockville HHS office she asked LaGretta to set up a meeting with Geoff Hale, head of the Agency for Healthcare Research and Quality and Dr. Mike Nichols, head of Actuarial Services, both in Rockville.

CHAPTER SIX

Maison Blanche Restaurant
Washington, D.C., two blocks west of the White House
Friday, October 16

"LaGretta had the *most* fun hearing about your date with Grant." Claudia was going to have a lot of fun at Merritt's expense about the 'hottie' at the Kennedy Center.

"God, Claudia, he was *not* my date," Merritt objected. "But, he sure is handsome. And I thought LaGretta was going to bust a gut laughing because she knew before I told her anything."

"You are the daughter she never had," said Claudia. "Did he call?"

Merritt stared at the menu. "No."

"Oh, he will. I bet he calls you today."

Claudia was a dear and really wanted Merritt to be happy. Merritt knew that but it was Friday. She'd met Grant a week ago. No call. Hadn't they made a connection? What was wrong with him? What was wrong with her? *We were close*, she thought. *It was going so well. Is he engaged or something? Was I …*

"Hello, earth to Merritt." Claudia brought Merritt back to the present.

A haughty pseudo-French waiter with excess ear hair leaned impatiently over the table. They were seated in the center of the restaurant, the 'A' tables. Reserved for the fast track, young and beautiful. The real power ringed the room not wanting the spotlight of attention. Claudia liked attention.

"I'll have a cup of mushroom soup and the chicken Caesar salad." Merritt tried not to look at his ears. "Please grill the chicken well done."

Claudia giggled. Claudia was entertained by nearly everything. *Maybe she really doesn't get out much,* Merritt thought.

"And I'll have the asparagus starter and the sea bass. And bring us each mineral water and a glass of chardonnay. Merritt, I want to treat you for your birthday."

Merritt guessed Claudia felt a little guilty for pushing about the 'hottie' thing. "Claudia, you're so sweet. Thank you. So, if he doesn't call me maybe I should call him?"

"Honestly, I don't think you should. Besides he *will* call."

Merritt absolutely wasn't going to call first but wanted some support for that notion. After all, it had been quite a dry spell.

Merritt almost never drank at lunch but was on her second glass of wine and very relaxed with this friend she hadn't seen in months. "It's a good thing LaGretta cleared my calendar this afternoon. I think I'll go home after this."

"Honey, is there something wrong?" Claudia was concerned at the tone in Merritt's voice.

"It's just that …" Merritt twirled her wine glass. "I don't know, sometimes I'm okay with life and then sometimes I just wish I could find the right man and settle down. You know, you get lost in what you're doing, career and, well, it's like I'm on a ride with no end."

Claudia seemed content with her life – her job, her family, her friends. That didn't include a man and that didn't seem to matter. Maybe Claudia had found the right formula for Claudia.

"Merritt, each of us has a path we are traveling. I'm comfortable with mine. Yours, I think, has many turns and many forks ahead. You're going places, Merritt, so it won't be easy and it won't be without some big bumps but, in the end, you will find your path, too." Claudia took a long easy sip of the buttery chardonnay.

Merritt looked at Claudia like a puppy hearing a frog for the first time. "Where the hell did that come from?"

"Hey, we're different for sure. I mean look at you. You're young; you're gorgeous. But I've been through some of what you're thrashing around inside your head. Maybe that's it." Claudia put down her fork and put her hands flat on her chest. "It's not so much your head as your heart."

"So maybe I've been absorbed with the job and not with…?" Merritt shook her head. "You know, that sounds a lot like what my mother thinks."

"Well, maybe you don't want a guy hanging around," Claudia offered.

"I don't think that's it. I'm just looking for the right guy. Like …" Merritt stopped as the waiter offered dessert. Before Claudia could say 'yes' Merritt said, "No thanks, just coffee, black."

"Like who? Go on." Claudia was anxious for Merritt to finish what she had started to say.

"Since school there has always been that drive to succeed, so unlike my Mom, and so like my Dad. I did have a steady boyfriend after I bought that small condo in Old Town Alexandria. We met at the furniture consignment store. You know, down by the Torpedo Factory. New love is so fresh and exciting."

Maybe Claudia couldn't identify with that but she was nodding her head and listening.

"He was fun loving and a caring, sensitive guy. Like me he was concerned with career. But his job over at Commerce just wasn't going anywhere. We shared just about everything – similar goals and dreams, but he just couldn't seem to grow. I don't know, maybe I changed."

"Sounds like you drifted apart."

"It happened so fast. One moment we're in love, talking about the future and the next, squabbling over the nits of life." Merritt really didn't like thinking of that relationship. It had soured her to love and channeled her attention even more to success in Washington's big government society.

Claudia and Merritt stood outside the restaurant chatting awhile looking over toward the Old Executive Office Building near the White House grounds. Seeing a cab pull up Claudia gave Merritt a hug, "Honey, happy birthday again and let's not let it be so many months next time. And Merritt, things are going to be just fine. You'll see."

"You're such a good friend. Thanks, Claudia." Merritt waved and thought to herself, *she is so sweet.*

Merritt drove home and looked forward to playing hooky for the rest of the day. She called LaGretta to tell her she had a great lunch and that she would get to the office some time over the weekend.

Meatball was waiting. "Hi, Meatie! She thumbed through the mail and checked for messages. Voice mail had a message from last night. She didn't recognize the Virginia number.

"Hi, Merritt, this is Grant. Grant Launder. We met at the insurance party last week. Say, I'm having some friends over Saturday for a cookout and wondered if you would like to come. I'd love to see you. About 6 o'clock Saturday, casual. Hope you can come. You can call me at home or the office…" Grant left his numbers and his address in McLean, Virginia.

Merritt grinned, spun around in the kitchen and then picked up Meatball and gave him a kiss on the mouth. She could almost hear Meatball say 'ick.' Merritt listened to the message two more times before she called Grant's work number. Not much advance notice, she thought to herself as she waited for an answer. But he said it was just a cookout so…

"Launder."

"Grant, it's Merritt Royce."

"Merritt, I'm glad you called. This week has been nuts at the firm, but I wondered if you could come over Saturday for a cookout. I'm having a few friends over."

Merritt wondered if any of those friends were *girl*friends. "It would be nice to see you again." *I don't want to appear too anxious,* she cautioned herself.

"Great. I think you'll like these people, even if they *are* all lawyers."

Merritt liked his easy laugh. "Oh, I work with lots of lawyers. They're usually pretty harmless. Can I bring something?"

"No, really. Just your beautiful self. And it's casual. Jeans and an appetite."

He gave her directions and they talked a little about how nice the gala had been.

She didn't know what to think when she hung up. She was excited about seeing him and a little nervous about going to his place rather than going out to lunch at a neutral setting for their first date. *First date!* She looked for Meatball to love him up again.

CHAPTER SEVEN

Brown Palace Hotel
Denver, Colorado
Friday, October 16

At precisely 9 am chief executive Marc Friedersdorf strode into the opulent boardroom of the Brown Palace Hotel. His aura made the eleven members uncomfortable, one in particular.

Elliot Weekly, a frail and quiet Mensa caliber operative, knew his place in the organization. He was employee number 006 at Gatwick Research and proud of his tenure and service. He'd started at the company even before Friedersdorf. Elliot had for 10 years been a loyal and productive 'Member.' He and the others were known as Members because theirs was not a traditional company.

Elliot watched as Friedersdorf first opened a leather folder and then surveyed those seated around the heavy walnut table, recognizing each and, it seemed, categorizing their accomplishments as he penetrated them with noble, steely eyes. Friedersdorf paused for a moment as his eyes met Elliot's. Elliot could feel the connection though neither acknowledged the arrangement they had.

Elliot only knew the others by their first names. Because he had been with the company since the beginning, he had pieced together a little about where they focused their efforts and how long they had been with the company. There was only one Elliot didn't recognize. He assumed this underdressed young male was a Member as only Members were invited. Elliot knew Friedersdorf would not be introducing him. *I wonder where* he *came from?*

Through his own experience Elliot guessed that each Member had half a dozen agents as direct reports. Maybe the more experienced of them could have the responsibility of having more agents to manage, but Elliot had special assignments. Maybe the chief executive felt six was enough for Elliot. He didn't really want more agents. They were difficult to control, such free spirits. Each held responsibility for a city or region of the United States. Typically, Elliot managed his own set of policies but also acted as manager of his agents. The agents didn't know each other, nor any of the other members or agents at Gatwick – another of Friedersdorf's rules.

The CEO's reputation was legion at Gatwick Research. He was little known by Elliot and the others and worked at keeping it that way. Yet he preferred to be addressed as Marc, or at least he said he preferred being called Marc. That anomalous familiarity made Elliot uncomfortable, too. The Members knew only enough to make them successful. Friedersdorf was a heavy-handed proponent of compartmentalized intelligence.

The tall and lean, almost gaunt, executive stood at the head of the conference table. To the left in the low-lit room Elliot recognized chief operating officer Jeff Dunlop, a witty, back slapping yahoo who knew everything. The loquacious yet thoughtful Dunlop had difficulty containing himself – he was always in motion, swearing, scribbling on yellow pads, tie undone even at 9 am. On the right side was a pretty and very young woman who had accompanied Friedersdorf into the conference room. Elliot didn't recognize her. *This is unusual,* Elliot thought.

Friedersdorf began: "Ladies and gentlemen, welcome to the tenth annual operations review of Gatwick Research. The agenda includes a financial and strategic overview, an operations discussion led by our chief operating officer, Jeff, and, finally, a recruiting segment as we will be expanding substantially next year."

Elliot recognized what his boss did not say: these one-day meetings were risky but necessary to give the members a sense of belonging, to move them to stay with the business. *But then joining Gatwick was a lifetime venture, wasn't it?*

"Two additions to the discussions," Friedersdorf continued. "Jeff and I have scheduled sessions with each of you individually this evening and tomorrow morning to discuss a range of issues, including compensation increases."

I think he almost smiled. My, he really is trying to motivate the members. Elliot didn't know what the other members were paid, but compensation certainly hadn't been an issue for him. Gatwick paid him just over one million dollars last year in base salary and bonuses.

"And the second addition to the agenda is that I have asked Dr. Linda Kingston to give us a briefing on the recent and rather startling improvements to the drug you have been administering. Linda's postdoctoral work focused on neural synapse effects of certain curare derivatives and these formulations have proven valuable in our research efforts here at Gatwick. Today she directs Gatwick's experimental drug unit. I think you will find the improved drug a measured advance in predictability. Dr. Kingston…"

More data than we usually get from Friedersdorf, Elliot mused. *This should be good. And she is elegantly dressed in what looks like a Chanel suit. Hmm, very young, though.*

Dr. Kingston began: "Good morning. As you may know, curare derivatives are used extensively in the operating room to induce neuromuscular blockage. Originally synthesized by Venezuelan natives from the bark of *Strychnos toxifera*, curare has proven – through advanced therapeutic methods – a principal source for blocking depolarization and preventing muscle contraction. For our uses here, the reformulations we have synthesized are significantly more predictable than, say, succinylcholine. Acetylcholine, as an essential neurotransmitter in the autonomic nervous system, is distorted by curare with precisely negotiable impacts on the nicotinic receptors on the motor end plate…"

Elliot was able to follow the next 15 minutes of extremely technical data as the scientist briefed the members. The research M.D.-Ph.D. fidgeted with her notes and too frequently changed her weight from one foot to the other. Elliot liked to critique speakers though he never spoke in front of groups. As he noticed the other Members beginning to wilt under the weight of jargon and, just as the complexity seemed to be peaking, Dr. Kingston put down her notes and stopped the somewhat irritating movement. She took off her glasses and took a deep breath, relaxing a little. Her bobbed black hair framed her pale complexion.

Her youthfulness belies her competence, Elliot thought.

Then with straightforward language that all could understand she summed up: "The drug is immediately available in two applications. The first acts in three hours, give or take about 30 minutes depending on the size, age and condition of the patient. The second is time delayed 36 hours, plus or minus a few hours, again depending on the patient. We have named them Hemloxin 2 and Hemloxin 3, respectively. There is no change in dosage size or application methodology. Your hardware remains the same. Delivery through the mail will not be affected as the drug is tolerant to extremes of heat, although we have not yet completed testing impacts of freezing on Hemloxin 3."

Elliot noted the way she glanced at Friedersdorf as she explained the unfinished testing. Friedersdorf did not react. Elliot amused himself with thoughts of people failing to meet the Gatwick CEO's rigid schedules.

"Shelf life is easily more than a year and allows cost effective production of the drug," Dr. Kingston continued, "although I understand this is of little consequence to you directly as you are apportioned vials as needed."

Friedersdorf reacted to this unnecessary information with a clearing of his throat.

Dr. Kingston realized her error and rushed to finish: "Uh, yes, and there is one significant change. There is now an antidote should one of your agents, ah, mishandle the application. The antidote has been produced as a nasal spray for ease of application and concealment purposes. Fortunately there has been no need for an antidote to date but with increased activity the probability of a mishap…"

"Linda, thank you so much for that excellent briefing," Friedersdorf said, cutting her off, to Elliot's delight, "and especially for your top notch work to improve timing of the drug and in developing an antidote."

The Members joined Friedersdorf in offering Dr. Kingston polite applause.

Dr. Kingston scurried to put her notes together as Jeff Dunlop, the chief operating officer, rose to escort her out of the room. "Marc, how 'bout a short break for some coffee?" Jeff suggested.

The pleasantries over coffee and elaborate pastries in the rear of the boardroom were strained but typical of these gatherings. Members knew better than to discuss anything of substance or even to make small talk about families or vacations or pets. There were just truncated comments of "nice to see you" and "excellent progress on the drug." Before the break was over, Elliot, and probably most of the other Members, overheard Dunlop speak to Friedersdorf, a conversation meant to be overheard.

"Marc, I'm sure the members will enjoy the opportunity to speak with you in our private sessions," said Dunlop before taking a large bite of a jelly filled donut.

"Yes, they should be helpful," replied Friedersdorf.

Elliot noticed Dunlop struggle to swallow and wipe his mouth with a linen napkin so he could continue his scripted dialogue. "There are unique situations which require some discussion. For example, Wendell has mentioned to me the difficulty of accessing small, special care facilities where security is tight, and Elliot has suggested increased use of agent teams rather than solo efforts."

Elliot turned to see Wendell, another of Gatwick's long-standing members and employee number 011, listening closely to Dunlop.

Friedersdorf eyed the spot of jelly on Dunlop's tie, "And I think all the members could use some corporate assistance in finding new agents that are worthy of our trust."

Only Jeff Dunlop spoke to Friedersdorf. It occurred to Elliot that Dunlop was the human translator between Friedersdorf and the members. Dunlop seemed so real, so approachable, maybe because of his disheveled look and bad haircut. On the other hand, Friedersdorf acted so proper in his buttoned up suit, overly starched white shirt and thinning gray hair.

Before Elliot could make his way to the new member to find out something about him, Friederdorf moved to begin the session again. "Before we turn to the operations side of the business, let me offer a few thoughts," said Friedersdorf. "Financial performance of Gatwick Research improved in nearly every category this past fiscal year. We continue to invest heavily in drug research with, as you have just witnessed, good progress on the efficacy of applications. The parent company is pleased with our contribution both financially and, I might add, as a confidential repository for sensitive data and for the most difficult job of analyzing that mountain of data."

Friedersdorf's piercing blue eyes moved deliberately from member to member. Elliot could now hear Friedersdorf's voice fill with purpose, with pride. Even Dunlop stopped scrubbing at his tie to focus on the chief executive. "Ours is a most challenging mission, a mission we approach as a team of professionals. Rarely do we come together to meet, but together, in spirit, we stand as the vanguard of success for our corporation and as a catalyst for societal change." Friedersdorf lowered his eyes to the table. "Yes, of course, it is the intelligent analysis of health claims data and the timely and sensitive fulfillment of insurance policies. We carry out the wishes of our policyholders efficiently, without one error in a decade. But beyond that…" Friedersdorf raised his arms visually surrounding his loyal members, his eyes beacons into their inner thoughts "…is our contribution to life's most valuable gift to humankind: the gift of *choice*. Of cherishing our dignity. Of preserving the best of each of us – without enduring the humiliation of decline."

Elliot was a believer. He had been from the very beginning. Friederdorf's talk was nearly identical year after year. Elliot could feel the room glisten with emotion as each of the members relived in their own minds the hundreds of lives they had touched. They, too, were proud. They were committed.

CHAPTER EIGHT

McLean, Virginia, about 8 miles from Georgetown
Saturday, October 17

Merritt wore True Religion jeans and a royal blue cashmere sweater to the cookout at Grant's. And, a pair of platform sandals that showed off her pedicure. As she pulled up out front of his townhouse, she felt a little nervous. *God, maybe I should have worn a bra,* she thought. She checked her hair and lipstick in the visor mirror and took a deep breath. *First date, good luck, Merritt,* she told herself.

The door to Grant's townhouse opened and a very tall, very muscular guy in shorts, an overly tight golf shirt and monstrous basketball shoes stood in the doorway. Merritt hadn't been prepared for meeting this huge man.

"Hey, there. Come on in. Grant's in the kitchen."

Merritt walked behind the 'hulk,' as she immediately nicknamed him. Grant was squeezing raw hamburger with what looked like a mixture of onions, spices, mustard and pieces of cubed cheese.

"Hi, Grant," she said.

"Merritt, thanks for coming. You look great."

She saw Grant start to reach to give her a hug and thought better of the idea with a shrug of his shoulders. *Good reaction,* Merritt thought, given all of that whatever on his hands.

She walked over next to Grant in the kitchen and put down the bottle of merlot she had brought. He leaned over and kissed her on the cheek. She raised her eyebrows at the concoction in the large stainless steel bowl in front of him.

Grant grinned. "It's my own recipe."

"I see why you need the fancy apron. 'Swedish Bikini Team'," Merritt read the front text and noted the blonde preference.

"The big guy, Brett, you met at the door gave it to me. My birthday is coming up. Thanks for the vino."

Oh my God, Merritt thought to herself. *We're both Libras. This is either going to be really good or really bad.* "Can I help?" she said.

"Sure. Help yourself to a drink and meet some of my friends."

She poured herself a glass of wine from the kitchen bar. A few more people were arriving. She saw the hulk, Brett, having fun leering down on them as they arrived. "Okay, I'll catch up with you after you and the bikini team finish your masterpiece." Merritt walked toward the front door thinking she would make Brett a project. "So, Brett, where did you play ball?" Merritt was guessing retired college football, lineman, probably a tackle – he didn't look very fast.

"Huh, oh, Maryland," Brett answered.

"Defensive tackle?"

"Yeah," said Brett with a predictable 'howdjuno' look on his face.

Merritt saw that she had his attention. "I'm Merritt. Have you known Grant long?"

"Nice to meet you. Yeah, since college. And he and I were in law school together."

Interesting, Merritt thought. *Hulk has a law degree.* Her dad had always told her earning a law degree depended much more on money and friends than on intellect. *Dad forgot football scholarships,* she thought to herself. "Grant play ball with you?"

"Yeah, quarterback for two years and then he blew out a knee. Then he majored in girls." Brett laughed sheepishly.

Well, at least he realizes he said something stupid, Merritt thought, looking at Brett trying to think of something to say which would recoup that thought. *May as well ask,* "So is Grant's girlfriend here?" Merritt tried to look innocent as she glanced around the townhouse.

"Oh, no, they broke up about a month ago," Brett answered while he opened the front door again.

Merritt stood with Brett and met the couple just arriving.

When Grant found Merritt she was out on the small deck talking with a couple in their late 40's. He walked up behind her, put both hands on her shoulders, and then slid his arm around her stomach. "Greg and Jackie, I see you met Merritt."

Jackie Best, a senior partner in the Baker and Jensen law firm said with a smile, "Grant, it's healthy to invite non lawyers to your parties. And especially such a cultured young lady as Merritt."

Before Grant had come on to the deck, Jackie and Greg had filled Merritt in on Grant's extended list of former girlfriends. Merritt guessed they disapproved of Grant's typical fare of younger women. Greg had described them as 'bimbettes'.

Merritt stepped aside just a little and turned to face Grant, wondering why she was completely comfortable with this man she had just met. "So who do you have cooking the Grant-burgers?" she asked.

"Don't worry, everything is under control," he said. "Come on, let me show you around my little place."

Jackie put her hand on Merritt's arm. "We'll catch you a little later."

The three-story townhouse was modest compared to Merritt's Georgetown home, but nicely decorated in an uncluttered, metallic motif. Merritt liked the organized look of his house. When he showed her the master bedroom she noticed his closet was absent women's clothing. Merritt was attracted to this man, although she couldn't entirely figure out why. As he led the way down the stairs, she was sorting those thoughts.

At the bottom of the stairs, Grant stopped and turned around with Merritt one step above him and her eyes just an inch or two higher than his. He moved his left hand gently behind her along her waist, his right hand lower near the top of her thigh and drew her near to him. She felt his lips on hers; his tongue touched hers. Her auburn hair draped forward as she felt her arms move around his neck and her breasts touch his chest. The lingering kiss softened for a moment harshness of the outside world. Merritt leaned forward and then arched her head back, her hair falling behind her, her breasts coming close, so close to Grant's face.

Not that it mattered to Merritt but others at the party didn't seem to notice the budding passion displayed on the stairway. Merritt took Grant's arm as they walked, without talking, back to the kitchen.

"There he is," said Brett. "Grant we need some executive direction here. Where's the potato salad? You have any more cashews?"

Merritt could see that Jackie and Greg got a kick out of big Brett. They were in the kitchen, along with everyone else, when Brett gave Grant a huge bear hug and yelled, "Happy Birthday, dude!"

Grant, with his arm around Merritt, protested mildly, "Hey, big guy, I have another four days."

Brett responded, "Yeah, but you know we're all a little too tight-assed at the firm to do much in the way of a birthday bash mid week. So... this is it!"

Several of Grant's friends brought in a big layer cake with 38 candles and a couple of the men used their cigar lighters to bring the near dark room to a flickering finale. "Make a wish! Make a wish!"

"May all my friends be happy, live long and see another Redskins Super Bowl win in their lifetime," proclaimed Grant, raising his glass.

Merritt gave Grant a big smooch on the lips and joined the collective toast.

No, no, Merritt thought to herself. *I will go home with everyone else. My God, I don't know this man. I just can't – hmm, I'd like to though.* She closed her eyes at the thought. Her nipples were still caressing the cashmere from her kiss on the stairway.

Merritt left with the others around eleven giving Grant a more PG-rated kiss as she left. But her hazel eyes spoke to Grant of feelings untapped. *That ought to rate a return engagement,* Merritt thought as she unlocked her car.

⇌⇋

Last to leave were Jackie and Greg. As Jackie gave Grant an air kiss following Greg out the door, she said, "Merritt is delightful for such a government heavyweight. How did you meet her?"

Grant looked quizzical.

Jackie, amazed Grant didn't get it, continued the thought: "Grant, this isn't just another pretty face. She runs most of the health care apparatus at HHS. This girl is *way* up there. Beautiful, yes, but a *serious* policy wonk with major access. 'Night..."

On the way home, Jackie said to her husband, "He's such a nice guy. But, you know, it's no wonder Grant hasn't made partner. I'm not sure he has the horsepower. I mean he had no clue his date is like number 4 or 5 over at HHS."

Merritt had just made it upstairs to her bedroom when the phone rang.

"You looked fabulous tonight. Thanks so much for coming," said Grant.

"Grant, I'm glad you called. Nice party. And your mystery burgers were delicious." Merritt was excited he called. She couldn't get him out of her mind.

"The burgers were okay. It's your *lips* that are delicious," said Grant. Before she could respond he continued, "Merritt, I'd like to take you out on a proper date. Would you have dinner with me Wednesday night at the Palm? I know it's a work day, but it's my birthday and… I want to spend it with you."

"I would love to, Grant. And the Palm sounds wonderful." Merritt just wasn't going to say 'no.' She had testimony Thursday to give at another congressional hearing, but she could prepare for that early. And this was a real date, not just a cookout with other people. Maybe she had worried too much about that anyway because now he had asked her out to a nice restaurant.

"Super. How about if I pick you up at your place, say at seven?" asked Grant.

"That sounds perfect," said Merritt. As they talked about Brett 'the hulk,' Jackie and Greg and others at the party, Merritt wondered where this relationship would take her. *He seems genuinely interested and attentive. But I guess I still need to be careful*, she thought. *I don't know very much about him, but I really do like being with him.*

CHAPTER NINE

Merritt's office in Rockville
Monday afternoon, October 19

LaGretta's smile preceded her as she popped her head in Merritt's office. "Your three o'clock is here."

Hearing the sing-song way LaGretta announced the meeting, Merritt looked up from her PC, "LaGretta, you are absolutely beside yourself today."

"Honey, if I was beside myself no one would be able to get through these big office doors of yours," LaGretta responded, hands on her voluminous hips. "I'm just *so* happy you found yourself a *man*," she said leaning around the doorframe.

Merritt raised her index finger in mild objection, "Sshh! Now, please show them in."

As they all sat at Merritt's conference table, she asked, "Okay, what did you find?"

Geoff Hale, director of the Agency for Healthcare Research and Quality went first. "You asked us to see if we could find out why Delaware General has, relatively speaking, higher profitability than other similar firms in the industry. This is somewhat outside our scope, but…"

Merritt interrupted, "Geoff, your agency's charter is research designed to improve the quality of healthcare, *reduce its cost* and improve patient safety. It may not be a typical request for AHRQ, but I think it is squarely in your charter." Hale was a holdover from the prior administration and Merritt didn't cut him any slack. She viewed him as on the bubble: either produce or get out.

"Yes," he continued, oblivious to Merritt's comment, "first, we sorted all the data Amy Dennis sent you from the IRIS database and added available data from financials submitted by Delaware General to the Delaware Insurance Commissioner. We segmented the data so just healthcare data was analyzed, stripping out casualty, life, etc. Here's a chart of the findings."

Hale passed to everyone at the table copies of the color line graph showing Delaware General operating income compared to the mean of similar companies over the last 10 years. "What we see here corroborates what NAIC found: DG's profit performance is better than average by a significant amount."

"And the differential between Delaware General and other companies is widening over time." A young analyst Hale brought with him to the meeting added, "See the difference here in the last three years."

Merritt nodded to the analyst. "Good observation. So any thoughts on why?"

"No specifics," the analyst responded, "but whatever they are doing as a business to generate these margins appears to be a rapidly growing piece of their healthcare segment."

Merritt looked at Dr. Mike Nichols, head of Actuarial Services. "Mike, you've been quiet. What gives?" Merritt liked Nichols. A bit of a rebel, he looked like a surfer and had the untamed bleached blond hair to match the label. *Way too many days in the sun,* she thought. Nichols drove a 'go to hell green' restored '65 GTO convertible. His staff admired his mathematical genius and his open style management.

"I procrastinated," he said. "About par when I haven't figured out how to tunnel in. Some of our folks had ideas on a methodology, but... well, like I said, I just kept thinking about it. Anyway, I couldn't figure out why either so... I called 'em."

Merritt, and everyone else at the table, looked at Nichols. "You called them? You called who?" asked Merritt.

"All of 'em," said Nichols. "I wanted to know why, so I called 'em all – their actuary chief, the chief financial officer – boy, what a dick he is – the head of the healthcare division, the CEO, the senior V.P. of business development, the head of public relations, and maybe a dozen others. Anyway, can't say they're the most cooperative bunch."

Merritt was clearly amused. "Well, that should light up the switchboard downtown."

"Hmm, yeah, guess I should've run that approach by you. Sorry, boss," said Nichols.

"No, I like it, Mike. Any useful reactions from them?" she asked.

Nichols responded, "The CEO didn't take my call, a few of the others said they'd have to get back to me, the CFO, well, like I said... but what I *did* pick up from the six or so people I talked to that ought to know is that each believes it's something different. I mean, the healthcare division head said it was pricing, the actuary guy said it was mortality, the controller in accounting said it was business efficiency, the top sales guy said it was volume, the systems guy said it was their advanced claims processing, and the PR lady said it was the management team – whoa, was *she* an airhead."

"Okay," concluded Merritt. "Not a bad start. We have confirmed the better than average profits for Delaware General. And we have started a process – a rather novel approach – which will likely result in some answers on why. After that, assuming we get some cooperation from Delaware General, we may be able to share with other companies how they are doing so well in the face of a difficult market and regulatory climate. Thanks everyone, and Geoff, would you email Amy Dennis your chart and tell her where we are?"

CHAPTER TEN

Dover, Delaware
Monday, October 19

"Ang, I'm feeling pissy today. I'm not going to the office. Hell, they don't need me anyway." Burroughs stood staring out the large bay window in the kitchen of his Jacobethan-style mansion. The kitchen overlooked an expansive washed marble veranda used for entertaining. Gardeners were already busy below tending the roses and shoveling over flowerbeds along the wide circular drive.

Angela came over to her husband from the refrigerator where she was getting some orange juice. "What's the matter, honey? You don't feel well?"

"I'm not sick. Just don't feel like doing much." Burroughs sat down at the big round table in the kitchen. Chuck, his golden retriever sat down beside him and looked up for attention.

"Why don't you take Chuck for a long walk around the grounds. See, he wants to go chase squirrels and bunnies." Angela leaned over and gave Chuck a hug. The dog recognized 'walk' and 'bunnies' and was now agitated. Angela knew that would work. She didn't want her husband to be down on himself.

"So you think I should get some exercise?" asked Burroughs.

"You did say you were going to try to get in shape." Angela reminded him.

"I *am* in shape," protested Burroughs, now standing giving her a big hug. "Round is a shape." He undid her fluffy, long robe to find she had nothing on. "Oh, look here, Chuck, a nude Angela." He squeezed her butt with one hand and cupped his hand under one of her creamy white breasts with the other. "I think Chuck can wait a while, " he whispered to her.

Angela wiggled free with a giggle and said, "No, now you and Chuck go outside and enjoy this beautiful fall morning. Go on. Maybe you can have some of this... later." Leaning over just a little, Angela pulled the robe back and put one hand on her exquisite rear.

Burroughs felt energized now and headed down the back stone staircase to the grounds below, Chuck in the lead, spinning and jumping and then tearing off to greet the gardeners.

As he reached the private road leading to the gated entrance, Burroughs pulled his cell phone from his pocket. The tall oak trees lining the road filled the sky with red and orange as Burroughs looked east to the bright morning sun. "Good morning, Anita. I'll be at home today, if you need me. Anything going on there?"

Anita had been Burrough's executive secretary for twelve years. He liked her because she didn't gossip, was loyal to a fault, and knew absolutely everyone in the country, or so it seemed.

"Good morning, Mr. Burroughs. Your schedule is clear until Wednesday morning at 10, your weekly meeting with Hanson, Greenberg and Scheier in your office. Wednesday evening a 7pm dinner in Washington with senior staff of the National Association of Insurance Companies and Thursday at 10:30am on Capitol Hill testifying before the House Subcommittee on Health."

"So Hanson doesn't want to let me out of the testimony Thursday?" inquired Burroughs. *Leaving the company to Hanson to run on a day-to-day basis was one of my better decisions,* Burroughs thought to himself. *Not the kind of guy to pal around with, maybe, but a no bullshit CEO nonetheless.* Hanson had been with Delaware General for 16 years, coming up through the ranks in sales and, later, operations. He knew the business cold— well, there was Gatwick he didn't know much about, but then no one at Delaware General did.

"Sir, he thought since you are this year's National Association of Insurance Companies chairman that you should be the spokesperson." Anita always reported what Burrough's management team said, verbatim, no filtering.

"He's right, of course. I just don't care for Congressmen. Egos an big as my house; brains the size of Chuck's." Chuck came back to Burroughs and looked up. "For Wednesday morning let Scheier know I'm interested in seeing the latest demographic research and actuarial forecasts for ages 45 to 60, and make sure Greenberg has the budget variances and margin forecasts for Q3."

Burroughs was an active chairman and wanted to stay current on the business. He was particularly concerned – and had been since he bought a minority interest in the business 34 years ago – about impacts of the baby boomer generation on the life and health insurance business segments. Burroughs felt those companies who best anticipated the needs of 'boomers' would lead the industry.

Also of prime importance to Burroughs was information technology. He had relied on Hanson, the CEO, for much of the expertise here because Burroughs was less comfortable with the high tech world. Yet Burroughs appreciated the value it would bring his company. As with his focus on the boomer generation, Burroughs had applied substantial internal resources to ensure Delaware General would break through the clutter of insurance paperwork with best of breed computer technology.

Burrough's elderly father had retired in Connecticut and turned over to his only child close to one hundred million dollars in securities, not in insurance but in defense industry companies. After earning his MBA at Wharton and shortly after his father's death, Burroughs concluded that not defense, but life and health insurance, was the business for him. He sold the defense company bonds and stock and bought 19.9 percent of Delaware General for 88 million dollars. Over time, Burroughs increased his ownership to 62 percent and increased his net worth to 2.2 billion dollars. The minority holders of Delaware General securities were trusts, endowments and pension funds: silent, non-intrusive partners and Burroughs liked it that way. Burroughs employed a marquis Board of Directors, which met quarterly to hear about the business, but usually heard more of the company's sponsorship of various philanthropic causes. The Board was window dressing.

Burroughs had never had an interest in taking his company public, or 'demutualizing' as it was known, counsel he had taken from his father. *Just too much SEC crap, too many reports to submit, too many questions from auditors, too many shareholders to satisfy – just way too much visibility,* he thought. It was tough enough to keep State Insurance Commissioners out of his shorts.

"I'll take care of those requests, Mr. Burroughs," said Anita.

"Say, Anita, has Greenberg been behaving himself?" asked Burroughs. She understood. The chief financial officer, promoted by Hanson when Burroughs relinquished the CEO role to Hanson two years ago, had an unintentional knack for asking questions the chairman didn't want answered.

"Mostly, sir," she said with a forced, little laugh, "but nothing that relates to the Denver division. I hope you and that big, happy dog have a wonderful day, sir," said Anita.

Burroughs noticed the absence of reference to Angela. As usual, he let it go. Anita considered Mr. Burroughs hers. Burroughs expected that brand of loyalty.

CHAPTER ELEVEN

Melbourne Beach, Florida
Home of Gatwick Research sales executive, Tracy Madson
Monday, October 19

Tracy's call from the week before with prospect Albert Thompson had been interrupted by a request from an existing policyholder, but she knew Thompson was curious enough to take a call from her when they connected.

"Hi, Mr. Thompson. This is Tracy Madson with the Chairman's office at Delaware General"

"Yes, I've been curious about your call."

"Yes," she said. "I hope you have a few minutes for me now."

"Yeah, I have a few minutes, but I don't have a lot of money and can't afford another insurance policy."

"Al, when we first spoke, I told you this policy was special and recommended by the Chairman. What I didn't tell you was why you and Cathy and your children Wally and Rebecca need you to have this policy."

Tracy continued, "Two years ago my dad died of dementia and emphysema. It was a terrible death, maybe a little like what you and your family went through with your grandmother, Adeline." Tracy paused just a second. "I know you just bought a policy for long-term care protection. That gives you a nursing home when you or Cathy needs it so your savings, for your kids, are protected. Al, you ever visited a nursing home?"

"Yeah," he said quietly.

"What were your thoughts?" she asked.

"That I never want to live like that," said Thompson.

"Me neither, Al. I made that decision after seeing my dad, every Thursday and Sunday for six years. When he died he… he just wasn't Dad anymore. I mean he was, but he wasn't. Do you know what I mean, Al?" Tracy didn't use a script. She didn't need one.

"Yeah. When I go, I hope I just drop over one day," said Thompson.

"Sure, me, too. Go peacefully in your sleep, or sitting in your chair watching a ball game, or down by the water fishing."

"Well, it doesn't always happen that way," said Thompson.

Boom, it's done, this one's in the bag, Tracy thought to herself. "It can, Al. We can give you that choice. Obviously we don't advertise this kind of policy, but…"

"Is that what you're talking about? How would you do that?" Thompson had lots of questions now.

"What would you say if you could be covered by a policy that guaranteed you would never be a burden to your family or friends, that you would go peacefully, that you would never be a vegetable with tubes hanging off you? That if you did come down with Alzheimer's you would go at the right time, before you forgot your kids' names, before you couldn't feed yourself, before you needed someone to change your diaper."

It was time for Tracy to let him think about it. He would call her in a couple days with questions. If not, she knew Thompson would take her call when she phoned back to close the policy.

CHAPTER TWELVE

Chicago, Illinois
Home of member Elliot Weekly
Monday, October 19

Elliot's online review hadn't taken long. The Gatwick weekly list of fulfillments had been waiting for him when he logged on to his home PC early Monday morning. Elliot sent encrypted emails to five of his agents with their assignments for the week – the sixth agent was on vacation. It was shaping up as a busy week. Eleven Contract policies. *None of the fulfillments look untidy or out of the ordinary,* Elliot thought, *except maybe the one in Detroit. Hmm, a home care fulfillment. Those always require a certain creative approach.* Elliot had an agent in mind. Tony was very good at those, so when Tony called in after his Chicago Methodist Hospital assignment, Elliot would talk to him about the Detroit policy.

Elliot knew Tony's Contract policy fulfillment today would not be a particularly difficult. Agent Tony Scalzo worked for member Elliot Weekly, though Elliot felt Tony did pretty much as he pleased.

Elliot put up with the independence because Tony was an exceptional agent: 62 years old, well mannered, innocuous, a master of disguise, and a veteran of 399 Contract fulfillments. Today would mark his 400th. In the backwater parlance of Gatwick agents, this accomplishment matched Hank Aaron hitting 700 homeruns.

Helen Halverson and her husband, Marvin, had each purchased a Contract policy eight years ago. Marvin had passed peacefully in his sleep two years earlier, though Elliot hadn't bothered to check the cause. Probably a heart attack, Elliot thought. Helen was now in intensive care at Chicago Methodist. Her massive stroke Thursday morning had left her mostly paralyzed, unable to talk, taking nourishment intravenously. Until Thursday, her 73 years had worn easily on Helen. A spry little lady with a kind word for all those who lived around her in the old south neighborhood of well-kept row houses, she had collapsed while tending her garden.

Elliot saw from the computer log that the first indication of Helen's condition appeared at the Medicare claims processing center when she was admitted Thursday at 8:45am. Her Medicare healthcare coverage had been validated and the necessary procedures had been approved. Since Helen was covered by Medicare, rather than Delaware General's healthcare coverage, a delay of a day or two was typical in retrieving government electronic files. The first detailed health claims data arrived at Gatwick's processing center Saturday afternoon from the Medicare claims database housed in the Social Security Administration's main computer complex in Maryland. Gatwick Research screening software flagged her policy Saturday night during the nightly batch computer run of all Medicare health claims. Gatwick claims adjudicators confirmed Helen's status Sunday morning and an M.D. on Gatwick's medical staff phoned the hospital Sunday afternoon to speak with the attending resident.

The conversation was recorded by Gatwick's central switch and transcribed in the log Elliot was reviewing:

"Dr. Syad, this is Dr. Roger Gramm, a friend of the family, calling to inquire about the condition of a patient, Helen Halverson, admitted Thursday morning."

"Yes, doctor," replied the resident. "I have her chart here. Mrs. Halverson is in ICU, patient is unresponsive, prognosis: poor. In all likelihood, she will require 24-hour care. Recovery of most motor, speech and quite possibly esophageal capabilities is not expected."

"I see," said the Gatwick M.D. "Next steps?"

"Not much, I'm afraid. We will keep her comfortable and she should be ready to transfer to a full care facility some time next week. At some point, after further review by the neurological staff, surgery may be indicated to clear the second carotid artery," said the resident.

"Thank you, doctor, for the update. I appreciate it."

Shortly after the call, Elliot could see from the log that Dr. Gramm categorized Helen Halverson as a 'gamma' and placed her on the list for Contract policy fulfillment. Policyholders were rated as alpha, beta, or gamma depending on their condition. Gammas were occasionally, and indelicately Elliot thought, referred to as 'gomers' by the doctors. They were patients whose quality of life was now severely impaired – either in a persistent vegetative state or alert mentally but physically unable to care for themselves. Gomers always made the list. *Mrs. Halverson is a gamma but not a …* Elliot just didn't like that description. *It's so callous.*

The list was apportioned by Jeff Dunlop's operations staff, roughly by geography, to members via encrypted email each Sunday night. Flash updates for the list were added each Tuesday and Thursday evening. The Sunday evening list for the week of October 19 included 137 names.

CHAPTER THIRTEEN

Chicago Methodist Hospital
Monday, October 19

He walked past the information and check-in desk with his topcoat buttoned up and took the elevators to the sixth floor. He removed the coat and folded it neatly over his arm. Exiting the elevator, he glanced in both directions and walked deliberately to the nurses' station. "Good afternoon, nurse. My name is Father Evangelista. I am here to visit Mrs. Helen Halverson."

"Mrs. Halverson is here," noted the nurse, "but the doctor has recommended against visitors. She is in intensive care and her condition…"

"Please, Nurse Langford," he noted her nametag, "her *condition* requires that I administer Last Rites and the reception of Holy Communion – the Viaticum, food for the journey. It will only take a few moments. Besides," he said smiling with omniscience, "I am not a visitor. I am her Monsignor and, since her husband, Marvin, died two years ago, her family." His eyes and his voice sincere and caring, he waited for the right response. As she looked around for her supervisor, he walked to Helen's ICU room, "Bless you Nurse Langford. And say a prayer for Mrs. Halverson. Poor dear needs God's care now." Before the nurse could object further, Father Evangelista, also known as Gatwick agent Tony Scalzo, was 20 yards down the hall and entering Helen's room. Confirming her name by the band on her wrist, his left hand lightly grasped her thin, tired arm.

His black suit and white cleric collar were properly pressed and cleaned for the occasion. He saw Mrs. Halverson awake and turn her head ever so slightly in his direction. "Helen, I'm here to bring you some comfort," he said. As he gently held her forearm, his right index finger touched the distinctive black onyx and titanium ring on the third finger of his left hand. With his touch to the ring's stone, an extremely fine gauge needle pricked her forearm and injected a single dose of Hemloxin 2. He released his touch and the needle retracted. He continued to administer Last Rites in the manner he had done many times before: "… anointing him with oil in the name of the Lord. And the prayer of faith shall save the sick, and the Lord shall raise him up. And if he has committed sins, they shall be forgiven him." He noticed a nurse watching from outside the glassed room. He could tell Mrs. Halverson tried to smile and say something. Tears talked for her. He kissed her hand and left.

Alone in the elevator he put on the dark overcoat. In his car on the way home, Tony began wiping off makeup he had used to darken his complexion.

Elliot was expecting calls this evening. He asked that his agents place a brief call to him after each fulfillment. It served as closure for the Contract policy and a handoff, of sorts, back to corporate.

Tony phoned on a secure line at 6pm. "Good evening, Elliot. The assignment was successfully completed at 1:30pm today. I have confirmed fulfillment – approximately 4pm."

"Thank you, Tony." Elliot knew enough about Tony to understand he didn't keep score like some of the other agents and accounting 'beaners' at corporate did. So Elliot spoke to Tony of the weather, a new restaurant in the city and then of their leader, Marc, without mentioning his name. "The chief executive counts you among his most valuable assets, Tony. You have become a living legend he speaks of with reverence. He asked me to pass along to you his highest regards. Tony, in all the years I have been around him, he has never said something as glowing as that about anyone – ever."

"I am honored to serve the cause. Please tell him that," said Tony.

"I shall," promised Elliot. "And now, there is a Contract policy in Detroit that will be a challenge." Elliot was certain this would elicit a concerted effort by Tony to quickly manage the next assignment. "Please pull up your file on Mr. Andrew Bartholomew of Detroit…"

CHAPTER FOURTEEN

Headquarters of Delaware General Insurance Company
Dover, Delaware
Wednesday, October 21

Chairman Delbert Burroughs arrived at his office in time to scan the papers and start preparing for the hearing Thursday in Washington. His testimony had been prepared by Delaware General's legal staff with assistance from the company's outside counsel of 20 years, the Washington-based law firm, Baker and Jensen.

Anita knocked on his open office door. "Sir, your ten o'clock is ready in the executive conference room." Burroughs' weekly meeting with chief executive officer Phil Hanson, chief financial officer Alan Greenberg, and president of the insurance division Robert Scheier was ready.

Hanson was first to speak as Burroughs entered the small but elaborately decorated ante room to the main boardroom. The dark cherry paneling and large brass sculptures stood in contrast to whimsical, brightly colored acrylic paintings adorning the walls. "Del, good morning. Hope you and Angela had a relaxing week in Aspen."

"We had a great time, Phil," Burroughs said. "Alan, Robert, good morning. Gentlemen, I only have a few things to go over with you today and then I'd like to get your take on how we're doing. First off, guess I'll sacrifice myself and go before the House Subcommittee tomorrow in Washington." Burroughs gave Hanson a wry smile. "Looks like they want to focus on increasing health care costs."

"So what else is new?" quipped Scheier.

"HHS will also be testifying, Del, before you go on, I believe," Hanson added.

"Why don't we see if we can find out what they are going to say?" Burroughs said to Hanson. "I'd rather not get blind-sided."

"Phil, I'll handle that," Scheier said, jotting a note to himself. "The folks at Baker and Jensen can usually get a heads up on that kind of thing. Speaking of the Department, Del, I took a call from the head of actuarial services at HHS a couple days ago and he wanted to know why Delaware General was so profitable. It's nice to see someone in government noticed." Scheier commented.

"What?!" Burroughs' square jaw clenched and he turned and stared right through Scheier.

Before the unsuspecting Scheier could recover and respond, Greenberg said, "He called me, too."

Incredulous, Burroughs turned his harsh stare at Greenberg.

"Hang on a second," Hanson punched a button on the speakerphone next to him. "Vicki, who from HHS called me? I think it was Monday."

"Let me check, Mr. Hanson. Yes, sir, Monday morning at 9:20 we received a call from a Dr. Mike Nichols, head of Actuarial Services at HHS."

"Thanks." Hanson clicked off the phone. The executives looked at each other.

Not wanting to appear too concerned and sensing he'd over reacted, Burroughs sat back in his chair with his hands clenching the chair arms and managed a thin smile at Scheier. "Well, I hope we gave him what he needed."

Hanson spoke for Scheier. "Del, regardless of why they are asking, I don't like them nosing around. I'll find out who else he called."

"Better get what our answers were, too," Greenberg added.

Burroughs managed his emotions during the rest of the session, but throughout those 30 minutes he kept asking himself: why are they asking and where are they going with this?

On the way out Hanson stopped and turned to Burroughs. "I'll find out what I can about the HHS guy who called and get the information to you before you head to Washington tonight."

"Yeah, Phil, thanks," Burroughs said, looking down and shaking his head. "Maybe it's a science project for this guy. But you're right, I don't like Feds nosing around either."

I really don't like this, Burroughs thought to himself, *maybe I should...* He saw Greenberg leave, "Say Alan, you have a minute?" Chief financial officer Greenberg followed Burroughs to his office. "Alan, my CPA keeps telling me to diversify. You think now would be a reasonable time to sell part of my interest?"

"Well," said Greenberg, "the business is at an all time high in quarterly revenue, cash flow and operating margin, so the answer is probably 'yes.' Your holdings of Delaware General total 62.4 percent. You could sell around 12 percent to retain outright control or you could..."

"No, I don't want to sell past majority control," Burroughs interjected.

"Okay. So 12 percent would be worth about..." Greenberg did the math in his head "...well, roughly 425 million."

Burroughs sat down in the black leather executive chair behind his desk and looked out at the field of trees surrounding the Delaware General campus. "Alan, make a call to Arnie over at Goldman Sachs and let's get this started. Oh, and I'll let Phil know, but let's keep it between the three of us for now." Greenberg left, now a man with a mission. *I don't like the feeling I've got in my gut*, Burroughs thought. *A simple question from an actuary at HHS and it sends me sideways. Maybe there's just too much risk in this Gatwick notion. It's the right thing to do. It fills a need. Someday we can shut it down. Drugs, gene therapy, surgical techniques – we won't need it. Maybe Marc was right. Maybe the size of it exposes us.* Burroughs continued to stare out the windows behind his desk. Over the trees he watched a gaggle of geese headed south for the winter.

CHAPTER FIFTEEN

Merritt's townhouse
Georgetown
Wednesday evening, October 21

Merritt remembered what LaGretta had told her: "If he's a good man, he'll treat you right." *So far so good*, Merritt thought. *He's so different from Dad. Dad was cerebral and cautious, methodical and well mannered. Not that Grant isn't those things, but he's more social, light hearted and definitely very handsome.* She had told her mom and sister Amy about Grant and they were excited for her.

Mom is maybe a little too happy about all this. As Merritt fed Meatball his "din din," she rolled her eyes at her Mom saying, again, "Don't work so hard, honey, maybe this guy will be the one for you."

Now upstairs in her bedroom, she wasn't concerned about the hearing tomorrow. She was prepared. In fact, she was going to stay after her testimony and listen to the industry representatives to hear what they had to say about controlling rising health care costs. She was more than casually interested in what Delbert Burroughs of Delaware General would have to say.

In her closet after a quick shower, Merritt had narrowed to two possibilities her outfit for the evening: either the turquoise sweater dress or the short red silk dress. "Meatball," she called. "Get in here and help me choose." *Guess I'm going to have to figure this out myself.* "Deciding something at work is easy. But pick an outfit? I'm Libra-impaired in the closet," she said out loud "Enough," she said to herself. She selected the red silk dress. No question about the bra and panties, she had slipped on the La Perla lacy orange and lemon colored set. *Who knows, maybe I'll get lucky tonight,* she thought to herself rather nervously. *Shoes?* It was warm enough tonight for sandals so she went for her sassy Giuseppe Zanotti's.

After turning on a few more lights, Merritt poured herself a glass of wine. *I need to relax,* she counseled herself.

At a few minutes before seven, the doorbell chimed. Grant had a big smile and a bouquet of fresh flowers. "Wow, you look fabulous."

"Thanks, Grant, please come in. The flowers are beautiful. Let's go upstairs. I'll put them in a vase." Merritt led the way up the stairs and noticed Grant checking out her legs in the short red dress. *I hope I didn't go overboard on the dress,* she worried.

"Girl, you wear the sexiest shoes," he said.

Grant wore a dark charcoal suit with light blue shirt and deep burgundy tie. *His dark wavy hair and blue eyes are perfectly complemented by his clothes.* As Merritt arranged the flowers in the kitchen, she offered him a glass of wine.

"Thanks, Merritt. I must say you have an incredible place."

"Here, let's take a quick tour," Merritt said. "Grab your wine."

It was now nearing darkness and from Merritt's living room balcony they could see the lights of Washington. "My God, Merritt, this view is killer. You can see the Kennedy Center. Cool view of Rosslyn across the river. Impressive."

"One more level," said Merritt.

"Government must pay better than I thought," mused Grant.

"Insurance policy from my dad when he died," Merritt said matter-of-factly.

"Sorry, I didn't mean to pry. Wow, this balcony is even bigger than the one off the living room," Grant said as he walked through the master bedroom to the glassed in view. "And who is this?"

Merritt saw that Grant was looking on her bed. "That is Meatball. Meaty, meet Grant Launder." Grant ignored him. Meatball ignored both of them.

Grant put his arm around Merritt as they looked out toward the river below. "Thanks for being with me today," he said.

"Which reminds me," said Merritt. She took his hand and led him down to the main level. "Bye, Meaty," she said. Merritt wondered why Grant didn't seem to pay any attention to her little guy. She had Grant sit down in the living room on the big sofa. "Looks like you need another glass of wine and… something I hope you like."

"Hmm, what's up?" he said.

She hoped he wasn't thinking she was going to strip for him like one of his former 'bimbettes.' "Happy Birthday!" Merritt handed him a present wrapped in bright green foil paper and a big gold ribbon.

"Thanks, but Merritt, you didn't… I mean, you shouldn't have done that," he said.

She sat down close beside him and said, "Open your present."

Grant carefully opened the big package and opened the box. "Hey, great basketball shoes. Black Nikes. And you… how'd you get the size right?"

Merritt giggled because Grant sounded surprised. "The hulk."

"Brett, the rat, he didn't tell me you two did this."

"He promised me he wouldn't tell you. I told him I'd tell everyone my nickname for him if he did," Merritt laughed.

"Thank you, baby." Grant leaned over and kissed her softly on the lips. He put his hand on her thigh and kissed her again, this time a deep, wet kiss. "Guess we should go to dinner... not that I wouldn't rather stay here and kiss you, but I want us to go on our date."

"I'm glad you like the shoes. Let me get my coat," said Merritt. Before she got up she ran her fingers through his hair, gave him another kiss and said, "Happy birthday." As she stood up she thought, *what is it about this guy? – I can't seem to get enough of him. This is so different for me.*

Their dinner at the Palm was memorable: big lobsters, big potatoes, big pickles, big waiters. Merritt loved it but tried not to eat too much. She saw that Grant liked it, too. And it looked as though he did eat too much, and maybe drank too much red wine. "I'll drive home," she offered.

"Whoa, chauffeured on my birthday. Okay, no dessert. Besides I have a ton of cake leftover from Saturday." He paid the bill and the valet pulled up his big Toyota SUV.

Grant talked all the way to Merritt's place about his job at the law firm, mostly complaining about not getting good assignments. *Must be the wine,* she thought, *because I haven't heard him be negative before.* He tried playing with her hair and her legs and kissing her ear, all this more awkward with the console in between them. Merritt dodged some of his advances with well-timed left hand turns. When she turned in to her driveway she turned off the SUV and they kissed for a few minutes. "Grant, I'd have you in, but I have a hearing in the morning."

He straightened up a bit and said, "Oh, for sure, Merritt." He walked her to her front door. At the front door he pulled her close to him and they kissed.

As his hands started to hike up her dress, she gently broke the lip lock and said "Good night."

"Thanks again for being with me on my birthday," he said. "Good luck at your hearing. Can I call you tomorrow night?"

As Merritt opened her door she said, "Sure, and I loved dinner and our date."

She opened the door to find Meatball waiting for her. "Hi, Meaty." She climbed the stairs slowly. In the kitchen, she touched the flowers he had brought her, took a bottle of water and went up the stairs to her bedroom. Kicking off her shoes in the closet, she stood there looking in the mirror. A torrent of thoughts flooded her mind.

CHAPTER SIXTEEN

Hearing before the Subcommittee on Health
Rayburn House Office Building
Washington, D.C.
Thursday, October 22

The cavernous committee room filled early with lobbyists, healthcare and pharmaceutical company employees. While only one of many committees with responsibility for some aspect of healthcare, this was the subcommittee where the issues were vetted, where decisions were made affecting all Americans.

Merritt had stepped in front of the witness table and walked up to the curved dais to shake hands with the chairman and Congressman Suben, the ranking democrat of the subcommittee, and to wave at several staff she knew sitting behind the congressmen.

Suben beamed at Merritt: "Miss Royce, again so nice to see you."

Merritt nodded and returned to her seat at the witness table. She could see the committee chairman looking at her trying to figure out what that was about.

The chairman, a republican from Ohio, gaveled the committee to order: "The Subcommittee on Health of the House Committee on Energy and Commerce is now in session. We have testimony today from the Department of Health and Human Services and, importantly, from several insurance industry executives. Given the time constraints of our industry participants, we will dispense with opening statements by the committee. Those remarks will be included in the record. We will begin with testimony. The Chair calls Assistant Deputy Secretary Merritt Royce. Secretary Royce, nice to have you before the committee again representing HHS. Please proceed."

"Thank you, Mr. Chairman," Merritt began. "If I may, Mr. Chairman, I will submit testimony for the record and summarize."

"Without objection, so ordered," muttered the chairman.

These arcane procedures add stuffiness to an already formal protocol, thought Merritt. Of course, the department wasn't helping things much. *This prepared testimony would bore the piss out of a saguaro cactus.* Written by HHS congressional affairs staff with input from a platoon of lawyers and policy analysts, with requisite last minute tweaking by the Office of Management and Budget, the 27 pages, though filled with excellent data, was a tedious read. So she summarized, both to save her reputation as a non-bureaucratic Fed and to allow for extemporizing on her part – OMB couldn't tweak that.

This was her twelfth appearance before a congressional committee. She actually preferred the Senate side to the House – fewer personalities to deal with. And it seemed House Members were always trying to make press, probably because with two-year terms they were always running for reelection. She learned after only a couple of appearances before congressional committees that 'this is all about them, not me.' *Make them look good and they think you are magical.* Today she would try to remember that.

Summarizing her testimony in less than fifteen minutes, Merritt focused on the primary contributors to increasing healthcare costs: drugs, hospital infrastructure and labor. She had Ben from the congressional affairs staff of the department flip through a series of large charts as she summarized her testimony. The visuals helped dramatize the increases, increases in cost the congressmen heard about daily from their constituents. Finishing, Merritt said, "Mr. Chairman, that concludes the department's remarks; I would be happy to take questions."

"Thank you Secretary Royce," said the chairman. "Just a few questions. You have presented data that categorizes cost increases. You said that prescription cost increases play a role, that too many hospitals or hospitals in the wrong places have added to costs, and that increasing costs of doctors and nurses, lab technicians and researchers all add to the cost."

"Yes, Mr. Chairman, those are the primary inflationary items." Merritt wasn't quite sure where the chairman was going with this but she reminded herself she was just there for the ride.

The chairman continued, "Maybe we should look at the data from another perspective. I'm sure our Ranking Member, the distinguished gentleman from Florida, Mr. Suben, will add to this thought when he has questions for you, but shouldn't we look more at *when* in the human life cycle the costs begin to soar?" The chairman nodded respectfully to Congressman Suben sitting to the immediate left of the chairman.

Okay, Merritt thought to herself, *I guess this is going to be Suben appreciation day.* "Yes, Mr. Chairman both you and Congressman Suben have been active in helping control costs for senior citizens. Cost increases affect the elderly more because many are on fixed incomes. Life cycle here, as you put it, is important. After the age of 55, pharmaceutical costs begin to escalate. And more outpatient procedures are required. Major surgery becomes more frequent. And certainly 24-hour care increases. Parts of the country where we have concentrations of seniors are seeing their local economies shift in support of this population segment and their healthcare needs. Medicare carries a large portion of the burden for those over 65, but our economy will increasingly feel the impact of baby boomer healthcare costs."

For the next 35 minutes, several congressmen, with Suben the most active, discussed rising costs for older Americans, and Merritt helped where she could with HHS data and several more charts. Each of the congressmen, and Merritt too, judiciously avoided the single largest cost component for seniors' healthcare: the last sixty days of life.

"Well this has been most helpful, Secretary Royce," said the chairman wrapping up. "Let's take a ten minute recess and then begin with the first of four industry representatives, Mr. Delbert Lee Burroughs, chairman of the National Association of Insurance Companies and chairman of the board of Delaware General Insurance Company.

Merritt picked up her notes and, after thanking Ben for his help with all the big charts, she looked up to the dais. Suben was there looking her way and she motioned discreetly with her hand to catch his eye. She saw the congressman wave her up behind the dais. With Suben and aides for both the chairman and Suben listening, Merritt made a suggestion: "We have some data that you may want to pursue at this hearing."

"Yes, Miss Royce?" Suben leaned in to listen. The subcommittee chairman had now joined the informal meeting.

Merritt took a deep breath. "You know the state insurance commissioners have an association that helps them work between states since most insurers cross state boundaries. Those people forwarded us some interesting data you may want to ask your next witness about."

"What's that, Miss Royce?" asked the chairman.

"The data says, and we have confirmed, that Delaware General has generated increasing profits over the last half dozen years or so. The profits seem to come from their healthcare business and they are accelerating. This in the face of other healthcare companies screaming about cost controls and deteriorating profits. One of our people called Delaware General and asked a number of their senior executives why they were doing so well when others were not. Here are their answers." Merritt gave the chairman and Suben a page of responses from the company along with who said what.

The congressmen, with staff looking over their shoulders, scanned the page. Suben was first to comment: "Remarkable. Both that the company is making so much money and that internally they don't agree on why."

"Good read, Joel," the chairman said, nodding. "I think it would be fine to ask Mr. Burroughs about this. Why don't you take the lead?"

"Happy to, Mr. Chairman." Suben stood rather straight, smiled and left with his aide to the meeting room behind the dais.

The chairman winked at Merritt, handed the page to his staffer, and then walked out front of the dais to meet the industry executives. Other congressmen at the hearing also greeted the insurance executives, yet it seemed that there was a special, and curious, deference to Burroughs. Merritt knew the chairman didn't want to confront such a powerful industry figure, not to mention an important campaign donor, with what could be considered intrusive questioning about profits. She spoke for a minute with the chairman's aide to make sure the staffer knew the context of the Delaware General discussion – that this was *good* news, if one company could find a way to make money in this market, maybe others could.

The chairman gaveled the subcommittee back to order. "The Chair is pleased to welcome Mr. Delbert Burroughs, chairman of Delaware General and this year's chairman of the National Association of Insurance Companies."

"Thank you, Mr. Chairman, members of the committee," began Burroughs. "I'm happy to be here today to give you a view of the healthcare industry from the perspective of the 300 members of the National Association of Insurance Companies."

Burroughs had received his briefing from Hanson before leaving for Washington. Hanson had for Burroughs the list of calls made by the nettlesome Dr. Mike Nichols to senior Delaware General executives, along with answers the executives said they gave to Nichols. Burroughs thought maybe he could find out what those calls were about when he was in Washington.

Burroughs also had a synopsis of HHS testimony that had been given. The synopsis was prepared by Baker and Jensen after a quickly arranged late lunch Wednesday between Jackie Best of the firm, the senior partner who managed the Delaware General relationship, and a young female GS-7 on the HHS congressional affairs staff. Burroughs liked this kind of intelligence and was willing to pay for it.

Testimony prepared by the association was pretty good, Burroughs thought. Well written, and good arguments for reduced regulation and price controls, and he knew from dinner the night before with NAI staff that his testimony had been preceded by a barrage of lobbying of each of the subcommittee members.

After completing his remarks, Burroughs knew it was the congressmen's turn. *But lobbying by association staff, complete with suggested questions* – he had the answers scripted in front of him – *should make this easier,* thought Burroughs.

The chairman asked Burroughs the expected questions. Nice of him to ask them in the same order as my notes, Burroughs smirked to himself. Amazing what a timely contribution to reelection will do.

Though Burroughs' politics were generally not a topic of conversation and he certainly didn't wear them on his sleeve, he had strong ties to senior administration officials, including the President, which made him a republican with a capital 'R', in Washington, D.C. anyway.

"The Chair recognizes the gentleman from Florida."

"Thank you, Mr. Chairman," said Congressman Suben. "Mr. Burroughs, welcome. Your stewardship with the association is a first in a few years. Yours is a profitable company. Your predecessors complained of low profits or losses in healthcare. You make money and they didn't. Enlighten us, please, with the secret of your success."

Burroughs' teeth clenched but he managed a benign look of indifference. *Jesus, I can't believe this,* he thought. *How the fuck...?*

"Congressman, we at Delaware General have worked hard to serve our customers, our employees and our community. That we profit from our hard work and innovation in healthcare is also a testament to our focus..." He thought maybe a lengthy, general answer would get this congressman on to another subject. *How did the congressman get on this? That dickhead down at HHS on his science project must have leaked the congressman the question to ask. Christ, what else does he have,* Burroughs wondered to himself.

"Yes, yes, Mr. Burroughs, a fine company you have and successful as we can all see. But perhaps you can share with us *why* your company excels, specifically if you would," Congressman Suben pressed.

Cornered, Burroughs opted for the direct route. "Congressman, apparently there is a zealous bureaucrat down at HHS who has been asking the same question. In fact, he took it upon himself to call several of my senior staff and ask them. I guess he could have waited a few days and listened here today." Burroughs smiled and reached for the folded page of notes in his suit pocket from Hanson. Burroughs didn't like this, but it seemed Suben was prepared with unknown amounts of data. *Maybe if I beat him to the punch,* Burroughs thought, *it will disarm him.* "Let me share with you what Delaware General executives said in response to those calls from Washington. Why are we profitable? The president of our insurance division said it was pricing." Burroughs looked up at the congressmen and smiled again, "Very reasonable pricing for our healthcare insurance, I assure you. Our executive vice president of sales answered that we are so profitable because of sales volume." Again, Burroughs looked up, "Of *course* a sales guy would say that sales volume is the reason. Our CFO said it was regional demographics. The head of information technology said it was our advanced software for automated claims processing. Our head of accounting said it was business efficiency. Not sure what *that* means," said Burroughs laughing. Burroughs could see his approach was working with the congressmen. They were being entertained. "And our chief of public relations said the reason we are so profitable is that we have a top notch management team." Pushing the paper away from him, Burroughs said, "Well, I certainly don't disagree with that."

"Mr. Burroughs, helpful, very helpful," said Suben, now also smiling.

The chairman interjected in support of Burroughs' response: "Mr. Burroughs, which of those answers do you think is right?"

Burroughs felt he could now be magnanimous. "Why Mr. Chairman, I think they *all* are. They each approach their area of responsibility with pride. And when they hear that we are doing well as a company, they naturally want to feel like they are a part of that success. So, perhaps they view a bit too narrowly the reason for our success…"

The chairman interrupted, "But very successful you are, Mr. Burroughs, and you and your many employees are a model for the industry."

"Yes, yes," added Suben, "a model you are."

Burroughs thought to himself, *maybe we should send some money to Congressman Suben's campaign. I'd like to reinforce the support he's giving us today, even if he is a strange bird.*

The subcommittee chairman wrapped it up: "Mr. Burroughs, thank you so much for coming today to share your thoughts. You have been most gracious with your time."

Exiting the hearing room, Burroughs saw a familiar face in the back among the scores of people. He thought to himself, *now who is that and where was it I met her?*

Outside the hearing room, Burroughs noticed a man had followed him out the massive doors to the marble tiled hallway.

"Excuse me, sir," said the man.

Burroughs turned and at the same time waved off his chauffeur bodyguard who had taken a protective step toward the man. "Yes?" said Burroughs.

"You are the Chairman of Delaware General?" inquired the man.

Burroughs nodded and motioned the chauffeur to step away.

The man took a deep breath, offered his hand to Burroughs and said slowly and quietly, "Sir, I just wanted to thank you and shake your hand. My partner had AIDS and… it could have been so very difficult, but we had your policy and… he went so peacefully. It was the right time, before he…"

Burroughs gently put his hand on the man's shoulder, "Sharing life brings so much joy. I'm sure it did with you and your partner. Sharing death should bring peace, not torment. Thanks for saying something to me." Burroughs watched as the man walked solemnly back toward the big doors outside the hearing room. The man's eyes focused on the floor. Burroughs called after him as the man reached for the door. "You gave him dignity and peace. He knows you did the right thing."

Holding open the massive oak door, the man looked back at Burroughs, and with tightened lips of a man crushed with deeply felt pain, he nodded.

Jackie Best of Baker and Jensen had been waiting for Burroughs outside the hearing room and now stepped forward to join Burroughs. "Walk with me," he ordered. The chauffeur took Burroughs' black leather valise and led the way to the underground parking garage. "Jackie, I didn't like what happened in there today with that Congressman Suben. Someone at HHS is trying to stir up interest in Delaware General and I want it put to bed – quickly."

"You handled the question superbly, Mr. Burroughs," offered Jackie.

"I got lucky because my CEO had me prepared," snapped Burroughs. "Suben – he must have gotten the question from that guy at HHS. I think his name is Nichols, a Ph.D. type. So find out who Nichols works for so I can have him castrated for fuckin' with me." Burroughs saw that his tense reaction to what had happened in the hearing room was making Jackie nervous. *Guess I'm overreacting again,* he thought. He realized her reaction was entirely appropriate: he had deflected a relatively harmless question with humor. He tried to smooth the tone a little: "And Jackie, as you can tell, these hearings upset me. Please try to keep me away from them. It's not good for my blood pressure."

Relieved somewhat, Jackie said, "Yes, sir, of course, Mr. Burroughs." As Burroughs got in the limo she said, "Oh, and I will send you a summary of reaction to your testimony today, sir."

Through the remainder of the hearing, Merritt sat in the back arms folded, then making notes, then looking off to the side, trying to figure out the Delaware General puzzle. *Why did I do this,* she asked herself. She had seen Burroughs smile at her when he left. *He'll connect me to the questions, so I had better do some damage control with Secretary Vickers. But first, I need to get reaction from the chairman and Suben. I wonder what they think; they know him better than I do. I mean, it sounded plausible. God, this certainly didn't go the way I thought it would. Maybe that's the problem: I didn't think it through. Why did he get so pissed? Maybe I'm reading this wrong.*

After the hearing, Merritt tried to catch the chairman, but he had other business. She did manage a few minutes with Suben and his aide.

Always dapperly attired with suit coat buttoned Suben said, "Well, Miss Royce, stayed to the very end? I hope you heard something from the industry people to help with programs for our seniors."

"I think so, Congressman. I wanted to ask you your impression of Mr. Burroughs' answer to the question on profitability." Merritt couldn't help it. She felt exposed and needed some moral support, even if it was from a congressman on the other side of the aisle.

"Clever fellow," said Suben. "He was ready – you saw his paper – though probably did not expect the question at a public setting. A bit theatrical in his response. When I first asked the question, I sensed he showed anger. Miss Royce, universal disclaimers of the guilty." Nodding his head, Suben continued, "Classical responses of someone hiding something. The chairman feels I may be interpreting this incorrectly, but he also felt Burroughs may be too protective of his company's reasons for success."

At this point Suben's young aide, who still had Merritt's page of names and responses from Delaware General, said, "Excuse me Congressman, but when Mr.

Burroughs went through the list of responses, it's curious he omitted one, only one."

"And which is that, Jeremy?" asked Suben, turning his full attention to the aide.

"Sir, the actuary at the company – the only executive omitted by the chairman – said the reason for higher profitability was 'mortality rate of policyholders'," said the aide.

"Hmm, interesting," Suben paused a moment. "Ah yes, well, there you have it, Miss Royce," quipped Suben. "Detect some measure of deception from Mr. Burroughs I did, and Jeremy concludes it must be about the single item Mr. Burroughs failed to mention." With a wry smile Suben turned to face Merritt and clasped his hands neatly in front of him, "So, using my finely honed congressional logic, we conclude... the man doesn't want us to know his customers are dying more quickly than the competition's customers." Both the congressman and his aide laughed as they said goodbye to Merritt.

On the way back to Rockville, Merritt picked up her cell phone. "Mike Nichols."

"Mike, this is Merritt. Meet me in my office. I'll be there in about 20 minutes. The data you gave me from Delaware General caused... a stir today at the hearing. I need to give you cover for a while, and... we have more work to do on this. I think we're on to something."

CHAPTER SEVENTEEN

Challenger 350 en route from Washington to Dover
Thursday, October 22

"Hello, Anita, this is Del."

"Oh, Mr. Burroughs. I have been wondering how the hearing went for you today. Is there anything I can do for you, sir?"

"I survived, in fact I think it went well, but I do *not* want to do any more testifying before Congress. I told Jackie at the law firm to keep me away from those damn things. She said she would send a summary or something like that. I don't care, just remind me never to do any more of those. Association staff can handle the hearings."

"Yes, sir," said Anita.

"See if you can get Phil for me on a secure phone. Call me back. I'm in Air Boss." Burroughs liked the nickname for his new jet. Scheier came up with that, though no one other than Phil Hanson had ever been on the jet – for business anyway. Burroughs had sent Anita home to Seattle to see her ailing mother on the jet a couple of months earlier. And when the plane wasn't busy, he asked the crew to volunteer for Angel Flights. Burroughs had donated nearly 70 hours of flight time the year before to carrying kids who needed transportation for medical treatment and their families.

Air Boss, a Bombardier Challenger 350, was fitted with a full galley and bar up front and a black marble bathroom in the rear. Normally decorated to accommodate twelve or so business travelers, Burroughs customized the interior for only four, plus the two pilots and a seat for a flight attendant in the galley. The interior was deep chocolate leather and dark cherry wood with a warm taupe carpet and matching interior fuselage. A large flat screen against the bulkhead served as display for the computer as well as TV or DVD. Near the rear of the plane, just before the bathroom, was a plush leather sofa. Diagonally across from the sofa, which folded out to a queen size bed, was a desk from which Burroughs made most of his calls. Secure telecommunications gear was installed to allow for encrypted voice and email traffic while cruising at 40,000 feet and 540 miles per hour. Burroughs promised himself that if he ever ran out of money he would spend his last thousand bucks to buy fuel for the plane and have it taxi around the airport.

"Del, this is Phil. Anita said you needed me. How did the hearing go?"

"Phil, hope I didn't interrupt you. Yes, the hearing was… full of Congressmen," Burroughs laughed, wanting to keep this light. "NAI staff did a nice job preparing for the hearing so, it went well. I did have a question from that Miami prick Suben about profitability. Somebody at HHS must have teed him up. He didn't let up so I took it head on and read the list of responses you gave me. Thanks for the notes. It took care of it."

"Glad to hear it," said Hanson. "Say, Jackie phoned me from Baker and Jensen and said you wanted to know who that Dr. Mike Nichols at HHS worked for."

"Yeah, I got a little crisp with her. She probably let Nathan Jensen know I went sideways. Anyway, who is the fucker at HHS so I can have him strung up?"

"It's not a 'him.' It's a 'her,' assistant deputy secretary Merritt Royce," said Hanson. She reports to the number two guy at the department, some former congressman whom I've never heard of, and he reports to your friend Vickers."

"Merritt Royce?" said Burroughs trying to remember where that name fit. "The NAI annual reception, the good looking redhead. And she was at the hearing today in the back."

"What's her problem?" asked Hanson.

"Maybe nothing. Maybe it's just that Mike Nichols. Phil, don't worry about it. I'll handle it with Jackie and maybe give Vickers a call. You have more important things to worry about like the automation project you were going to brief me on…"

Burroughs wrote off the questions for now. *Vickers wouldn't have one of his people getting in my business. But I'll get NAI staff to lean on Merritt Royce to find out what Nichols is up to.*

Next, Burroughs placed a secure call to Friedersdorf. Burroughs knew the call would concern Friedersdorf because they rarely spoke by phone.

"Marc, maybe it's my imagination, but I believe the operational audit we discussed may be of increased importance."

"Any specific event cause this shift in thinking, sir?"

"No. No, I just think you are right that we should become more vigilant, given our fast growth, additional employees, increased number of policies." Burroughs knew that would be enough to put Friedersdorf in overdrive.

"I will double our resources on the audit and accelerate the pace, sir."

Burroughs walked up to the galley of the jet and looked over the wine selection. Since it was a short hop from Reagan National Airport to Dover, no attendant was on the flight. Trying to distance himself from the tenseness he felt over the last 24 hours, Burroughs sighed deeply. Angela had been more than a little interested in his selection of a flight attendant. The attendant was 23, blonde and petite, buxom and cute, and had a penchant for short skirts and tight red sweaters. She had told him about school in Nebraska before moving to Delaware. *Go Big Red,* he thought. He selected a '91 Caymus cabernet and smiled about Angela's mild jealous streak. *It's good for her. Besides, 23 is* way *too young.*

⸺⸺

"Mike, thanks for coming right over," Merritt said as she slid into a seat across from him at the conference table. "My piece of the hearing went as expected today, but an idea I had for the Delaware General chairman backfired."

"Whaddya mean?" Dr. Mike Nichols leaned back in his chair with his hands behind his head.

"Guess I didn't follow this through well enough, but I suggested to a couple congressmen that they may want to ask Delbert Burroughs why Delaware General is so profitable. You said they weren't terribly helpful to you when you called."

"Heh, heh, that's pretty cool, Merritt," laughed Nichols. "I have the dumb idea to call a bunch of those people and you put it on the front page. Think there are any HHS offices in Nome, Alaska, 'cause that's where you and I are goin' soon as the Secretary gets a call from buddy billionaire Burroughs." Nichols grinned and shook his head.

"I have a meeting with Vickers but it's not until next Wednesday," said Merritt. "He's in London for a conference."

"So chances are he's out of pocket for tiny issues like 'Merritt and Mike get the HHS dumb and dumber award of the week.'"

"Mike, don't worry, Vickers isn't going to beat us up for trying to do the right thing. Besides, you have five whole days to get this figured out so I have something to tell the Secretary next Wednesday." Merritt managed a laugh.

"Thanks for including Saturday and Sunday, boss. And just what am I figuring out, and shouldn't this be 'we' not just moi?"

"Drill is the same, Mike. Why is Delaware General so profitable? Except I want you to focus on just one possible reason. We have Congressman Suben to thank for this lead, although he and his staff guy thought the idea was… funny. Funny as in funny preposterous." Merritt went through the 'congressional logic' discussion with Nichols. "Mike, as improbable as this may be, I'd like to check it out. It may be that the most obvious and yet unlikely conclusion is the correct one.

"Hmm, congressional logic," said Nichols. "Might that be analogous to 'military intelligence,' in an oxymoronic sort of way?"

"Five days," insisted Merritt.

"Okay, boss. Five days to figure out if Delaware General Insurance Company is more profitable than the competition because its policyholders are dying faster than the competition's policyholders."

"Perfect assignment. After all, you *are* an actuary."

CHAPTER EIGHTEEN

The Law Offices of Baker and Jensen
H Street, NW, Washington, D.C.
Thursday, late afternoon, October 22

Senior partner Jackie Best had no notes for this meeting with the managing partner. It was a brief update on her work with Delbert Burroughs while he was in the city. As she climbed the circular staircase to the top floor of the H Street building, she thought about her 22 years with the firm. She had started right out of law school as an associate and eagerly consumed the vast amounts of lobbying support work they had thrown at her. She didn't want to litigate – not her style – and she didn't want to work on the same case for the rest of her career. She had seen where antitrust cases had droned on for over a decade. But advocacy for the right causes, that fit.

"Ms. Best, Mr. Jensen is ready for you."
"Thank you, Elizabeth."

Jackie smiled at the 'gatekeeper,' Elizabeth, as she walked with confidence into the penthouse office suite that was home, literally and figuratively, to Nathan Jensen. Jensen, half of the founding team of Baker and Jensen, directed the day-to-day activities of the firm though his age, 68, had slowed his pace a little. *He still moves more quickly than half the 130 lawyers in the building,* Jackie thought to herself. A striking man six feet tall with erect posture, his chiseled features were complemented by a mane of gray hair and the most elegant taste in Brioni suits. Jackie truly admired this man. He had created a personal residence as well as office suite on the top floor, breaking all sorts of building codes. Jackie's countenance warmed immediately as Jensen rose and greeted her.

"Jackie, my dear, how are you this evening?" said Jensen. "I haven't seen you all week."

"Nathan, you are looking dapper and fit as usual."

"Why thank you. Walking in the crisp fall weather agrees with me. You know I enjoy my late morning walks. So many friends to see."

Jackie understood. Somewhat of a loner, Jensen had his driver take him to the National Zoo where, weather allowing, he took his walks and visited the animals, especially the lions, bears, wolves, elephants and rhinos.

"It's a very peaceful place, sir."

"It is. I confess my joy of walking among God's beasts occasionally surpasses my love for humankind. I would prefer them in their natural habitat but, properly architected and managed, zoos and sanctuaries can help educate our little ones to the beauty, grace and nobleness of wildlife, and the need to protect them from those who would do them harm."

Jackie responded, "I think it is wonderful that you are so generous in your contributions to Friends of the National Zoo."

"My, you must have been busy with our friend Delbert Burroughs."

"Yes, Mr. Burroughs had a busy week, as did I," said Jackie.

"Please sit and tell me all about it," said Jensen. "You know, Del is also committed to saving our wildlife. Some day I will share with you his novel efforts in that regard." He offered her a seat in one of the large burl and leather chairs in his sitting area. The decorating style was eclectic gathered from years of Jensen's travels: richly colored hand woven Persian rugs, vases from Athens, a floor lamp from Stockholm, a large antique table and armoire from Paris.

Elizabeth brought in tea for them as Jackie summed up the week. Jensen listened intently. Burroughs had been a client for 20 of the 33 years that Baker and Jensen had been a chartered firm. Burroughs and Delaware General generated 3.9 million dollars in revenue for the firm last year plus another half million dollars or so from Capitol Investigators, Baker and Jensen's wholly owned private investigator subsidiary.

"So work with the association and the hearing itself went well," concluded Jackie. She turned to make sure the door to Jensen's office suite was closed. "Nathan, there *was* a concern. Mr. Burroughs became incensed that Congressman Suben asked him about Delaware General's financials, their profitability. The actuary at HHS was asking questions of company staff last week and the actuary's boss – a woman I've met, by the way – must have fed the question to the congressman. We both know how paranoid Mr. Burroughs can get when he thinks someone may be trying to get information about *his* company."

Jensen understood. 'His company' was code for Gatwick. Neither he, nor Jackie, ever spoke of it by name.

"There is absolutely no evidence to suggest that," asserted Jackie. "Frankly, I think the question was harmless, an attempt to find out how Delaware General can do so well as a company when others like it are faltering."

"Just keep it close," said Jensen. He rose and smiled, "We don't want one of our principal clients to become agitated. And I'll see how he is the end of this month when I visit him in Dover. He's invited me up for the weekend."

CHAPTER NINETEEN

Merritt's townhouse in Georgetown
Thursday evening, October 22

"Hi, Claudia," said Merritt, sinking into a chair with the phone. "Sorry I didn't get back to you at the office today but it was crazy. Hearing in the morning, then meetings. I'm exhausted."

"Poor girl," said Claudia. "I had called to see how the hearing went. When I couldn't get you, I talked with the chairman's staff guy, you know, Tim. So, Tim said there was some excitement when Congressman Suben cornered the Delaware General chairman on profitability." Claudia snickered. Tim had told her Merritt set it up. "Why in the world did you do that?"

Merritt saw Claudia was having fun at her expense, again. She explained to Claudia the data on Delaware General and the company's responses. "Suben thought he was hiding something," offered Merritt.

"Well, maybe so, but Delbert Burroughs *is* an influential republican and I know my senator certainly doesn't want him irritated at us. So," Claudia said, still enjoying the moment, "when you come over here to testify, please don't ask Senator Tidwell to pummel Delaware General with profit questions. Okay?"

"Oh God, I have had *so* many better days." Merritt exhaled heavily.

"All right, I know a bright subject. Instead of congressional hearings, let's talk about Grant. Have you consummated this relationship yet?" giggled Claudia.

"Claudia Kelly, aren't we being the little gossip? And 'no' we haven't. I'm just not sure about him. I mean, I am – he's so good looking. He's a nice guy with great friends. But, I don't know." Merritt told Claudia about dinner the night before.

"A quandary for the beautiful. Say, why don't you come over to the Senate side for lunch some time next week and I'll introduce you to some new committee staff. It may be helpful next time you come up to testify."

"Thank you, Claudia, that would be really good." *I could use more exposure to staff of the Senate Committee on Health, Education and Labor,* she thought.

⇌

"Merritt, hi, it's Grant."

"Hello."

"Merritt, please forgive me for being a little drunk and a little grabby last night. I'm sorry."

"Hammered and handsy," said Merritt with a reluctant smile in her voice.

"Oh God, I was, wasn't I? Shit. This is terrible. We just met. Oh, man, I really am sorry, Merritt. You are so beautiful and successful and I was just kickin' back on my birthday and… oh, wow, how can I make it right, Merritt? God I can't believe I did that. I wanted things to be so proper."

Merritt felt bad that Grant was so upset. *Maybe this is right after all,* she thought. *He's a good guy. He just got a little carried away. It* was *his birthday.* "It's okay, Grant. Why don't we try again?"

"Oh, you are just the best. Why didn't we meet years ago? Try again, how 'bout tonight?"

"Grant, it's 9 o'clock and we *do* have work tomorrow."

"Okay, okay. How about tomorrow? It's Friday. I'll pick you up… early, and we'll… we'll have happy hour in Georgetown and dinner at 1789. We can walk."

"That sounds… good. I like it."

Merritt and Grant talked for nearly an hour. She felt relieved, and now she felt it may work. *I sure hope this works*, she thought. *He's such a sexy guy; maybe I can settle him down. Maybe we…*

CHAPTER TWENTY

Aspen, Colorado
Friday, October 23

Burroughs watched MSNBC while he dressed for lunch with Friedersdorf. "Don't those assholes at the State Department get it?" he growled at the segment on Saudi peace proposals. "Saudi Arabia is the *problem*, not the solution. We oughta neutron bomb those fuckin' ragheads and take over their oilfields." Burroughs stomped over to a long cowhide covered bench to put on his socks, complaining as he went.

"Del, sweetheart, it doesn't do any good to yell at the TV." Angela had come to accept, and expect, her husband's verbal barrage against one thing or another.

"Angie, you'd think those buzzards at State would figure out this is a crusade, not a matter of diplomacy. It's simple: Arabs against the West; radical Islamists against Christians and Jews, hell, everybody else."

Angela came over to the bench and sat down with her husband. "Did you take your blood pressure medicine this morning?" she asked in a sweet, concerned voice.

"Ah, fuck it. Let those bleeding hearts screw things up." He clicked off the TV and turned to Angela patting her on the leg, "Honey, I'm fine. One day when you and I are queen and king, we'll fix this mess. Until then, well, we'll just have to get along with the fruitcakes out there."

As Burroughs walked out of the house he kissed his wife, "I'll be back in a couple hours. It's that lunch meeting with the guy from our Denver division."

One of Burroughs' favored haunts, Montagna at the Little Nell Hotel featured Rocky Mountain cuisine in an Aspen casual setting. Friedersdorf was already seated and drinking ice water when Burroughs arrived. He rose to meet his boss. "Mr. Burroughs, nice to see you."

"Marc, good of you to come out here so we can talk. Let's have some lunch and then take a walk. By the way, two good drinks here at Montagna: Aspen tap, which I see you've discovered, or just about anything in their wine cellar. Richard, the master sommelier, took me through the 15,000-bottle cellar. Too much French Bordeaux for my liking but plenty of big California cabs." Burroughs genuinely liked Friedersdorf and wanted him to be at ease. And he liked discussing business while he walked. It helped him relax and, besides, he knew he needed the exercise.

At Angela's suggestion Burroughs kept his lunch light and managed to limit his Diet Coke intake to two large glasses. He remembered her saying, "Not too much caffeine, love."

As they walked along the nearly deserted streets of the resort town, Friedersdorf gave Burroughs a detailed briefing on the Gatwick operations review, including the individual sessions with members. Friedersdorf had served in several positions at Delaware General before Burroughs had appointed him president and CEO of Gatwick Research. Burroughs had kept near constant surveillance of Friedersdorf for two years before talking to him about taking the helm at the recently formed Gatwick.

Burroughs knew this man well. He understood Friedersdorf's heritage, his family, his health, his finances. He identified with Friedersdorf's driven psyche. He shared his beliefs, and his personal tragedies. And Burroughs had entrusted him to direct Gatwick Research for the past decade and manage the fulfillment of Delaware General's secretive, and most profitable, insurance policies.

Now walking on the outskirts of town in the Victorian west end, Burroughs fought the urge to remember his mom, her last days, the absolute helplessness he felt even with all the resources he could bring to bear. In that instant his eyes welled with tears of a loving son. Burroughs accepted without embarrassment that Friedersdorf sensed his sadness. He knew Friedersdorf had those kinds of memories, too. That was something they shared. It was their bond. Together, at the formation of their executive relationship, they had vowed to spare others the same wasting fate.

"Mr. Burroughs, there are several issues we need to address at Gatwick." Friedersdorf's pace slowed.

"Yes, Marc," acknowledged Burroughs, "we do have some policy issues to resolve." Burroughs had a couple changes he wanted to make, but wanted to break them gently to Friedersdorf.

"Sir, when we last met in the spring, I gave you a quantitative assessment of the changes you made four years ago. As I briefed you in April, the change to allow policyholders to bind others to the Contract has markedly increased our level of activity."

"You're suggesting you can't keep up with policy fulfillment?" Burroughs was listening but not concerned. Friedersdorf, he felt, occasionally overstated the impact of modifications to the business that Burroughs felt were necessary to grow and increase profitability.

"No, we have been able to keep pace. Dunlop, myself and a number of the more senior members have recruited and trained agents to handle the workload. It's more of a moral question, sir."

Burroughs stopped walking and stared at Friedersdorf. "What?" Burroughs liked Friedersdorf's bluntness and today, it seemed, he was going to get some of that straight talk.

"At your suggestion I did not inform members of the change. Only Dunlop and my sales executives have known of the change we made three years ago. Of course, the members and sales execs still have no contact with each other. We simply loaded the additional case files from Delaware General into Gatwick's database of active policies. All of that is transparent to the members: they only see the active files. The members believe all of those active files are policyholders. Of course, with the change, we allowed policyholders to also buy a Contract policy for family, friends, whoever."

"Yes, yes, so what's the issue?" Burroughs wanted to know the problem, if there was one.

"But in the individual member meetings Dunlop and I held at the ops review, two of the members raised a concern voiced by their agents. The agents felt a number of their Contract fulfillments were with policyholders who seemed totally unprepared. That anecdotal data supports what Dunlop and I have seen over the last year in about 20 of the 'state of mind reports' prepared for us by Capitol Investigators."

"Marc, you and I know very well it's not unusual for policyholders to appear unprepared," countered Burroughs. "Here, let's walk." Even on a walk around town, Burroughs did not want to attract attention. "A massive stroke, a car accident causing brain damage – we've had many cases where an agent was called in quickly, the Contract fulfilled and the policyholder and family seemed unprepared. I mean, that's exactly the point: you can't prepare for the unimaginable." Burroughs sensed Friedersdorf needed reminders of the fundamentals.

"Of course, sir," responded Friedersdorf.

"Besides those cases, I still think it's the right decision, as well as good for business, that we allow policies to be purchased for those who don't have a clue that they are covered. First it was 'well, I'd like to also cover my wife,' then it was 'my mother,' then it was 'my ex-wife' – no doubt driven by alimony avoidance – and then it was 'my management team.' I'm convinced we did the right thing." Burroughs reached out and pulled a few needles from a big fur tree while he waited for Friedersdorf to regroup. Friedersdorf continued, "Combine those impressions from our agents with Dunlop's belief that several of our members know the identity of the parent company is Delaware General."

Burroughs gritted his teeth and gave Friedersdorf a look rarely displayed by the chairman. "I *certainly* don't have to tell *you* of the need to maintain *absolute* separation between Gatwick and Delaware General. The *last* thing we need is for a bunch of independent insurance salesmen to get a whiff of the existence of this kind of insurance policy, not to *mention* the authorities."

"No, sir. But there's one more piece."

Burroughs didn't like the sound of that, either. "What's that?"

"We can control Gatwick people. We can't control those we sell to – our policyholders. Some of them talk. And our sales staff offer reference inducements. There's enough history now and other data that…"

"Marc, we've gone over this dozens of times." Burroughs was relieved it was just rehashed concerns from Friedersdorf. "We have layers of control in place. Jesus, Marc, you put most of them in place yourself. Outside assertions of the existence of a Contract policy can't be proved. There is no trace. Anywhere in the process. None in fulfillment, and none in setting up the insurance policy."

Burroughs was agitated and believed he needed to make a stand, again, with Friedersdorf. As he looked around to make sure no one was nearby he stopped and faced Friedersdorf, putting his hand on Friedersdorf's shoulder. "Okay, where's the hole?" Now Burroughs pointed to fingers on his other hand, one finger for each piece of the process, a process on which he knew Friedersdorf needed no lecture: "Your people get sales leads from signed Delaware General insurance policies – life, health, long-term care, catastrophic. All contacts are over the phone after thorough background checks by Gatwick. Those interested are given a local number to call routed to God knows where so Gatwick sales staff can, after rigorously screening callers, answer their questions. Again, your technology makes it untraceable. Policyholders pay only by direct debit from their bank. Software – real fuckin' expensive software, I might add – keeps the accounts rotating and not traceable. We pass data to Gatwick on policyholder status. You monitor policyholder data, and select policies where a Contract is to be fulfilled. Gatwick agents, having no contact with others in Gatwick, get the job done. Untraceable. Complete deniability."

They were now walking again. Burroughs knew that Friedersdorf felt more comfortable having shared his concerns with his boss and mentor.

"Yes, sir," responded Friedersdorf. "Perhaps it is the size of the business, our rapid growth. I just don't want any... sloppiness."

Burroughs continued to put Friedersdorf at ease. "Marc, there *will* be mistakes. Hopefully they won't be cluster fucks. And, yes, growth of the business may open up opportunities for mistakes that weren't apparent with a smaller organization. Frankly, I've always thought the weakest part of our system is sales." Noting Friedersdorf's reaction Burroughs clarified his point. "Not the process, the humans. Sales guys. It's their personality. Too much ego. Loose lips."

Friedersdorf nodded in agreement.

"Tell you what, Marc, why don't you have Dunlop – that crazy fucker always thinks out of the box – go through the entire process, cradle to grave, so to speak. See if he can break it. Have one of your former cops and a techie work with him. Give it priority. We'll meet again in, say, 30 days and review the findings. What do you think?"

"Mr. Burroughs, that's an excellent idea. I'll put together a team. And we will focus on how the system may have become weaker because we are dealing with more volume."

It seemed to Burroughs that Friedersdorf really liked the idea. Sometimes Friedersdorf sucked up to Burroughs. *But, no, he seems to think this operational audit will yield results,* Burroughs thought to himself.

"Okay, now I do have a minor change I'd like to make and then a special request." Burroughs knew Friedersdorf wouldn't like either, especially the special request. "When a policyholder stops paying on the Contract policy prior to paid up status, for whatever reason, we have historically taken them off Gatwick's active list of policyholders. I'd like you to change that. In the future, even if they only make one payment, I'd like you to maintain their active status as long as they are still covered by our health insurance – unless, of course, they want out. By the way, had any of those this year?"

"None this year. Only three since inception and salesman talked all of those out of changing. But to your main point, yes, the change you suggest can be made quickly. We can make that retroactive to last January 1, if you would like," offered the now pliant Friedersdorf.

"Fine. The other matter..." Burroughs took out his wallet and from it a small, folded newspaper article "...is this guy. I understand he's out on bail pending trial." Burroughs handed the article to Friedersdorf. "Let's not burden the judicial process, shall we?"

"We will handle it, sir." Now back at the town center Friedersdorf offered Burroughs his hand in a firm handshake. "I look forward to meeting with you in one month with results of our..."

"Let's call it an operational audit." Burroughs said approvingly. "Marc, you're doing a stellar job. I sincerely appreciate your loyalty and your dedication." Turning to walk back to the cottage Burroughs said, "By the way, I have revised your compensation for the new fiscal year. This will put you in the eight figure bracket."

CHAPTER TWENTY-ONE

Home of Gatwick Research sales executive Tracy Madson
Melbourne Beach, Florida
Friday, October 23

The cool, wet breeze from an onshore wind refreshed Tracy. She pulled her sun lightened brown hair back in a ponytail and viewed the dark tan on her flat stomach. She loved the salt spray; it smelled of ocean and life. She enjoyed an early morning walk barefoot on the beach before starting her day. Tracy's home was also her office. She ventured out to help prevent feeling cooped up. She watched as a flock of pelicans flew across the beach toward the marsh grasses. *They are so prehistoric looking*, she thought.

Enjoying a mug of black coffee after her shower, Tracy began her brief morning ritual of first cleaning the two thin profile and conjoined PC monitors and the large digital flat screen on the wall and then using a pencil-sized compressed air device to clean the keyboards. The computer processors, communications gear and security components were housed in an enclosed temperature controlled and filtered air cabinet behind the rather ordinary looking smoked glass rack of shelves, which contained Tracy's stereo equipment. Tracy's supervisor had insisted on the hidden and enclosed cabinet. She could access the locked cabinet from her laundry room. He told her the special cabinet was needed because of the corrosive effects of salt air. She felt there was probably a more important reason, like security. *What would one of my friends say if they saw all that computer stuff?*

Tracy enjoyed having friends over to her condo. Drinks and a light dinner on the balcony were always a hit at Tracy's. People loved her place. The ocean drew them in. There was something soothing about watching the waves break, rush forward in a foamy slosh and then disappear back into the blue. Sea birds added to the constant motion of life. She didn't have a steady boyfriend – male friends, but no romantic connections. The local guys she hung out with seemed too young and the older, really together guys were married.

When she got the usual questions about where do you work, her stock answer was marketing research, or sales for the market research division of a big insurance company. She was permitted to say the name of the company, Delaware General. She was not allowed to discuss compensation, though her friends could see she did very well. She had strict instructions against disclosing anything about the hardware or communications gear, not that Tracy could have explained it to anyone anyway.

Tracy didn't know she really worked for Gatwick Research. There was no need for her to know. Her contacts were her policyholders and as far as Tracy and her customers were concerned, she was calling on behalf of the Chairman of the Board of Delaware General, just like she said in her calls.

Her salary and sales commissions were automatically deposited every month in her bank account. Her monthly statement showed

The Socratic Contract

only a bank name in the Cayman Islands, although recently she noticed the bank name changed and it looked like a French name.

The company didn't provide business cards so Tracy had some printed up. The cards showed her name, her unlisted home phone number, no address other than Melbourne Beach, Florida – Tracy thought that it was a smart idea not to have the street address – and indicated her title and company as 'Sales Executive, Market Research Division, Delaware General Insurance Company.' The embossed cards were a nice touch, Tracy thought, helped her hook up and impressed the guys who thought she was maybe just a store clerk or something.

Tracy was proud of her success and felt strongly about what she was doing. Her dad had turned her on to Delaware General four years ago when she finished her cosmetology training at Eastern Florida State. He introduced her to an older, well dressed gentleman from Washington, D.C., who had a long discussion with her about careers, how she felt about a wide range of topics, sales, and strangely, she thought at the time, about her mom and how sick she had been. All that became clear to Tracy, of course, when she met the man who was now her supervisor.

Next Tracy logged on to the database. The screen read 'Delaware General Health Claims Information System.' In reality, it was the online system of Gatwick Research. No matter, Tracy just called it 'the database.' The logon process was routine but thorough: three layers of passwords. The first brought the always-on system from sleep mode to active, the second opened the software and the third accessed the online database.

This last password access was designed to offer the sales executive an out if he or she were being forced to log on. The security protocol activated in this event would be transparent to the sales executive and whoever was forcing the logon, but it activated a whole set of draconian measures at Gatwick. Tracy had been told they were effective and would protect her. There was something in the manner in which her supervisor had explained the procedure that cautioned Tracy from probing the issue further.

The last step of the secure logon procedure required Tracy to phone the central switch so her voice could be validated. Only after her voice was validated did Tracy gain active access to the database. It was an automated procedure with a short script: "Hello, this is Tracy Madson, sales executive for Delaware General. I am requesting access authorization. Please confirm." The system analyzed Tracy's voice against an earlier recording. The system also required her to include the key words 'sales executive for Delaware General' and 'please confirm.' If she failed to include those words, the system transferred to a live operator. On one particularly hung over morning, Tracy had messed up her script and the call had been routed to a Gatwick supervisor. After validating through yet another script that this was indeed Tracy and that she was not under any duress, nothing that couldn't be fixed with a couple Excedrin and a lot of water anyway, she was counseled to "stick to protocol." To avoid that supervisor hassle on nights when she expected to party she occasionally left the system on so she wouldn't have to log in when she got home. Tracy was conscientious and wanted to check messages from the company and customers at night after she had been gone several hours but she didn't want to talk to a supervisor after drinking.

With the five minute housekeeping routine out of the way, Tracy checked her list of callbacks. She usually liked to start with those and save the first time calls for after lunch. First on her list was Mr. Albert Thompson of Clearwater. *Oh yes,* she thought, *I talked to Al on Monday. Let's see, he didn't call back with questions so... let's talk to Al.*

"This is Al Thompson. May I help you?" Thompson had just finished briefing his sales associates and completed the Walmart store-opening checklist.

"Good morning, Al. We spoke earlier in the week. This is Tracy Madson with Delaware General. Just wondered if you had a chance to talk with Cathy about the policy we discussed Monday."

"Hang on a minute," Thompson said before he lowered the phone. "Larry, get those lawn tractors moved inside this morning... Yeah I know, but I want to put the winter inventory there... Okay, yeah, fine." Thompson brought the phone back up to his ear. "Uh, sorry, it's busy here. We just opened up and we've got a big sale this weekend. Want to buy a riding mower?"

That made Tracy laugh. "I live in a small condo, Al. No lawn. Maybe someday, though. Tell you what, the day I need one, I'll come and buy it from you. So, you had some questions when we talked. Maybe we could take just a few minutes and you can tell me what Cathy thinks." Tracy wanted Thompson to buy a policy for both himself and his wife. She knew cost might be an issue, but Thompson had said he would talk to Cathy about the policy. Tracy had the Thompson's other policies and family health history on her screens.

"Yeah, I have questions. I wrote them down so I would remember the ones Cathy wanted answers for, too. Uh, hold on a minute while I switch phones." Thompson put Tracy on hold and moved to a phone away from the front of the store. "You still there?"

"Yes, Al, go ahead."

"I'm not sure where to start. This insurance policy. It's... it's obviously illegal, isn't it? I mean you're putting people down like what's done with an old dog."

Tracy closed her eyes, inhaled deeply through her nose and sighed as she looked out the window toward the surf. "I had to put my old German Shepard, Princess, to sleep because she was in bad pain with cancer, Al. That was the hardest thing I ever had to do. I grew up with that dog. She was my constant companion; she protected me, slept with me, walked me to school; she ate the food I didn't want. She was my best friend. I loved her to death.

I went with my dad to the vet's that day, the day I found out why she cried at night, why she couldn't eat, why she peed on the floor. She had cancer. The vet said the cancer had spread and there was nothing he could do. My dad said we had to put her to sleep, that she had the best life a dog could have because I loved her so much. He told me if I really loved her, I wouldn't let her suffer any more. So, I kissed Princess goodbye and she licked the tears on my face." Tracy paused to compose herself.

"Sorry, Al, I get pretty emotional when I talk about her." Tracy breathed deeply again and continued, "When we said goodbye, I cried for a week. I was 15. Someday maybe someone will love me as much as I loved Princess. If I'm lucky enough to find someone like that, I hope in the end he lets me die in peace without suffering."

Al took a few seconds to respond. "I understand. Cathy and I agree with the idea. It's just that, well we don't understand how it works."

"Okay, I certainly understand that. Let me see if I can help by answering the four questions I hear most. First, people want to know if they can change their mind later. The answer is 'yes,' but the Chairman doesn't want you to do this unless you're sure. Second, they want to know how it's done. The answer is it's painless; it's not noticeable to anyone, including medical professionals. The third question is what happens after Medicare kicks in at age 65. Delaware General has a hook into the government so we know what's going on with your claims and health even after we don't pay for your health claims. And the fourth question is how do we know when the right time is. The answer there depends on the condition. If, because of an accident or sudden problem like aneurysm, stroke or seizure, the policyholder becomes nearly lifeless – the doctors call it persistent vegetative state – then that obviously is the time. Debilitating diseases like Parkinson's, Alzheimer's, Multiple Sclerosis, each have their own set of criteria our doctors review. Basically it comes down to quality of life. When the mind is no longer able to comprehend family, can no longer control the body's functions, then it is time. Or when the body can no longer move, breathe, eat or feel, even though the mind is active, then it is time."

"Has anyone with one of these policies... By the way, what do you call it?" asked Thompson.

"I'll get to that in a few minutes," Tracy said. "Go ahead with your question."

"Yeah, okay, well has anyone with one of these policies ever changed their mind?"

"The answer is 'no,' but let's think it through, Al," said Tracy. Why would you change your mind? Not because you all of a sudden don't believe in the idea. The notion is one that seems to stay constant regardless of age, financial status, or change in religion." Tracy was referring to a script on the large monitor now. She was comfortable talking about most of the subjects but sometimes she referred to scripts when a policyholder had a question about a certain disease or, in this case, about 'changing your mind.' Tracy wasn't sure she agreed with the company on this one so she read the script.

"Well, I could change my mind if there was a new kind of treatment for a supposedly inoperable kind of cancer or something like that," said Al.

Returning to the script Tracy said, "There *will* be new drugs, new procedures, gene splicing, things we can't even imagine to cure us. Nothing in the policy interferes with that." Now Tracy added her own views. "It's best to view this policy as a last resort. When everything else has failed – all the drugs and alternative medicine and prayer – then the policy is there to prevent you from unnecessary suffering and humiliation. It also prevents draining your family's financial resources to nothing."

"Yes, I see that," said Thompson. "Okay, well Cathy and I talked about this. We talked about it a lot. We want to do it, but, well, we just can't afford it right now. You said it was one thousand a year for five years. We aren't going to do this unless both of us have the policy, and, well we can't afford two thousand a year. So, I think what we want to do is wait until…"

"Al, I think I have a solution for you and Cathy. We have a discount if you both buy a policy at the same time. One of the plans for those under the age of 50…"

"Yeah, we are," added Thompson.

"… allows you to pay one thousand dollars a year for ten years instead of five, and that buys a husband and wife policy."

"Hmm, yeah, I think that makes it better," said Thompson.

"Then I think we're there. Just a couple more things. First, if you find someone covered by Delaware General health insurance who feels like you and Cathy do about this and they buy a policy, then we take off your last payment. You save a thousand dollars. We will take off one payment for every person you refer to us who buys a policy, up to five. You understand? You bring me five and Cathy gets hers free." Tracy liked this part. Now her customers became her best sales leads. She thought she understood why the company limited the number to five. *We don't want people making cold calls on* this *policy.*

"Really? I bet we can get some other people to buy a policy. I know my brother feels the way I do," said Al.

"This is important, Al. Only *you* can call me about this. No one else, not even Cathy. You call me at the number I gave you before. You still have it?" The number was a local Clearwater, Florida number where Thompson lived, but the call would be forwarded to the Gatwick switch where Thompson's voice would be authenticated by voice analyzers before forwarding the call to Tracy.

"Yes, I have it here. It's 523-0523."

"You can call any time. It's an automated system. It will ask you a couple of questions. Ask for me. If I'm available right then, it will transfer to me. Otherwise leave a message and I'll call you back. Then we can talk. Okay?"

"I understand. But how will I know if the person I referred to you bought a policy?" asked Thompson.

"Because I'll call you and tell you, Al. Remember, they must be covered by Delaware General health insurance. And only you are to call me and give me the lead. They are not to call me directly. Our system will not let the call through. Some companies, like Walmart where you work, allow their people to choose the health plan they want, so even if they aren't with Delaware General today it doesn't mean they can't change. Okay, the second thing is I need the numbers on the bottom of your check from your bank where you want the money taken out."

Thompson read the ABA routing number and account numbers from the bottom left of his checkbook.

"Almost done now," said Tracy. "When you see your bank statement, the one thousand dollar deduction each October 23rd will say Delaware General, just like your other health and life insurance payments."

"That's fine, but where's the paperwork on this?" said Thompson a little uneasily.

"I think you understand why there is no paperwork, Al. Since society hasn't accepted this choice we are making, we need to be careful about how it's done. So maybe a thought crossing your mind is 'how can I make sure this is for real.' I have two examples for you of the chairman's policy. Oh, you asked that earlier, Al. You asked what I call it. I call it the Chairman's Policy. Two examples." Tracy pulled up another screen and sat down so she could read the detail. "Al, do you know Dan and Laura McKenzie? They live near you."

"Yeah, Cathy knows Laura. They teach Sunday school together," said Al.

"Okay, well Laura's mom – she lived in Tampa – fell off a stepladder and broke her back. She was paralyzed from the neck down and couldn't breathe without a respirator. She was fed by tube. She had other tubes. The doctors said she would always be paralyzed. She died while she was still in ICU. Nine years ago, her husband bought the chairman's policy for them both. You understand what I'm telling you?"

"Yeah, I understand. And I wouldn't want to live like that either."

"Okay, Al, here's one more example. Your boss at the store, name is Tom, right?"

"Yeah, Tom Cordova," said Al.

"Tom's oldest brother died six months ago in Phoenix. He had MS. It had advanced to the stage where his brother had little control of his body. He couldn't talk and they had to switch him to feeding through a tube because he was choking on anything by mouth. Two days after they started feeding him by tube he died."

"How many policies like this are there?" asked Thompson.

"I've been selling these policies for four years and I'm told they have been around for about ten years. I've also been told that about 190,000 people have signed up."

"Holy cow," remarked Thompson. "How can it stay a secret if that many people know about it?"

Tracy remembered this question and answer from the scripts: "People protect what they believe in." She turned in her swivel desk chair and closed the database screen on the Thompson family. "Al, just one last thing. Since there is no paper here, the Chairman of the Board of Delaware General has asked me to share with you something from him, from the Chairman personally. I told you I call it the Chairman's Policy. Well, the Chairman calls it something else." Tracy's tone changed from conversational to deliberate, precise language. "He views it as a verbal *contract* between *you* and *him*." Tracy glanced at the other computer screen but knew the

The Socratic Contract

dialogue. "Early in his career the Chairman became convinced that modern medicine, with physicians sworn to the Hippocratic oath, was in many instances *prolonging* life with too little regard for the *quality* of life. Hippocrates believed physicians should first and foremost cause no harm to their patients. Our chairman feels that oath has failed to keep pace with medical technology. Another Greek philosopher, Socrates, believed that *quality* of life was more important than… existing. So, the chairman calls this insurance policy *the Socratic Contract*."

"Yes, okay," said Thompson with the phone pressed against his ear.

Tracy continued, "The Contract says: …" She stood up from behind the PC and took a couple steps toward the sliding glass doors of her balcony. The same flock of pelicans she had seen on her walk flew back over the surf, so ancient looking yet so natural. "… In the winter of my life, as the drifts swell over my soul, I will not burden my family and friends. I will go with my dignity, cherishing the time I have had, and know the grace of God will comfort me."

"That is exactly how Cathy and I feel," Thompson said emphatically. "Can I write that down? I want to tell her those words. That's *exactly* the way we feel."

CHAPTER TWENTY-TWO

Headquarters of Gatwick Research
Denver, Colorado
Friday, October 23

The building had a small, discreet brass sign: Gatwick Research Corporation. Friedersdorf swiped his security card at the dark glass revolving door. "Good morning, Mr. Friedersdorf," said the security supervisor as the chief executive walked the ten paces to the front desk. Gatwick exclusively hired retired police officers for their large security division.

"Good morning, Officer Henderson. Have a big weekend planned?" Friedersdorf took enormous pride in his security team. He viewed each as an unappreciated hero. His officers earned more in retirement than they had on the force. They were well schooled in the mechanics of Gatwick's information systems, communications technology and layered security protocols. They had the best health insurance package offered by Delaware General and, of course, each had been briefed on, believed in and was covered by the Socratic Contract. All Gatwick employees were.

"We're having the grandkids over for a little birthday party tomorrow," said the officer. "Six of them. Think I'll take home my ear mufflers from the shooting range. Supervisor Dawson will be out front here Sunday afternoon if you come in." The front desk carried far more responsibility than the typical corporate reception area. It also served as the human interface to the central switch, the computerized phone system, which fed calls from sales agents who deviated from logon procedures and which intercepted calls made to local numbers around the country when a caller failed the automated voice analyzer comparison.

The three-story brick building stood among half a dozen widely separated office buildings in an office park in residential southeastern Denver. Groves of trees added privacy around the parking lot and building. Gatwick headquarters housed 97 employees. Underground, the computer center rivaled any operations environment on the planet for lights out, online, fault tolerant database processing.

Friedersdorf didn't have a secretary. When he walked into his office on this Friday morning, he carefully took off his suit coat, hung it on a wooden hangar and placed the hangar on a hook behind his office door. The office was modest and no larger than any of the other offices at Gatwick. His office door was usually open. Today would be an exception.

After logging on to the system and quickly dispensing with a dozen emails from financial and technology staff, Friedersdorf pushed intercom button number one.

"Yes, Marc, we're ready for you in Par 4." On a rather slow day a few years back, COO Jeff Dunlop had named each of the conference rooms and asked staff to decorate them with art appropriate the appellation.

Friedersdorf joined the group taking his customary seat along the long side of the table. Dunlop stood at the front of the room scribbling notes on the white board. Member Elliot Weekly had flown in from Chicago and stood to shake Friedersdorf's hand. Also present were Ed Vaughn, the executive who from day one had managed Gatwick's sales staff, and several staff hand picked by Dunlop for their expertise in communications technology, encryption and, importantly, criminal investigation methodology.

Elliot knew all the staff present but felt a certain ominous undercurrent given the inclusion of the criminalist, former Philadelphia chief of detectives, David Angelo. Elliot had met Angelo only once, also at Gatwick headquarters, at a meeting Friedersdorf held to buttress Gatwick's already formidable array of security procedures. On that day the discussion had focused on improvements designed by Angelo to ensure background checks on new agents, sales executives and headquarters technology staff prevented infiltration into Gatwick by undercover police or the FBI.

Dunlop turned from the wall where he had been writing and began, "Marc, I believe we are ready to present you with an outline of what we've come up with. First, for Elliot who represents the members and for Eddie and his super sales guys, let me sum up what I believe is our charge."

Elliot liked being included in sessions like these. He wanted to contribute in ways more than just as a manager of agents. *I'll work hard at this,* Elliot thought, *so Marc will include me more often.*

Dunlop loosened his already loose tie and hitched up his trousers a little causing his shirt to bulge a little more around his expansive waist. "We want to conduct a thorough operational audit of Gatwick procedures and identify areas where our *growth* as a company may have introduced weakness or threat of exposure."

"Precisely," said Friedersdorf, "well put."

"The outline we have developed this week – I've jotted it on the board here – suggests two person teams reviewing procedures for each of three areas: operations here in Denver, that is the processing of data from the parent company; sales; and agents. We…"

"Excuse me, Jeff," said Friedersdorf. I'm sure you have made the point repeatedly, but let me emphasize something. It is *critical* that this group not discuss these proceedings with colleagues. We keep the three areas of Gatwick separate for reasons of security and we never discuss the parent company. Sorry, Jeff, go ahead."

"Yes, Marc, in fact a component of this review should include the point of contact of each of the three functional areas. So, anyway, we have concluded that each of the three areas – operations, sales and agents – has several pieces to look at: technology, communications and the human connection." Dunlop continued, "Now here's the novel feature of this review. Each two person team will review this, um…"

"Three by three matrix," interjected Elliot. He could see Dunlop was searching for a descriptor of the methodology they had suggested.

"Yes, each team will review this 3x3 matrix but without talking to the other teams. The teams will be comprised of the six people in this room," said Dunlop. After the teams take one week to review each of the three areas, a total of three weeks, then we will meet and go over our findings."

Friedersdorf sat back in his chair. Elliot could see he was thinking about what had been recommended. *Maybe he didn't like it,* thought Elliot.

With elbows on the arm rests of the chair and fingers of each hand lightly bouncing off the opposing hand Friedersdorf asked, "But how do we get at whether the procedures are actually being implemented the way they are designed?"

Dunlop scratched his head and sat down at the head of the table. Elliot saw Angelo and the others nod their head in agreement.

Friedersdorf continued, "The procedures may be air tight, but if they are adhered to only erratically or, more likely, if nine out of ten do it right and one does it sometimes, then…"

"Then we need to try and break it," said Elliot. Friedersdorf turned toward Elliot as he finished his thought. "We *do* need to review the procedures for our now higher volume business, and the team reviews will accomplish that. But perhaps we also need…" Now Elliot was struggling for the right description. "We need operatives in our business who try to break the system in each of the three functional areas. Undercover people." Elliot could see the sales exec, Ed Vaughn, wasn't following so he explained further. "For example, in your area, Ed. We could have someone – like me – pose as a health insurance policyholder of the parent company so that my name comes up for one of your sales executives to call about the Contract policy. And I try to get them to compromise security, to deviate from protocol, to tell me something they shouldn't…"

"That's entrapment," objected Vaughn. "Besides, we already record all their conversations and randomly listen to the recordings to make sure they are following procedure."

"I think Elliot is correct," detective David Angelo interjected. "If an investigator is able to figure out how to get a call from a sales executive, then the investigator tries to get the salesman to say something that incriminates him. With that as leverage, the investigator sets up a meet and beats on the salesman until he cooperates in disclosing the rest of the apparatus. That's how I'd do it."

The group sat for a few seconds without discussion. Elliot squirmed a little. This kind of talk made him nervous.

Friedersdorf sat back up in his chair and pulled forward. "Okay, people. Go ahead with your plan to audit the procedures with two person teams. That sounds good. Time frames need to be accelerated though. Get the 3x3 matrix done in two weeks, less if at all possible, then we'll meet." He turned to Dunlop who had a concerned look on his face, "I also want a parallel track targeted at our external contacts, the sales executives. Get David to help you set it up. See if our sales execs have enough technology and training to avoid getting sucked in by an investigator. If not, put together a plan to fix it. Top priority." Friedersdorf turned to Vaughn and leaned forward. "I need you on board with this, Ed. If we have an exposure, it's our contact with those we can't control: our policyholders. And your guys own that."

"Yes, sir," said Vaughn.

Friedersdorf stood up to leave. "Thanks everyone. Jeff, check in with me later and let me know how things look. And let me borrow Elliot for a few minutes."

Elliot rose to follow Friedersdorf. *Oh dear*, Elliot thought. *I wonder if I said something to offend him.*

Walking the empty hallway together back to his office Friedersdorf said, "Good suggestion in there, Elliot. Ed may be too protective of his troops. If we get in trouble, it's going to be because a salesman gets cornered and blows it." They entered Friedersdorf's office and he shut the door behind Elliot. "Have a seat."

Elliot was more comfortable now. He guessed he was about to get a special assignment.

"I have a fulfillment for you, for you *personally* to handle," said Friedersdorf, now opening his desk center drawer. Friedersdorf handed Elliot the folded newspaper clipping Burroughs had given him in Aspen. "Let's not burden the judicial process, shall we?" Friedersdorf said as he handed the clipping to Elliot.

Elliot felt Friedersdorf didn't agree with these fulfillments and noted that his boss failed to make eye contact with him. *And besides*, Elliot thought, *Marc doesn't even talk like that.* "Suspected Child Molester Out on Bail," read Elliot aloud. *Maybe that was gratuitous, but I want him to know how much I do for him. I don't object to these special assignments. In fact, they are fine with me. Each of the cases I have been asked to fulfill were worthy. I know it's not from Marc but from Marc's boss. I wonder if I will ever meet him.*

"Any questions?" asked Friedersdorf.

"No, sir. I am happy to handle these assignments, Marc. It's fine, really."

CHAPTER TWENTY-THREE

HHS Headquarters
Washington, D.C.
Friday, October 23

Before LaGretta let in the next appointment she came in to Merritt's office and over to her desk. "Charlene from the Office of the Secretary called. She let me know the National Association of Insurance Companies president called for Secretary Vickers about an hour ago. This guy, his name is Dr. Gust, was ranting about how you had Mike Nichols ask a bunch of questions and embarrass an insurance big wig. Maybe it was at the hearing yesterday. She didn't get all the scoop because she was listening to the Secretary's executive assistant take the call."

"Oh, geez," groaned Merritt.

"I called Mike," said LaGretta, "to warn him and he said Cliff from the NAI staff had already called him. And your three o'clock appointment is here. After that, you're free."

"Thanks, LaGretta. Your network is amazing. Remind me to give you a million dollar bonus for Christmas," said Merritt.

"Sure, that will be the sixth one this year. Pretty soon I can retire." LaGretta sashayed out of the office and brought in the Washington vice president for the pharmaceutical association.

"LaGretta, please see if Mike Nichols is downtown today. If so, I'd like him to stop by here a little later," said Merritt, "and I'll call Cliff after I finish here."

The courtesy call from yet another lobbyist was over in twenty minutes. As she picked up the phone to call Cliff at the National Association of Insurance Companies, she wondered how much the last visitor was paid. *Probably 300,* she thought shaking her head, *plus a big expense account.* Merritt talked to Cliff and got the details on the NAI president's call to Secretary Vickers. "So, Burroughs called your boss, Gust, and wanted to know why we were picking on Delaware General?" concluded Merritt.

"Yeah and he was steamed about it," said Cliff. "So what's going on anyway?"

"That's just it, Cliff," she said. "Nothing. A few questions trying to figure out why Delaware General does so well when others don't. Why should they get mad about that?"

"Dunno, Merritt, but Gust said Burroughs was hot. And when the chairman is hot, we're hot. So can you help us out here and back off a little?" pleaded Cliff.

"I'll see what I can do Cliff," said Merritt. She hung up and buzzed LaGretta to ask if she had found Dr. Nichols.

"LaGretta, why don't you go home now," said Merritt. "No objections. Go have a nice weekend. Oh, and say 'hi' to Mo from me if you get a chance to talk to him. I hear Virginia Tech is supposed to win this weekend."

"Thank you, honey. Hope you get some lovin' this weekend," giggled LaGretta.

Mike Nichols walked in Merritt's office, sat down on the couch and put up his feet. "I hear LaGretta's son, Mo, is some kind of football player. I sure like that lady."

"Nice boat shoes, Mike," said Merritt as she sat down in a leather chair opposite him.

"Oh, sorry," said Nichols. "We're kind of relaxed down in the bowels of Actuarial Services on Fridays and I guess I forgot I had meetings downtown today. I told the team in Rockville they can dress down if they want. We may have hit a new low this summer. But it'll be cold enough soon to get 'em out of shorts and sandals."

Merritt got to the point. "I called Cliff. Apparently, Del Burroughs called the NAI president, Dr. Gust. Gust called Secretary Vickers. Point of the call was why are we – you, actually," Merritt said, grinning, "singling out Delaware General."

"Interesting," said Nichols slumping down in the couch. "How 'bout if we bag this and go to happy hour somewhere? I've got the top down on the GTO."

"Sounds nice, but you're too young for me." *He's not usually a flirt,* thought Merritt.

"Yeah, sure, I'm 18 months younger than you. Your loss, the goat is spanked and ready to run today." Nichols sat up. "So, I called the actuary back at DG and told him what happened at the hearing and asked him why Burroughs hadn't mentioned *his* reason when he had mentioned the reasons all the other senior DG staff had given. Knew that would get him. Us actuaries are *so* vain about our science. About two-thirds the way through a cogent explanation, he pulled himself up short. Guess he realized he was screwin' the pooch – again. So here's the deal at DG." Nichols stood up and paced around the office for a few seconds.

I wonder what's with Mike today, Merritt thought.

"Seriously, I think we should do this at a bar," said Nichols now sitting on the back of the couch. "This is spooky stuff."

"What? You worried the office is bugged?" joked Merritt. She saw from Nichols' face that he seemed to be genuinely concerned. "What did the actuary say to get you nervous?"

Nichols was pacing again and then, noticing the open office door, he looked outside where LaGretta's desk was and then shut the door. Still walking around with his hands in his jeans pockets he said, "Merritt, actuaries are a pretty strange bunch. There aren't very many of us. Takes years to get certified. We calculate risk, life expectancy, insurance premiums. Advanced statistics, math models. Boring to most people. But we stick together. Nothing to compromise competition in business, but… well, more like a fraternity." Nichols sat down again across from Merritt. "This actuary up at Delaware General, he and I had a good discussion. He knows his stuff. Went to University of California at Berkeley. Those guys came up with the original mortality database. We talked Lexis diagrams and observed death rates and… you know the level of detail he has is extraordinary. He has deaths organized by individual triangles of the Lexis diagrams on fine levels of…"

"Mike, I'm not an actuary," said Merritt shaking her head.

"Right. Okay. He says the reason they're making money in their health insurance business is their mortality rate for policyholders with diseases causing death is seven times higher than the national average. Seven times!"

"Obviously seven times the national average is huge," said Merritt, "but what is…"

"Here," said Mike as he pulled several pages from his pants pocket, "these are the numbers."

Merritt looked at the pages of notes from Nichols' phone call. It had diagrams and rows of statistics, descriptions: cohorts, intercensal periods. But the notes specified a particular demographic event.

"Check this out," said Mike pointing to the unfolded page, "where it says 'onset of diseases classified as terminal.'"

The Socratic Contract

On the last page, she saw two columns with Mike's notes and then his summary: National mean of U.S. born, white, male and female, age > 40, diseases causing death: nqx = .13039. Delaware General: nqx = .91120.

"Mike, does this mean what I think it does?" Merritt was stunned. "Congressman Suben joked about this yesterday: they are more profitable than the competition because their policyholders with serious diseases are dying faster."

"Yup," said Nichols. "The net of this is if you have a health insurance policy with Delaware General and you get a serious disease, you are seven times more likely to die within a year than the national average."

"Which means the insurance company doesn't have to pay for the most expensive last months of life," added Merritt. "They save millions of dollars in hospital claims."

"Correction, Merritt," he said, folding the notes and putting them back in his pocket. "They save *hundreds* of millions of dollars. Over time, billions."

"My God," she said, slumping back in her chair. "Was that why Burroughs was so mad about us asking questions?"

Nichols also slid back. Looking at the ceiling he said, "As you said when you called me after yesterday's hearing: I think we're on to something."

Merritt twirled her hair in her fingers. "Yeah, the question is… on to what?"

"Can't say for sure, boss, but what I *can* say is we need some help figuring this out." Nichols stood up. "How 'bout if I get a couple folks from my staff digging on this?"

"No, Mike. Your description of this as 'spooky' fits the way I'm feeling. Having billionaire insurance CEOs pissed off is one thing. We can probably handle that… note I said *probably*. But how does an insurance company orchestrate a higher mortality rate? Maybe it's something simple like they don't cover expensive procedures, so policyholders don't have them done, so they die more quickly. Who knows."

Nichols sat back down. "Hey, the reason I said this is spooky is…" He sighed noisily and tried to smile. "Did you know that an actuary would rather be absolutely wrong than approximately correct?"

"You're about to tell me I've missed the obvious? You know I hate it when you do that."

Nichols managed a grin. "The reason I said we need help figuring this out is I'd like to be absolutely correct about this. Listen, the numbers on Delaware General aren't an accident."

Now Merritt stood up and walked around to the back of her chair. "So, if it's not an accident, then they *planned* it this way?" She raised her eyebrows, shook her head and pushed the air in front of her with open palms, "I don't like where this is going."

"Me neither," said Nichols.

"I don't suppose your new actuary friend at Delaware General would help you more." Answering her own question she said, "No, let's not push him right now. Let's find another route and then come back to him." Merritt thought about it while Nichols sat there with his arms folded. "Okay, have a couple of your staff find the companies that have their health insurance through Delaware General. Don't tell your staff what's going on. Use secondary research only. No more discussions with anyone. You and I will go over the list and call contacts at those companies where we know somebody. We may have to get some outside help there, but let me handle that. We'll ask questions until they stop answering: why did they go with DG, what is their experience, do their employees like the insurance, what kind of other DG policies do they have, do they have cost comparisons with other health insurance carriers. We need to find out what would affect mortality rates for those with serious diseases so dramatically."

"Got it," said Nichols. "And I'll keep it to myself. Whatever 'it' is," he mumbled to himself as he opened the office door. "We'll have the list Monday. Still think we should have done this at a bar. Later."

CHAPTER TWENTY-FOUR

Merritt's Townhouse
Georgetown
Friday evening, October 23

Merritt leaned forward her palms resting against the slate shower wall as the pulsing jets of hot water worked their magic on her tight shoulders and neck. She tried to relax in the shower, but her life was full of questions.

I have so many things going on and then I step into a mess with Delaware General. But what are they doing? Why should I care? It's not like I don't have enough to do trying to help control hospital costs. And why is Grant driving me crazy? I want him; he's such a hottie, but is he just a girl chaser? Is there something for us, a future?

"Merritt, I'm almost there," said Grant from his cell phone. "I know I'm early so if you're not ready, I'll wait in the car."

"Hi. No, no just come in. I'll unlock the door. Be down in a couple minutes," said Merritt.

Grant launched himself anxiously up the front steps of Merritt's townhouse and opened the black lacquered door. "Hello Gorgeous, I'm here," he called out. Grant took the stairs to the main floor and pulled out a stool at the counter in the kitchen. Meatball jumped up on the counter expectantly just as Merritt came down from the bedroom.

"Did you give Meaty a snack?" asked Merritt.

"You look incredible!" said Grant as he got up and gave Merritt a hug and a kiss on the cheek. "Snack?"

Meatball's eyes got big at the word and Merritt opened the top counter drawer. "Here you go, Meaty," she said with a loving touch to the side of his head. "He's crazy about these things."

"I think he likes the lovin'," said Grant as he pulled Merritt close to him and nuzzled her neck.

"Hmm, you guys are all alike," she said. "Where to first? I wore shoes I can walk in."

From Merritt's townhouse to M Street, one long block toward the river, a vertical drop of 100 feet caused foot traffic to move carefully. They walked holding hands taking the leisurely less steep route first along Prospect Street, then on 35th to the busy street below. Merritt showed Grant the neighborhood of colonial row houses, each with a long history, several dating back to the early 1800s.

"I like the narrow streets and brick sidewalks," said Grant playfully angling his foot steps to match the chevron design of the red brick. "The houses are so old and full of character." He touched one of the black wrought iron hand railings leading up to a late Victorian Queen Anne row house. "What made you pick Georgetown as a place to live?"

"The history, the architecture. It's close to everything and yet a private sanctuary above the river. A friend of my Dad's sold it to me. Must have been as a special favor to my Dad, because I know it was worth a lot more than I paid for it. The biggest purchase I'll probably ever make."

"It sounds like you were close to your dad." Grant put his arm around her.

"He taught me so much. And cared for me. But he always let me choose."

"Was your dad in government?"

Merritt smiled. "Yes, and his father, too. At least early in his career and then Grandpa was a consultant."

"You mean lobbyist?"

"Probably," said Merritt. "I really never understood how Grandpa made his money. But he was … very well off."

"Lobbyists can make a ton of money, especially the smaller firms with just a few partners. My firm makes half its revenue in lobbying. They call it consulting. Helping companies get things done through the Congress. I like casework better than advocacy, though. Nothing like a good lawsuit."

Merritt looked a Grant with mock disdain. "You're kidding, I hope."

"Yes, I'm pulling your … hair," he laughed as he tugged at the hair she had pulled back in a ponytail and tickled her a little."

She liked his easy-going style. He was interested in his work, just not consumed by it, although from their date on Grant's birthday she had seen a side of him that seemed to be dissatisfied with the types of assignments he was given. "My Dad used to say that if we could find a way to put all the lobbyists in Washington and all the analysts on Wall Street in real jobs, America's innovation and productivity would move a generation ahead."

"So when you leave government you're not going to be a lobbyist?"

"Good question," said Merritt. "I'm not sure when I'll leave, or if I'll leave government. I like public policy. I think I'm good at it. But elections and politics may have something to say about when I leave before I can figure that out."

Grant slowed down as they turned the corner onto M Street. "You know, Merritt, work isn't all there is out there." He put his arm around her neck and pulled her face to his kissing her lightly on the lips. He stopped and kissed her again, slowly, taking in her lips. He pulled her toward him and as they were cheek to cheek he said, "I think we are very good together."

Merritt felt flushed like the first time she had danced with Grant. "I think you're right." They started walking again, the evening air growing colder on the noisy main thoroughfare of Georgetown. There was that thought again: all work and no play…

Merritt looked up at him and put her arm on his shoulder. "See that place just down the street? It's called the Old Stone House. It was built in 1765 – the oldest surviving building in Georgetown on its original lot. Did you know that Georgetown is more than 250 years old?

"Girlfriend, you're ignoring me."

"Girlfriend?" she said resisting.

"Well it's too early to call you fiancé, so yeah, girlfriend."

Merritt slapped at Grant's coat. "Stop it. You are *such* a player."

Grant grabbed her shoulders and turned Merritt to face him. "Hey, I'm not kidding. You really do it for me. I mean, I know we just met but you are it, girl.

"I like you, too, *boy*." Merritt was having trouble figuring out this man.

"So we'll take it slow and, uh, get to know each other. How's that feel?"

"It feels like happy hour and Clyde's is just across the street and down a little." Merritt pulled on Grant's jacket and they crossed M Street by the gold dome of PNC Bank.

As they were about to enter Clyde's, one of Georgetown's more resilient watering holes, a familiar voice yelled from across the block: "Hey, Grant. Wait up."

"Well, look who's here," said Merritt. "It's the hulk."

"Brett, what up?" yelled Grant back at the charging lineman and a petite blonde who looked like she was being dragged by a shaved Kodiak bear. After a collective hug at the door, the foursome caught a couple of stools at the end of the bar as a couple was leaving.

"Cool, a place to sit!" said the blonde with a voice at least an octave higher than Merritt thought humanly possible. Her name was Nanci. "That's with an 'i' because most other Nancy's are with a 'y' and I wanted to be different, ya know?"

"For sure," Merritt said with a grin noticing Grant give her a look and mouth the words 'be nice.'

Nanci continued, "Brett says you work in government. Is it boring? I've heard it's like *so* hard to get anywhere in government. Do you like it? How long have you worked there?"

God she talks fast, Merritt thought. "Sometimes, but any job is what you make it; yes; and only about a year and a half in this latest job," answered Merritt while she picked out an appetizer and chardonnay by the glass.

Merritt watched as Brett leaned over and excitedly whispered to Grant something about a 'road trip.' It was obvious Brett didn't want Nanci to hear what was going on.

"Wanna go to the ladies'?" asked Nanci of Merritt.

"No, honey, I'm fine," said Merritt.

Nanci rolled her eyes a little as she slid off the bar stool and headed to the restroom. Merritt saw Brett eye up his petite friend and then motion to Grant.

"You would not believe the bubble butt on that girl," Brett whispered to Grant but clearly in Merritt's earshot.

Grant seemed to ignore Brett's comment and put his hand on Merritt's leg excitedly. "Merritt, listen to this. Brett heard about this band tour put together by Power 98."

"Yeah," said Brett leaning over in Merritt's face. "It's very hot. Three primo concerts. Three cities in three days. The station is chartering a big jet and they have about a dozen tickets left. They're calling it Party Tour."

"When is it?" asked Merritt.

"November 5, 6, and 7," said Brett.

"That's a Thursday through Saturday. We'd get home Sunday afternoon," said Grant. "We'd only have to take off half of Thursday because the plane leaves Reagan National at 3pm. What do you say, Merritt? Let's go!"

Merritt could see Grant was really pumped about the idea but she was concerned about work and this meant lots of things she didn't know if she was ready for. "What about hotels and…"

"Brett says the price for a couple is two grand and that includes everything except food and drink. Deluxe hotel rooms, transportation, concert tickets – all of it. Merritt, my late birthday present to you. How 'bout it?"

She had not seen Grant this excited. "Well, I can't think of a conflict at work and as long as I'm back Sunday afternoon because I can't miss Monday staff meetings – yeah, I guess so."

"Yes," said Grant giving her a big squeeze. "Merritt, you're the best. Wait until you hear the list of bands. And the tickets are all on the floor, up close. The first concert is in Charlotte, North Carolina and the next two in Florida, Orlando and Melbourne Beach."

The three of them raised their glasses in a toast to the Party Tour just as Nanci returned. Merritt wondered who Brett was thinking of bringing along on the tour and hoped it wasn't one of Grant's hand-me-down bimbettes. Maybe the hulk was waiting to see if Grant was going.

"What did I miss?" asked Nanci bouncing her way back up on the stool.

Merritt briefly entertained herself with the thought of the hulk and the petite soprano hooking up.

"Not a thing, buttercup" answered Brett pulling Nanci's stool closer to him. "You know, baby, you are just the cutest little thing. I could eat you up."

That bit of imagery was over the top for Merritt. *That high-pitched giggle,* she thought. *It reminds me of something. I just can't place it.*

On the way out of Nathan's Grant whispered in Merritt's ear. "I think I've got it. You know what you sound like after you suck on a helium balloon? Okay, so add a young Dolly Parton with straight hair."

Merritt laughed. "Was that amazing? So is Brett taking Nanci on the tour?"

"He's trying to figure out if he wants to take her or a girl from the office. Nanci is definitely his type. They've been on a few dates." Grant looked at Merritt. "I think he wanted to know if we were interested in going – mostly you. He knows I'm up for a good concert."

"We'll talk about it more when we get some of the details, but, yes, I would like to go – with you." Merritt was struck by the fact she had said 'yes' so easily to Grant's invitation. It started to sink in. *Three nights together. What if it doesn't go well? Geez.*

"I promise. It'll be a huge time. And, no strings, no…"

"I like the plan, Grant. We'll talk about it later," said Merritt.

It had turned cold and blustery and neither of them was dressed for a long walk in the weather.

"Maybe we should head back toward your place," he said, "and warm up a little before dinner."

"That would be good. I'm getting cold."

"The 1789 is so close to your place. Do you go there much?"

"No, I really don't but I love it, and The Tombs downstairs is a great place to catch a burger and a football game" Merritt said as they began walking back. "I'll change and we can zip across the street."

"And how 'bout wearing another pair of sexy shoes for me?" Grant had his arm around her as they approached the parking garage on the south side of Prospect just a block from Merritt's townhouse.

"I admit it. I love shoes," she said.

Now just at the parking garage Grant tugged at her coat and pulled her around the corner into the brick area recessed from the street. "Warm up break." His back to the wall he unbuttoned his overcoat and motioned Merritt toward him.

She came close to him. "You needed a break just a block from my house?"

Grant unbuttoned her coat. "The wind was fierce and I thought…"

Merritt kissed him deeply and put her arms around his waist inside his sports coat. She leaned into him. Grant grabbed her lowrider jeans below her navel and drew her closer toward him. His cold hands slipped inside her sweater and climbed her sides to her waiting breasts. Still taking in his lips she exhaled with a short squeal as he held her, his icy fingers gently squeezing her nipples. She spun around pulling her long coat to the side now grinding her butt against him and slipping her hand behind her touching his upper thigh.

Merritt yanked down her sweater as she heard someone come up the stairs of the garage. She turned to face Grant and laughed out loud at the expression on his face. Buttoning her coat and watching him try to right himself she said, "you look a little bewildered."

"Be-wild-ed would be more like it. God girl, you're amazing, ravenous, incredi…"

Merritt put her hand over his mouth as the couple from the garage walked by them. "Come on, let's get to the house."

"I'm up for that, so to speak." He adjusted his coat and hiked up his trousers. "You sure you want to go to dinner?"

"Yeah, I'm hungry. Aren't you?" she asked with a grin.

They walked quickly to the house. Meatball met them at the door but quickly scurried away up into the living room.

"Grant, why don't you sit down in the living room and relax while I go put on something more dressy for dinner. And turn on the fireplace so we can warm the place up. The remote is on the coffee table." Merritt started up the stairs and looked back to see Meatball and Grant stare at each other. *I wonder if those two boys are going to get along.*

Grant felt the heat of the fireplace and watched as the flickering light from the flames danced against the walls. He walked to the glassed in porch and viewed the lights of Georgetown below and left and, beyond that, down the river to the sparkling white marble of the Kennedy Center where he and Merritt had first met, where they had danced, where he had felt a connection.

As Merritt came down the stairs, Grant walked toward her. "So I see you're all ready to go, coat and all. Let's see what shoes you picked out for tonight."

Merritt stopped in front of the fireplace to model. "Round toe casual pumps by Stella McCartney," she said, twirling with her trench coat wrapped around her. "Do you like them?"

"Sassy," said Grant. "You *are* a girly girl, aren't you? So pretty, so sexy – even in your overcoat." Grant moved close to her and, putting his hands on her hips, kissed her, slowly taking in her lips, touching her tongue with his. "I want you. Let's skip dinner and…"

"Well, I'm still a little hungry," said Merritt with a teasing half smile, but maybe we could start with some dessert." She took half a step back toward the fireplace and let her coat slip off and fall to the floor. The flames from the fireplace flickered on her bared silhouette.

"Whoa, you are a vision of perfection," said Grant as he put his arms around her bare waist and kissed her passionately.

Merritt felt her temperature soar as he touched her skin, moving his hands over her body. She gave herself to him, releasing her control, nearly collapsing in his arms.

They fell on to the overstuffed sofa, she on top of him. Grant kicked at his shoes. As he pulled at his pants to get them off, he said: "Be gentle, it's my first time and I …"

Merritt pushed her arms straight against his chest, her back arched, her auburn hair cascading in his face: "Grant Launder, kiss me and shut up!"

From his perch on the large green leather chair next to the fireplace Meatball occasionally looked over at the couple, responding to the sounds of passion.

Grant helped Merritt pull the white knit throw over them as they lay facing the fire, aglow in the sweat of their intimacy.

"I'm going to need bigger condoms. You make me absolutely huge," said Grant.

"You were absolutely adequate," said Merritt with a wry smile. "And speaking of being prepared, did you bring a toothbrush?"

"My 'merit' badge in overnight stays is well deserved. Ya like that? 'Merit' badge?"

They wrestled on the sofa over where they would end their next date, his place or hers.

"I am also absolutely famished. How 'bout a run to Blimpie's? We can just throw on some clothes," said Grant.

"Okay, but I'll make breakfast here in the morning – just before I kick you out," responded Merritt. She sat up, put on Grant's sweater and ran to the stairs.

He tossed off the knit throw and ran after her, catching her by the sweater as she reached the second stair. Spinning her around he pulled off the sweater causing her breasts to bounce in his face. "Hmm, maybe Blimpie's can wait."

"Let's stick to the plan," she said. "You drive, I'll run in and get the subs while you go around the block." Merritt's nude saunter in heels up the stairs held his attention. Merritt liked the attention. And she loved what was happening.

CHAPTER TWENTY-FIVE

Merritt's Townhouse
Georgetown
Saturday morning, October 24

Merritt awoke to the smell of … "What *is* that," she wondered aloud. *My God, what is he doing?* She hurriedly put on pajama bottoms. She still had the top on but had lost the bottoms sometime during the night. She cooed at that as she made her way down the stairs trying to fix her hair a little as she went.

"There she is. Sleeping beauty!" said Grant as he poured into a hot pan full of crispy fried bacon pieces and its oily residue what looked like an egg mixture – an egg mixture voluminous enough to feed a platoon of hungry troops. He popped bread in the toaster and turned to face Merritt. "Grab a plate and pour some OJ. Breakfast a la Grant is just about ready."

Merritt came over to see the egg, bacon and grease puddle bubble with male pride. "Morning, lover," she said to him with a hug and a peck, remembering she hadn't brushed her teeth. "Is this another Grant masterpiece?"

"Well, given the scarce resources, it'll be a 'lite' version of Grant's best. Hey, you, come here. I need a better hug than that. And I like that – lover."

Merritt felt him squeeze her from top to bottom, literally. He has such nice big hands, she thought to herself. "Nice PJs," she said. She admired his buffed, tanned chest and six pack abs.

"Oh, these are my running shorts. I don't own any pajamas. Maybe you noticed last night. I sleep in the raw."

"Hmm, no, I didn't notice," she said pouring the juice. She flashed back to their raucous lovemaking at four in the morning. He had taken her, powerfully, without mercy. And she had given herself to him. She felt wet and blinked her eyes. She caught herself before she spilled the orange juice.

"I don't want to overstay my welcome," said Grant as they sat at the round kitchen table to eat, "but you said you wanted to cook breakfast and, well, you looked so peaceful and pretty as you slept that I didn't want to wake you."

"I loved last night, and you are not overstaying your welcome."

They talked of Georgetown, of the up coming Power98 party tour and then jostled over who got which part of the Saturday *Washington Post* to read first.

Merritt watched Grant as he devoured the sports section and mumbled about some football trade. She saw on page two of the front section an article on rising insurance costs. She recalled from a recent *USA Today* a similar article that said for the first time in 20 years, small businesses named rapidly rising healthcare costs as their biggest concern. She stared at the table. *The number one headache for small businesses – taxes – replaced by soaring health insurance costs. It's getting worse.*

"So, what are you thinking about?" asked Grant. "By the way, why were the eggs brown?"

"They are organic." She could tell by the look on his face that didn't mean much. *Men*, she thought. *Just amazing.*

"Humph. And the bacon was weird. I had to add some grease."

"It's turkey bacon. You *added* grease? No, no, I do *not* have grease in this kitchen!"

"Okay, oil. So what were you thinking about?"

"Oh, I was reading about how much healthcare insurance is going up. It means businesses are putting more of the cost burden on employees or higher deductibles for families, or both," she said.

"Yeah, the law firm has been good about that, though." Grant still had his head in the paper. "Ours has stayed about the same. I don't get the juicy litigation assignments, really a bummer, but I can't complain about the benefits."

"Really? What health insurance do you have?" asked Merritt looking up from the paper.

"It's called 'Preferred.' Pretty good, too, although I haven't had to use it much. Just for my knee. I'm in fair shape so I don't need…"

"No, I mean what insurance company?"

Grant put down the paper and picked up another slice of bacon viewing it suspiciously, "Delaware General."

Merritt's mouth fell open. "Your firm uses Delaware General?"

"Yeah. So, what's the big deal?" asked Grant somewhat defensively. "A lot of people do. Well not so many in this area yet, but they're big elsewhere on the east coast."

"I'm … I'm having some issues with Delaware General right now."

"You mean you have a claim with them that they won't pay or…?"

"No, Grant, I, uh … I'm trying to figure out why they are doing well – profit wise – when other companies, like these I'm reading about," Merritt said as she waved the paper, "are either losing money or are raising rates through the roof." She tossed the paper on a vacant chair. "Oh, just work stuff."

"I mostly work on cases between the Feds and our energy clients. Natural gas and also fuel pricing – gasoline, diesel, jet fuel,

fuel oil. Sometimes we can negotiate with the Department of Energy or the Federal Trade Commission. Sometimes they just want to beat us up. This Administration has been better about that, though. I don't know much about what we do for Delaware General."

Merritt was incredulous. "You do work for Delaware General?"

"No, *I* don't. But the firm has had them as a client for longer than I've been there. I think for something like 20 years."

Merritt continued her look of disbelief.

"You know I really don't know, Merritt. If I had to guess, I'd say regulatory stuff and maybe some lobbying. Guess I could find out if you're curious."

"No, no. Guess I'm stressed by the job some these days. Didn't mean to bring work up."

"Hey, it's okay. I remember I unloaded on you on my birthday about my job. Gets to me sometimes. The crummy assignments. But, hey, that's what friends are for. Sounding boards." Grant stood and walked over to Merritt, leaned over her and said, "Yep, that's what friends are for. And lovers are for..." He nuzzled her neck and gave her wet ear kisses.

Merritt screamed in fun and raced up the stairs passing Meatball who she saw had a look of terror on his face.

Grant ran after her but couldn't catch her before she locked herself in the bathroom. "Mer-ritt," he sang in a baritone voice.

"Not before I brush my teeth..."

Grant looked back at Meatball on the stairs for support. Meatball saw him but turned his head away disinterested.

CHAPTER TWENTY-SIX

The Burroughs Mansion
Dover, Delaware
Saturday, October 24

"Angela, do you want to come along?" Burroughs liked it when his wife went on these Saturday jaunts to homes for seniors but could see she really wasn't interested in going today. He gave Chuck a quick grooming with a wire brush and took a short braided leather lead from the line of tack hooks near the side door leading to the eight-car garage of the Dover mansion.

"No, honey. You and Chuck go talk to the old folks and I'll call the caterers about next weekend. Remember, you won't be able to go next Saturday. We invited Nathan Jensen and the Tidwells up for the weekend and we have a big dinner party next Saturday night."

"Right. It'll be good to see Nathan again. Well, we're off to Greenside Village – back in a few hours."

Angela kissed her husband goodbye and petted the big golden retriever. "Chuck, you kiss the old folks for me and be a good boy.

Del, you didn't mention the Tidwells. You're not happy to see them next weekend?"

"He's a pompous ass and she's a social climber with painted eyebrows."

"Oh, you like him, and I'll keep her away from you. Besides, you said you would help him with his reelection."

"Yeah, Senator 'Pompous.'" Burroughs opened the back door to the black Range Rover and the Golden jumped up and in, tail wagging. "Yes, you're a good boy and we're going for a ride. Bye, hon."

Burroughs' estate included a half mile of frontage along the west side of the St. James River, a waterway less fit for recreation than for the view from the mansion's veranda. The leisurely drive to the south side of Delaware's capital city took 30 minutes, passing from rolling hills of tall oak and maple to the flat suburbs.

Greenside Village spanned 102 acres just east of the interstate. *It's one of the nicer places for older folks*, Burroughs thought to himself. Plenty of things to do for the residents and, like many of the larger developments for seniors, a choice of independent living, assisted living or nursing home care. Burroughs remembered the slow, painful progression his own mother had gone through after his dad had passed away. Of course, she had the financial resources to live at home with fulltime nurses, a maid and a cook. *Better to live at home*, he thought, *but then not everyone has that option*.

He and the dog had visited nearly all of the homes for seniors in Dover. The most difficult visits were to the nursing homes. More difficult yet would be to hospices, where terminally ill people went to await their death, though Burroughs never went to a hospice. He didn't believe in letting life slip that much.

Burroughs opened the door to the Greenside Village nursing home and Chuck, pick of the litter of grand champion golden retrievers, trotted in tail wagging. He loved the dog's happy demeanor. He knew Chuck's attention, licks and soothing presence meant more to the residents than his human visit. As Burroughs walked to the reception desk the sight of wheel chairs and antiseptic scent of adult diapers tugged at his chest. He noticed Chuck's sensitivity to the old people, many still in their night clothing sitting in chairs lining the hallways. The dog always seemed to, instinctively, dial it down for older people. *Animals are smarter then we give them credit for*, he thought.

Joining a 'conversation' Chuck was having with one of the residents, Burroughs approached an elderly man who had been awakened by the dog's attention. "My, you are a handsome puppy," said the old man. "What's your name?"

"My name is Chuck," said Burroughs answering for the dog, "and I'm six years old."

The old man didn't look up but reached to hold the dog's big head and floppy soft ears in his hands. Burroughs could see the man's callused hands had worked in the fields and now felt the ravages of arthritis.

"My son has a dog like you. Big, pretty dog. Yep, with lots of fur just like you," said the old man as he stroked Chuck's ears and neck.

Burroughs knew better than to ask about the old man's son. Nursing homes like these were not a favorite of sons and daughters. As Chuck licked the old man's hand and continued his 'conversation,' Burroughs looked down the long hallway of chair-bound seniors. *Such long hallways*, he thought. *Bet more than half these people never see a relative.*

"Well, hope we see you on our next trip here to Greenside," said Burroughs to the old man.

For the first time since meeting Chuck and Burroughs the old man looked up and nodded, "Yep, I'd like that." The old man slumped back in his wheel chair. "Better make that soon, though. Doc says my heart isn't gonna hold out much more."

Next, Chuck walked briskly up to a nurse. "Well, look who's here," said the nurse. "We're always glad to have you and your beautiful golden visit. You know, I can just feel the blood pressure go down when that dog strolls through."

Burroughs nodded and followed Chuck down the hallway.

A bent over little woman with a walker was Chuck's next contact. Burroughs remembered this lady from a prior visit. "Good morning," said Burroughs.

The little lady slowed her shuffling slippers to a stop and, looking at Chuck, said, "Cats are smarter than dogs."

"Yes, I've heard that. And, at least with Chuck here, you won't get any argument from me," Burroughs laughed. Chuck was sniffing the yellow tennis balls covering the walker's legs.

"Why don't you bring a cat next time," insisted the little lady.

"Hmm, I don't have a cat," he responded.

The little lady started shuffling again. "Nobody ever has what I want around here."

Chuck moved on and slowed his walk as he came to a very pale old man in a wheel chair being fed what looked like baby food by a young nurse. The dog sniffed at the man's knee with no reaction from the old man. The nurse gave Burroughs and his dog a wan smile. Burroughs watched as Chuck rested his head on the old man's leg. *It seems God's furry empath is at work again*, thought Burroughs.

The chairman and his dog visited with about 20 old folks that Saturday. On the way home he made a mental note to sneak out from Angela's dinner party preparations next Saturday so Chuck could have another 'conversation' with the old man with the weak heart.

"Tom Cordova?" Tracy had his Walmart work number on this Saturday afternoon and wanted to make sure she caught him, even if it was from her cell phone after two sets of tennis.

"Yes, this is Tom."

"Hi. Tracy Madson with Delaware General. Just wanted to let you know that Al Thompson and his wife signed up for the chairman's policy. So, first of all, thank you for the referral and, second, you and your wife get a $2,000 referral discount off your policy."

"Well, nice to hear that. I thought Al might be a good candidate. But his wife signed up, too. That's a bonus."

"Now, just a reminder, Tom. Please do *not* discuss this with Al or anyone else. By the way, since you were curious about it, he didn't ask if someone had referred him. If you have other referrals, you have my number. Okay?"

"Thanks, Tracy. Say, something's been on my mind since we signed up for the policy." Tom closed the door to his small office near the front of the store and sat down again.

"Go ahead, Tom." Tracy walked to the corner of the tennis court complex and leaned up against the chain link fence.

"Well, my wife and I aren't what you would call active church goers. I mean we go with her Mom to church a few times a year but our beliefs are more private. Guess we just don't talk about it much." Tom put his head down a little and cupped his hand into his receding hairline as he spoke, now a little more softly. "Do people who buy the policy, are they… are they all religious, I mean really bible thumping types or are they… or don't they go to church at all? Guess I'm having trouble trying to say what I mean."

Tracy didn't have her answer scripts in front of her but was comfortable with the questions of faith and the Contract. "I think I can help, Tom. There really is no religious or church-going profile of those who buy the policy. Christians, Jews, active and inactive, agnostics, atheists and probably some eastern religions, too. They all have bought the policy. The policy doesn't say you have to believe. It is an insurance policy. Your beliefs are yours and yours alone."

"Separate," he mumbled.

"And, Tom, I get the question a lot. Anytime you start thinking about your own mortality, the end of life, the finality of it, you – I'm sure all my clients – start to wonder what else is there? What happens next? The decision to buy the chairman's policy doesn't say anything about your faith except that you don't want to suffer, that you don't want your family and friends to bear a huge burden. The Contract doesn't say you're not afraid to go. Most of us just try not to think about it. But you can be prepared."

"Yeah, I guess, and the rest is between you and your God."

"That's a good way to look at it," responded Tracy.

"Maybe my wife and I watch too many movies. Seems to come up a lot, though."

"What's that, Tom?"

"The notion that, well, like the soldier said to his buddy in that Vietnam movie... what was it – *Hamburger Hill*? Anyway, where another soldier had been badly wounded with his guts hanging out, the soldier in the background said: 'Better to check out than to go home all fucked up.' Then the medic shot the guy up with a lethal dose of morphine."

Tracy listened. She knew when to listen and when to stay quiet. Vetting of the Socratic Contract took different forms for her clients. It was a deeply moving experience for many of them. But then they would accept and file it away, resolute in their decision.

"And then in *Million Dollar Baby* the proud girl boxer who had been hurt badly, paralyzed, and was on a respirator said to her manager by her bedside... remember that movie? Hillary Swank and Clint Eastwood... 'I need you to do me a favor. I need you to do for me what Daddy did for Axel.'"

Tracy could hear the pain in Tom's voice.

"Tracy, I remember when we first talked you told me about your German shepherd, Princess, and what happened. Axel was also a shepherd. I think it's the right thing. Whether for dogs or humans. God doesn't want us to suffer."

Tracy was now standing upright her hand over her mouth thinking of her beautiful furry friend of so many years. "Thank you so much for remembering my Princess, Tom. Thank you."

CHAPTER TWENTY-SEVEN

Saturday afternoon, October 24
Phoenix, Arizona

Elliot had flown first class to Phoenix from his home in Chicago. After all, this was a special assignment directly from the CEO of Gatwick. *I'm quite sure the chief executive at Delaware General Insurance Company gave the assignment to Marc Friedersdorf personally,* Elliot thought. He wasn't supposed to know the parent company's identity. That jewel of data had come to him from one of his agents. During a fulfillment the agent had found a Delaware General long-term care policy in the same file with handwritten notes describing the Socratic Contract. Elliot had discounted the file to his agent as meaningless and had never discussed the discovery with management at Gatwick. He liked having these little secrets.

On his cab ride from Sky Harbor Airport to the Cricket Pavilion where the concert would be later, Elliot went over all the preparations in his head but quickly shifted to thoughts more pleasing.

Actually, this should be rather fun, he thought. *I've only met her once in the flesh. She was exquisite, and all our phone conversations since have been personal and productive. Shana is so very cool, even if she is a bit pedestrian, and such a pretty girl. Oh, and the clothes. To-die-for outfits. Her voice can be so angelic, yet I just cannot seem to become an aficionado of country music. It's so... rural.*

As the taxi pulled up to the concert arena's back entrance, Elliot took his laminated backstage credentials from his shoulder bag and put them around his neck. He slipped off his jacket and stuffed it in the bag. His black short sleeved jersey had 'Event Staff' in large yellow block letters on the back and 'Elliot Weekly' and 'Security' embroidered in small script on the front. He had never gone backstage at a major event, but Shana had made arrangements for his visit and told him what to expect.

Elliot knocked on the large door of the center backstage area. The door opened with a metallic groan and he could feel suspicious eyes of 'Event Staff' working him over. *Oh my,* thought Elliot. *They are all so big. And they fill out their jerseys and I look like a 90-pound weakling. Why did she want my last name on the shirt? I just know these men are laughing at me.*

The large black man who opened the door reached for Elliot's credentials. Elliot recoiled a little not knowing what this beast with the bulging biceps was going to do to him. Taken aback, the security guard said, "Hey, I just need to check your picture ID."

"Oh, yes, of course."

"Okay," said the guard. He yelled behind him to a group of several similarly clad men inside, "The computer guy is here: Weekly." Turning to face Elliot he said, "Okay, Mr. Weekly you can come in. I need to look in your bag first, since you're new around here."

"Yes, no problem," said Elliot.

"So why does Shana need a computer security expert," asked the guard.

Elliot's creative side went into high gear. "She wants to stop illegal recording of her concerts and posting them on the net. Lots of pirating going on."

"Hmm," said the guard with the biceps. "How do you do that?"

Okay, you want more? Elliot threw the bag over his shoulder and looked calmly at the large black man. "I've developed interspatial neural scoring software which, when filtered through preamp processors and then downloaded through the PA system, interrupts recording of Shana's voice by sucking inaudible data bits from the mid and high frequency bands – but is undetectable by the audience. Works like a charm. Where can I find Shana?"

"Uh, yeah, Mr. Weekly, right up the stairs, red door with the star on it."

Pleased with his performance Elliot strode past the other security guards and up the stairs.

"Come on in," she answered. Shana was sitting in front of her dressing room mirror applying mascara, barefoot and dressed in bra and panties. "Elliot, nice to see you again. Sit down. Care to do a line with me?"

Oh my, I don't remember her like this, he thought. Elliot could see the hand mirror on the dressing table had four lines of what he assumed was cocaine and a short straw. "Thanks, no. I'll stay straight so we can do this tonight."

"Straight? Right. Well, I need the bump now. I told the guy to come before the concert, instead of after. We're leaving right away for L.A. I hate that fuckin' bus."

"Shana, the plan was for *after* the concert. Lot's of people backstage; easy to disguise what we've done. This is too exposed. It's..."

The country singer put down her mascara. "Look, Elliot, I do this for Friedersdorf because I think it's the right thing. God knows he's helped me out with my family, and I appreciate it, sincerely. But plans change, so let's just do this and move on."

Elliot sat down and looked at the floor. *This is not going the way I planned. Maybe I should call it off and reschedule – no, Shana may not be the right one for this. I'm going to have to go think about this.*

"Don't worry, this creep won't know what hit him. I'll have him so worked up, he'll be thinking with his little head, not his big one."

Okay, adapt, improvise, Elliot thought. "Shana, how will you explain my being in here with you? And I'm not ready yet. I thought I'd have about three hours before we did this."

"Lord, Elliot, would you calm down." Shana stopped putting on her makeup again and poured a shot from the Wild Turkey bottle on the dressing table. "Here, drink this. Drink it!"

Elliot followed her order and the bourbon burned all the way down.

"Now listen. He'll be here in…" She looked at the wall clock. "He'll be here in 10 minutes or so. Security will call me first and escort him in. I have four other back stage visits before I go on in an hour. When the visitor after him comes in, I'll give the creep a hug and let him grope me while you stick him. Easy. Here have another shot. I'm serious, Elliot, drink!"

Again, Elliot did as she ordered. *My God, this is so harsh,* he thought. *Oh, I don't know. Maybe she's right. But what happened to my pretty Shana? This girl is raunchy and bossy and…*

"Here, help me zip this up." The very short white skirt flared from the waist and was a little tight.

"Okay." *I can't get over how different she looks from when I first met her,* he thought. *But then it was at a formal reception and she was all dressed up.*

Shana stood in front of her full-length mirror. "Shit, I'm not getting any younger." She unclasped her bra and threw it across the dressing room. "Hand me that pink top on the rack."

Eyes wide open, Elliot complied. He watched as she shimmied into the translucent hot pink top.

"There now, that'll wow 'em. How 'bout you, Elliot? Like what you see?"

"Of course, Shana, you always look spectacular. Uh, so what shoes will you wear?"

"You know, Elliot, it's okay to be gay or bi or whatever you are. Just go with what God gave ya. Know what I mean?"

Elliot could feel himself flush as he protectively shut his eyes and sighed deeply. "Shana, please, let's think about doing this some other time."

She had her hands on her hips and got in Elliot's face. "Look, Elliot. It's happening tonight, right now, or it's not happening. Listen, I've done your 'Contracts' before by myself: kids' wing of a cancer center, a fat politician at NIH, some rich bitch in Palm Springs. Eight times. I've helped whenever Marc needed special access, whenever I could. Fine. But now you show up with all these special plans and, I mean, what's the big fuckin' deal?"

The phone rang and there was a knock on the door at the same time. Shana reached for her platform heels, answered the phone and yelled at the door, "Come in."

A burly security man opened the door and motioned him in. Cautiously entering the dressing room, the man had a big grin on his face. In his late 30's, balding, nicely dressed with a bouquet of flowers in his hand, he gushed, "Shana, I am so very pleased to meet you. You are my favorite country star. I love your work. Thank you so much for inviting me here. This is the biggest thrill for me."

Shana's mood swung to Nashville elite. "Darlin', thank *you* for being such a great fan of mine. Come sit for a minute. Elliot, take the flowers and put them in water, will you?"

Elliot took the flowers and put them in one of a series of expectant vases and stood in the corner of the room listening to them converse. *I think it will be some time before I see Shana again*, he thought. *I can't believe how she is effusing over this disgusting human. I must remember this is an act. She is an actress. And I am the closing curtain on this miscreant.*

A few minutes later the door knocked again and Elliot answered. The next set of backstage visitors was anxious to see their country idol. Shana stood, as did her first guest. "Thanks again, darlin', for coming to see me." Shana looked at Elliot as she said to the man, "Come on now, give me a big luscious squeeze."

On cue, unrehearsed as it was, Elliot approached the man's back.

The man put his arms around Shana and then pulled her waist toward him. Shana cooed and wrapped her arms around the man's neck.

Elliot moved quickly. His left hand touched the man above the exposed right elbow and then, leaning into the man, his right hand touched his black onyx ring. As he touched the ring he said to the man, "You are a most cooperative fan. We'll have someone take you to your seat."

It seemed to Elliot the man didn't feel the prick from the ring. Perhaps, as Shana planned, he was caught up in the moment. Certainly it had never been an issue before, yet he was always relieved when the recipient failed to notice. Elliot escorted the man three steps to the dressing room door where another of the 'Event Staff' took him to front row seats of Cricket Pavilion.

Elliot went through timing. *Two hours plus until the concert is over, an hour to get where he's staying, and, given his good health, maybe an hour cushion before he falls over dead. No problem, but the original plan was still better.*

After the next set of guests left her dressing room, Shana asked Elliot, "So, that guy, the first guy, the creep, he raped and killed little kids?"

"Three boys, ten years old or younger," said Elliot coldly. "Each on their way home from school or soccer practice. All in the last year: Phoenix and L.A. And then, he mutilated them... in a most horrid manner." He reached for his shoulder bag to get his jacket. "The guy probably was a molester first, but then he graduated to murder. Really sick. Apparently there were miscues in the L.A. investigation, but our research shows solid evidence by the prosecutor here in Phoenix, including DNA, tying 'the creep,' as you called him, to the crimes. His family has money so he hired a big gun lawyer, who claims there have been crime lab screw-ups. Anyway, the judge let him out on eight hundred thousand bail and took his passport. He has no priors, at least here or in L.A. He did it, though. Absolutely, no question." Job done, Elliot put on his jacket.

"Elliot, I could have handled this," Shana said matter of factly.

"Yes, you could. But this is *not* a Socratic Contract. This is special."

CHAPTER TWENTY-EIGHT

Early Sunday evening, October 25
HHS Actuarial Services
Rockville, Maryland

Suppose I could have done this from home, he thought. *Except I said print it and then delete the files. First time they've heard me ask for confidentiality about anything in the two years I've been here. Okay, what do we have…*

Dr. Mike Nichols, chief actuary of HHS had cut short an NFL Sunday barbeque with friends and driven to his Rockville office to review what his staff had pulled together.

Four Coors Lite should help this process, he thought, although not entirely convinced of his prognostication. *Let's see, we have 14 pages of companies who enlist the services of Delaware General for health insurance. Whoa, would you look at this? The staff knew I was being weird so they… My God, they went to a lot of work.*

Nichols' four key staff, whom he referred to as the four musketeers, had worked the weekend to craft what he wanted, with a little extra. The list of companies showed addresses, person in charge of the benefits division, and phone numbers. The 'extra' was they had cross-referenced Nichols' graduating class at Stanford plus a year on either side with names of corporate officers of these companies to give him entree. They didn't know because their work experience had been exclusively government, but he had told them so many times that personal relationships in the actuary business form the core of success. The Stanford alumni were highlighted. The list also indicated the alumni's home address, home phone number, and cell number and email address, if available.

So, Merritt should be pretty happy with this, thought Nichols. *Heck, since I'm here, I may as well try a few of these guys. Guys, he thought. I can count the number of female actuaries I know from Stanford on my two big toes. The field is definitely not a chick magnet. Okay, here we go: assistant personnel manager, and well known college dork, Bain Mason at HyperNet Systems, Inc. in Cupertino, California. Yep, I see Bain has already exceeded his potential, but oh, could he put away a lot of beer at Phi Gamma Delta.*

"Hello?"

"Yeah, Bain. This is frat brother Mike Nichols. How are you?"

"Yo, Mike. Damn, it's been a few years. S'up with you? Still have that GTO?"

"Sure. Could never part with that ride. Lookin' good, too. Say, sorry to bust in on your Sunday, but I'm at work and could use a little help."

"What's up? I don't know what company you're at."

"I work in Washington for the government, the Department of Health and Human Services. I'm their actuary."

"Damn, you done good, bro."

Lord, help me, thought Nichols. "Yeah. Listen, I'm trying to track down some data on Delaware General and I see that your company does business with them."

"Uh, yeah, we do. In fact we just re-upped for another two years because their rates were so good. I think they're trying to break into the California market in a big way and we like what we see. Why, what's goin' on?"

"Only good news, Bain. We noticed they are doing well, relative to other insurance companies, and wanted to know why."

"I dunno, why don't you ask them?"

"They are privately held and not the most open on the subject."

"Hmm, well, I can tell you our employees like their service and have very few claims issues. Delaware General offers a full range of insurance products and, from my perspective, since I ran the cost comparisons, overall they beat the competition by at least ten percent. And in health insurance, they were almost 15 percent better priced."

"I see," said Nichols. "How many years has HyperNet Systems been with DG? And how many employees do you have covered?"

"Four years. We have 1,200 staff and, with dependents, the total is about 3,000. Is there a problem with them? I mean if they're under some kind of Federal investigation, my ass is grass. I negotiated the contract."

Nichols tried to cool off his fraternity brother. "No, really, we're just trying to help other companies do as well so we can get national health costs under control."

"Oh, okay. Well, what else can I tell you? Hey, you ever come out to the homeland? Love to have you stop by and meet my wife and we could go have a few brews."

"Thanks, I hope to get out there next year. Just one more question. You have four years with DG. Since you are a software company, the mean age is, what, like 30 years old?"

Interesting you ask. Our COO just asked for that. We have staff spread over 15 states so data collection is a drill. Average age is 32."

"How about mortality data on employees and dependents?"

"Guess I'd have to look that up, but only a short handful a year."

Nichols asked the next question with anticipation. "In those few cases, any serious illnesses that seemed to end in death earlier than might have been expected?" Nichols was surprised at himself by the way he phrased the question. It seemed more obvious now than when he had discussed the data with Merritt.

Mason was clearly surprised by the question since it strayed outside the bounds of cost control. "Mike, I think the company would be happy to get you whatever data you need but I'm not sure where you're going with this."

Nichols asked again. "What I want to hear is: did any of your deaths occur in less time than you would expect given the illness?"

"Mike, I need to know where you're going with this."

"Relax, Bain, this has nothing to do with you, your company or your management and this is the last you will hear of it. I just need some data."

The Stanford-trained actuary, Bain Mason, while not at the top of his class, did trust his fraternity brother and did have a better grasp on his company's employee history than he had let on. "In the last four years, HyperNet has lost nine staff and dependents: two from a car accident, one drowned, one suicide, and five from apparent heart attack or stroke."

"Bain, can you tell me anything about those five?"

Mason sighed into the phone and continued. "Of those five, two had been diagnosed with inoperable cancer, one each with brain and pancreatic cancer, and another with a terminal blood disorder. Now, are you going to tell me why you called?"

"So those three employees, the ones diagnosed as terminal — how long after they were found to have terminal conditions did they die?" asked Nichols.

"Well, mercifully each died soon after, as I said from heart attack or stroke. And as I remember, each was within several months of their diagnosis."

Nichols pressed a bit more. "Bain, 'merciful' is an interesting descriptor for those young deaths."

"You know, Mike, I haven't talked to you in years. And now, out of the blue, you're drilling me, I guess to figure out why our insurance carrier is doing well, but you are focusing on deaths that you seem to be concluding were premature. Jesus, Mike, these people were going to die anyway, in all likelihood painful, terrible deaths. What is it you're really after?"

"Yeah, you're right, Bain. Guess I'm pressing for answers when there isn't a question. Sorry again for interrupting your Sunday. I'll look you up when I get out that way." Nichols hung up anxious to phone more of his actuary brethren on the list connected to companies covered by Delaware General. *Let's see if I can find a company with an older demographic. More deaths, more data. I need more data.*

CHAPTER TWENTY-NINE

Monday morning, October 26
HHS Headquarters
Washington, D.C.

Merritt sat in her usual place but a few minutes earlier than usual. This was his first day back after the heart attack and major surgery and she was curious about the group's reaction.

Deputy Secretary Marlin Houghton opened the 8am staff meeting with a prayer: "Thank you Lord for allowing us the privilege of serving our country. Thank you also for allowing me a speedy recovery so that I might again be with these patriotic souls. We do your work here for our countrymen aiding them in basic requirements of health, formal learning and care for those who need assistance. We pray for your spiritual guidance in our work. Amen."

Merritt tried not to look at her colleagues' reaction but it was difficult to avoid.

"He found the Lord while he was in the hospital," whispered a deputy bureau chief next to her.

Merritt nodded but did not respond. *A prayer to start? Interesting. Hmm, he looks thin but otherwise good. This staff meeting is shaping up as another memorable one.*

The 68-year old Houghton continued, "I have always been a religious person though I held those views to myself. The life-changing ordeal I experienced over the last couple of months has shown me I need to be more public with my faith and my love of Jesus Christ. I understand some of you may not be comfortable with my views and my new found openness. But, please, just give it a chance. I think it may grow on you.

"Secretary Vickers is still in Europe but returns late tomorrow. For my own benefit and to give the Secretary a full briefing on his return, I'd like your updates this morning to be in somewhat more detail. And please have your brief put in writing – not more than two pages – and delivered to me by close of business tonight. Okay, let's start with Congressional Affairs. Emily…"

Merritt could see she was not alone in the group as she text messaged, pushing back appointments two hours to allow for the 'somewhat more detail' requested by Houghton. *I hope he listens. Sometimes he just likes to hear himself talk, holding court with a captive audience. Geez, why couldn't he still be in Congress?*

―✦―

"Thank you LaGretta for changing my schedule," said Merritt hurriedly. She stopped abruptly and turned to LaGretta, "And you are such a dear for splitting time between here and the Rockville office. It makes my life *so* much easier."

"Not a problem, honey, and I have Mike Nichols waiting for you. He says you two will need a few hours to make some phone calls so I pushed the appointments back to after 2. Okay?" LaGretta wanted a 'man' update but saw that Merritt was busy.

Merritt closed the door behind her. "Mike, hope I didn't mess up your weekend too badly for you."

Nichols looked up from his wireless laptop on the conference table. "Nope, the four musketeers did most of the work. Great team. I did have some fun on the phone last night. Got through to a handful of guys I know. Good data. Scary, but good." Nichols had another laptop at the other end of the table for Merritt with identical files loaded and cell phones set up each with Bluetooth wireless headsets. "Caller ID on these phones will show 'HHS Headquarters' in Washington. May as well make this comfortable. Didn't think you'd want to record any of these conversations so none of that hardware here. Ready to hear what I found?"

"The 'scary' word bothers me. Is that an actuarial term?"

Nichols was still focusing on the PC screen. Merritt sat at the table.

"Scroll down to the first company," Nichols started, "so I can show you the spreadsheet components. I put this format together after talking to the first three companies. We can add more elements if we need to."

Merritt scanned the spreadsheet. "Okay, I understand the approach. You talked to five companies?" She could tell Nichols was in a zone and all business.

"Four," said Nichols. "Two guys from INSCOM, the controller and the HR chief. Some questions don't seem to be helpful – dead ends. Hope you can read my shorthand for those and the questions that seem to hit the mark. Rough estimate here, and you know how actuaries dislike estimates, but we should be able to quantitatively assess the delta between Delaware General and the set of other companies in some statistically significant way if we get data from a total of, say, 20 companies. If the data trends continue as solidly as from the first four companies, that should be enough for us to turn this over to the Inspector General or the Justice Department or wherever you think we should take this."

"What! Whoa, Mike. Justice Department? Why don't you back up and tell me what you found out."

Nichols looked up from the laptop. "Sorry, I got ahead of myself. Data so far is unambiguous, which is why I'm anxious to add more companies to the mix and see if the trend holds."

"What trend?" pressed Merritt.

"Uh, right," responded Nichols apologetically. "Deaths where a terminal condition had been diagnosed occurred well in advance of predicted life expectancy in 80 percent of cases where DG was the health insurer, regardless of age, ethnicity or sex or the employee. Here's an example: an INSCOM employee was told he had lung and liver cancer with less than a year to live; he died before manifesting significant symptoms six months after the diagnosis."

Merritt stood and walked to her desk. Pushing the intercom button she said, "LaGretta, this is going to take longer than I thought. See if you can clear my schedule for the rest of the day." She returned to the table and took her seat. "Mike, let me listen to one of your calls before I do my list."

Four hours and a couple of half eaten sandwiches later, the phone work was completed, and 21 companies had been questioned. Merritt returned a few calls from messages taken by LaGretta while Nichols compiled the data.

"Okay, Merritt. The spreadsheet is ready."

"So what do we have?" she asked.

Nichols, stretching his back near the leather sofa in Merritt's office, sat down, leaned back and propped his loafers on the coffee table. He spoke to the 14-foot ceiling: "We have directional though not conclusory evidence of premature, or perhaps I should say 'managed,' death where Delaware General is the healthcare provider. Premature death presents under DG management a) when a patient had been diagnosed with a terminal condition or b) as we heard in our later calls, when an employee had an accident leading to a coma or other persistent vegetative state. I could suggest some next steps to…"

"Mike, let's sit on this a while." Merritt was pacing her office. "We need to digest what we have before we can say what the next steps are or whom to involve. We started this exercise because we thought other companies could share the good news profits of Delaware General if they were more like DG. Now we see directional evidence, as you put it, that DG's profits are managed by premature deaths of their sick or dying customers. And the billionaire CEO of Delaware General is a 30-year friend of the Secretary's!"

"Mind if I make a few more calls to companies covered by DG? It may give us an easy or at least non-criminal explanation for how this is happening. Besides, this managed death phenomenon doesn't occur in *all* cases where DG is the healthcare provider."

Merritt stared at Nichols. "First you mention the Department of Justice and now you say the word criminal. Dial it down a little, will you? You're the actuary for God's sake and we don't have much here other than a pissed off CEO, some directional data and a pack of hunches."

"Roger that," said Nichols.

"And fine on more calls, but don't have the musketeers involved. If we're petting the wrong end of the elephant I don't want to have more damage control, or political casualties, than necessary." *And I don't want to be one of those casualties.*

Nichols, a laptop under each arm, whispered to LaGretta on the way out of the office suite, "She's going to need some time to breathe. We've been digging in some really big piles of poop and she has to figure out a way to stay clean, and yet do the right thing."

CHAPTER THIRTY

Melbourne Beach, FL
Home of Gatwick Research sales executive Tracy Madson
Tuesday, October 27

Tracy was out on the small deck of her beach condo when then call came through. The client had phoned a local Orlando number Tracy had given him and the call had been routed through Gatwick's central switch in Denver, first confirming through voice analyzers the caller was in fact who he said he was and then routing the call to Tracy in Melbourne Beach. The process took under two minutes and was transparent to the caller.

"Tracy, this is Neal Harkin. You sold me and my wife the chairman's policy a couple years ago."

"Of course, Neal," said Tracy who now had moved inside and was viewing Harkin's case file on the big flat screen monitor, "it's nice to hear from you. What can I do for you?" Tracy handled a few calls each week with follow-up questions from her clients.

Questions varied from administrative 'who do I call if I move?' to unique as the one Harkin would ask today.

"My son, Corky, well that's what we call him. His name is William Neal Harkin."

Tracy could tell she was going to listen, listen for quite some time.

"Corky is 17. He broke his arm pitching varsity baseball ten days ago. When the orthopedic surgeon took x-rays and set the arm, he asked for more tests and a consulting oncologist to assist." Harkin paused, breathing deeply. "The doctors say Corky has bone cancer. It's a rare type. It's virulent and quite often fatal."

"I'm so sorry to hear that, Neal," offered Tracy.

"Yeah, it's going to be tough. We have two options: treat him aggressively with some new radiation and chemo treatments, or not. If we treat him as they suggest, it may kill him or damage his musculature so badly he may spend the rest of his life in bed. Or it may cure him. If we do nothing, he will likely die within 12 months and the cancer doctor said it would be a difficult death. My question is this: Can I add Corky to the chairman's policy? We want to make sure his wishes are respected and he doesn't want to live if he is bed-bound from the treatment or in huge pain from no treatment at all. I'll pay the $5,000 or whatever it costs upfront."

"Neal, I know you called to get an answer and I want to give you one, but I need to check with my supervisor because the condition is now present and I've not had this situation before."

Tracy put Neal on hold and speed dialed the on duty supervisor in Denver.

"Supervisor Bell. How may I help you?"

"Hi, this is Tracy Madson, Melbourne sales. You just forwarded me this call. It's outside anything I have dealt with. I need guidance."

Thirty seconds later when Tracy reached the point where the Contract policy prospect was known to likely have a terminal condition, Supervisor Bell said, "Hold. I'm getting an executive on the line. Tell your client to keep holding and come back on this secure line."

The supervisor dialed Marc Friedersdorf. "Sir, we have an out of bounds request from a sales rep in Florida. Tracy Madson is her name, verified, and the line is secure."

Gatwick CEO Marc Friedersdorf responded, "Okay, set conference."

"Hello, Supervisor Bell, I'm back," said Tracy. The client said he could hold."

Without identifying himself Friedersdorf said, "Hi Tracy, why don't you start over and we'll resolve this."

Wonder who that is, thought Tracy. *They told me in training if I call with an exception to make the call crisp and to the point.* "Orlando client bought the policy, sorry, Contract, two years ago for him and his wife. He now wants to buy it for his boy, 17, who has been diagnosed with bone cancer." Tracy briefly explained the treatment and prognosis.

"Thank you, Tracy," said Marc. "You were right to call in. We view the Contract as insurance, not as a way out. Yet the emotional state of the father and the fact that the son has made his own wishes clear need to be considered. Tell the father 'okay.' Anything else?"

Relieved, Tracy said, "No, sir, I can handle the rest."

The secure line to Gatwick clicked.

"Neal, I have an answer for you. We will add your son, Corky, and he will be covered by the chairman's policy. Since you and your wife paid up front the price to you is $3,000. Shall I debit your same account?"

"Yes, yes. Thank you so much, Tracy. You don't know what peace of mind this gives us. After finding out the terrible news from the doctors and then learning Corky could lie in bed for so long and suffer and never get any better or die a painful death from the cancer, well, we were heartbroken, especially knowing we could have bought a policy for Corky when we bought ours. We just never thought… I mean he is so young we thought…"

"It's okay now, Neal," reassured Tracy. "Corky is covered."

Friedersdorf walked out front to Supervisor Bell's position. "There is some risk here of exposure of the Contract if we did not grant his request, and there is some risk that fulfilling the Contract may be complicated by the parents present at bedside should we need to fulfill the Contract."

"Yes, sir. Not an easy one," said the supervisor. "If the boy goes south, the agent we put on this fulfillment will have to be very good."

Friedersdorf nodded and walked back to his office, adding this episode to the growing list of exposures to be assessed in the operational audit.

CHAPTER THIRTY-ONE

Delaware General Headquarters
Dover, Delaware
Late Tuesday afternoon, October 27

Delaware General CEO Phil Hanson walked with purpose into the chairman's office. "Good afternoon, Anita. I have an item for Del. Is he in?"

Hearing Hanson's voice Burroughs rose from his desk, "Phil, come on in."

"Mr. Hanson, would you care for tea or coffee?" asked Anita. "And I brought some of your favorite oatmeal cookies in today. I was going to save them for Mr. Burroughs' staff meeting in the morning but since you're here…"

"Thanks, Anita. I'll grab a couple on the way out." Hanson shut the door behind him.

"Have a seat." The two sat in large, high-backed cordovan leather chairs in a sitting area of Burroughs' expansive office.

"Del, I thought you would want to hear this before staff meeting. Scheier brought it to me this afternoon and was concerned, given your reaction last week."

"Not more Fed meddling, I hope." Burroughs shook his head.

"Afraid so. This is odd, though." Hanson continued, "Scheier said that since yesterday morning his regional directors have been fielding calls from customers, companies where we have a range of policies in force. The company reps, most from the benefits divisions, are asking why the Department of Health and Human Services is asking questions about Delaware General."

"Jesus. Fucking bureaucrats." Burroughs stood and walked over to an ornate server. "Care for a drink?"

"Thanks, I'll pass."

Burroughs poured himself an XO cognac in a delicately etched snifter and, holding the glass by the bottom rim, gently swirled the amber solution to his suddenly ragged nerves.

"Extra old." *Something I don't think I want to be myself,* Burroughs thought. "Cognac has a magical way of soothing one's soul from the fracas of life's bullshit."

"Scheier will bring notes from the calls to our weekly meeting tomorrow," Hanson said as he unfolded a sheet of hand-written points for the chairman. "The questions have to do with everything from how long has the company done business with us to how many employee deaths have there been, the causes and any cases of early death of those classified as terminally ill. And it's the same government people asking the questions. The HHS actuary, Dr. Mike Nichols and the woman you said you've met, assistant deputy secretary Merritt Royce. Del, I don't think this is a science project. Or, if it was, it graduated."

Burroughs took a long draw from the snifter. "Damn, that's smooth. All right, thanks, Phil. I asked the association guys to lean on the Department a bit. That obviously had no impact.

Vickers has been in Europe so I wanted to wait until he returned. Why don't you have Scheier drop those notes off now and I'll call Vickers this evening and make sure he knows we're concerned about snooping Feds. Calls like that stress our customer base and we've worked hard to earn that business."

"Agreed."

"Speaking of nosy," Burroughs said with a smile, "I asked our illustrious CFO Greenberg to have Goldman Sachs search for buyers of twelve percent of my holdings in the firm. That leaves me with controlling interest but it's time I diversify. Arnie at Goldman says he has some interest already – trusts, pension funds and the like – so it shouldn't take long to get done. It's worth more than Greenberg guessed so I'm going to carve off one of the 12 percent for the management team with you getting one-third of that."

"Well, that's quite a surprise and very generous of you, Del."

"Your piece should be worth close to $13 million if the valuation holds as Arnie suggests."

"That's incredible, I don't know what to say." Hanson folded the piece of paper and shoved it in his pocket, discarding the notion of asking Burroughs more about the Federal interest in their company.

Burroughs beamed at his own magnanimity. "You're welcome. Now grab a couple of Anita's cookies so I don't eat them all and have Scheier bring by those notes."

CHAPTER THIRTY-TWO

The Burroughs Mansion Library
Dover Delaware
Tuesday evening, October 27

"Angela, honey, I'm going to make a call or two then I'll join you in the great room." Burroughs closed the double mahogany doors to the library.

Angela Burroughs was in the large catering kitchen helping the family cook clean up from supper. She had two containers for the leftover tenderloin and vegetables. Her husband loved leftovers and she remembered him saying the packaged goodies made it almost worth going to work.

Delbert Burroughs had the notes from calls fielded by his regional insurance directors. The companies had called their insurance carrier because officials of the Federal Government had been asking pointed questions about coverage illnesses and mortality of their employees. The president of the insurance division, Robert Scheier, had handed Chairman Burroughs the notes and tried to quickly escape. Burroughs' reaction the week before, upon learning of government questions to their headquarters offices, was something Scheier did not want to revisit, if he had the choice. As it turned out, he did not. Burroughs grilled him. It was time to reach out to his long time friend, former U.S. Senator and now Health and Human Services Secretary, Donald Vickers to help call off the intrusive government questioning.

"Don, this is Del Burroughs."

"Nice to hear from you, Del," responded a weary Vickers. "I just got to the house about an hour ago. International travel is just not all it's cracked up to be. So how is America's favorite insurance icon?"

"I realize you are just back from a grueling trip, Don, but I could use some help."

"Well, this will be a first. I seem to be the one always calling for help. When I was in the Senate, hell before that, it was campaign contributions. Last couple of years it's been donations, corralling some of your association members to tone down rhetoric, or jawboning a few in Congress for one thing or another."

Burroughs recounted for Vickers the questions posed of Delaware General executives by the HHS actuary and the difficult Congressional hearing where the profit questions planted by HHS officials had been made public.

"You know, Don, from my perspective," Burroughs continued, "our roadmap to improved profitability is a proprietary matter. We are not a public company and I have majority control so, as long as we report to the state insurance commissioners and pay our taxes, I don't see why we should have to put up with rogue intrusions by agents of HHS." *So much for not wanting to overstate my case.*

"Sounds like you managed through it, but I'll certainly look into it, and I'll do it tomorrow," Vickers said, somewhat surprised by Burroughs' tone.

"That's not the half of it. Now the same department officers, your actuary, Dr. Nichols is his name, and his boss, a Merritt Royce, have been calling our customers – dozens of companies from what I can tell – and asking them a whole ream of questions about our coverage, what we're like to do business with, what kind of illnesses and death experience we have covered. Don, they are setting off alarms and scaring our corporate customers."

"Well that's damn curious. I wonder what kind of a …"

"Either a science project or a vendetta," Burroughs said. *I've said enough. Better let him go sort it.*

"I promise you, Del, I'll get to the bottom of this."

"You're a good friend, Donald. I knew I could count on you. Now I better let you get some sleep and shake off that British jet lag."

That should take care of it. If it doesn't…

CHAPTER THIRTY-THREE

Office of the Secretary
Department of Health and Human Services
Washington, D.C.
Wednesday morning, October 28

Just across Independence Avenue and past the Botanical Gardens soared the white marble dome of the Capitol. As Merritt waited in Secretary Vickers' formal office she could see the U.S. Capitol where she had worked until Senator Tidwell had asked her to join the President's transition team.

Occasionally she missed the personalities and drama that the tangled politics of the Hill generated on a daily basis. Progress there was deliberate but at least measurable: legislation enacted, appropriations approved, history made with moving speeches from the floor of the Senate and House, coalitions forged to articulate positions of the Legislative Branch.

The Executive Branch could move with speed if not stealth. Sunshine in government meant open proceedings and a full airing of policy development. For Merritt, however, movement of government around her had not been speedy. In fact, it had been glacial recently except, of course, for the disturbing data uncovered about Delaware General.

The premature or 'managed' deaths, as Mike Nichols had described it, of clients of Delaware General Insurance Company were more than curious. What had begun as a simple exercise in asking the insurance company to share information about how they recorded solid profits in a tough industry and regulatory environment had morphed into something else, something Merritt knew was not explainable by statistics or medicine, something she needed to take to the Secretary.

When Merritt met with Secretary Vickers the location was often his smaller private office. The walls in the anti-room were filled with memorabilia from his years in the Senate. Around his desk and sitting area were photo displays of him with family, colleagues, Presidents and captains of industry. Merritt preferred that less pretentious office to the ostentatious and grand style of the formal office. It wasn't the size of the main office that she reacted to but its lack of warmth.

The Secretary entered from the side entrance, which connected to a suite housing his three executive assistants, the kitchen and his private elevator to the garage. "Merritt, good morning."

She stood and shook his hand. "Thanks for seeing me this morning, Mr. Secretary. I know you have some catching up to do so I'll try to make this brief."

"I had the most peculiar and disturbing call last night," said Vickers.

Merritt's heart sank to her stomach. Her face froze as the blood drained from her head. *Damn, Burroughs got to him first. Shit, shit, shit.*

"I see you know who called me." Vickers eyed Merritt's ashen demeanor.

Merritt sat up straight. "I had hoped I could speak with you before you took calls on the matter." She had expected the National Association of Insurance Companies to call, but certainly not Vickers.

The Secretary settled in his ornate blue brocade armchair just a couple feet from Merritt. "Well, Merritt, maybe you could tell me why my ace healthcare executive and her chief actuary are snooping, scaring customers, and irritating the hell out of my life-long friend, Del Burroughs."

Okay, keep it under control, remember what Dad said, "Smile, steady voice, eye contact – and don't blabber." "It's been an interesting couple of weeks," Merritt began. "I took a call from the National Association of Insurance Commissioners. Their analysis showed declining profits by healthcare insurers except for Delaware General. They suggested, and we concurred, that knowing *why* might help other companies perform better. So far all of this seemed innocuous enough."

Merritt could tell from the Secretary's reaction that he agreed. But next was the hard part.

"We asked Delaware General *why* in phone calls to their staff. They told us a variety of reasons which Mr. Burroughs repeated to Congress in a hearing on healthcare costs he and others, including me, testified at." Merritt chose to omit that she had set up the questions to Burroughs at the hearing. "Except he left out one of the reasons for better profitability – mortality rates. So, our actuary called DG's actuary again for more data on the mortality of their policyholders. It turns out that Delaware General has a higher rate of deaths among its terminally ill and dying policyholders than other companies. Seven times higher. Our actuary says that is not possible without managing to that death rate."

Vickers reacted quickly. "So then you and Nichols, smelling something sour, decided to call their customers directly? And, I hear, ask them about cause of death?" The Secretary was getting more animated. "Can you imagine the reaction of a company manager to getting a call from a Federal official asking, in an accusatory way, about their healthcare insurer and death rates?"

"We were simply trying to determine…"

"What you were *doing* was scaring the bejeezus out of Delaware General customers," said a distressed Vickers. "And on a supposition that DG was doing something very wrong when this exercise *began* as something *positive*."

Merritt found it difficult to keep the smile on her face as her dad had suggested. "We selected companies where Mike and I had contacts, where we knew people. Mr. Secretary, the questions were focused on number of early deaths in cases where a terminal illness had been diagnosed. And what we found…"

"Merritt, listen," said Vickers relaxing a bit, "Del Burroughs is a pillar of success in the insurance business. He is widely respected. He is Chairman of the National Association of Insurance Companies. He's a big deal Republican. He's on our side for God sakes."

Vickers leaned forward a little toward Merritt. "What you found can probably be explained by any number of things, but I don't see it as our job to figure that out. I really don't want HHS, on my watch anyway, to become a heavy handed Federal detective snooping around healthcare companies. God knows we're already viewed as a cop in a lot of areas. This intrusiveness just isn't my agenda."

"Yes, sir." Merritt resigned herself to backing off. *A cushy lobbyist job sounds pretty good right now.*

Vickers stood up and walked over to the long conference table. "On paper you report to Marlin Houghton."

Geez, where is this going?

"In his absence over the past two months you stepped up to the job and, without getting a big head about it, directed his responsibilities extremely well."

"Thank you, sir," said a relieved Merritt.

"In the next month or so I'll be talking with Marlin about his retirement. Obviously I'm sharing this with you in strictest confidence," Vickers said motioning with his hand.

Merritt nodded, and she could feel herself flush at the thoughts starting to rush through her head.

"I saw in Marlin's absence that operations improved. More direct communications, less staff infighting, better progress in key areas. I think you are a big reason for that." Vickers smiled, "If I can talk Marlin into retiring, I'd like to know you are ready to accept more responsibility as Deputy Secretary."

Oh my God! My dream. What I've worked for. It may happen! Her spirits lifted as high as the magnificent office ceiling. She felt her body lighten, her head become numb with noise, her heart pound. "I am… gratified, Mr. Secretary, that you would consider me for the post," said Merritt, the excitement in her voice noticeable. "That would be a great honor."

"Merritt, several things need to happen to make this a reality. First, of course, Marlin needs to come to terms with his recovery and the pace of action around here. I'll take that one on. But I need you to be successful in several other areas."

"Yes, sir?"

"Continue to pull the team together. As my deputy you would act as chief operating officer. This disparate bunch of political appointees is hard to keep going in the same direction. You've had good success with that in Marlin's absence, but once you are named to the job, alliances and working relationships may change. You're younger than many of those who would view themselves as candidates for the position. You're also an attractive female and, while that probably worked for you in the past, it may now be a burden if you vie for the number two job here at HHS.

"Second," Vickers returned to the armchair and sat across from Merritt, "I need to make sure that *your* agenda is *my* agenda. This exercise with Delaware General and profits and calling their customers, this is an example of a direction that can hurt us and an example of you going off on a subject that just doesn't match my objectives. Sure it started off well intentioned but... Do you understand, Merritt? I need to be able to count on you."

"Yes, Mr. Secretary, I *do* understand. Merritt's excitement continued to build. *Dad would be so proud. I can't mess this up.* "When I worked on Senate staff I tried to become an extension of the Senator's persona – his goals became mine, his priorities became mine."

Vickers nodded. "Similar concept here. I remember when I worked in the Senate some of my staff required a very short leash because they'd go off on tangents. Others I'd never have to worry about. Here at the department, though, we're talking about 80,000 employees. There's a huge potential for wasted effort if we're not all moving in the same direction."

"You can count on me, sir."

"Okay then. The last area is pretty easy given your Hill experience. You have to be confirmed by the Senate. And, of course, I'll need to get you up to the White House and take you around to domestic policy staff there in the West Wing and at OMB in the Old Executive Office Building where you need to know the staff. The President and Vice President will want to meet you and they need to be comfortable with the selection."

The President and the Vice President. "Sir, I'm excited about this. Public policy has always been my career choice and this will be a dream come true."

"Wonderful," said Vickers rising from his chair and extending his hand to Merritt. "I'll pick the right time to have my talk with Deputy Secretary Houghton and then I'll give you a call," he continued, shaking her hand. "Oh, and I'll give Del Burroughs a call back so he knows my ace healthcare executive is on track and headed for bigger things." Walking her to the substantial bronzed metal double doors of his office he said, "You know, Merritt, Del Burroughs could be very helpful to you in the confirmation process."

She walked down the long marble tiled corridor to her office deep in thought. The glow on her face barely cloaked lines of conscience.

CHAPTER THIRTY-FOUR

Office of the HHS Chief Actuary
Rockville, MD
Friday, October 30

Wednesday afternoon, nervous about how Merritt's meeting had gone with the Secretary that morning, Mike Nichols phoned her office in Washington for an update. LaGretta told him the meeting had gone very well, that she seemed to be less stressed, and that she was tied up on a number of catch-up projects but she wanted to meet with him after her staff meeting on Monday.

Nichols had continued his calls to Delaware General clients, talking to contacts where he had an 'in,' collecting more data on mortality rates and refining his thoughts. The anecdotal information he gathered on policyholder deaths helped focus each successive call. He shifted his calling technique to portray the data gathering as a research project so companies viewed the calls with less alarm. Still, Nichols often dealt with company representatives who became defensive or resistant to his questions.

Initially he had thought a sampling of two dozens firms would provide sufficient basis for thoughts on Delaware General versus other healthcare insurers. The more companies he called, however, the more curious he became about the true nature of this Delaware General phenomenon. Each call provided more context, more clarity to the math model he began to construct in his mind – a model capable of explaining this puzzle.

So Nichols called more Delaware General customers, now including companies who used more than one insurer for healthcare coverage. *Why does there appear to be premature death among diagnosed terminally ill patients only with DG and then in clusters or not at all? The pattern is not uniform, nor is it random.*

Nichols recalled a conversation he just had on a call to a vice president of human resources at a large Phoenix headquartered manufacturer. The VP was a classmate from Berkley who had opted out of the rigorous actuarial program in favor of an MBA. It was something the guy had said: "Mike, maybe you're looking at this from the wrong angle. Maybe it's not something that Delaware General does. Maybe it's something the policyholder does."

Nichols was now consumed by the project. He let the musketeers handle his other workload. *I* am *going to figure this out. Merritt thinks I'm out to lunch suggesting criminal activity. Crap, it even bothers me to say the word. I have to get this done before I show her results of more calls. Otherwise she'll think I'm being alarmist.*

Before Nichols could make the next call, his secretary buzzed him on the intercom. "Dr. Nichols, you asked me not to disturb you, but there is a Bain Mason on the phone who says it's very important."

"I'll take it. Thanks." Nichols clicked on line 1, his Bluetooth headset taking the call. "Bain, twice in a week. What's up?"

"Nothing good," said Mason dejectedly. "HyperNet just announced a downsizing and I guess I am expendable." Mason sighed, "I'm calling to ask you to keep your ears open for an HR or actuarial position."

"Damn, Bain, I'm sorry to hear that. You were with them awhile, too, weren't you?"

"Five years," said Mason, "and I thought the business was doing pretty well." Mason explained to Nichols a little more about the situation and the kind of position he was looking for.

"Since you want to stay on the west coast, I can't offer you anything with my office, but email me your resume and I'll get you in the government system for actuarial and personnel manager jobs in California."

"Thanks, brother," said Mason. "They put us all on the street already. Pretty shitty, huh?"

Hmm, this may be just what I needed to crack the DG code. "Bain, you know that call I made to you? I'm still trying to figure out what's going on at Delaware General. I have contracting budget. I could hire you on a temporary basis to work with me on this project. You've worked with Delaware General; you could be a major asset. You don't need to come out here for this. You could do it from home – your PC and phone. Contracting pay is really good."

"HyperNet only gave me six weeks severance pay," admitted Mason. "I could use the money."

Nichols felt he was on to something with the addition of Mason. *He knows DG. He can handle the calls while I build the model.*

"This wouldn't have anything to do with HypetNet," added Nichols, "I'm just trying to figure out the mortality issue at DG."

"Like I care about HyperNet now," said Mason. "You know, it was always strange to me how much employees liked Delaware General. But then DG didn't say much to us HR types except the party line. Impressive financials and growth, and, like I said before, really good pricing for healthcare."

"So, Bain, we're a go on this?" asked Nichols.

"Yep, and I appreciate it, Mike."

"I'll email you a contract and our personnel office will call you when we get a faxed, signed copy. You can start making calls right away. Seriously, I think you're going to be a big help."

Mason thought a moment. "You may want me to talk to some of the employees rather than just company representatives. And for those deceased employees, talk to their husband or wife."

"Because…"

"Because," said Mason, "the company can't tell you any more than I did about reasons and timing of death, but I bet the families can."

"Interesting," said Nichols. "And you would do this under the guise of research?"

"That's what this is, right?"

"Sold," said Nichols. "Okay, let me share with you the questions I'm trying to get answered. And then the model I've been screwing around with to predict annual number of premature deaths from DG compared to other companies. I want a macro view of this."

"Bro, you made my day," said Mason. "Man, sacked and hired all in one day and doin' 'impotent' stuff with my man Mike."

Geez.

CHAPTER THIRTY-FIVE

Clyde's in Georgetown
Friday, October 30

The intense week downtown at HHS had drained Merritt. Her call to Grant in the afternoon was a plea for escape from politics and bureaucracy, planning and budgets. She was also trying hard to force from her consciousness a tug of guilt. She had left Mike Nichols with no feedback from her meeting with the Secretary, in part because she was still sorting what to do next, if anything, about Delaware General. The lack of ambiguity in the Secretary's approach had startled Merritt. The more she chewed over the meeting, the more it unsettled her. He had not wanted to hear all she and Nichols had uncovered. While she still dreamed about the possibility of becoming Vickers' deputy, the velvet hammer approach he had used on her to stand down from her analysis and work toward his agenda stirred queasiness in her stomach.

"Goochie-goo," said 'the hulk' as he snuck up behind Merritt at the double doors of Clyde's Restaurant on the south side of M Street in Georgetown. He tickled her sides and made her giggle.

"So where's Nanci with an 'i'?" asked Merritt playfully looking under Brett's jacket to see if the petite blonde was hiding amongst his immenseness.

"She's probably inside already," responded Brett. "She and a couple girl friends were going to get an early start. Your call to Grant really got things moving for a Friday charge."

"Charge?" asked Merritt as they made their way through the noisy crowd to the long bar of varnished wood and brass foot rails.

"You know, happy hour, bar hopping... charge." Seeing Grant at the bar Brett yelled over the crowd, "Hey buddy, look who I found."

"Hey girl," gushed Grant as he gave Merritt a kiss on the cheek. "I haven't seen you since that quick lunch Tuesday. I was like having Merritt withdrawals!"

Merritt had stopped by her house to feed Meatball, love up the little guy and change out of government blahs into black leather pants and turquoise cashmere sweater. The brisk walk down to M Street had helped, but she was still tight from stress at the office.

"This has been a wicked week." She started to sit at the stool where Grant had been sitting and changed her mind. "I've been sitting too much today – think I'll stand. We can give the seat to Nanci," said Merritt turning to Brett. "I know how you like to watch her bounce up on a stool."

"Ah, transparency, one of my more affable characteristics," sighed Brett.

Maybe there's more to the hulk than meets the eye, thought Merritt.

"There she is at the end of the bar with, oh my God, a brunette and a redhead. Trifecta!" Brett parted bodies as he inched his way down the bar. "Later, you guys."

"Your chardonnay is on its way," said Grant. "Happy hour until six so you just made it. How 'bout some oysters. I need to be prepared," Grant grinned sheepishly.

Merritt avoided the bait. "I hope I can relax. Thanks for meeting me here and setting this up. I need this… charge," she said trying to smile.

"Sit. Tell me all about your week. In fact we'll take turns 'cause I've had a real shit-bird week."

Merritt didn't want to say anything about the possible promotion or grouse about her workload. *Maybe an abridged version will make me feel better.* She took another sip of the chardonnay. *Too much citrus and bite, not enough butter and oak.* She looked at Grant, pursed her lips in an air kiss and scoped out the busy restaurant. *Lots of suits; lots of players,* she thought. *God, Merritt, relax!*

Grant loosened his tie, took a long draw on his Amstel Light and began, "I told you Tuesday that assignments were being made for two new big deal clients. Brett got one and the other went to a woman who has only been with the firm three years. I mean I understand giving Brett the Transaction Processing, Inc. account. He may not look or sound like it, but he's an expert on computer equipment. You should see his setup at home."

"Jock, yes," remarked Merritt. "Computer jock, I would not have guessed."

"I don't know, maybe I should try another firm. Baker and Jensen just isn't giving me opportunities to show what I can do."

"Maybe your boss thinks the clients you have now are more important," offered Merritt.

"That's part of the problem," said Grant. "Not the clients. My boss. He's a partner who's been there forever, okay 15 years, but hasn't done anything for the firm in the last decade."

"No sunshine under a boulder." Merritt was still sipping but thinking of ordering something else.

"So you think I should try to get with a different partner," said Grant puzzled by Merritt's response.

"Yes. There *are* risks in riding with a fast track boss – you may end up with an out of control dragster – but you won't be stuck in neutral, unless, of course, there are other issues."

Merritt, gazing at the bar crowd, didn't seem to realize the deflating impact of her comment.

"What's the matter?" he asked.

Merritt turned to see the look on Grant's face. She put her hand on his. "I'm not a good source for lawyer job counseling. I just don't know enough about how Baker and Jensen works or how cases and clients are parsed out to attorneys."

"Hmm, yeah. Well, I know how it works. It's just not working for me right now. So what's been going on with you this week?"

The cabernet blend Merritt ordered was much more to her liking. As she tasted the wine again she said, "Better. Smooth, no bite, nice finish. Deep garnet color, lots of forward fruit." She swept her auburn hair back and crossed her legs, relaxing a bit. "Well, this week I learned more about that insurance company I told you we are looking at – Delaware General."

"Be nice to them. They made sure I didn't pay a dime for all the work on my knee."

"Something strange about them," said Merritt. "Please, just between us. Okay?"

"Sure," said Grant. "What's strange?"

"I thought I should try to figure this out. Now I'm not sure." She recalled vividly the stern message from the Secretary. "They're acting like they have something to hide." Merritt's voice lowered and she leaned toward Grant, "And it appears from the data we have, admittedly most of that is anecdotal, that their increasing profits may come from premature deaths of their terminally ill patients."

Grant cocked his head and lowered his chin. "Premature deaths of terminally ill patients," he repeated. "How... If they are going to die anyway, how do you know the deaths are premature?"

"Our actuary can measure it, sort of, and calls to companies who use Delaware General confirm it."

"You called some companies?" he asked.

"Yes, a couple dozen."

Merritt suddenly remembered she had told actuary Mike Nichols he could continue calling firms. *I need to have Mike stop or I'll get sideways with the Secretary. Hopefully he didn't make more than a few other calls. I have a meeting with Mike Monday. I can fix it then. And try to explain to him why we should chill on this analysis. I know he's not going to like that.*

Grant thought while he finished his beer and ran his hand up her thigh. "Nice pants. Why would a company do whatever 'this' is?"

"Why? Higher profits. Covering sick and dying patients is very expensive," she answered. The discussion was less abstract with Grant, more understandable, even as she had immersed herself with the issue for days now.

"How do you get a 'premature' death?" asked Grant.

As obvious as the question was, the simplicity of it surprised Merritt, and concerned her. "Lawyers *do* have a way of asking questions." She tried to think of this as he was, *de novo*.

Grant saw he was on a roll so he continued, careful in the crowded bar so no one eavesdropped on their conversation. "I assume that a healthcare provider could deny services, or some services, that would accelerate a terminally ill patient's death. That seems most likely as the only other possibility is..."

"Much less benign," Merritt interrupted. "That scary thought has occurred to us. That's why this is between just you and me." Merritt patted Grant's chest for effect. "Listen," she stood and put on her black leather jacket, "why don't we see if the hulk and his adoring trifecta want to go to the 1789 with us. I moved our reservation for last week and made it for four, though I'm sure I can make it six if the other two girls want to come along." Merritt ran her fingers through Grant's thick wavy black hair and landed a scorching kiss in front of the throng of suits.

As they made their way to the end of the bar where Brett held the rapt attention of the three young ladies, Grant ran his hand over the smooth leather adorning Merritt's rear and whispered over her shoulder, "Black leather and bossy."

CHAPTER THIRTY-SIX

The Burroughs Mansion
Dover, Delaware
Saturday, October 31

Angela Burroughs did know how to throw a party. And tonight's reception and dinner event would qualify for the *New York Times* society page, except that her husband had nixed the idea of press coverage. He knew only the outline and invitee list for the evening's festivities and didn't care to know the details. In addition to Senator and Mrs. Tidwell and Nathan Jensen, the managing partner of Baker and Jensen, all of whom would spend the weekend at the Burroughs mansion, there would be 11 others attending. The three weekend houseguests would be arriving about four o'clock. Burroughs had sent the jet to Washington to pick up his friends. The reception was set for six o'clock with cocktails and crudités on the marble veranda to the rear of the mansion.

"Quiet, Chuck," whispered Burroughs to his Golden Retriever. "Mommy's busy with the caterers so we're going bye-byes." This week the trip back to Greenside Village would have to be shorter.

⊷⊶

Burroughs parked the Range Rover and pulled an envelope from his jacket pocket. Chuck recognized where he was and whimpered excitedly for Burroughs to let him out. As Chuck exited the rear of the SUV, Burroughs asked the dog to sit. He kneeled down by his companion. "Chuck, we're here to say 'hi' to the old man with the bad heart. You have to be a good dog. Okay? Now, *take*." The big Golden gently took the envelope in his mouth and walked off Burroughs' left knee without a lead to the entrance of Greenside Village.

Inside there was a little more activity than Burroughs expected so he and the dog waited near the sitting area for the nurse he wanted to see. The nurse, now free, recognized Burroughs and the dog and came over to them.

"Chuck, *give*," said Burroughs.

"What do we have here?" said the matronly nurse leaning over to take the envelope from Chuck's mouth.

Smiling and meeting her eyes Burroughs said, "Thanks for being helpful. We just want to see the man we visited with last week. Third door down on the left." His eyes lowered to the envelope, then he eyed the hallway looking for the old man. "I see him. Thank you." He and Chuck started walking toward the man's room. The old man with callused hands was slumped over in his wheel chair in the hall.

The nurse opened the envelope, read the note, folded the three crisp one hundred dollar bills and slid them deep into her dress pocket. She called after Burroughs, "His name is Myron."

Chuck nosed the old man's arm, waking him from his nap.

"Well, look who's here." He took Chuck's head in his weathered hands and looked up at Burroughs.

"Let's go outside and get some fresh air," said Burroughs going to the back of the old man's chair and starting to wheel him toward the side entrance.

"Oh, they don't let us go out." Trying to turn a little in his chair to talk to Burroughs, the man objected, "And this door has an alarm on it."

"I don't think we have to worry about that today," said Burroughs. The nurse walked in front of them, entered a code in the keypad by the door and unlatched the dead bolt. She walked away without comment. Burroughs backed the chair through the door and out to a small courtyard.

"You must be a pretty important guy," said the old man his head up looking at billowy white clouds against a bright blue sky.

The dried leaves rustled as Chuck returned to the man's side asking for attention with a nudge from his wet black nose.

Petting the needy retriever the old man said, "You sure are a nice dog. Sorry, I don't remember your name. Never thought I'd see you again."

"Chuck," said Burroughs. "Want to walk a little?"

"I don't do much walking anymore… but, hell, I'll give it a try."

Burroughs flipped up the foot paddles on the chair and carefully helped the man to his feet. He offered him his hand, "My name is Del and you are Myron, right?"

The old man grimaced at trying to stand straight but extended his hand and met Burroughs' eyes with neglected pride, "Yes sir, my name is Myron. Myron Berger."

The autumn breeze wisped through the old man's strands of gray hair, and the sun sparkled in his blue gray eyes.

They walked a few yards, Burroughs holding the back of Myron's belt to steady him. They sat on a concrete bench, Burroughs easing him down slowly. Chuck was now chasing a blowing leaf and the old man watched with a smile.

"Don't know why you're here," said the old man still watching Chuck play, "but I thank you."

"Everyone deserves a little sunshine," said Burroughs also watching the dog.

They sat quietly for a few minutes breathing the crisp fall air. The nearly bare trees had but a few leaves remaining.

The cold concrete bench reminded the old man of the approaching season. "I always enjoyed taking care of the animals in the winter. The cows and horses on the farm, they needed me."

Delbert and Angela Burroughs stood outside their front door as the limousine pulled into the circular drive. The chauffeur had discreetly phoned from a couple of miles away so they would be ready.

"Should we have met them at the airport?" asked Angela as she waved and walked down the short flight of stone stairs.

"Remember, keep her away from me," Burroughs said, smiling at the arriving guests. "God, what did she do to her hair?"

The Burroughs greeted their guests warmly and escorted them into the entry.

Mrs. Tidwell was still trying to rub the lipstick off Burroughs' cheek with a highly perfumed kerchief as the Senator spoke, "Angela, Delbert, thank you so much for inviting us to your home again and for hosting this fundraiser. You are most gracious."

As Angela took the guests into the formal living room for tea she offered them the powder room to freshen up or the option of first seeing their rooms.

Burroughs motioned to Nathan Jensen in amusement as the chauffeur and butler carried three large suitcases up the stairs to the Tidwell's guest suite.

"Delbert, you have invited me for the evening," said Jensen, "yet it appears you have invited the Tidwell's for a fortnight."

"Great to have you here, Nathan. We'll have some fun. I made sure there will be lots of pretty ladies here tonight for you to admire. And, selfishly, there's a lot going on. I could use your counsel."

"Ah, you've invited breasts and legs. Marvelous. I continue to be amazed at how you old rich men attract such young beauties. And fashion these days is so... revealing."

"Careful, Nathan, your prostate."

Burroughs and Jensen joined the others for tea. Jewel tone fabrics and a richly detailed 20 by 30 foot Persian rug complemented the formal living room's walk-in limestone fireplace and dark cherry wood floor.

"My goodness, Del, you new plane is just *so* beautiful," chattered the handsome Mrs. Tidwell, nervously adjusted her ruffled white blouse. "I know it was just a short flight but I just had to see the bathroom. Nathan, you missed it. Black marble! And the faucets, my, what *are* they made of, Del?"

Burroughs started to answer.

"The pretty flight attendant made us feel right at home," Mrs. Tidwell continued. "She met us outside Reagan National airport and arranged for our bags and... did you know she's from Nebraska?"

Angela noticed Jensen wink at Burroughs at the mention of the flight attendant.

Mrs. Tidwell's chitchat was nonstop. "Your driver was just so very helpful. You know the Senator has a bad back on occasion so it was most thoughtful..."

Burroughs tuned out Mrs. Tidwell's barrage of consciousness though he shook his head slightly at her reference to her husband as 'Senator.'

"Sweetheart, I'll take care of it," Angela whispered as she served her husband.

A few minutes later as promised, Angela, having waited for Mrs. Tidwell to take a breath, said, "Hon, why don't you come with me to the kitchen and dining room and I can show you how we have things organized for tonight, just so you are comfortable with everything." She stood, smiling, and took Mrs. Tidwell by the arm, the Senator's wife now speaking to an audience of one.

"Gentlemen, why don't we walk out to the veranda?" suggested Burroughs. A servant cleared the tea service and the men walked from the living room through the large mahogany paneled family room to the set of bi-fold French doors leading out to the veranda.

"Senator, this is where we will have cocktails and a few appetizers this evening." The expansive view of the sculpted grounds below and the Delaware River beyond drew a pleased look from Burroughs. "Would you care to say a few words to the guests here or would you prefer a more formal setting at the dinner table?"

It was customary at fund-raising events to have the principal speak to the group, not of money, as that was managed by administrative staff, but of broad political objectives. As the senior U.S. Senator from Delaware, Senator Tidwell was well ensconced in the Republican Party elite. Though only two years into his fourth six-year term, the Senator wanted to build an insurmountable war chest to stave off possible primary competition from those young Turks who would seek to topple him and certainly from the several ambitious likely Democrat contenders. Those invited this evening, not all Republicans, were all past contributors to Tidwell's campaigns and to friendly political action committees where the Senator garnered even greater funding support.

"Let's do it right here, Del," Tidwell said. "That should help keep dinner fun, with the business side already taken care of." They discussed the particulars for a couple minutes, including the introduction to be given by Burroughs.

"Senator, your wife is energized today," Jensen noted with a wry smile as they were about to go back inside.

Burroughs winced at the dig but Jensen kept smiling.

Tidwell stopped before the doors, turned to Jensen and tried to return the pleasantry, "Yes, Nathan." He started to open the door and closed it again. Turning back to Jensen he said, "It's not lost on me that her singular repartee appears as a command performance. She sucks the oxygen out of the room. No one else can get a word in. But, on the positive side, after she settles down, she listens pretty well. I've explained the problem to her and we have a signal when she needs to turn it off." Then Tidwell laughed and opened the door, "And she can still give great head."

The three men chuckled as they walked back through the family room. Jensen, with his hand on the Senator's shoulder, asked, "So how much do I have to contribute to your PAC to learn what the signal is?"

The Senator's brief talk on the veranda was well received and led guests to offer their polite congratulations and good wishes going forward. Burroughs knew the soiree would bring the Senator needed good will among the well heeled in Dover as well as campaign funds, both direct and soft money through a dozen separate political action committees.

Burroughs was enjoying the evening. Conversation at the dinner had been absent politics, save Nathan Jensen's quiver of sharpened arrows at the Washington establishment. Jensen's decades of insider experience and dry wit entertained the men and his playful banter, never quite flirtatious, enticed the women.

Angela Burroughs had arranged dessert, after dinner drinks and coffee in the mansion's family room, an opportunity for guests to stretch their legs and mingle more with those not seated near them at the stylishly appointed dining room table. Crisply dressed catering staff offered a variety of finger-sized sweets. The

Burroughs' butler served liqueurs from the elaborately carved mahogany bar. Guests began to leave around 10:30.

"Angela, magnificent job," Burroughs said as they waived goodbye to the last couple. "Well done. The guests all enjoyed themselves, including me. Thank you, Sweetheart."

"A perfectly planned evening Angela," said Senator Tidwell while Mrs. Tidwell gave her a big hug.

"Gentlemen, perhaps a cognac and cigar in the library?" asked Burroughs.

"Cognac would be delightful," offered Jensen, "but may I suggest the veranda? If you must smoke those carcinogenic pieces of fancy moss, I need fresh air to waft away the bilge."

Seeing the Senator nod, Burroughs obliged, "Veranda it is."

The butler quickly arranged a tray of cognacs and several snifters etched with a large 'B.' While a caterer brought the large silver tray to the Veranda, the butler retrieved Burroughs' cigar humidor from the library. Noting the chill, the butler lit the gas fire pit and brushed off the cushion sections surrounding the round structure. Lava stones in the pit immediately emanated a flickering light and welcome heat. The Senator and Burroughs selected cigars and watched without discussion as the butler, wearing soft gray gloves, clipped the ends.

"Thank you, Jeffrey," said Burroughs. "Nicely done this evening."

Handing Burroughs an engraved gold lighter, the butler silently withdrew shutting the series of doors behind him.

The three men sat facing the gas-fired warmth of the pit and listened as the breeze pushed a few dried leaves from the marble steps.

Burroughs offered to light the Senator's cigar first, but Tidwell waited. "After you, Del."

As Burroughs clicked open the lighter, Jensen spoke: "Your man servant is remarkable."

Burroughs handed the lighter to Tidwell. The Senator turned the torpedo shaped cigar slowly as he drew flame to the tobacco tip.

"Delbert, what is this inscription on the lighter?" asked Tidwell. "It's difficult for me to make out."

"'Not life, but good life, is to be chiefly valued. Socrates.' My father gave me the lighter. I had it engraved after my Mom passed away."

"A mantra of your life," said Jensen.

Looking at Jensen, Burroughs nodded affirmatively, "Yes."

"A noble one indeed," said Jensen.

Tidwell stretched out his legs, exhaled skyward. "Before hearing of your Socratic Contract from Nathan, I believe my greatest fear in life was dying as my father had," he told Burroughs. "The peace of mind knowing that will never happen to me or my wife is a great burden lifted."

Burroughs, turning his snifter so he could watch the flames through the cognac, nodded again and then sipped the mind-soothing brandy.

Looking toward the tree line down by the river Tidwell eyed Jensen. "Del, Nathan here was quite dramatic as he explained the Contract."

"I remember it well, Senator," said Jensen, "because I tell many potential policyholders the same thing."

Tidwell said, "Please, Nathan, share with Del your conversation."

Jensen sat his snifter of cognac on a limestone pedestal near the fire pit and motioned, his hands open toward the soft flames: "The most difficult death belies its presence. Would you wish your last days as a shell, empty of heart, void of thought, absent even the ability to feel anger at your sorry state? No, take me with heart full of love, yea even hate, but let me go with my God given dignity. Should your mind be crisp but leave you with body full of pain, unable to touch life or smile, then let me go. Please, let me go. It is my right."

Tidwell turned to Burroughs. "That argument, however compelling, is not politically acceptable, except perhaps in the

Netherlands and in a few states. Nor is it acceptable to most religions and certainly not to our Republican party. Yet here we are." Tidwell took another short draw from the cigar. "From the polls I've seen, most Americans believe as we do."

Picking up his glass again, Jensen raised it in a toast, "To continuing the work of the silent majority."

The Chairman of Delaware General, the managing partner of Baker and Jensen and the senior U.S. Senator from Delaware shared the distinctive sound of crystal glassware ringing in the night.

"I have an issue with the company I need counsel on," said Burroughs.

The men looked at Burroughs, Tidwell pulling his feet back toward him, Jensen clasping his hands.

"I have a problem with a couple of bureaucrats down at Don Vickers' department in Washington."

"Health and Human Services?" asked Tidwell.

Nodding, Burroughs continued, "They have been asking a great number of questions of company personnel and of our customers about profitability in the healthcare business, about mortality rates, about timing of deaths of our policyholders with terminal illnesses."

Incredulous, Tidwell pressed, "Why would Secretary Vickers allow such meddling?"

"No, Senator. I'm convinced he didn't know anything about it until I phoned him to lodge a complaint. He called me back a couple days ago to say he fixed it. But my CEO let me know yesterday afternoon that the phone calls to Delaware General customers have continued."

"Why are they asking questions?" asked Tidwell still trying to understand.

"Evidently it has its genesis in simply wanting to know why the company is more profitable than similar companies," Jensen told him. "But when the HHS actuary discovered that Delaware General's higher profits were coming from accelerated mortality of terminally ill clients, they pushed for more answers."

Tidwell turned back to Burroughs, "Is that who's asking all the questions?"

"The other person," said Burroughs, "is a political employee, a senior staffer to Vickers – although the calls by her seemed to have stopped after Vickers said he fixed the problem."

"Maybe she is being clever," suggested Jensen, "saying she stopped the prying, yet letting the actuary, whom I assume is not a political type, continue asking questions. So... a vituperative cunt we need to neuter?"

Burroughs frowned, "No, no, I really don't think so. She has Vickers' ear and respect. Hell, I've met her. Pretty redhead. I just think she needs to be steered. It's the other one, the actuary, Dr. Mike Nichols, who's the problem."

"Never heard of him," said Tidwell. "What's the woman's name? Maybe my staff can help lean on her."

"Merritt Royce," Burroughs said.

Tidwell reacted with a look of surprise. "I know Merritt. She worked on Senate staff. Smart, works hard, a loyalist. Her father was FTC Chairman years ago." He shook his head, "Damnation, I brought her into the Administration through the Office of the President Elect."

"I remember her dad," Jensen added. "Brilliant man. And difficult to 'steer,' as you put it, Delbert. Hopefully she is not as hard-headed as her father."

"Gentlemen, you don't know the logistics of the Socratic Contract. You don't need to know. Moreover, you don't want to know. Suffice it to say the mechanics are invisible, totally insulated – financially and through state of the art technology. And it is bulletproof. A huge investment in technology and people has been made to keep it that way."

"We know that, Delbert," said Jensen. "And I think we can help. Don't you agree, Senator?"

"Absolutely. I'll meet with Merritt personally, early next week," said Tidwell.

"And I will spend time on this personally as well, Delbert," said Jensen. "We have a number of resources at our disposal. I'll put Jackie Best on this – she said she has met Ms. Royce – and I'll run… an investigation of Dr. Nichols."

Noticeably uncomfortable, Senator Tidwell placed his half smoked cigar in the heavy lead crystal ashtray and stood, offering his hand to Burroughs. "Delbert, I'm sure this will all work out. Thanks again for such a lovely evening. You are a most gracious host."

After Senator Tidwell retired, the two old friends sat staring at the fire.

Jensen took a last sip of the XO cognac, "I'll work the issue, Delbert. We'll fix this and then you can get back to enjoying life to the fullest."

Holding the stem of the snifter, Burroughs deliberately swirled the remaining cognac. Then, he snapped the glass toward the flame, the brandy flashing in the fire pit.

"Nathan, I feel the stank breath of Government wet on my neck."

CHAPTER THIRTY-SEVEN

The Law Offices of Baker and Jensen
Washington, D.C.
Monday, November 1

Elizabeth fidgeted with her calendar, waiting, knowing the managing director was anxious. He had appeared in his office suite adjacent to his living quarters on the top floor of the building a full hour earlier than usual this Monday morning. She had just turned on the lights in his office and her adjoining entry alcove when he appeared. He had made the request immediately.

"Thank you for coming right up, Ms. Best," said Elizabeth. Senior Partner Jackie Best had just reached the top of the circular stairs to the upper suite. "Mr. Jensen rarely gets in a huff, but he is very nervous this morning and anxious to see you."

"Do you know what the issue is?" asked Jackie.

Standing to escort Jackie into Jensen's office, Elizabeth, in her perfectly starched white pleated blouse, responded in a quiet voice. "I'm almost positive it has something to do with his trip over the weekend to see Mr. and Mrs. Burroughs in Dover." Elizabeth dispensed with the coffee and sweets pleasantries, as she could tell her boss was intensely focused on whatever had happened in Dover. She shut the door to his office.

"Yes, Jackie, let's sit here at the table," said Jensen with a smile but matter of factly. "We have some work to do."

Jensen brought his yellow legal pad with him and sat at the head of the table. His written notes were a trademark. No fancy leather portfolio, simply inked kernels of thought ordered by margin scribbles and arrows.

He was comfortable with a PC, at least from a business perspective. Networks of personal computers had advanced productivity immensely in his time with the law firm. Yet he required the yellow pad to think and organize his thoughts. It was with these legal length yellow pads that he crafted his now legendary closings in trials. Using a silver Cartier fountain pen added art to the process and thoughtfulness to each word. Less frequently now than in years before, when he needed to draft a brief, a letter or an argument, he would, with legal pad in hand, dictate to Elizabeth while she entered the document in the PC. He stood over her shoulder watching as the words flew onto the screen, the clicking of her nails on the keyboard a staccato symphony of logic.

Jackie sat on a long side of the table and opened a leather folder containing a yellow pad and a few papers summarizing recent Delaware General account activity.

"The seemingly harmless set of questions posed to Delaware General a couple of weeks ago have apparently taken a more ominous and insistent tone," Jensen said. "The questions, initially asked of executives at Delaware General, are now being asked of *client companies* – dozens of them. We don't know what conclusions HHS is taking from these interviews, but it is having a chilling effect on customers."

"Obviously then calls by the National Association of Insurance Companies had little impact," Jackie said.

"No, though that's not entirely surprising." Jensen had little respect for political strength of association staff, though he believed they proved valuable in member communications. "Delbert had phoned Secretary Vickers about the matter with Vickers calling back to say he had taken care of the problem. Yet, the questions continue days later."

"The same HHS staff?"

"The actuary, Dr. Nichols, yes. Merritt Royce – initially, yes, but Vickers may have stopped her. It is essential we stop this analysis early before it spins beyond our ability to control it." Jensen pointed at his notes with the impressive silver pen. "We need information. What do they know, or what do they think they know? Who at HHS is involved? Is there an investigation or did Vickers shut it off?" Jensen put down his pen and looked up at Jackie.

Jackie sat back in her chair, her hands on the armrests. "Okay, Nathan, here's what I suggest. I will handle this myself. I will need Capitol Investigators for background on Nichols and surveillance to catch his phone and PC traffic." She crossed her legs and folded her hands in her lap. "Ms. Royce... requires a more delicate approach. Vickers said he fixed the problem which means he probably talked to her." Jackie turned her head toward the center of the office collecting her thoughts and then looked directly at Jensen. "We need to know what that conversation was – from Royce's perspective. And we need to know what she plans to do now." Jackie inhaled and exhaled through her mouth.

"Yes?" said Jensen expectantly.

"One of our associates is dating Ms. Royce. Grant Launder."

The rarest hint of a smirk crossed Jensen's lips, his right eyebrow raised slightly. "Ms. Best, what are you suggesting?"

Jackie moved forward on her seat and leaned her forearms on the table. "I have heard that Grant is not happy with his caseload. He wants more responsibility, better assignments – an opportunity to make partner. Grant is a capable attorney, not a star. Perhaps if he were helpful to us here..."

Now smiling, Jensen pushed his chair back and stood. "Jackie, my faith in your ingenuity and directness continue to be rewarded. I'll let Elizabeth know to interrupt me any time you have progress to report."

CHAPTER THIRTY-EIGHT

Office of Assistant Deputy Secretary Merritt Royce
Department of Health and Human Services
Rockville, MD
Monday, November 1

The 35-minute drive from her Washington office to the Rockville office provided Merritt time to consider her predicament with Chief Actuary Mike Nichols. She knew Nichols to be a laid back guy but he had a stubborn streak. *Must be an Aries*, she thought. *We're not on a witch-hunt. Delaware General is a good company. Delbert Burroughs is a solid citizen. Why else would the Secretary stick up for him like that? And I have an opportunity to get an incredible promotion! But Mike thinks there's something wrong. God, he said 'criminal.'*

She had asked LaGretta to stay at the Washington office and nose around. LaGretta's personal network at HHS was unmatched. Merritt had only asked Lagretta to walk around and listen, especially to what's going on with the Secretary and Deputy Secretary, but the wink in Merritt's eye would spirit Lagretta to new heights in word of mouth. Merritt didn't particularly care for gossip and certainly didn't engage in that malicious sniping herself, yet was inured to the benefit of occasional hallway intelligence.

Nichols strode into Merrit's office in a pressed striped long sleeve shirt with a pair of ivory Polo pants. "You been dodging me or just playing hard to get?" He plopped himself down on her leather sofa, his blonde mop of hair parachuting to a landing after he did.

"Sorry, the Secretary has me running in dozen directions." *How straight should I be with Mike? May as well fess up, except for…* "The Chairman of Delaware General called the Secretary and asked him why his customers were being hounded by HHS staff. Secretary Vickers asked me to lay off. So I'm glad we did. We did, didn't we?"

Nichols sat up, surprised. "Didn't you tell him what we found, that DG policyholders with –"

"Of course, but he believes the early deaths can be explained by any number of reasons, *not* including nefarious acts."

"Man, Merritt, he just blew you off." Nichols stood and paced around the sofa. "I knew we should have gone to him after we had the analysis done, not half baked. He didn't believe us, did he?"

"He thinks Delaware General, and Burroughs in particular, are above reproach and that if we were alarming their customers with so little to go on, then we were off base. Not 'his agenda,' as he put it." Merritt felt caught in the middle – not wanting to disappoint Nichols, not wanting to lose a chance to excel in the Secretary's mind.

"Like I said, he didn't believe us. Damn."

"So backing off while we sort this is probably for the best." Merritt was having a tough time believing the words she was saying.

Back in his own office Nichols took the blame for not convincing the Secretary. *My fault. I know better than that. All my training warns against half-assed, bullshit analysis. That's the last time I take data up the chain without finishing the job. Damn. I'm not taking this back to Merritt until it's done. Then Secretary Vickers will be convinced. Bain will have the data and without calling more customers because he's going to call policyholders directly. And I'll have the model done. We can have it done this week. Then I can get Merritt revved up again.*

CHAPTER THIRTY-NINE

Senate Dining Room
U.S. Capitol
Tuesday, November 3

Merritt and Claudia, Senator Tidwell's long-time administrative assistant, had taken the brief underground electric train ride from the Russell Senate Office Building to the Capitol to have lunch at the Senate formal dining room. The Russell building had a small cafeteria but Claudia had insisted. Merritt remembered fondly her days on Senate staff, taking a late lunch in the cafeteria. The ladies who worked there became like family. She recalled a day when she was in line behind a Senator of some age and girth: the lady serving his requested Rubin sandwich had admonished him, "You watch your pressure now, hear? No salt on those fries."

On their short walk and elevator ride the Capitol halls enveloped them with a palpable sense of history. Merritt knew the Senate dining room was reserved for members but senior staff also dined there. The high ceiling room was small with tables appropriate for several people. The setting was quiet, the sounds were of cordial discussions, clinking of glassware and ice, and silver service against monogrammed china. And, of course, the subtle aroma of Senate bean soup.

As a waiter in starched white served ice water, Merritt saw several Senators having lunch with constituents and staff. "So Claudia, we are not having lunch with other staff from the subcommittee?"

"In fact, yesterday when I mentioned you were coming up for lunch, Senator Tidwell asked to join us," said Claudia.

Merritt took a deep breath and laid down the one-page daily menu.

The Senator appeared and, after politely acknowledging colleagues, sat down. "Ladies, thanks for letting me join you. Merritt, good to see you. We didn't get to talk very much at the NAI reception so I thought we could chat here."

The three had a brief lunch of soup and fish and made small talk on a potpourri of subjects, from the Washington Nationals to Iraq to the NAI reception to family. Merritt found the Senator charming and refined and fluent on most any subject.

As they stood to leave Tidwell said, "Merritt, if you have a few minutes perhaps you would walk with me." Claudia gave Merritt a quick hug and disappeared.

Merritt was apprehensive but excited. She guessed the Senator had wanted to talk with her about moving up in HHS, although she didn't see how Secretary Vickers could have had time to talk with Tidwell. They walked the long ornately tiled hallway toward the Senate chamber.

"Mrs. Tidwell and I had a lovely weekend in Dover with the Burroughs this last weekend," said Tidwell.

Merritt's heart plummeted.

"You met Del Burroughs at the NAI reception, didn't you?"

"Yes, Senator, an impressive man."

"He and Angela treated us so well, helping with fund raising, introducing us to new people. You know, Merritt, Del made his money in insurance by concentrating on baby boomers, the post World War II babies now reaching retirement age, 50s to late 60s. Better than other chief executives he has focused on improving life insurance and, particularly, health insurance that cares for this age group." Tidwell stopped in front of the Senate chamber entrance and spoke directly to Merritt. "Yes, his products are innovative, some might say novel or perhaps even avant-garde. To the extent his company has found a niche in providing this… *before-its-time* set of services, I think he should be applauded."

The Senator offered his hand. Merritt took it in a firm handshake. He put his other hand on top of hers and deliberately proffered a last thought.

"Those in today's society who are *true* innovators, whether they conform to some set notion of what is acceptable policy or law, should be offered help, help to mute their risk. Take care, Merritt." With that Tidwell turned and walked through the massive bronze double doors to the Senate chamber. The clerks for the Senate Sergeant-at-Arms opened the doors and nodded deferentially as he entered.

CHAPTER FORTY

Merritt's Townhouse
Georgetown
Tuesday evening, November 3

Merritt sat on a stool at the kitchen counter using chop-sticks to pick from two Chinese take-out boxes, neither deserving the courtesy of a plate. Meatball lay on the counter, tail swishing at the paltry offering, but hopeful nonetheless that a pleasing morsel might appear.

"It was great to see you again, too, Claudia." Merritt had hoped the call was from Grant. She needed a lift, a diversion from today.

Claudia's curiosity was screaming. "What was the private conversation about?"

"Nothing heavy, really. The Senator just wanted to talk a little about healthcare for baby boomers and the importance of public policy in that arena."

"He didn't say anything to me, which was a little strange."

"Claudia, I have another call coming in. I think it's from the 'hottie,' Grant. Talk to you soon and thanks again for lunch." Merritt could see caller ID this time. It was Grant. She was happy to stop trying to improvise with Claudia about the Senator's talk with her after lunch.

"Hey good lookin'. What are you up to tonight?" asked Grant.

"I'm trying to decide which is worse, the kung pao chicken or tofu and pea pods. Meatball seems to think neither." Merritt pushed the containers away from her. "And how is Grant, the hottie?" she giggled.

"Why, thank you. You've never called me that before."

"No, it's not my nickname for you. My friend Claudia on the Hill calls you that."

"Okay," said Grant, "then what do you call me?"

"Hmm," purred Merritt standing up and caressing Meatball's back, "I don't think I have a pet name for you just yet."

"I loved our time together this weekend," said Grant. "And I can't wait to have you all to myself for the road trip. Are you pumped?"

"You know at first I was a little nervous to leave work right now. There's just so much going on. But I think I got over that today. Yes, I'm excited and ready for your road trip."

"It's 'Party Tour' and that's why I called, that and to find out what you're wearing. Heels and no panties, I hope."

"Grant Launder, you have a one track mind. You and the hulk are a real pair. Did he decide if bubble butt Nanci is going on the trip?"

"Yep, she's coming."

"*Won*derful," Merritt said sarcastically.

"She's okay, really, and Brett thinks she's cute and likes her a lot."

"We'll see," Merritt said. "By the way, her friends at Clyde's Friday at happy hour?"

"Yeah?"

"I think they're lesbian."

"Why, what makes you think that?" Brett asked.

"Gay-dar. That and each one had her hand on the other's… bubble, but I'll admit my faculties there are better at detecting gay women than men." She remembered her date with Billy from the Majority Leader's office. "Not a concern at all, just wondered if Nanci was."

He laughed, "I'll ask Brett."

"Oh geez, don't do that!" Changing subjects she asked, "Now tell me again about the trip so I can get myself organized."

"I'll pick you up at your place at 1pm Thursday. The Party Tour charter leaves at three from Reagan National. Brett and Nanci will meet us at the gate. First stop is Charlotte, then off to Florida for the next two nights and back to DC Sunday about 2pm. Dress like a rock star for the concerts and bring a couple bikinis for Jacuzzis at the hotel and maybe the beach in Florida. Oh and we have some free time so maybe a couple dressier things, you know, low-cut tops, heels, thongs…"

"You do have a way of taking my mind off work."

"So, tell me about that."

"Oh, I don't want to lay that on you," sighed Merritt.

"It's okay. You told me at happy hour Friday about premature deaths from terminally ill patients. How do you think Delaware General could do that?"

"I don't know, and with the pressure I've been getting to leave the company alone, I'm not sure I ever will."

"Pressure?"

"Very *convincing* pressure," said Merritt.

"So," said Grant, "what next?"

"I don't know. Maybe nothing."

"So, what *are* you wearing?"

CHAPTER FORTY-ONE

HHS Offices
Rockville, MD
Wednesday, November 4

Dressed in shirtsleeves, ties undone, the two men looked like a couple of civil servants sitting in their car having lunch. The windows on the white Chevy were rolled down. Sandwiches and bags of chips were on the dashboard. Erwin and HB had settled in the HHS Rockville parking lot for an afternoon of listening and enjoying the fall breeze. Their earpieces were not noticeable to those who walked by. Knobs on the car's radio and CD unit controlled the recorders and transmitting equipment located in the trunk.

"I like the car scene," said HB opening another bag of potato chips. "Get to watch the government babes stroll back from lunch and enjoy some fresh air. Much better than that closed up stinky van."

"The van smells because you smell," said Erwin calmly adjusting his earpiece. "Are you sure you have his phone and PC tracked?

"Yep," grinned HB. "Bugs in both his office phones. And give me ten minutes back at the office and I'll have whatever you want off his hard drive. No electronic fingerprints and I'll leave a beacon so I can get back in whenever we need to."

"Think it's his laptop or one that stays in the office?"

"Definitely his. Sony notebook. New. Very fast, all the add-ons. Government doesn't issue those to bureaucrats, not even to wizards like this guy. Say, that lady that took us in the building today, who is she again?"

"She's a senior lawyer at Baker and Jensen."

"Not much to look at," snorted HB. "This is sure a lot more interesting than those reports we do. What are they?"

"'State of mind' reports," answered Erwin, "and for once I don't disagree. This is serious detective work. Listen up, he's back from lunch."

Actuary Nichols had just returned from lunch with his team, the four musketeers, where he had tried to explain at a macro level what he was doing for Merritt Royce and why he couldn't talk about it. He had failed to do either convincingly so he bought lunch.

"Did Bain Mason call while I was out?" he yelled over his shoulder at his executive assistant as he hurriedly walked back to his conference table.

"No, but the phone people were in to make some changes so he may not have been able to get through," replied his assistant.

Great. "Do they work now?"

"Yes, no problem."

"Okay, I'm going to be on the phone for at least an hour. Please keep the hoards at bay."

Nichols again sorted the spread of charts on his table and reviewed the model on his PC. He had wrangled more data from the National Association of Insurance Commissioners, including some that Amy Dennis, their Director of Financial Reporting and Analysis, had been reluctant to provide. Ms. Dennis had agreed only after Nichols had promised her results of his modeling efforts. Nichols now had a barrage of data on Delaware General. The county-by-county breakdown on health insurance policies in force, other policies purchased by the clients, age of the clients' relationship with the company, along with additional and current mortality data, gave him the final pieces necessary to complete a predictive mathematical view of the Delaware General phenomenon. Now he needed to test and tune the model against specific data points being collected by Bain's phone calls.

"Hey, Bain. Ready to give me what you have?"

"Bro! Man this phone work is ugly. I mean I'm glad to do it for you. Happy to have the work. Like I said, my wife and I need the money. California living isn't cheap and we, well, we spend what we make, or made."

"Listen, Bain, I'm the one who appreciates your help," said Nichols. "This drill you're going through here is *extremely* important for the Department. Hell, Bain, it's important for *me*."

"Well, I can see why you guys are interested," Mason remarked offhandedly.

"Why's that?" Nichols was at attention at his conference table chair.

"The answer isn't with the guys like me in a company's personnel office. We don't hear much that isn't filtered and fit for corporate consumption. I finally concluded that Friday night, after calling, like, another 30 companies with Delaware General coverage."

A neuron synapse bolt sparked Nichol's memory. His Berkeley colleague in Phoenix had said, "Maybe it's not something that Delaware General does. Maybe it's something the policyholder does."

"I really got nowhere calling more companies," Mason continued, "not like I didn't try or stick to your suggested set of questions. The HR people just didn't know." Mason paused. "The families knew."

"Knew what?" Nichols was now standing in anticipation.

"You know, Mike, I always had a notion that there was something different or special that attracted such a loyal following to Delaware General. But, like I said, HR types are sometimes the last to know the real skinny…"

"What did the families tell you?" insisted Nichols.

"I made calls all weekend. The more people I called, mostly spouses although there were a couple of children and one mother of a deceased employee, well, the better feel I got for what was going on. By the way dude, do I get overtime pay for working all weekend?"

"Yeah, I'll get you time and a half. Email me a breakdown by day of your hours and I'll get a bank transfer to you this week. So?"

"It's not like they told me directly. Some spouses wouldn't say anything to me. The more calls I made the better at the routine I got. Sunday about noon – must have been church, huh? – I changed my story to the folks I was calling. It was like I had an epiphany. Appropriate, right? Church, epiphany? Yeah. I said I was doing research for Delaware General and wanted to know if they were okay after the loss of their loved one."

"Ouch," responded Nichols. *I could get my ass in a sling for this.*

"I know," said Mason, "I wasn't real truthful, but it worked. It was like a door opened. The conversations I've been having with people the last couple of days have been amazing. The conversation I just had with a lady whose husband passed away four months ago is a good example."

"Go ahead, Bain. By the way, you logged all the calls and you have notes of the discussions?" Nichols wanted Merritt to have all of this data.

"Sure, I'll email it to you, probably tomorrow after I organize it better. So, like I was saying, this lady really opened up, kind of an emotional outburst, when I asked her how she was doing. She said that what the company had done – she was talking about Delaware General – was a Godsend. That's the word she used, 'Godsend.' She said that her husband had lung cancer but that he died peacefully before it became unbearable, again, her words, 'peacefully' and 'unbearable.' And then she thanked me for working for such a wonderful company and asked me to thank the chairman of the company for her."

"The chairman?"

"Yeah, have no friggin' clue what that meant. You know, Mike, these people have been telling me in so many words that Delaware General offed their husband or their wife or their mom. I mean I know that sounds crazy but that's the message that's coming through. I'll keep making calls. Maybe one of these people will tell me how it's done."

"Listen, Bain, great work. What you have here is really important. I want you to be here Monday morning, in Washington, to present what you have. Email it all to me first, tomorrow is fine if you need to work on the presentation. Fly in Sunday, I'll pick you up so we can go over what you have."

Nichols mentally put together a plan, first to put indisputable evidence in front of Merritt and next to work with her to convince the reluctant Secretary of Health and Human Services. *Delaware General has an agreement with dying policyholders, an agreement to end the policyholder's life.*

Erwin and HB looked at each other. HB put his chips down and wiped his mouth with the back of his hand. Erwin took the cell phone from the clip on his belt and pressed a speed dial number.

"Did you get the number he called?" Erwin asked nervously.

"Yep," HB said, "and I'll put the whole conversation in a packet and secure email it to HQ."

"Hold on that to HQ," Erwin directed. "Ms. Best? This is Erwin with Capitol Investigators. We have an urgent packet for you. Email okay? It will be encrypted." Erwin gave her synopsis of what they had just overheard. "Yes, ma'am, right away. Thank you, Ms. Best."

"What'd she say?" asked HB anxiously.

"She said email her the packet and that we get a five hundred dollar bonus each because we did well and that this is sensitive."

"Yeah, no shit, Sherlock. Wow, five hundred bucks!"

Erwin and HB looked at each other again. HB attached the audio clip to Jackie Best's Baker and Jensen email address using a keyboard from under the dash. He typed in the phone number of the call Nichols made to California. Erwin confirmed the proper email address, and HB, using the scrambler, sent the encrypted packet 'highest priority.'

CHAPTER FORTY-TWO

Reagan National Airport
Washington, D.C.
Thursday, November 5

"Hey, Brett, over here." Grant waved to get his attention in the crowded afternoon terminal.

Standing in front of Grant, Merritt turned from the Delta Airlines check-in counter to see Brett 'the hulk' grab Nanci's big rolling suitcase and his own and move quickly toward the counter, leaving Nanci to grab her small bag and purse and scurry after Brett, her perky breasts bouncing in a sunshine yellow tube top. Merritt was again amused at the size differential between Brett and Nanci.

Her stiletto boot heels clicking to a stop, Nanci squealed buoyantly, "Hi, you guys! Road trip! Wow, Merritt, I love those jeans. You look fab. What are those?" She lunged to give Merritt an air kiss.

"Hi Nanci. Oh, thanks, they're Joey distressed by True Religion." Modeling her ripped low riders, Merritt turned and put her hand on her hip.

"Nice butt, too," giggled Nanci.

"Yeah," said Grant, "nicely put together, but you'd think a senior government type could afford jeans that weren't shredded."

"Geez," remarked Merritt as she turned to finish check-in.

Brett joined Merritt at the counter tossing the big bags underneath. "Okay, I'm TSA'd and checked in."

Merritt looked puzzled at Brett.

"TSA'd. You know: frowned at, frisked, bag scanned and bothered," said Brett, giving Merritt a hug around the shoulder. "I just need bag tags, checked in online at home."

"So you *are* a computer whiz?" asked Merritt taking her boarding pass from the airline agent.

"Yes, the hulk knows hardware. Software is a different animal. Difficult to be really good at both."

Merritt turned to see Grant leering down Nanci's tube top. "I think the quarterback is horny."

"So what else is new," commented Brett. "Guess we better get those two on the plane. So, he told you the incredibly good news?"

Merritt cocked her head.

"Oops. Crap." Brett put his large frame between the other two and Merritt. "I just thought he would have told you already," he whispered.

"Well, we haven't talked all that much. You know – work, trying to get ready for this trip," she offered defensively.

"Okay, then act surprised when he tells you. A senior partner at the firm, oh, you met her at Grant's house, Jackie Best, talked to Brett about a new assignment and getting on a track to partner. Cool, huh?"

Merritt's mouth fell open in surprise. "Great!" She pushed the hulk aside and stepping over bags and interrupting Nanci's banter, she bounded on Grant. "Brett told me the super news. On path to partner and better assignments. That's just what you wanted." Merritt was really happy for Grant.

"Oh, way to go big mouth," snarled Grant as he punched good-naturedly at Brett's arm. Turning to Merritt he said sheepishly, "I was saving it until I actually got the assignment and a new boss. I mean it's not really final, but at least they seem to be noticing me now." Grant leaned over and picked up his carry on. "So everybody, let's go on Party Tour."

CHAPTER FORTY-THREE

Law Offices of Baker and Jensen
H Street, NW, Washington, D.C.
Thursday, November 5

"Elizabeth, you look lovely today," remarked Jackie Best as she walked from the circular stairway to the executive assistant's reception area. "Beautiful dress. Is it new?"

"Yes, thank you." The proper and perfectly put together Elizabeth said with appreciation. "I bought it at Neiman's. A departure from my wardrobe of suits, but Mr. Jensen said he liked it, too."

"Indeed I do. Feminine and fetching, don't you think, Jackie?" remarked Jensen walking out of his office into the reception area. "I do prefer dresses on women to suits, but perhaps I'm a little old fashioned."

Elizabeth blushed as she finished preparing a tray of tea and cookies.

"Please, Jackie, come in. Let's sit here and have afternoon tea," said Jensen. "The view is marvelous this time of year." The wide floor-to-ceiling window took full advantage of the view southeast to the north side of the White House and beyond that to the south, the Washington Monument.

The two quietly enjoyed the hot tea as the sun angled further past the White House down Constitution Avenue toward Virginia.

"Nathan, the news I bring is not good."

Jensen broke his gaze from the fall afternoon in Washington and placed his cup on the saucer. Leaning forward he pushed a small button underneath the round cherry wood table between the high backed chairs. Elizabeth came to the door.

"Elizabeth, please see if Mr. Burroughs can accept a secure land line call."

Jensen turned his attention to Jackie. "While she is locating Delbert, why don't you tell me where we are?"

Jackie briefed her boss on information gleaned from Grant Launder and from Capitol Investigators. While they spoke Elizabeth phoned Burroughs' executive assistant, Anita, and tracked him to his garage where he said he would call back from his library where there was a secure phone.

The attorneys moved to Jensen's desk, Jackie taking the armchair, and awaited the call.

"Hello, Delbert. Thank you for calling us. Jackie Best has information for you. Ordinarily we would meet with you on this subject but this data is time sensitive."

"Nathan, nice to hear your voice again and Jackie thank you for working this issue. It is, of course, of critical importance to me. By the way, I had my people check this phone and lines to your office just a few days ago anticipating our conversations, and we are secure. Tell me what you have found."

Jensen motioned for Jackie to begin.

"Yes, Mr. Burroughs. We have three findings. First, Merritt Royce from HHS has told our source directly that she has had compelling pressure to stop her inquiry into Delaware General. And, apparently, she has done exactly that."

"Good news," said Burroughs. "I believe I have Don Vickers and Senator Tidwell to thank for that."

"Yes, Delbert," said Jensen. "But she does believe there are… How did she put it, Jackie?"

"Ms. Royce told our source that the company is somehow causing, and I quote, 'premature deaths of terminally ill patients,' that this activity is not benign and that profit is the motivator."

Jensen added, "Royce, as of this moment, has been steered away."

"That was the good news." Jackie shifted in her chair and reviewed her notes. "Second, the chief actuary at HHS, Mike Nichols, has proceeded without Ms. Royce to investigate Delaware General claims experience from aggregate data and has continued directing phone calls to companies with DG coverage. By that, sir, I mean Dr. Nichols is putting together what he calls a predictive model of Delaware General's client mortality. The detailed data came from NAI."

"Jackie, you said Nichols is continuing to call our customers?" asked Burroughs.

"Yes, but not directly, and that is the third and most damaging data. While Nichols is directing further calls to DG customers, he is not conducting the research himself. He has contracted with an individual in California, who was released in a corporate restructuring earlier this week, to make the calls. This fellow – Bain Mason is his name – first called DG corporate customers and then, of his own volition, started calling families of deceased policyholders. He evidently has some experience with Delaware General in his former job."

Jensen pointed to Jackie's notes, a transcript from the audio clip captured by Capitol Investigators. "Delbert, Jackie has the conversation between Nichols and Mason."

Jackie flipped through the emailed notes and transcript typed up by Elizabeth. "Mr. Burroughs, here in the conversation Mason, the fellow in California, says, referring to a call he has just made to a spouse of an employee covered by DG: 'She said that her husband had lung cancer but that he died peacefully before it became unbearable… And then she thanked me for working for such a wonderful company and asked me to thank the chairman of the company for her.'"

There was silence for a few seconds and then Burroughs sighed, "Oh, God."

Jackie continued, "The conversation continues with Mason saying to Nichols: 'You know, Mike, these people have been telling me in so many words that Delaware General offed their husband or their wife or their mom. I mean I know that sounds crazy, but that's the message that's coming through. I'll keep making calls. Maybe one of these people will tell me how it's done.'"

"Mr. Burroughs, Nichols then asks Mason to come to Washington to brief Merritt Royce on Monday."

Burroughs remained silent. Jensen could feel his friend's pain and shook his head. "Delbert, we have the capability to intercept a copy of the presentation that will be emailed to Nichols tomorrow from Mason," said Jensen. "And, of course, Jackie will pursue this with full effort to get you more information. Perhaps…"

"Uh, Nathan, Jackie, thank you for your thoroughness on this matter." Burroughs speech was halting and subdued, his thoughts lost in a mad sea of ripping currents.

Jensen sensed his long time associate's dismay. "Jackie, would you mind terribly excusing us. I'll finish up with Delbert and we'll speak again this evening. Oh, and leave the transcript and report from Capitol Investigators."

Jackie gathered her notes and retreated quickly, relieved as her own thoughts wandered to what these powerful men would do now. Gathering the intelligence was one thing. Sorting it and coming up with a plan, one that was within the bounds of even a stretched set of morality would be far more difficult.

She thought ahead to her meeting later with Jensen. *At least we have a boyfriend willing to share some insider data. And the policyholder discussions with that Mason are purely anecdotal – there is no proof.*

CHAPTER FORTY-FOUR

The Burroughs Mansion
Dover, Delaware
Thursday, November 5

A single leather shaded lamp and diffused sunlight afforded by the drizzling late afternoon rain provided the only light in the mansion library. Burroughs sat with his elbows on his desk, his head leaning forward, his hands cupped over his head barely touching the short cropped cut of gray hair.

Though bureaucrats threatened his life's work, he calmly, if sullenly, reviewed his position.

The political appointee, Merritt Royce, is contained, although that could change depending on data brought to her by the actuary and the contractor. He scribbled on a pad of company stationery. *The zealot actuary, how to turn him off... He's immune to pressure from Vickers, or any other political type. This is a science project for him and he is fully engaged. God, he's as pig-headed as I am.* That observation brought Burroughs one of the few smiles he would enjoy today.

The contractor – he's out of a job, he brought us into his old company. He… can be bought. The inducement will have to be sizable enough to cut short his work with the actuary. What's left? The science project then will have little science.

Burroughs picked up his phone and hit speed dial 3. "Phil, glad I caught you. I need you to hire someone and there are a few particulars that are important."

The CEO of Delaware General responded, "Sure thing, Del, shoot…"

CHAPTER FORTY-FIVE

Headquarters of Gatwick Research
Denver, Colorado
Friday, November 6

Marc Friedersdorf, CEO of Gatwick Research, had just joined the meeting. The chief operating officer, Jeff Dunlop drew boxes and made notes on the white board while David Angelo, head of security and a former chief of detectives in Philadelphia, passed out a dozen page report. Elliot Weekly sat near the end of the conference table hands folded in his lap waiting with the several other staff for the operational audit meeting to begin. The plan was to put final touches on the audit today with an action plan to follow next week after Friedersdorf briefed his superior.

Elliot felt at ease with the group at the table but uncomfortable with his team's findings. His team had been critical of the sales apparatus and their perceived loose style, at least as compared to the strict codes of what Elliot was familiar with as a member and with his agents. *I really don't know the sales process so how am I to judge them? I hope I'm not called on to defend these conclusions.*

"Hello everyone," said Friedersdorf with a thin smile. "Jeff tells me you have done great work on the operational audit and I am anxious to see the results. Strengthening our information systems, sales procedures and agent training is critical to our next decade of success."

Dunlop finished writing on the board and turned to the group. "Morning. Well, Marc, I have met with each of the three audit teams and they have brought to us a number of areas where we can improve with a particular focus on sales reps and their contacts with prospects and our policyholders."

"Good, where would you like to begin?' asked Friedersdorf.

Dunlop hitched up his slacks. "Each of the three teams has selected someone to present its findings. There are a large number of issues, but the ones that will be presented here in written form – David Angelo has passed out the report – are the top five, in the considered judgment of the team. These items represent the team's view of issues that could compromise security or introduce error in fulfilling Contracts. Until today each team has not seen what the other has concluded. It is interesting, and discomforting, to see two of these weaknesses on all three sets of analysis. I've noted those on the board."

Elliot saw Friedersdorf immediately turn to the board. Silence greeted Dunlop's scribbled notes. *Well, at least our team agreed with the other teams on the sales issue,* thought Elliot.

Dunlop pointed with an eraser to the first common issue on the white board. "All three teams agreed that lack of human contact with sales executives in the field…"

Suddenly, after two quick knocks, the conference door opened half way.

"Henderson, this is a confidential meeting," started Dunlop before Friedersdorf cut him off.

"Yes, Officer Henderson, what can we do for you?" said Friedersdorf.

"Sir, I was looking for Jeff or Ed. I have an out of bounds call from a sales executive that appears urgent."

Ed Vaughn, head of Gatwick sales rose to take the call but Friedersdorf motioned with his hand for Vaughn to stay seated. Smiling at Dunlop, Friedersdorf said, "Officer Henderson, we'll take the call in here."

As Henderson left Friedersdorf said to the group, "Let's use this as a piece of our audit. If the sales component has more risk, then maybe we will see some of that here. I'll handle the call." He leaned forward and moved his chair closer to the table. Elliot stood and moved the speakerphone toward the Gatwick CEO. Friedersdorf nodded at Elliot.

Maybe this will make us all more comfortable, thought Elliot. *We can see how Marc addresses these unique sales situations.*

"Go ahead, I have an executive on the phone," said Henderson patching in the conference room.

"Yes, sir. This is sales rep Thomas Belday in San Francisco."

"Yes, Thomas, go ahead and explain your situation," requested Friedersdorf.

The sales rep continued, "I just had a call from a policyholder – her voice was confirmed – who said she had a call from a guy who said he was calling from Delaware General conducting market research. The policyholder wanted to know if the call was legit. The policyholder's husband had passed away about four months ago, terminal cancer. Both the wife and the husband are covered by the Contract policy. The wife called me because she had second thoughts about the market research since I had told her, as our procedures state, that no one but me would contact her from Delaware General…"

Friedersdorf gritted his teeth at the disclosure of the parent company's name. Dunlop lowered his head and winced.

Uh oh, thought Elliot. *The boss surely didn't know the call was going to be* this *out of bounds.* This unexpected development both entertained and worried Elliot.

The sales rep continued, "I told the policyholder I would check and asked her what the researcher had asked. She said the researcher had asked about how she was doing given the loss of her husband and did she have any feedback for the company. The policyholder told him his passing was peaceful and saved him from months of pain and suffering. The policyholder said he thanked the researcher and said, and I quote, 'the chairman's policy was a gift, a gift that kept my husband from suffering needlessly.'"

Stone silence filled the conference room. The meeting attendees looked down at their papers. Except for Elliot. As he watched the pallor grow on Friedersdorf's face, he felt badly for him, knowing this breach in their system, this invasion from some outside investigator, would cause huge undercurrents at Gatwick in the weeks and months to come. Elliot quickly wrote a note to Friedersdorf and slid it across the table.

Friedersdorf nodded. "Did you get the researcher's name or location?" he asked the sales rep.

"One better," said the salesman. "The policyholder checked her caller ID and gave me the name and phone number of the market researcher."

Friedersdorf pointed at Angelo as the sales rep gave the name, Bain Mason, and the number. Angelo wrote down the number and left the room.

"Thomas, thank you for bringing this to our attention. You did exactly the right thing, and you were thorough and professional. You should know that, in fact, no market researcher from Delaware General called your policyholder. That was a fraudulent call. Please call your policyholder back and tell her we appreciate her call and that she should not speak with anyone but you about this policy. We will handle the matter with the market researcher from this end." Friedersdorf read another note slipped to him from Elliot. "And Thomas, please extend sympathies again to your policyholder for the passing of her husband. Thank you, Thomas." With that, Friedersdorf clicked the phone off.

"Well," said Friedersdorf to Dunlop pushing his chair from the table, "I didn't expect our operational audit to be quite so… illuminating. I need a short break."

"Back in ten minutes everyone," said Dunlop.

Friedersdorf asked Dunlop to bring Angelo and Elliot and meet him in his office.

"Find out anything about this market researcher, David?" asked Friedersdorf.

"He lives in Cupertino, California. That was his home number. I will have more data on him in an hour. Doesn't appear to be a Fed. Strange. We have a digital recording of the policyholder's conversation with our sales rep. I'll review that and see if there's any more to it than the sales rep said."

Dunlop interjected, "Good job by the sales guy, I thought." The executives and Elliot agreed.

"David, before joining us again check with your supervisors and see if any of them have fielded anything even remotely like this call lately. Before I call… hmph… my boss – guess the audit group knows who that is now – I'd like to have a feeling for whether this is a one-off or part of a larger research effort."

Elliot noted Friedersdorf stayed away from the term investigation. "For what it's worth, Marc," offered Elliot, "I've known for some years that our parent company was Delaware General. It's not widely known, but a few of the more senior staff understand the relationship."

"Thank you, Elliot. I guess I should have expected as much. Would you stay for a minute?" Dunlop and Angelo left Friedersdorf's office. Without sitting he took a step closer to Elliot. "I may have a special assignment for you, soon, so keep yourself clear for a week or so. Okay?"

"Yes, Marc." Elliot returned to the conference room wondering what that could mean. *He doesn't want a special assignment on that researcher, does he? That's not right. We don't know anything about that man. It may be an innocent call.*

But Elliot knew there wasn't anything innocent about the call to the policyholder or the questions. He also realized that Marc had never asked him to do anything Elliot felt was morally wrong. At least not yet.

CHAPTER FORTY-SIX

Westgate Lakes Resort
Orlando, Florida
Friday, November 6

"Wow, look at this!" Merritt's excitement was contagious. She grabbed Grant's arm as they entered the massive Universal Studios complex. "And thank you so much for the wonderful time at SeaWorld this afternoon. Great band, but I do think the whales would be better off in the wild."

"So you liked getting soaked by the whales?" Grant had insisted on stadium seats close to the water and the whales.

"You I'm just crazy about animals, and the whales are so huge." Merritt clung to Grant's arm as they walked through the Universal facilities on the way to the concert. "The water was *really* cold."

"I could tell," said Grant. "You know, Merritt, I think you'd do very well at a sports bar Brett and I go to in Vienna, Virginia."

"Do well?"

"Wet tee-shirt contest."

Merritt squeezed Grant's arm with feigned exasperation.

They walked several blocks past a small man-made lake where staged pyrotechnic chase scenes and water stunts were part of daily shows. In front of them lay a concourse of shops and restaurants. "We have good seats again tonight," explained Grant. "Not sure about tomorrow. I couldn't tell how far back they were from the seating chart."

"I think I'm getting a renewed appreciation for rock 'n roll," said Merritt matter-of-factly. "Some of the hip-hop I listen to on the radio is not very musical, and the lyrics – if that's what you call them – are less than inspired."

"I don't disagree. Course, each style of music has its masters and its boners."

Merritt dug in her purse hearing her cell phone's distinctive 'Amazing Grace' ring tone. "Hello? Oh, hi… No, we're just walking through Universal's huge resort in Orlando on the way to the concert… He does?… Okay, I'll call him. Thanks, LaGretta."

"Problem?" asked Grant.

"Oh, maybe. It's a guy I work with, the chief actuary. He says it's important. I asked LaGretta not to give out my cell number. Mind if I call him before the concert?"

"If you do me a favor."

"Yes?" Merritt answered with a suspicious look on her face.

"Brett said Nanci is acting stand-offish. Maybe you could try to find out what the deal is."

Merritt punched in Nichol's office number. "You want me to find out what's going on in Nanci's head? Right." She shook her head and rolled her eyes at Grant. The call went through. "Mike, it's Friday night," Merritt looked at her watch, "seven o'clock, and you're at the office?"

"Yes, Merritt thanks for calling back. Sorry to bother you on vacation. I mean I am, really, because I know you don't take much time off."

"It's okay, Mike." Merritt held Grant's hand as they continued to walk toward the concert hall.

"LaGretta told me you're back Monday. I wanted to give you a heads up on work I've been doing. I have what we need to convince the Secretary that Delaware General has been offing many of their terminally ill policyholders."

"You've been doing more work on Delaware General?" She stopped walking and dropped Grant's hand. She put her hand over the receiver and started to say something to Grant.

"Go ahead, take the call," said Grant motioning to an out of the way bench where they could sit."

Merritt mouthed "thank you" to Grant along with a quiet smooch.

In an animated voice Nichols responded, "The Secretary blew you off when you met with him because we didn't have our shit together. You said we needed to sort this out. Well, I've been sorting and I'm pretty close."

"Vickers wasn't convinced. We need to chill on this awhile."

"I understand why he wasn't convinced and why you felt we should back off. We didn't have more than some hunches and a few data points. Now, I have a predictive model and results from more calls – put together, it's a compelling picture."

"You called more companies? You know Burroughs will call the Secretary again and I'll get slammed for not listening." Merritt began to panic.

"I don't think that's going to be a problem," said Nichols.

"Of *course* it's a problem if DG gets more calls from companies wondering why the Feds are calling them."

"Well, the calls were made to individual policyholders, not to companies, and I didn't make the calls."

Merritt rolled her head back and ran her hand through her hair. "Well then who *did* call and… and why did whoever it is call individuals?"

"I had a guy, a Berkeley actuary I graduated with, make the calls. He was one of the people I knew when we made the first round of calls to companies. He got laid off and I contracted with him to help out because he knew Delaware General. His idea, not mine: call family of those who died prematurely, ask them about it. He posed it as market research. You know, how they were doing after the loss of their loved one and did they have any feedback for Delaware General."

"Mike, you *are* a wild one." Merritt felt better about this approach. *It seems to insulate me, a little anyway, and I would love to know what's really happening at Delaware General.* "Okay, so what's next?"

She appreciated Grant's relaxed attitude about taking the call, especially so close to concert time. She put her hand on Grant's leg and he wrapped his arm around her shoulder as she pressed the phone to her ear listening to Nichols. Nichols discussed the predictive model, general results of the calls, and the trip by Bain Mason to Washington for Monday meetings.

Nichols wrapped up, "I'll work the weekend on this and have it ready for you right after your staff meeting Monday. Bain will be with me. I'd like to be with you when you brief the Secretary, but you know how crappy I do around those political types. Except for you. Not that you're a political type but…"

"It's alright, Mike, no offense," said Merritt. "Let's see what we have Monday and then decide who we brief and who does the briefing. I know you're with me that, if we do this again, it has to be as airtight as we can get it."

"It will be actuary certified," responded a confident Nichols.

Merritt put away her phone and stood. She didn't listen to Grant as they started to walk. Her initial reaction to take time to sort the problem would no longer be viable. *I have to figure out if Vickers will ever be convinced, even if we find out how DG does this. If he won't be convinced, ever, then why take it back to him? All I do is screw up my chance for the Deputy Secretary post. Yet if something like this is really happening, don't I have a responsibility to report it? Or do I just let it go because… what did Senator Tidwell say, something like, 'true innovators in today's society should be offered help to mute their risk.'* Then it hit her. *The Senator and the Secretary know what's going on. I don't, and they don't want me to know.*

Merritt and Grant found their seats, right center and seven rows back from the stage.

"Great seats again," said Merritt. She tried to purge the issue from her mind.

"Not bad," said Grant proudly. "Say, why don't you people watch for a minute while I go call Brett and see where he is. He should have been here by now."

"Just call him from here."

"Better not, they said no cell phones. I have to hit the head anyway. Be right back." He patted her leg, got up quickly and left.

About ten seconds later from the other side of the aisle Brett called out as he and Nanci excused themselves past others already seated. "Merritt, sorry we're a little late. I know we were going to meet you for a pop before the concert, but we got hung up. Where's my buddy, Grant?"

"Hi." Merritt looked to where Grant had gone but couldn't see him. "You just missed him. He went to call you."

"He go that way?" Brett pointed to the aisle where Merritt had just looked.

Merritt nodded.

"I'll go catch him," said Brett as he stepped past Merritt into the aisle.

Nanci's face lit up as she sat down next to Merritt. "Hi, sweetie," said Nanci. "You look *so* hot tonight. Great top." She touched the leather spaghetti straps to the multi-colored cami top.

"Thanks, it's Roberto Cavalli. I bought it at home for the trip."

Nanci's mouth fell open. "Oh my God, he is like my favorite, but like *so* expensive. Want to exchange closets?"

Merritt remembered the favor Grant had asked. "You're way too cute. I couldn't fit into your clothes."

Nanci looked her over. "We're about the same size on top and bottom but you have legs, legs, legs. I think my jeans would all be Capri's on you," she giggled.

"So how do you like the Power 98 Party Tour so far?" asked Merritt, trying to be nonchalant.

"It's... good. Yeah, cool bands, fun stuff to do..."

"It sounds like there's a 'but' in there."

Nanci faced forward and sighed. "Brett's a nice guy, totally cool, generous, a nice man. But he's not real smooth personally." Nanci looked at Merritt and could tell she didn't know what she meant. "I mean he's such a... guy. Anyway, so we're not a match. It's so great to spend some time with new friends, though." She snuggled up against Merritt's arm.

"Look who's back," said Merritt, "and just as the lights go down. I see you two found each other."

"Please," said Brett now a little louder as the crowd got rowdy anticipating the first band, "he needed me to help him find a place to talk on the phone, he needed help to find the bathroom, he..."

"Come on boys, sit down," said Merritt patting the seat next her for Grant to sit.

Merritt's attention wandered as the first band proved to be head bangers. *Too loud, too raucous, too everything but talented*, she thought. She watched Grant's reaction, energized and happy. Next to her Nanci motioned and grooved but seemed to ignore Brett.

Finally, she thought, *they're done.* The first act departed to less than rousing applause and the audience, more sedate than most rock concert fans, stood to stretch.

"What *are* you grinning about," asked Merritt.

A little embarrassed she noticed, Grant said, "I got some good news. I checked messages at the office and my new assignment came through, a good one. And a new boss, a senior partner. Cool, huh?"

Merritt hugged Grant, "Way to go! We'll have to celebrate. How about champagne after the concert? My treat." She turned to Nanci and Brett and told them the news.

Though Nanci didn't react, Brett said, "And he deserves it. Champagne sounds great. In the hot tub?"

"It's agreed," confirmed Merritt. "A hot tub, champagne, post concert party."

Back at the resort, Merritt had ordered two iced bottles of Moet Chandon White Star to be delivered poolside to the hot tub nearest their rooms. When she and Grant arrived, Brett was in the hot tub adjusting the jets. Nanci sat at a small table nearby still in her sarong and flip-flops, sipping on a drink. Merritt sat next to Nanci.

"Start without us?" asked Merritt.

"Oh wow, this is *so* not working," said Nanci making a face. "I needed a drink."

"Here's our champagne," announced Merritt as the waitresses brought the bottles and buckets of ice. Before the men arrived at the table Merritt whispered to Nanci, "Maybe some champagne will make it better."

"Maybe the whole bottle," complained Nanci.

Merritt stood and poured for the four of them. "Let's toast to Grant's promotion and bright future."

"Here, here!" said Brett loudly now out of the hot tub with glass raised, his hugeness and swim trunks dripping on Nanci's sarong as she stood to join in.

"Well, that went quickly," commented Merritt on the empty first bottle.

"Let's order more." Nanci put down her glass and took off her sarong throwing it over a chair. She filled her glass and motioned for Merritt to get in the hot tub.

"Okay, one more," said Merritt. "Grant would you call room service and ask them to bring another, same card?" She joined Nanci in the hot tub.

Nanci took another drink of champagne and leaned over to Merritt as Brett climbed in the hot tub, "No thong bikini for me tonight. I don't want to encourage him." Sitting up again and smiling now as Grant made it a foursome she said, "Beautiful bikini. I bet it's Burberry."

Merritt raised her glass confirming Nanci's educated guess.

"You are *so* fashionista!" bubbled Nanci.

Grant and Brett talked about football; Nanci drank champagne and gabbed; and Merritt brooded over the conundrum facing her next week.

As Nanci got out of the roiling water to refill her glass, Grant stood and sloshed over to Merritt. "Hey, Sweetheart, Brett and I are going to catch the rest of the football game. Redskins. You want to watch with us?"

"I'll be there in a few minutes," answered Merritt who was looking over at Nanci teetering near the table as she poured the rest of the champagne. "I'll bring in Nanci when she's had enough hot tub."

"Good idea," said Brett shaking his head and ignoring his date.

Back in the hot tub Nanci asked Merritt, "Where did you meet Grant? He's cool and kind of pretty. Great hair but not hairy, know what I mean?"

"I met him at a reception at the Kennedy Center. He *is* a hottie." Merritt shook her head at the term Claudia used. *Geez, and now LaGretta calls him that, too.*

Noticing Merritt's champagne glass was near empty Nanci scooted next to Merritt. "You're empty. Here, have some of mine. She held the glass to Merritt's lips.

Well, she *certainly doesn't need any more,* thought Merritt as she accepted the drink.

Nanci raised the flute a little too much and champagne spilled over Merritt's lips, down her neck and on to her chest. "Oops,

I'll fix that," slurred Nanci as she swiveled toward Merritt. Nanci licked the champagne from Merritt's chin and caressed the bubbly as it flowed into Merritt's bikini top. Before Merritt could react, Nanci continued moving closer, sliding through the hot water, straddling Merritt's thighs, facing her. She kissed Merritt ever so gently on the lips. "You are *so* pretty."

Merritt put her hands on Nanci's hips. "Thanks for the compliment, sweetie. I'm sorry things aren't turning out for you and Brett." Merritt looked understandingly into Nanci's blurry eyes.

Nanci dropped her gaze and slid slowly off Merritt's legs. "Can't blame a girl for trying. Want some more?" Nanci offered Merritt the rest of her glass.

"Thanks." Merritt took a sip and returned the glass.

"I think maybe I'll go home tomorrow," said Nanci. "Brett and I talked some. He'll be okay with it. I hope I see you in Georgetown again." She sounded hopeful.

Merritt stood and with a grin offered Nanci a helping hand. "Count on it. Now, let's go bother those *boys*."

CHAPTER FORTY-SEVEN

The Burroughs Mansion Library
Dover, Delaware
Friday evening, November 6

After trying unsuccessfully to coax her husband downstairs to the great room for some TV, Angela Burroughs slowly walked toward the double doors of the dark wood paneled library, concerned he was spending hours at his desk fretting about work. She had seen him unusually consumed in thought today.

"Don't worry, Baby, I'm just going to make one call. Shouldn't be more than fifteen minutes. Have a problem in the Denver division and I may as well deal with it rather than think about it anymore." Burroughs placed the call from his secure phone to Friedersdorf's direct line.

The on-duty supervisor at Gatwick headquarters answered the after hours call. "Marc Friedersdorf, please." Burroughs provided the supervisor with the CEO connect code: "Prime 1 bear 2."

The supervisor checked his codebook confirming the November call code. "Yes, sir."

Friedersdorf's home phone rang, the secure line sounding an obnoxious fast metallic clink. "Hello?"

"Marc, this is Del. Look, I apologize for calling you at home but I was briefed on some data yesterday that I thought you should hear about before you give me results of the operational audit."

"That's fine, sir. In fact I was going to call you tomorrow morning. We took a call today from one of our sales executives. He had received a call from a policyholder who had been contacted by someone claiming to be doing market research for Delaware General…"

"Guess you don't need to go further with that Marc. That's why I wanted to talk to you. It's connected to some aggressive bureaucrats in Washington trying to figure out our Contract policy. HHS employees – an actuary and a political appointee. They're getting close. The 'someone' you refer to – the guy purporting to be conducting market research – we have identified him and he has been removed as an impediment. Pretty easy as it turned out. We offered him a job doing market research for Delaware General. I enjoy the irony there."

"Excellent," said Friedersdorf. "I was waiting to phone you in the morning to see if our sales execs have fielded any other calls of this nature recently. As of an hour ago this looks to be a solo effort."

"That's good data, Marc. Let me know immediately if any callers are identified."

"We also got the caller's name – just so we have the same guy, it's a Bain Mason – but did not have an immediate solution how to stop him. An issue I wanted to discuss with you. Of course, there is always the solution of last resort, a special assignment, though as you know we have never used that as an internal solution."

Both executives remained silent for a few seconds.

"I don't like that," Burroughs said in a quiet, quick voice.

"Yes, sir. You know of my own reservations on ever using that alternative."

"Ever?" responded Burroughs.

Friedersdorf felt he might have said too much. "I understand the special assignments. I agree with those we have undertaken. Yet the fact that we engage in these seems to legitimize extreme sanction outside the scope of our business."

Burroughs nodded to himself. "Yes, it does. Marc, only you and one of your members have knowledge of these special assignments. They are external, justified and one of the very few power trips I allow myself."

"Yes, sir." Friedersdorf paused. "Do you require our assistance on the two HHS employees you mentioned?"

"I don't think so."

"Yes, sir." Friedersdorf took a breath. "Thank you for calling. I will let the operational audit team know this problem has been contained. Are you still on for the meeting we have scheduled for Tuesday to discuss audit recommendations?"

"A couple questions first. Did the results of your matrix approach result in disparate findings or is there general agreement?"

"Surprising unanimity in the set of findings and recommendations, especially among the top several issues."

"And would I be correct to assume those issues focus on sales staff?"

"You are correct, sir." Friedersdorf could guess where Burroughs was going with this line of questions. "I can go over those briefly with you now if you wish and we can defer the meeting."

"Let's do that and just give me the top line, say a two minute drill, and then we'll get together for a session after I get these Feds under control." *I know he wants to meet and go over details so I don't change things after he's put them in place – I just can't afford the diversion right now.*

"That's fine, sir. First…"

"Marc, before you start, just let me assure you I'm not going to second-guess your internal audit group. They work with the processes on a daily basis. I just want to understand the weaknesses and the adjustments you are making."

"Thank you, sir, that is helpful and I'll pass along your confidence to the participants. First, the teams found that lack of human contact from Gatwick – supervisors, executives, and other sales staff – weaken the tie our salesmen have to the company to the point where they may become cavalier or slip-shod in protective procedures or stray from scripts markedly. Second, the teams believe we should strengthen sales executives' logon procedures to the Gatwick database. For example, presently there can be as much as six hours of inactivity while the salesman is logged on. Third…"

Burroughs trusted Friedersdorf implicitly to direct Gatwick and its complex technology, information management and human apparatus. And there was an explicit understanding that should Burroughs die, become ill or need to be silent in the business for some time that Friedersdorf would continue to execute the Gatwick charter, without interruption and without the need for outside instruction.

The Chairman of Delaware General and the CEO of Gatwick had arranged their business connection so Gatwick could maintain complete independence. Gatwick showed on the parent company's books as a line item: Delaware General Market Research Division. On paper, the division reported to Phil Hanson, Delaware General's CEO. In reality, it reported to Burroughs. The chairman had let the CEO know early on that the division was not a subject of discussion. Hanson never asked about it and Burroughs never volunteered. When CFO Alan Greenberg pressed or one of his staff asked for detailed financials, Hanson and Burroughs changed the subject. The division was never identified as Gatwick

Research and no one from Delaware General but Burroughs knew the location of the Gatwick headquarters facility.

Similarly, the division's financials were reported as a profit center with a slim but respectable margin, nothing that would draw attention. Revenues from the Contract policies were, by design, slightly more than expenditures for Gatwick personnel, security, and technology. Revenue was recognized as fulfillment of Contract policies was completed, not as sales. Rapid sales growth had necessitated a change in revenue recognition policies four years ago to the more conservative approach so margins could be managed appropriately. This year Gatwick's revenue – the Delaware General Market Research Division – would show as a $57 million line item among a sea of other far more impressive figures reported by DG's insurance businesses. Of course, the most significant impact of Gatwick's work rippled unseen throughout the parent company's health insurance division: huge profits from vastly lower end-of-life claims costs.

CHAPTER FORTY-EIGHT

Melbourne Beach, Florida
Saturday, November 7

The drive from Orlando southeast to the beach and site of the last of the Power 98 Party Tour concerts took 45 minutes, though a quiet Brett in the back seat of the rented SUV made that time pass slowly. Grant tried talking about the rock groups to be featured at the King Center in Melbourne that evening without much luck at getting Brett to put on a happier face. The dour hulk had taken Nanci to the airport before noon.

"Here we are," said Grant as he pulled into the parking lot of a new four-story condo building.

"Where's the hotel?" asked Merritt as she exited the SUV, wondering why they weren't at the Sheraton.

"Surprise," beamed a proud Grant. "I upgraded to a two bedroom condo for our last night. Right on the beach with bars and restaurants just across A1A." He pointed to a strip of seemingly unending asphalt: fish grills, surf shops, Mexican restaurants, sports bars, and Italian eateries.

The subject of food awakened the moribund hulk from his doldrums. He stretched his outsized body and grabbed the luggage. "So how 'bout some lunch and then hit the beach? And Merritt, this place has a pool and hot tub if you don't like the beach. I checked it out online with Grant when we signed up."

"No, I like the beach," said Merritt. "Great way to exfoliate your feet. Salt water and a little sun are good for your skin and hair – just not too much."

Grant grabbed Merritt in a hug, "Yeah, redheads are pussies! Oops, I mean…" He dropped her and ran behind the hulk for cover.

"Grant Launder!" squealed Merritt as she tried to get around Brett to get at Grant.

"Listen you two. Get a room, will ya?" said Brett keeping the two separated. "And while you're at it, get me a date for tonight."

Grant and Merritt stopped playing and agreed at the same time to help with an urgent 'get the hulk a date for the concert' plan. They helped with the luggage and started strategizing as they took the elevator to the third floor corner unit.

Merritt quickly hung her things in the small closet and put her jeans, shorts and a few surprises she had brought for Grant in the chest of drawers. *Haven't used any of those little things I brought*, she thought. *Maybe we have been too busy. Always seems like we're moving to the next place.* She opened the slider to the long balcony and stepped outside inhaling the mild salty scent of the ocean. Still reflecting on the state of love making with Grant she thought, *other than that quickie the night we arrived…*

"Hi."

Merritt turned to see a twenties-something, very tan girl on the next balcony.

"Just get here?" she said.

"All unpacked and ready for the Party Tour concert," replied Merritt. "Have you been here long?"

"Oh, I live here," she said leaning over the railing a little, her pony tail falling over her shoulder. "What's the Party Tour?"

Hmm, a candidate. Very cute, petite like Nanci, nice figure – okay, maybe no bubble butt. "Rock concert tonight. Hey, Grant," Merritt called over to the guys as they tried out the TV in the living room, "where's that concert tonight?"

Grant came outside from the living room sliding door with Brett behind him. Grant had the remote control in his hand; neither had a shirt on.

"The King Center on Wickham Road," said Grant.

"Who's your friend?" asked Brett, pushing past Grant to the railing.

Merritt winked at Grant, hoping the hulk would now have a date for the concert and that she and Grant could spend some time alone, away from Brett and football on TV.

"Hi, I'm Tracy," she said turning around with her hands now on the railing behind her. "Man, you are a big dude."

Brett flashed a twenty-inch flexed bicep at the tan brunette. "Thanks, I think." Pointing at Merritt, Brett said, "And don't tell her your nickname for me."

"Okay," said Merritt, "if you're nice the rest of the trip." Directing her attention to Tracy, Merritt said, "He's a great guy and smarter than his immenseness would lead you to believe – a lawyer, no less. Say, we were about to go get in a little beach time. How about joining us and you can tell us what's up in Melbourne?"

"Well, I guess I can leave the grind for awhile," Tracy said as she checked her watch. "Sure, I'll see you downstairs in a few minutes." She smiled demurely at Brett and closed the sliding glass door behind her.

Back inside their condo Brett said to Merritt, "Hey, thanks."

"Sure. You take it from here. She seems like a nice girl, maybe a little young for you…"

Grant piped in, "Pretty surfer girl. Hope she doesn't have a boyfriend."

Heading toward the bedroom to put on her bikini, Merritt said, "Just a guess, but I think she works at home, does well and has no steady boyfriend."

Grant and Brett looked at each other puzzled. Shaking his head and walking to his room Brett said, "Sure wish I could do that. It would save me a *huge* amount of time. Huge."

⇌

A tropical storm had passed the Florida coast two days before headed north, so the surf was up. Rather than small 2 to 3-foot waves the four watched surfers take 6-footers. Brett and Tracy sat on a towel together and talked easily. Merritt, relieved the couple was hitting it off, noticed Grant absorbed in a new sport – surfing. She snuggled up next to him on their beach towel, hooking her arm in his. She loved his broad shoulders and flat stomach. *He looks really good in those trunks.*

"That looks like way too much fun," said Grant, putting his arm around Merritt. He kicked off the running shoes he had worn to the beach and put his keys and phone in one of the shoes.

"You should try it some time," offered Tracy. "Not on this stuff. A little big to begin on. Usually it's pretty flat here, sloppy in the afternoon and hard to get up. And there are rocks here. A little south of here in Sebastian or maybe up at Cocoa would be a good place to learn."

Merritt sensed Tracy liked her beach and the environment she lived in.

"See the older guy in the yellow baggies?" Tracy continued. "He really handles the long board well. And those two guys there?"

She pointed to two boys on smaller boards. "Those two kids can really shred. When the waves get like this, surfers come from all over the state. Kind of like a fresh powder day in the Rockies – everybody's looking for first tracks."

"You surf?" asked Grant.

"I have a board and go out when it's small, 3-foot curls, glassy with an offshore breeze, but I'm not like those kids. I'd rather ocean kayak. Now tennis I'm good at."

Brett decided now was as good a time as any. "Hey, Tracy. We're here for a rock concert tonight and I have an extra ticket. We have great seats at the King Center and the bands are hot. How about it? I'd like for you to come along. Dinner, too, before the concert."

Merritt nodded her head in support.

"Well, I was supposed to meet some friends downtown but… um… sure, sounds good."

"Super," said Brett. "We'll leave for dinner at around six. That sound okay?"

"Sure, that sounds great." Tracy turned to Merritt, "What are you wearing? I haven't been to the King Center. I mean, I hear it's a great auditorium. I just haven't been there so I don't know how people dress."

"Speaking as rock concert experts now we can say that just about anything goes. Pretty crazy. May be better to dress for the restaurant. Where are we going, Grant?"

"I got two recommendations both not far from here on A1A, the Dove and the Cove. But maybe Tracy has other recommendations."

Tracy giggled. "The Cove… close your eyes, listen to the accents and you'll think you're in North Jersey. But the pink flamingoes painted on the wall bring it back to Florida. But it's something different now anyway. The Dove has great Italian, but moved to downtown."

"Damn, girl," said Brett, "you are a walking restaurant guide."

Tracy spoke up, "Mind if I make a suggestion?"

"Please, we need help," said Grant.

"It's called City Tropics. Good early crowd on Saturday. We'll need a res'y. Younger, partyers, good food – including sushi – and a great wine list. We can eat outside and catch some college football on the TVs."

The three looked at each other and offered high fives to Tracy.

"Whoa," said Brett giving Tracy a hug, "where have you been all my life?"

Merritt could tell the youthful Tracy was a little overwhelmed at the positive attention. "Grant, loan me your phone for a minute and Tracy and I will call for reservations."

Grant shook his cell phone out of the toe of his Nike's and gave it to Tracy. He and Brett started talking about which game would be playing around dinnertime.

"Okay, four at six o'clock outside at City Tropics. Done." Tracy handed the phone to Merritt.

"Mind if I check messages?" Merritt asked.

"Uh, I don't know if I have much juice. Yeah, go ahead," he said. He watched as Merritt dialed her cell voice message number. When she connected he returned his attention to college football with Brett.

Merritt had two messages, both from Mike Nichols. *God he sounds stressed. What possibly could...* She erased the messages. She stared at the flip phone. *I need to call him. Now. Should I call from here?* The battery was still full on Grant's phone. *He doesn't want me to use his phone.* Merritt looked up and saw Grant was in an animated discussion with Brett about Florida's college football teams and their rankings. She looked again at the phone. She pressed 'Recent', not understanding why she was doing it, and then 'Dialed' to see the log of calls made from the phone. The log showed the most recent calls first:

48) 321-723-1300
47) J Best cell
46) Office VM

Merritt closed the flip phone. She touched Grant on the arm, "Here, Hon, we're set for dinner at six."

Grant took the phone and stuffed it back in his shoe.

She took a deep breath and started to get up. "I have to call the guy I work with again. He says it's urgent."

Grant turned and faced Merritt. "You mean Mike Nichols?"

"Yes. I'll call from upstairs."

"Okay, I'll come up, too. I've had enough beach." Grant motioned to Brett and Tracy, "See you guys at 5:45."

Upstairs in the condo Merritt picked up her purse from the bedroom and retrieved her cell phone. "No need to arm wrestle for the shower. You first; I'm going to make that call." Moving to the main room she sat at the small desk near the sliding glass doors overlooking the ocean.

"Hello?"

"Mike, this is Merritt. You said it was…"

"Merritt," Nichols interrupted loudly, "I was just on my way out. Please call me in ten minutes at 301-472-2890. Same situation. Thanks." He repeated the number and then the phone clicked off.

What? She scribbled down the last seven digits. *That's not his cell phone.* Merritt turned and saw Grant come out of the bathroom, sans clothes. She could hear him opening a drawer. She stood, concerned about Nichols, and walked to the bedroom entrance.

"I don't know which view is better," said Merritt, "the ocean or you."

"Thanks, Baby. Just looking for that body lotion. I thought I put it… ah, here it is."

"Want me to put some on you?" offered Merritt in a sultry voice.

"Sure, after I shower," he grinned. "I thought you said Nichols wanted to talk to you?"

"He does, but he asked me to call him at a different phone."

"Well then, you have time for a shower." Grant took Merritt by the hand and pulled her toward the bathroom.

She tripped on her flip-flops as he led her to the running shower, her eyes focusing downward along his muscular torso. "I should call him soon so maybe we could wait until..."

Grant turned and drew her close, his nude body pressing against hers. He kissed her roughly and unhooked her bikini top throwing it on the floor.

I need to call... Oh my God, he feels good. I miss his touch, his lips on me...

His smell of sweat, the grit of sand on his chest, consumed her. The tightness of her own skin dried from the afternoon sun and sea breeze contrasted with the heat melting her from within. She succumbed to her cravings for love. Raw, unbridled lust she had missed those years driving her career.

He stepped into the warm shower and she followed. He turned her into the spray and stood behind her, his hands working liquid warmth through her hair washing away the ocean. His arms surrounded her and moved down her sides grabbing her bikini bottoms, caressing her thighs, pushing the wet garment down past her knees then slowly to her ankles and the tile. As she stepped out of the small triangles of modesty his hands followed the course back up her leg, one of his large, warm hands, softened by the sheets of water, moving between her thighs. He paused, kissing her, water pouring over his face. He stood unable to slow the pace, cupping his hand behind her, his other hand grabbing her breast. Her hands braced against the shower tile as he thrust against her.

They lay on the bed facing each other, a towel their only cover. "You are very good, Mr. Launder."

"Thanks, Gorgeous. The pleasure was all mine – well, I hope not *all* mine."

"Hmm, certainly not," she cooed.

Geez, I have to call Mike. Merritt glanced at the wall clock. *Ack, it's been 45 minutes!* "Not to rush away from this delicious moment, but…"

"Oh yeah, your guy is expecting a call, right?" said Grant. "Go ahead, you have plenty of time for the call and getting beautiful before we leave."

Merritt slipped on the orange silk Da-Nang pants she would wear to dinner and a sleeveless burgundy tank and hurried into the living room to make the call. She could hear Brett turning on the shower in the adjoining bedroom. She towel dried her hair with one hand as she punched in the number Nichols had given her with the other.

"Sorry, I'm late with the call, Mike. Where am I calling – sounds noisy."

"Sports bar down the street from my place. I had a couple beers while I waited. Think I probably needed them. Have you had your cell phone with you for the last week, no change of phones or repairs?" Nichols spoke in agitated short bursts.

Merritt sensed trouble. "Phone is the same; it's been with me. Why did you have me call this number, Mike?"

"My work phone is tapped. Must be. I'm thinking Wednesday afternoon. Wouldn't surprise me if they sucked my laptop hard drive, too. And they probably planted a keystroke monitor or spyware of some kind. Won't know until I have the office swept Monday and my PC checked."

"What!" yelled Merritt as she stood up at the desk. "Who?"

The door to the adjoining bedroom flew open and Brett came out into the living area dripping wet holding a towel around his waist. Grant came into the room wondering what the commotion was about.

"There is *no* hot water!" said Brett loudly, eyeing Merritt's wet hair and Grant in his towel. "You didn't. Aw holy shit. I have a hot date tonight and you two guys drain the water heater. Me? I'm androgynous. Totally without nuts. Wanna see?" Brett strode over to Merritt.

Merritt put her hand over the phone, turned to Brett and said sternly, "Hulk, not now!" She walked to the sliding glass door and faced the ocean. She saw Brett dejectedly walk back to his room.

"Mike, what's going on?"

"I got a call today from Bain Mason, the guy doing the work for me on DG. He says he can't come to Washington tomorrow because he has a new job. Guess who with?"

A streak of panic flashed through Merritt's gut. "Delaware General," she said slowly, hoping it wasn't true. Turning she saw Grant in the small kitchen at the other end of the room getting ice water.

"Bingo! Bain gave me this long song and dance about why they wanted him: they needed people with actuary backgrounds; they knew he had brought DG in when he was with HyperNet. They said they would give him a signing bonus if he started right away."

Merritt's thoughts raced. *Could this be on the up-and-up? Maybe they do need actuaries.*

"He's going to work from his home; they'll train him in Dover and somewhere else. Here's the kicker: he started *yesterday* afternoon after signing a confidentiality agreement that was emailed to him. He read me part of it. He had to stop any work being done for anyone else immediately. No contact with other insurance companies, clients or policyholders, and no contact with government agencies. Violation of the agreement means termination, return of the signing bonus and civil suit against him for God knows what."

"You didn't talk with anyone else about what Bain found in his calls with DG policyholders?"

"Nope," responded Nichols. "The only way anyone could have known would be to tap his phones or mine and no one knew he was doing this work, so... They had to bug me. They know Bain and I think Delaware General is... euthanizing policyholders when they get really sick to save on healthcare costs. They know that because they had me bugged. And they had tapped me because I called their corporate customers. They could have you bugged, too."

They both thought about that for a few seconds.

"Nah, doing that would require really big nads," concluded Nichols. "They may see me as the threat, not you. Shit, Merritt, I'm spooked. They may just try to off me like one of their terminally ill policyholders, before any of this makes it to prime time."

"Mike, let's not get to dramatic here. They – whoever 'they' are – are paying him to keep quiet. Maybe I can match their offer with a longer term contract for him." Merritt was groping for a solution.

"He already signed with them. They doubled his HyperNet salary. And the signing bonus? You're not going to believe this. Fifty grand now and another fifty in a year if he signs another employment contract. Deep pockets. We're outgunned. Merritt, I need some protection. Can we call someone?"

She read genuine fear in his voice. *I bet they don't have me bugged. I haven't called companies since when, a week ago, and no policyholders. They think I have been managed. Damn... they would be right.*

"Mike, let's think this through. Now that they know what you know, you aren't dangerous, are you? They neutralized your source."

"Yeah, maybe," said Nichols. "Hell, I don't even want to go home." Trying to stay focused he put down the long neck beer, rubbing his forehead with the heal of his hand. "I think the Federal Protective Service can do the sweep for devices. I still have the log of calls Bain made to policyholders and what they said. And I have the predictive model on Delaware General mortality rates. So if we can prove my phones are tapped, that should be plenty to get the FBI in this. Don't you think?"

Geez, the FBI? Is that where this is headed? In nano-blips of memory she relived the jarring discussion with Secretary Vickers and the promise of a promotion. The amorphous lecture by Senator Tidwell ground deeper still. The knot in her stomach tightened. Her queasiness deflated the afterglow of intimacy. *What am I doing here? Is this an escape?* She looked back at Grant still dawdling in the kitchen. *What would Dad do? Should I tell Mike to take a vacation, just leave it alone? Even if I agree to something less like going to the HHS Inspector General, Vickers will still come down on me with both feet. I'm not sure Mike would back off now anyway. Oh God, I need some time to sort through this. Yes, Dad, I know: 'Tough decisions don't go away by ignoring them.'*

"Okay, first step: Monday morning, before my staff meeting with the Secretary, I'll ask for an electronic sweep of your office and mine, including PC's. That a good place to start?" Merritt hoped that would work for Nichols. "I think we need to prove the assertion of surveillance before this goes any further."

"The question is: who is 'they'?" asked Nichols.

"'They' have to be some sort of appendage to DG. That's not nearly as hard as *what* exactly are we dealing with?"

CHAPTER FORTY-NINE

City Tropics
Indialantic, FL
Saturday, November 7

The outside bar was turning over from a late lunch and football-watching crowd to the first wave of Saturday evening revelers.

Brett was first to notice how many people said 'hi' to Tracy. He elbowed Grant as they made their way past outside tables to the semicircular bar, "Dude, she knows as many people here as you do at your sports bar back home."

Tracy grabbed Brett's hand and pulled him aside to meet some of her jeans clad friends.

"Looks like you helped the 'hulk' land a real cutie," Grant said to Merritt.

"I'm glad he has a date for tonight. And I think he's over not having much hot water for his shower. Look at him smile at all those young girls." *And it seems he's over Nanci, too.*

"Get things sorted out with Mike Nichols?" asked Grant.

Merritt sat down at a four top near the long curved bar and surveyed the growing number of partiers. "He's nervous." She caught the attention of a waitress.

"Why?" asked Grant as he opened the menu.

"He thinks… I can't believe he's being tapped. It's just too weird." Merritt stared blankly at the bar scene. "He has an overactive imagination. He's been working hard…"

"Hey, what's up?" Grant asked as he leaned toward Merritt.

"It's not that I don't believe him. It's… believing him means taking this to a place I can't go." Merritt's searching eyes met Grant's.

"Then, don't," said Grant. He put his hand on hers and ordered a bottle of chardonnay from the waitress now standing tableside. "And a spider roll and a California roll from the sushi bar, please."

"I can't just ignore the situation." Merritt remembered her Dad's advice: delaying a decision is a decision in itself. "Mike is very bright and hard working. He says he has enough data to go to the FBI about Delaware General."

"Whoa, that sounds pretty radical. He needs to settle down."

Merritt contemplated Grant's reaction as Brett and Tracy joined the table.

Brett scooted his chair close to Tracy's. "What's the discussion? You guys look serious." Not waiting for a reaction he continued, "Miss me that much? Say, Tracy suggested a condo crawl after the concert. Whaddya say?"

"Yeah," added Tracy, "since your place is next to mine and this other couple's place is downstairs, we can party wherever there's drinks left."

"Outstanding," said Grant, "we can stop by a store on the way home for eats and something to drink."

"We really don't want to be driving on A1A after drinking," Tracy said to Merritt. "Way too many beach cops, so this keeps it local. And we can stop by Goombays for take out."

"Sure," responded Merritt. "Goombays?"

"Tuna sticks, mahi tacos. Yum." Tracy grinned.

"This beach scene has me pumped," said Brett.

"Yum again," said Tracy as she felt Brett's bicep. Still hanging on Brett's big arm she said, "You guys all lawyers?"

"Brett and I work at the same firm," said Grant. "Merritt works for HHS."

"Hmm. Health and Human Services," said Tracy. "What area?"

"Mostly in analyzing healthcare costs and insurance," said Merritt. *This girl has so much more on the ball than Nanci.*

"How 'bout that. I work for an insurance company." Tracy pulled three business cards out of her little bag.

Grant and Merritt looked at Tracy's card and then at each other with eyes wide open and said together, "Delaware General?"

"Yes, you know them?"

Grant replied, "Delaware General is my insurance company for health and life." He looked at Merritt.

"Mine, too," said Brett.

"Oh, super!" said Tracy.

"So you are in market research?" asked Merritt looking at the card.

"Yeah. Great company to work for. I can work out of my place. Mostly phone and PC work," said Tracy. "I've worked for the company for four years. It's worked out really well."

Merritt put the card in her pocket. "I met the Chairman of your company at a reception in Washington not too long ago."

"Did you?" said Tracy.

"And saw him at a congressional hearing a couple weeks after that."

"I've not met him but I understand he's a wonderful man," said Tracy. "Well, I'm starved. Let's order some dinner."

Interesting, thought Merritt. *For a girl that's obviously a quick study, you would think she would be more curious about the head of her company.*

"Yes, we better get dinner so we're not late for the concert," added Grant. "I'm having the grouper."

CHAPTER FIFTY

Condo of Tracy Madsen
Melbourne Beach
Saturday night, November 7

Brett carried the food in. "Very cool place, Tracy. Much better than our condo next door."

"Thanks. I had a girlfriend help me with the painting and faux work." The leather like texture on the taupe colored walls of the living area added an immediate sense of warmth and comfort. Tracy put the wine in the refrigerator and rushed back out to the living room to show off her place to her new friends.

"Just about everyone has tile floors because of the humidity and salt spray." Tracy opened the long sliding glass doors. The surf pounding below continued the drumbeat of the night's concert. "I've been in this place a couple years and haven't had any problems, although people who have lived on the beach a long time say it has its drawbacks. I love it here, though."

"I can see why," said Merritt. "The sound of the surf is beautiful and your place is perfect."

"Thanks," gushed Tracy, pleased to be giving a tour to someone other than the flip-flop crowd she usually met. The men had bought nice wine from the wine boutique at City Tropics and the food at Goombays. That and dinner and the concert – certainly better treatment she got from locals who leaned on her way more than was fair for her to pay.

Tracy continued showing off her condo after stopping in the kitchen to serve wine. She wiped the glasses clean as they saw little use from her typical visitors.

Brett gave her a hug as she served him a glass of chardonnay. "Ever get up to the Washington area?" he asked. "I'd love to show you around the city and return the hospitality."

"I used to visit there." My Dad lives outside DC in Potomac, Maryland. My Mom passed away quite a few years ago. I haven't been there in awhile. Dad usually visits me here. He'd think you are wonderful. He's a lawyer, too, and a big guy like you. Well, not *quite* as big," she giggled. She punched at Brett's stomach with Brett exaggerating the impact.

"I love this setup," said Brett as he sat in her desk chair and swiveled around toward her keyboard and screens. "Beautiful brunette surfer girl and smart enough to manage this bad ass work station. What do you have here?" His eyes followed the monitor cabling to a wall port ending at the smoked glass cabinet.

One-third of the main living area was upscale high tech office furniture, a graceful segue from the contemporary living and dining areas to her open office environment.

"Oh, just several screens to help me with market research. You know girls and their multi-tasking," said Tracy. "How about some of those jerked tuna sticks from Goombays – you're gonna love the sauces, too."

Brett followed the others to the round glass top dining room table where Tracy had spread out the food. The door bell rang before he could pick up a plate. "I'll get it," said Brett

The neighbors from the condo just below Tracy's place stood with their mouths open staring at Brett as Tracy squeezed her way between Brett and the doorway to welcome them.

"Hi y'all, come in," said Tracy backing in to Brett to get him to move.

Merritt elbowed Grant motioning to the greeting. "I swear the hulk gets his entertainment from watching people's reaction to his hugeness. He ever do that at the office?"

"Naw, he's pretty buttoned up at the office," Grant responded while he snarfed a fish taco. "He's done really well there – better than me."

"Hey, you're getting a raise."

"Yeah, I think it's going better now, more visibility."

Two bottles of chardonnay and one of a too-sweet pinot grigio later, Tracy poured the last of the wine Brett and Grant had bought. "Time to condo crawl," announced Tracy.

The other couple invited everyone downstairs and led the procession. Brett gave Tracy an off the floor bear hug and said, "Be right there, I'll do a quick kitchen clean up and take out the trash." Tracy tried to argue but Brett insisted, "No, no, don't argue. Go."

Merritt added, "I'll help, use the restroom and be down in a sec."

Looking back to see Merritt and Brett clearing the table, Tracy left the door open and said, "Don't bother with that, come on down."

"It'll just take a minute," said Brett.

Merritt held a trash bag while Brett finished the quick cleanup. "Isn't that interesting that Tracy works for Delaware General?"

"Not nearly as interesting as her PC setup," said Brett. "Look." He pointed to the glass cabinet behind Tracy's computer monitors.

"What do you mean," asked Merritt.

"It's locked, but see behind the sound system components?"

Merritt checked the open doorway and walked over behind the monitors bending to look into the smoked glass cabinet. "Looks like the computer processor is in there. So?"

"Not just any processor. HP's newest, fastest, totally duplexed. And see those peripherals on the left? Looks like an encryption device and an extra processor for who knows what. This isn't market research gear. There must be thirty grand of equipment here plus the monitors."

Merritt looked again at the doorway not wanting to be caught snooping. "Then what is it?"

"One of the companies I work with has contracts with State Department Intelligence. Their office-to-office communications look like this – secure, state of the art. Tracy said she's worked for Delaware General for four years. This hardware can't be more than six or nine months old. Insurance companies don't spend this kind of money on market research hardware. And why lock it up like this and have encryption technology?"

She looked at the doorway again and then at the keyboard on Tracy's desk.

"You want me to see what she's working on?" offered Brett.

"Um..."

"Oh, come on. I'm as curious as you. I've been itching to do this as soon as I saw her hardware." Brett sat down at Tracy's desk.

"I don't want to have her see us. We can't..."

"It'll just take a second." said Brett as he touched the space key on the keyboard. "This will bring it out of sleep mode, if it's on. See, here it is. I'll go downstairs and keep her busy for a couple minutes while you take a look."

Brett, seeing the center monitor light up, stood and held the chair for Merritt. "Sit. Quick. Remember to return to the screen it was on when you started and use the mouse, like this," he leaned over to show Merritt, "to put it back in sleep mode." Brett bolted for the door. "Can't guarantee any more than like three minutes. And I want to know what you find."

Merritt listened to the heavy-footed bear bound down the outside stairs not taking her gaze off the screen. The page was on what looked to Merritt like an insurance policyholder's history:

Mary Alice Putnam *Policy Number 4,282,754*
45 Orchid Blvd., 2A *DOB 11/21/68*
Cocoa Beach, FL 32931

TSC 9/10/04
Long-Term Care 6/04/04
Universal Life 1/19/02
Health Premiere 8/03/01

Alright, she has health and life insurance, and long-term coverage. Wonder what 'TSC' is? She scrolled down to the next page:

TSC
Referrals:
Edward Putnam, $1000 *Policy Number 4,355,687*
Lynn Putnam Argent, $1000 *Policy Number 4,358,113*
Status:
Alpha 9/22/07
Last contact:

Called 3/23/07 to ask "Can I buy a Contract for my younger sister (Lynn Putnam Argent) who can't afford the policy herself?" Answered in the affirmative and gave her referral credit of $1000. Counseled Mary Alice not to discuss with Lynn.

Merritt heard steps approaching in the hallway. In a near panic she scrolled back to the first page and tried to return the machine to sleep mode as Brett had shown her. *Oh, get it right. Hurry!* The screen went dark and Merritt ran to the front door closing it behind her just as a delivery man passed Tracy's condo and knocked on the neighbor's door. Her heart still pounding Merritt briskly made her way downstairs and joined the boisterous group where Brett was showing Tracy the finer points of arm wrestling techniques. Merritt repeated the two pages of data to herself from the screen and jotted down the first policy number, date and address. She could remember the names. She made eye contact with Brett and gave him a shrug of the shoulders and raised eyebrows.

⇌

Lying on her back in bed, staring out the sliding doors at the sliver of moon, Merritt was still awake listening to the surf, trying to make sense of the mad rush of events in her life. She heard Brett stumble back into the condo, fish around in the refrigerator and then close the door to his bedroom. Grant had fallen asleep on the way to the bed, or so it seemed.

I can't get close to Grant. Close, yeah, but emotionally close, figured out close, in love close... What is the matter with me? And I can't get away from Delaware General. Tracy isn't who she says she is. She's not a market researcher. It looks like she's selling policies. But then why the cabinet full of expensive computer gear? What kind of policy is that? And why would she write in her notes not to talk about the 'Contract.' Maybe Mike can figure out what TSC means. I need to tell him what I found. Where am I going with this?

CHAPTER FIFTY-ONE

Melbourne Beach condo
Sunday morning, November 8

Merritt, packed and ready, was in the small kitchen looking for the croissants and other pastries they had bought for breakfast so they could get a quick start to the Orlando airport.

Brett lumbered into the main living area in only a pair of running shorts. "Uh, oh," he said and turned back toward his bedroom.

"Hulk! Did you eat *all* the pastries?" yelled Merritt.

"Um…"

"You didn't save me even *one* croissant, and you said when I bought them, 'why get those, there's nothing inside but air?' Come here you."

Brett stood arms at his side his head lowered like a berated puppy who had pooped on the carpet. Merritt, her face redder than her auburn hair, had her hands on hips looking straight up into Brett's sheepish grin.

"How could you do that, hulk? I need something to soak up all that wine we drank. How could you eat four donuts, two bear claws and three croissants?"

Hearing the one-sided argument, Grant came in the room with a towel around his waist. "What's going on?"

Brett answered, "You know those French croiss... however you say that, aren't too bad. Anyway, I owed you guys one for the hot water fiasco."

"Argh," yelled Merritt. She turned to walk away from Brett, who was still grinning, but then spun around and before he could react, she reached down and pulled the sides of his shorts down hard.

Grant laughed and hooted at Brett's knee high shorts and his rush to get them pulled up.

"What are you laughing at, sport?" said Merritt as she passed Grant on the way to the bedroom stopping long enough to yank off Grant's towel. Both men now scrambled to get their modest garments back in place. "Alright boys, get packed. And I need your help on something, so get moving. Oh, and I want to stop on the way and get some grease for breakfast. I'm buyin'. I'm feeling a little rough."

Brett and Grant looked at each other and exclaimed at the same time, "Grease!"

Still about 20 minutes from the airport and filled with fried hash browns loaded with salt, sausage and egg biscuits and black coffee, the three revelers relaxed.

"I can't believe I just ate that," said Merritt.

"Perfect hangover remedy, although I think you actually used the term 'grease' to describe breakfast." Grant enjoyed the moment.

"Geez," groaned Merritt. "I'll need to rest up from my vacation." She looked at Grant, "Thank you so much for the Party Tour. It really was fun."

"You're welcome. You made the trip," said Grant.

"Yeah," said Brett from the back seat. "You really are pretty cool, for a Fed. Say, you said you wanted our help. On what?"

"I do want your help." Merritt turned to look at Brett in the back seat. "You planning on seeing Tracy again? I mean, she's a smart, nice girl, but what I need help on involves her."

"If you mean 'is she the one,' I dunno," said Brett, "but she's a great date. Hell, I really don't know. Aw, don't worry about that. Ask your question."

From the driver's seat Grant eyed Brett in the rear view mirror.

Merritt said to Brett, "You got me into her system last night. What I saw was…"

Grant reacted. "You went in Tracy's computer? Jesus, Merritt!"

"What's the big deal, bro?" said Brett. "I was curious so we snooped a little."

Merritt studied Grant's reaction.

"You're a senior government employee," Grant continued. "You can't be caught doing that kind of stuff!"

Before she could respond, Brett piped in again from the back seat, this time leaning forward with his hands on the front seats, "Dude, what *is* your problem? Tracy is a cool surfer chick, but she's no market researcher. That computer rig is spook quality shit. Besides, Merritt only looked for a couple minutes." Turning to Merritt he asked, "What did you find out anyway?"

Racing through Merritt's head was, *Why is Grant being mean about this? It's like he's protecting her.* "Grant, no it's not right to poke around in someone's computer, but you know what I've been working on. This could be a big break. This could have led me to what it is that Delaware General is hiding."

"Whoa," said Brett, now leaning between the seats again. "You're after Delaware General? For what? How come you didn't tell me?"

"Brett, it's not a legal investigation. It's…"

"Well, it's illegal to be spying in someone's business PC," said Grant, stern faced and staring at the road ahead.

"All right, fine," said Merritt. "Let's just leave it then."

Brett slid back slumping in the back seat and looking out the side window at the palm trees whizzing by.

A few seconds later Grant broke the awkward silence. "Okay, Merritt, I'm sorry. I just don't want you to get in trouble. So, what *did* you see?"

Merritt had her arms crossed. "Policy numbers, dates, policy types."

"And that's not market research stuff?" asked Grant.

She uncrossed her arms and turned to Grant and Brett. "No. It showed when this policyholder, Mary Alice Putnam, 39 years old, had bought her several insurance policies – health, life, long-term care and something called 'TSC.' And the next screen had notes about this Mary Alice buying her sister a TSC policy and it also showed other referrals – looked like relatives – and that Mary Alice received a $1,000 bonus for each referral."

"Damn, girl," said Brett, "you have a photographic memory?"

"No," said Merritt, "I had to write down the policy number and date because I didn't want to forget them."

"Holy crap," said Brett. "Glad you're not my girlfriend. You'd remember every screw-up I ever made. Wish I'd known you wanted Delaware General data. Maybe I could have helped… *Bond, Brett Bond…* Whaddya think?"

"Stick to computer hardware and being a lawyer," said Merritt. "Have any idea what 'TSC' means? And, 'no' I don't want you to ask the company or anyone else."

Both Grant and Brett replied, "Nope."

"You're right, though," said Brett. "Not market research. More like sales. Phone sales."

Grant responded, "Never heard of phone sales of insurance policies that cost thousands of dollars. Course, I'm only a lawyer not a sales genius."

As the SUV pulled up to departures Merritt said, "Well, not a lot to go on but I'll work on it."

The three Party Tour participants waited for the flight, now delayed 30 minutes by thunderstorms, in the main concourse, each wandering off to a little shop. Merritt saw the men migrate to the PGA golf store. She started with the $10 store and looked at scarves. She meandered to a couple of other little places and then to a bookstore where she walked to the back to look at magazines. The isles were narrow and filled to seven feet off the floor full of the latest periodicals, fashion journals, sports weeklies and skin magazines. As she reached for *Vogue* she recognized Brett and Grant's voices one isle over. She turned to walk around the aisle to meet them and was about to surprise them when she overheard Grant answer his cell phone. She stopped in her tracks.

"Jackie, yeah, thanks for calling back." Grant tried to shield his conversation from Brett by turning away and cupping his hand over the phone. "I'm on my way back but I need to give you a quick update."

Merritt faced the magazines. *Jackie? The senior partner from Baker and Jensen? Why…*

"She's shopping. Our flight is delayed a little. I can't talk here but we met a girl last night who is a sales rep – well, she said she was a research analyst – for Delaware General… Yeah, her name is Tracy Madson." Grant looked around and saw Brett giving him the eye so he stepped away a couple steps still guarding the cell phone with his hand. He was now near the end of the aisle.

Merritt stood just a couple yards away on the other side of the tall rack of magazines. She stared blankly at the wall of periodicals just inches from her nose.

"Jackie, listen! No time. I'll brief you when I land, but Merritt got into this sales rep's PC and saw some files about policy types and dates. She wrote down numbers and names. She saw the computer arrangement... No, I don't have what she wrote down... Okay, I'll try. Gotta go." He flipped the phone closed.

The glass chard of betrayal ripped through Merrit's core, piercing her heart, knifing her tenuous hold on love, tearing at all she knew. She tried to steady herself against the rack, her knees rocking from under her. *No, no. My God, how could he?*

Brett stomped over to Grant. "What did you just do? That was Jackie at the firm? Dude, what are you doing? This thing you have with Merritt is so good, and you're going to fuck it up? For what? Shit, Grant, you did this to make partner? I can't fuckin' believe what you're doin'. Man, you are some certified piece of suck."

Grant grabbed Brett's arm and tried to quiet the big lineman before they made more of a scene.

Merritt quickly exited during their elevated argument, her face drained, her life in hell's basket of quandary.

The lump in her throat shortened her steps to the gate area. She sat holding her carry on bag in her lap pining for the comfort of home, of Meatballs's purr, of solitude away from hurt. When Grant and Brett showed up, the plane was ready to board. Merritt forced a weak smile and showed off her $10 store purchases – two brightly colored scarves. She closed her eyes on the return flight. She forced herself into light conversation on the ride back to her home. As she thanked Grant for the trip she summoned the strength for a quick poison kiss on the landing of her house. He would pay the price another time. A time she would choose.

CHAPTER FIFTY-TWO

HHS Headquarters, Washington, D.C.
Monday, 8:35 am, November 9

"Good morning, Mr. Secretary," said Merritt smiling as she stood from the long conference table and flipped her shining auburn hair over her shoulder. The HHS Secretary's staff meeting had just concluded and Merritt saw he was in a positive mood. As they walked together back toward his private office she said, "I have interesting news about Delaware General. I think it explains Mr. Burroughs sensitivity lately." She raised her eyebrows and continued smiling. "Have a few minutes?"

Secretary Vickers responded immediately. "Of course, Merritt, please come in." They went to his smaller private office, and he closed the door behind him. "I must say I had been wondering how you were doing, how you felt about our conversation a week or so ago."

Elegantly attired in a St. John Knit burgundy dress with a tailored black and burgundy tweed short jacket, she said with her hazel eyes twinkling and the slightest turn in her head, "Still excited about the prospect of becoming your deputy. And very much committed to *your* agenda, sir. Which is why I wanted to catch you this morning. The noise around Delaware General seems, now, rather easily explained."

Vickers leaned back in his chair. "Well, that's good news. I would hate to have another terse conversation with Del Burroughs. He is such a friend to this administration."

"Yes, I know he is," she said. "Here's what happened, although I'm still putting the pieces together. Chief Actuary Nichols correctly saw some anomalous figures on premature death pointing to Delaware General. But, his extrapolations were based on three pockets of data, all of which are explained by recent press accounts."

"What press? I didn't see anything on Delaware..."

"No, sir, not on Delaware General, but on *mercy killings* – a set of nine in San Francisco, all at the same hospital, the Coastal Medical Center, a male nurse was indicted. And another eleven deaths, again blamed on mercy killings at a hospital and Alzheimer facility in Paramus New Jersey, there by a long time administrative aide. And five deaths at a hospital – I don't recall the name – in Baltimore, there an oncologist has been charged."

"Mercy killings," repeated Vickers. "But why is..."

"Separate events, different indictments, different parts of the country, yet connected by the same timeframe and, unfortunately for Delaware General, the same insurance carrier. Those killed, that is 22 out of 25 deaths, were covered by Delaware General Health insurance. In fact, I ran into a Delaware General sales rep this weekend when I was in Florida and she said the company was concerned about the mercy killings and rumors that DG was somehow connected."

Merritt was confident she remembered the conversation with Vickers just 12 days before when he had cut her off. *This fits. He'll want to buy it because he needs the problem to go away. Question is, did Dad teach me to play poker well enough.*

⇌

"How was the Secretary's staff meeting?" asked LaGretta coming into Merritt's office.

"Secretary Vickers was there." Merritt was standing beside her desk staring at the corner with the phone remembering when she hoped the call, every call, would be from Grant. "And so was Deputy Secretary Houghton." She looked up at her loyal administrative assistant and tried to smile. "We have a full agenda this week. No hearings but several briefings. Thankfully I only have to organize one of those. It's on the House side and it shouldn't take too much time to prepare. And Mike Nichols will be here later this morning."

LaGretta walked over next to Merritt. Her empathy brushed Merritt's elbow. "Well now, we'll have some fun here this week then. Virginia Tech won Saturday while you were in... Florida and..."

Merritt rested her hand on LaGretta's arm. "I'm not good at hiding my feelings, am I? The trip was really good until yesterday. Then my rainbow faded." Merritt gave LaGretta a pat on the hand and walked briskly to her brief case on the couch. "Actually, it was one of the worst few minutes of my life." Now sitting at her desk, she said, "I outlined a plan last night for dealing with my... mess, but it has a lot of moving parts. I need your help."

From the door of her office a familiar voice rang out, "Count me in."

LaGretta turned, "Hello, Miss Claudia."

Merritt rose and greeted Claudia with a hug and then shut the door.

"Honey, I'll do whatever I can to help you," said LaGretta, "but can you tell us a little about what happened?"

"She told me on the phone last night. That pretty boy Grant used her to get a promotion!" Claudia's face tightened and reddened as she brought LaGretta up to date. LaGretta's mouth opened wider and wider as she heard the story.

Claudia and LaGretta sat across from Merritt as she fished in her valise for her notes. "Claudia, I hope I'm not intruding on your day too much."

"This works out perfectly," said Claudia. "Senator Tidwell is out of town until tonight and the Senate is not in session until later today. This is a girl's session to fix a problem, a man problem, and I have some ideas."

LaGretta got up and scurried back to her desk waving a hand above her head as she lit up the room with pantyhose friction. "You wait a minute. I need to get my desk covered and get my pad. Hang on, hang on…"

Back in their huddle the three played out options to figuratively castrate the offending pretty boy. They would connect the end of the day by phone to put the pieces together.

CHAPTER FIFTY-THREE

Office of HHS Actuary Mike Nichols
Rockville, Maryland
Monday 9:15 am, November 9

"Maybe I'm still a little drunk from last night, but that lawyer lady from Baker and Jensen looked pretty good this morning," said HB as he finished removing the tap to HHS Actuary Mike Nichols' desk phone where the phone wire ran to a wall port.

Erwin shook his head at his colleague's observation and put a nickel-sized harmonica bug from the other phone in his breast pocket. "You didn't even look at her face. All you saw was her short skirt and high heels. Hurry and get the PC handled. His secretary said his Monday staff meetings are short, and he's only two offices away."

"Won't take a sec. Watch this." HB plugged a FireWire into Nichols' Sony laptop and thumbed a command into his handheld device. Twenty seconds later he unplugged. "Let's go. I have his latest data and removed the beacon."

"Hmph," grunted Erwin. "So much for him thinking he could backtrack on us."

As they left the building they pulled their GSA hats down to cover their faces.

"How did the lawyer lady know he wouldn't be in his office at 9 am and that his laptop would be there?" asked HB.

Erwin responded, "Lawyer snoops are at a different level. Anyway, she gave us another 500 bucks each so I'm not asking questions. When you work with lawyers, you can't get in too much trouble."

"Can I keep the hat and jacket?" asked HB.

"Yeah, but not for wearing in public."

"Maybe she can get me a smaller jacket. This one's too big. What's GSA anyway?"

"General Services Administration," said Erwin. "They handle space, maintenance, phones, that kind of thing, for government."

"Sounds boring."

Erwin looked at HB and grinned, "Not the way we do it."

They chuckled as they walked to the back of the parking lot. After sending a short encrypted email to Jackie Best at Baker and Jensen, they drove off in their gray van. The email said simply: "Clear. Awaiting next instruction."

CHAPTER FIFTY-FOUR

Office of HHS Actuary Mike Nichols
Rockville, Maryland
Monday 9:40 am, November 9

Nichols whisked by his administrative assistant on the way into his office talking over his shoulder, "Have you heard from Merritt yet?"

She responded, "Yes, Miss Royce wants to meet with you later this morning after the Federal Protective Service is finished. What are they going to do?"

"They're going to…uh," Nichols decided to hold a little back, knowing how cautious Merritt had asked him to be, "…help me sort out a security problem."

"Well," said the assistant smiling at the man in the suit and two other uniformed men now standing in front of her desk, "ask and you shall receive. Are you gentlemen from Federal Protective Service?"

The man in the suit responded, "Yes. Is he expecting us?"

"Come on in," said Nichols from his desk.

The men entered the office, displayed their credentials and introduced themselves, one a special agent and the other two officers with the secure communications division. The security officers began looking around the office.

The special agent said, "Assistant Deputy Secretary Royce phoned last night and requested a priority sweep of your phones, lines and computer. She said you have reason to believe your office phone has been monitored by an outside agent.

Nichols started to answer but his assistant, about to close the door, cut in. "Mike, sorry, I overheard, GSA phone people were here about half an hour ago. They said everything looked fine." She began to shut the door.

"What!" yelled Nichols. "Wait a minute. Phone people were here this morning? GSA?" Nichols was now walking over to his aide who looked shocked at his reaction.

The Federal Protective Service officers looked at each other. The special agent spoke first. "I assume, Mr. Nichols, you did not request GSA assistance."

"Hell no," answered Nichols.

The agent said to the other officers, "Start here, also get the main box and router. And check Ms. Royce's office as well." He turned to Nichols, "You okay to stick around? These officers may need to ask you questions. I suggest we also sweep your home and cell phone. I'll be back after I quiz GSA and check with the front desk for sign-in sheets and front entry video." The agent moved quickly down the long hallway talking on his cell phone as he walked.

Nichols paced in front of his desk then reached for his cell phone to call Merritt.

"Wait one," said an officer taking the phone from Nichols. "Let me check it first."

CHAPTER FIFTY-FIVE

HHS Office of Assistant Deputy Secretary Merritt Royce
Rockville, Maryland
Monday, 1 pm, November 9

Nichols slumped in the long leather sofa eyeing the top of the window cornice in Merritt's office. "See, if we all had a small video camera right about *there* in our office," he pointed to where he was looking, "with wireless feed to an external harddrive, we would be a lot more secure, no need for the Federal Protective Service." He grunted, "They're part of the Department of Homeland Security. Not much help today, though. Maybe they should've stayed in GSA."

"We learned quite a bit," said Merritt crossing her legs as she sat in the big armchair across from the sofa.

"Yeah, like what?" Nichols leaned forward with his forearms parked on his knees. "FPS officers found no evidence of taps, bugs, PC spyware, nothing. The timeframe that fits has only two guys on the video with no sign-in names. One… a courier with baseball hat and sunglasses. No name, just the courier company name on the sign-in log. The only other guy with no name also had a hat, pulled down nicely, thank you, and was carrying a big box for the lawyer you know. And that delivery checked out. Files big Ben needed in Congressional Affairs. We did see two guys leaving about the right time with GSA outfits on but no ID and with GSA hats so we can't see their faces."

"Okay, here's what you're missing," said Merritt. "Whatever they put in, they took out – professionals. The FPS special agent confirmed no GSA staff were authorized to be here working on phones this morning. And, there's no match between incoming males and the two departing GSA impersonators. So…"

"So they changed identities from the time they entered to the time they left as GSA types."

"Yes," said Merritt, "and it's likely the courier and the box carrier with no sign-in names are the GSA impersonators. So…"

Nichols thought, "So…?"

"So, I think that implicates Jackie Best, the Baker and Jensen partner who signed in just in front of the guy carrying the box. The reception guard said she told him it was heavy and this guy would carry it in for her and she vouched for him."

"Pretty thin," said Nichols wincing.

"Not if you had the history I have with Jackie Best." Merritt stood and sighed. "Here's the short form. The guy I have dated for about a month is a lawyer with Baker and Jensen. I shared with him – I know I screwed up – some of the stuff, okay, a lot of the stuff, we were working on with Delaware General." Merritt waved her hand at Nichols to let her finish. "He told Jackie Best what I shared with him, and she… she is the Baker and Jensen partner managing the Delaware General account. That's how DG knew what we were doing. That's why they were tracking you. I'm the leak." She sat down with her head in her hands horrified at the words she had just spoken. *I am the leak!*

Nichols nodded slowly. "Man, your boyfriend is a real shit bird."

They sat silent for a few seconds.

"I'll get the *ex*-boyfriend end of things managed. By the way, he doesn't know I know."

"Hmm," said Nichols. "That could be useful."

"I'm counting on it."

"Not sure how you're going to *manage* that, but that's none of my business."

She added, "We could have FPS pull in Jackie Best for questioning but that would show our hand and she'd just say some nice man helped her with the box. What you weren't here for earlier was follow up by the FPS agent that Jackie Best was in the building here last week about the time you started getting worried about what was going on. There were two unidentifieds with her then, too."

"The lawyers… " Nichols stood. "She's senior partner and Delaware General is a principal client of Baker and Jensen which means executive management of the law firm and the chairman of DG, your billionaire buddy Burroughs, are in this up to their asses. I have quotes from DG policyholders from our now ex-contractor Bain Mason that talk about 'the chairman.' *He's* the architect of all this!"

"I expect that Burroughs will call again any time now for Secretary Vickers."

"Why's that?" said Nichols folding his arms behind his head and slouching further down in the chair. "Something else I need to know?"

"I think – I hope – I took care of that this morning when I talked with Vickers after the staff meeting. I briefed him on your predictive model." She tried to keep from smirking.

Nichols popped up on the edge of the sofa his hair stunned by the free fall. "How… without… What? You briefed him, but…"

"Actually, I made up some stuff. I think he bought it, though."

"And you said it was *my* model? Why… without *me*? No, I wouldn't want to brief that airbag anyway, but I didn't give you my charts and…"

Merritt explained to Nichols what she had told Vickers.

"He bought that crap? Seriously, Merritt, you need a tutorial on basic actuarial science. That line you fed him was total sheep dip. Okay, well, passable for a novice, but now he thinks I'm going to support this?" Nichols head was now bobbing between his knees like a surfboard between swells.

"I had to cut off another flank attack by Burroughs. Because of what I saw, and what Burroughs knows, about this last weekend" said Merritt.

"Crap. Something positive, I hope."

"This would be under the 'good news' column," said Merritt. "Well, mostly. When I was in Florida over the weekend, my *ex*-boyfriend and I and another guy that traveled with us…"

Nichols tilted his head, "Wha…"

"…met a girl who said she did market research for Delaware General. She didn't want to talk about it though when she heard I worked at HHS and that I had met the chairman. And the other guy with us, another lawyer with Baker and Jensen and a computer expert, said her hardware setup wasn't market research. He said there was 30k worth of processors, communications and encryption technology in her cabinet."

"What possible reason would there be for all that gear, unless it's classified, secret stuff," mused Nichols.

"I looked at her PC screen when the party moved downstairs, after we finished all the wine at her place…"

Nichols' head tilted again in the 'puppy wants to know what you're talking about way' with a modest grin forming, "Some day I'd like to hear the unabridged, X-rated version of your weekend. You are quite the party animal. Go on," he motioned.

Merritt ignored the surfer-GTO ripping persona and concentrated on the actuary component of the blond-haired dude sitting across from her. "I only looked at the screens for a few minutes so I wouldn't get caught. It showed the client, the client's policies, numbers, dates. It also showed referral bonuses and notes from the last contact. Here are my notes." Merritt handed Nichols her page of notes from the PC screen.

"What's this? 'TSC'?"

"I don't know," said Merritt. "Must be a type of policy. She referred to it as a 'Contract.' A relatively expensive one, thousands of dollars anyway, and one that generates referral bonuses."

"All sales by this girl were by phone, it seems. No paper? All that fits," said Nichols nodding again.

Merritt thought out loud, "Secret type of insurance policy sold over the phone with high tech gear, an insurance policy the chairman sponsors, one that he and his law form are willing to break the law to protect by spying on us with expensive talent…"

Nichols continued the stream of thought, "One that accelerates the death of terminally ill policyholders, one that saves Delaware General billions of dollars over time in end-of-life intensive medical care costs."

Nichols added, "The predictive model I have and, who knows, they may have it, too, pirated from my PC, indicates a population of between 200,000 and 400,000 of these policies in force. That's with a bunch – actuarial term there – of assumptions, but I can say, with certainty now, given all the data I have, there must be an agreement of some type between the policyholder and DG."

"A euthanasia policy?" Merritt asked.

"Hmm, yeah." He thought about that for a few seconds. "But looks like you found the real name for it: TSC." Nichols read Merritt's notes again. "Why don't we call Mary Alice Putnam. Looks like you have her address and policy data. You could pretend to be the girl you met, the policy sales girl."

"Not bad. Pretend to be Delaware General sales rep Tracy Madson and see what the policyholder tells us." Merritt took a few seconds to study her chief actuary.

"What?' asked Nichols.

"You know, you could have really blasted me – with good reason – for being the leak, for causing you all kinds of grief, for putting you in potential danger. But, you didn't."

"Hey, this isn't your fault. We just got sucked up in it."

"Yeah, well, thanks for not blowing up. I feel terrible enough about this." She stood up and paced.

Nichols looked up at her. "Hey, you *do* know we're now in a place we can't come back from. We are now officially, collegially fucked with the Secretary of Health and Human Services."

She nodded. "You try to do the right thing," her eyes tracing the carpet's design while she paced. "My Dad tried to teach me to recognize the black and white in public policy. And, when to be watchful because the government palette of gray tones would confuse me." She stopped pacing. "I'm *not* confused. And it's *not* shades of gray. A rainbow of life's colors shines on us every day, with texture, time, relevance and emotion acting as a prism. You just try the best you can with what God gave you, and do it in a way that… your Dad would be proud of."

"What's next?" Nichols said standing.

"I need your help on something outside your job description."

"Cool."

CHAPTER FIFTY-SIX

HHS Office of Merritt Royce
Rockville, Maryland
Monday, late afternoon, November 9

"Grant called. I told him you were in budget meetings all day. Claudia's on line 1," said LaGretta as she closed Merritt's office door and walked quickly over to the big walnut desk. She pushed the button for speakerphone.

"Okay, ladies, what have you come up with?" asked Merritt.

"Seems to me," started LaGretta, "you need to play offense 'cause your defense is weak and the other side is using big guys to beat you up."

Merritt groaned. "I like the football analogy and you're right. I'm getting sacked every day."

Claudia giggled on the speaker, "Not by that bad boy Grant any longer."

"Geez, guess 'sacked' was an unfortunate selection of words," said Merritt shaking her head.

LaGretta continued undeterred, "I have an executive assistant friend at Baker and Jensen and I think I should put out the word that Grant Launder is a user, a betrayer of women, a bad man. I talked to her some and she said that Grant already has a street rep for dumping girls."

"LaGretta, that's perfect," responded Claudia. "I have a girlfriend there, too. She's a partner in the firm. I can spin it a different way including the part about Grant ratting on Merritt to get a promotion and that would hammer that Jackie Best there, too. I do need to be careful getting my name involved in this since my Senator knows the managing partner over there."

"Ladies," said Merritt, "thank you so much. Between the women support staff and the female lawyers hearing this from you girls we should have a distracting undercurrent of Grant bashing going on very soon. And Claudia, if you would, let me know if Senator Tidwell gets a call from Delbert Burroughs at Delaware General. LaGretta, see if you can get some intel from the Secretary's office about calls from Burroughs."

Claudia and LaGretta agreed.

"Okay, girls, I appreciate it. We'll connect late Wednesday and see where we are," said Merritt. "I have a few other things in mind to keep from getting 'sacked,' maybe literally, since Burroughs and the Secretary are good friends." *And then a few other plays to take on the big guys.*

CHAPTER FIFTY-SEVEN

Headquarters of Gatwick Research
Office of CEO Marc Friedersdorf
Denver, Colorado
Monday, 5 pm, November 9

"Come in gentlemen. You said you found something while making calls to our sales reps?" Friedersdorf pulled his chair closer to the desk.

COO Jeff Dunlop began. "Marc, the operational audit concluded we need to have more personal contact with our 68 sales reps, including reminding them of procedures, security protocols and a few recent changes such as frequency of logins."

"The calls have been made by Jeff and myself, together," former police chief detective David Angelo added. "At your suggestion we have not involved supervisors or sales executive management here at headquarters."

Friedersdorf said, "Yes, Ed didn't care for that but I spoke to him and he understands. You can brief him on your calls later. What did you find of concern?"

Dunlop spread his notes in front of him, knowing Friedersdorf was anxious to get to the issue. "Only one sales rep so far with a problem, Marc, and we're about 80 percent done with the interviews. We thought we should bring this to you before finishing…"

"Yes, yes…" said Friedersdorf motioning to continue with his hand.

Dunlop pointed to the notes. "Tracy Madson, Melbourne Beach, central and northern Florida sales rep for four years. Good producer, sold 752 Contract policies last year. No issues with phone or email scans by human resources staff. One login error last year, handled without incident by the on duty supervisor. His log says she wasn't feeling well when it happened."

"When Jeff and I spoke with her, she became nervous about procedure," said Angelo, "and this after the proper notification sent to her by secure email asking her – as we have asked the other reps – to call our central switch at a set time for the interview."

"David, that's true," said Dunlop, "although probably a dozen of our reps have been pretty nervous by the interview. It's not like we talk to them every day."

Friedersdorf nodded and squeezed a pen on his desk.

"Anyway," continued Dunlop, "she told us she had a call from one of her clients this afternoon who said someone had called her, the client, around 2 pm today saying they were doing follow-up to see if she needed anything. This woman who called the client identified herself as a customer service manager for Delaware General and wanted to know if she had any comments about service from her sales rep, Tracy Madson. Was Tracy responsive, did she answer questions fully, that kind of thing. Here's the full transcript of the call, including the originating phone number – thought you would want to see it."

Friedersdorf took the two typed pages from Dunlop and read stopping at the word. "She used the word 'contract'?"

Dunlop watched Friedersdorf rub his forehead. "Yes, sir."

Angelo added, "It was in the context of…"

"Yes, I see it," snapped Friedersdorf. "No wonder Ms. Madson was nervous. Either she has been talking or someone hacked into her system."

"Not possible," said Dunlop.

Friedersdorf rifled an eye at Dunlop.

Dunlop quickly explained, "No evidence of hacking. Madson's system was searching this client's records three days ago, that is Saturday. Our IT guys confirmed that a few minutes ago. Ms. Madson's system was logged onto the database from 10:15 am Saturday, November 7 until 10:02 am Sunday, November 8. She logged in this morning, Monday, at 8:52 am."

Friedersdorf pushed away the transcript and, with his elbows on the desk, lowered his head cupping his hands over the back of his closely cropped head.

Angelo spoke next. "We think someone was in her home and saw the computer screens she had up; someone with an interest in what we're doing; someone who took the trouble to call a client. Fortunately the client called Ms. Madson. Unfortunately the call originated from what is probably a disposable cell phone. The area code is 202. Washington."

Friedersdorf straightened up and spoke to Dunlop. "No one that doesn't have eyes on this already needs to be involved further. Put a lid on it. We're going to need to talk with Ms. Madson again to see who was at her place Saturday, and then we…

There was a knock and the office door opened. The on duty supervisor said, "Sorry, Mr. Friedersdorf, there is a validated secure line call for you from prime 1 bear 2."

"Gentlemen, I'll get back with you a little later," said Friedersdorf as Angelo and Dunlop left and shut the door. "Yes, Mr. Burroughs."

"Hello, Marc," said Burroughs. I'm afraid we have a Gatwick sales rep who has been compromised."

Friedersdorf gritted his teeth. "I was just briefed by my staff who found the problem during the course of the operational audit follow-up. Tracy Madson, Melbourne Beach?

"Yeah. Well, looks like the audit worked, if a little late."

Still clenching his teeth Friedersdorf said, "We should know soon *who* in particular saw Ms. Madson's PC display, although if you're calling me about this, you probably already know that." The dejection in his voice was apparent.

"Same Fed, plus a couple lawyers from Baker and Jensen who are on our side and fed me the data." He took a breath and sighed. "I thought I could count on HHS Secretary, Don Vickers, to help us out. I've known him for, oh, 30 years." Burroughs was now thinking out loud knowing his loyal Gatwick CEO would be a good listener. "No joy there. He called me this morning excited that one of his assistants – the Fed I told you saw your sales rep's screens this weekend – had come to him and explained all the 'noise' about Delaware General was three sets of mercy killings. She said that explained it and then Don Vickers says to me, 'that should take care of it.' Guess he didn't understand why I wasn't more pleased with his call. Not like I could tell him, 'It's not mercy killings, dumb ass, it's euthanasia agreed to by our customers in a verbal contract and your assistant has *you* totally mind fucked.'" Burroughs measured his next statement carefully. "We need to ensure we are ready for *solo*."

"Understood."

CHAPTER FIFTY-EIGHT

Merritt's Washington, D.C. office
Tuesday morning, November 10

On the way out of her Washington office Merritt spoke to her loyal administrative assistant. "I'll be at the Longworth Office Building. My phone will be off. Back in an hour or two. Keep my afternoon clear, please."

"Okay, Hon. I'll leave you a voice mail if there's something hot," replied LaGretta.

Merritt mindlessly went through security check-in procedures at the Longworth House Office Building replaying in her mind the conversation she wanted to have with the ranking Democrat on the House Subcommittee on Health. *An ally on the other side will give me some cover.*

Congressman Joel Suben enjoyed a first floor corner suite in the oldest of the House office buildings with a postcard view of the Capitol to the north. Seniority had its privileges and the Congress presupposed its arcane machinery with a motorpool full of seniority vehicles.

"The Congressman will see you now," said the bowed over little lady at the end of a tightly clad row of cubicles full of staffers. "And, as you asked, no staff will be with the Congressman."

He rose to meet her. A generous smile accompanied the friendly welcome. She sat across from him, he behind an imposing desk organized neatly with a small antique brass clock near the corner and several paperweights, none with paperwork underneath.

Merritt began, "Congressman, you have been a valuable counsel to me in the past. I need more of your sage advice today."

"My dear, I would be happy to assist. Your diligence at the Department is helpful, most helpful to my constituents. My staff person, Jeremy. You have an issue with him?"

"No, no, Congressman. That's not it. Jeremy is a fine staffer. But this... this is too sensitive. I'm concerned..."

"Miss Royce. Okay, then. Please begin."

"You remember the questions asked of Delaware General on why they were so profitable," said Merritt. "Well, the actuary at HHS and I have figured out why."

"And what did you find?"

Merritt sat on the edge of the chair. "Delaware General has been selling insurance policies which promise to euthanize policyholders if they become terminally ill or have an accident that puts them in a persistent vegetative state." She waited for a shocked response from the Congressman but instead he waited for her to continue. "I talked to a person who had just bought one of these policies. I met a woman who sells the policies. There are maybe hundreds of thousands of these policies in force. Our actuary has estimated thousands of deaths from the policies. We don't actually know how they terminate the people, but we know it is happening and can localize areas where it is most prevalent."

"I see," said Suben. "The rumors…" he muttered under his breath.

"Congressman, this is murder on a massive scale!" Merritt shook her head ever so slightly as she tried to understand the Congressman's seeming indifference.

Suben rose slowly from his executive chair and motioned to a worn black leather couch along the back wall in his crowded office – crowded with ghosts of constituents in need, with unrepentant lobbyists squealing for more, with unbending bureaucrats quoting worn books of rules, with colleagues asking for favors now for favors later. "Miss Royce, come sit by me, please, so we can discuss this dilemma." He looked at his polished shoes as he took those few deliberate steps across a congressional patterned blue and gold area rug. Motioning for her to sit he sat next to her, close enough to see the conundrum in her hazel-hued eyes. He placed his hands on his knees and looked straight ahead. Taking a full breath of the vocation he loved and lived, he turned to the young woman from the executive branch.

"My people live in Miami beach. An eclectic population, diverse, rich in an array of cultures. *My* people, though, are not the affluent, jet setters with big boats on Fisher Island. Those… they can take care of themselves. My people are the middle class and the elderly. Yes, *especially* the older people. Many have but one home or apartment, and a small one at that. It's not what television or movies portray. Many are on fixed income. They have insurance and Medicare and Social Security and some have or will have other retirement money as well, but they live in the middle." Suben broke his straight ahead stare with a faster cadence and a brief nod to Merritt. "Of course, many in Florida and across our nation fit this 'in the middle' socioeconomic strata." Suben leaned back against the cracked leather that had cradled his naps these many years and closed his eyes. "My father lived in a small South Beach hotel after Mother died." Suben opened his eyes and turned

The Socratic Contract

his head slightly to Merritt. "You see, in the 50s and 60s, the elderly Jewish community in Miami congregated in these beach hotels. Perhaps less informed care than in a nursing home, yet those around them... *cared*. Enough to share a casserole, enough to take time to sit and talk, enough to hold..." his voiced cracked, "enough to hold a lonely hand in need of companionship."

The congressman leaned forward and then stood, adjusting his suit coat and tie. Suben faced Merritt his hands folded in front of him. "I was probably too busy to take care of him like I should have," he confessed looking down at the floor. "But he had his friends. They looked after each other in their final days." Suben looked at Merritt and returned to the couch turning to face her as he sat. An unforgotten pain weighed on his chest. "The barrios of South Beach became known as God's waiting room."

"Miss Royce, if there *is* such an insurance policy, or if it is the work of friends doing the bidding of those they love, then... so be it." He took a deep breath and exhaled slowly. "I will not interfere. No." Then, in an allegro, staccato cadence, he continued: "Nor will I prosecute. Nor will I debate the subject in public. I will do as I have for 22 years: work for the health, happiness and protection of those I serve, and now, in particular, the elderly who have few other voices to speak for them." Suben relaxed a little and put his hand on Merritt's. "You said this policy was for terminal cases or for those in a vegetative state." He shook his head. "To allow the dying a last wish of dignity – is this mass murder? I think not. Auschwitz. *That* was murder." He stood and walked Merritt to the door. "Of course you must do as your conscience directs, Miss Royce, but on this..." He offered his hand, "... some considerable thought first. Yes?"

A cold wind from the north blew her hair over her face as she tried to hail a cab. *Suben's response helps explain why this special policy has so much traction. Thought he might be more sympathetic, though.*

Taking this all the way only leaves tough options: Justice and the FBI, the department's Inspector General, another congressman – this time a right-winger? Each one with issues and I lose control of the outcome. If I race after this, I get run over. So, one step at a time.

CHAPTER FIFTY-NINE

Beach condo of Gatwick Research sales rep Tracy Madson
Melbourne Beach, Florida
Tuesday, 8:30 am, November 10

"Please come in," said Tracy.

"Hi Tracy, I'm Jeff Dunlop," he said smiling and shaking her hand.

"I thought you said on the phone that there would be three of you," she said nervously.

"Yes, a supervisor and one of our techies will be along shortly, but they are arranging for a truck and packaging for your equipment." Dunlop looked around and walked past her workstation to the sliding glass doors with the view of the Atlantic. "Looks like it's going to be a beautiful day. You get nice morning sun."

"Yes, sir, I enjoy the condo." Tracy walked quickly up to the relaxed Dunlop who was wearing khakis and a blue polo shirt. "I'm sorry those people saw a couple of screens. I know I should have had the system off, but I was doing work earlier and…"

Dunlop turned, "Tracy, I'm not here to punish you or fire you." He motioned to the small couch and chair in the living room. "Here, let's talk. I can imagine since what we do is automated and without much contact with people that you are concerned."

"I love what I do, Mr. Dunlop, and I don't want to mess it up." She started sobbing. "Please I'll do whatever you want to fix this. I'm so sorry that…"

"I know. It's… something the company should have been better at – talking with our sales reps. You've been doing a good job for us, Tracy, and we want you to continue that work. Unfortunately we will need you to move because we can't have those people come back with… investigators. We have to remember that what we do is not socially accepted, regardless of how we feel about it."

"Okay, like I said in the interview, I'll move." Her sobbing slowed as the reality of changing her life settled in.

"We need to do this quickly," said Dunlop. "The first thing I'd like to do is have you call Mary Alice Putnam with me and tell her I will be the contact going forward. She should contact me if she gets any other calls about Delaware General or her policies. Here is a script you can use."

"Sure, let's sit over at my office. I just finished logging on and verifying before you arrived so we could begin." Tracy read the script. "Mr. Dunlop, it says here that I am being moved because I'm being promoted?"

Dunlop laughed. "Yes, I should have told you that up front. We have to put you through an ordeal here to move and settle in a different city and you have been a good producer for us so we want to give you a bigger territory and a raise. Your title will now be 'Senior Sales Executive.' Your new home base will be San Antonio. Let's make that call."

After the call, Dunlop and Tracy continued to talk.

"That must be the other two gentlemen," said Tracy getting up to answer the door.

Dunlop introduced them. "Tracy, this is Supervisor Joe Henderson and technical advisor Elliot Weekly. They will help move out the computer equipment. Your other movers will be here before noon."

"You arranged for movers?" she asked.

"Like I said, we need to move quickly. All right, gentleman, get to it. Tracy, pack enough for a month on the road. We're going to give you a paid vacation in Key West and you leave… " Dunlop looked at his watch "… in three hours from the Melbourne Airport in our corporate jet. I'll help you and go over some ground rules for the next month."

Tracy scurried to her bedroom to pull out her suitcases.

Elliot approached Dunlop. "Jeff?"

Dunlop watched as Tracy excitedly prepared for her vacation, move, and new assignment. He looked at Elliot in the eye and shook his head.

CHAPTER SIXTY

Delaware General Headquarters
Dover, Delaware
Tuesday, 11:45 am, November 10

Anita scurried into the office. "Mr. Burroughs, I was just calling to set up the meeting you requested and… it's *him*, she blurted.

"Mr. President, this is a surprise. And here I was just trying to get an appointment." Burroughs laughed and looked out his expansive office window. "I find myself standing to talk to you."

"Del, it's been too long since we've shared a cognac and shot the bull. How's that gorgeous wife of yours, Angela?"

"She's a handful."

"Double down there," the President hooted. "When are you getting down to Washington? Bring Angela, we'll have a night of it. You can stay in the Lincoln Bedroom if you want. I think the Secret Service has finally cleared all of Monica's DNA out of there."

"Nice visual. And I'd love to have your famous rubbed ribeye and onion rings. Angela won't let me eat that here, but if we're at the White House, not much she can say about it."

"Del, my secretary, Norma, told me you wanted a meeting but, unless it's today, I'm jammed for about a week. Something I can help you with before we get together?"

"That's thoughtful of you, Mr. President. I'll give you a précis of the issue and then we can discuss it more in a week or so."

"Shoot."

"Tax advantages notwithstanding, I have elected to keep Delaware General private, partly to keep nosy State and Federal types out of our business."

"Yes, Del, I know you to be a private man."

"A couple of Don Vickers' people over at HHS want to roast my company because we are making decent profits in healthcare and because they think we're doing that by shaving benefits from terminally ill patients – something that is patently untrue and to which I take great offense. And they have been calling dozens of our business customers and individual policyholders with all kinds of questions, and that's causing big problems for us."

"As far as I know, Del, your company has always been a leader. Not sure why Vickers would buy off on this."

"I don't think he has. One of his appointees, Merritt Royce, told him she was pursuing this vendetta against Delaware General because of early deaths of dying patients of ours then, when pushed, she made up some cover story about how it was a mistake and the deaths were random mercy killings." Burroughs tried to slow himself down. "Point is, Mr. President, Vickers has lost control of a couple key bureaucrats, and it is about to cause my company and me great public humiliation – all for no good reason. Hell, I just sold a minority interest in the company for nearly half a billion dollars. If these unfounded and untrue allegations get out, my buyers are going to go sideways."

"Whoa now, Del, let me do some checking here and see if before we see each other I can get this sorted out. We sure don't want Delaware General or its chairman to be sullied undeservedly."

"Sorry to get emotional about this but, hell, this company is my life and it gripes me when intrusive bureaucrats stir up my customers." Burroughs tried to wind down knowing his dime was up.

"Del, I'll have Norma get back with you when I get clear in a week or so and in the meantime I'll work this for you."

Good, Burroughs thought, *I got my message through to the man loud and clear. Hopefully in a week this will all be behind us.* He thought to himself, *political contributions – big ones – work.*

CHAPTER SIXTY-ONE

Office of Merritt Royce
HHS Headquarters, Washington, D.C.
Tuesday, around noon, November 11

"Merritt, it's the call you've been expecting," said LaGretta, "line 1." The door closed.

"Hi, Mr. Johnson, thanks for calling me back."

"Dammit now Miss Royce, I told you to call me 'Red.' Everybody does. Now, let's start over. Hello, *Merritt*."

"Hello, *Red*," she said in a sultry voice.

"Alrighty then," he said with a belly laugh. "We going to get together and talk insurance?"

"Yes… Red, but right now I could use some help." *May as well come right out with it.*

"Whaddya need? Speak up, I'm on my G6. Just left Teterboro. Been in New York with a slew of portfolio managers and investment analysts. Wall Street MBAs think they know my business. Hell, *I* don't even know my business."

Merritt took a breath. "I have a problem with Delbert Burroughs and Delaware General."

He laughed again. "Damn, Girl, why don't you start with somethin' a little easier?"

I need to know how he feels about Burroughs. "Hey, Red, you're chief executive of the midwest's biggest insurance company. You can handle this. But if you guys are best friends, this may not be…"

"Can't say we're all that friendly, Merritt. Oh, we socialize like when I met you – what was that, like a month ago? Shit fire, I can't believe I just said 'like' twice in the same sentence – my teenage daughters are rubbin' off on me. But, no, we are competitors. So what's the prob? My kids say that, too. 'Prob.' Next thing ya know, I'll be text messaging."

"Delaware General, with Burroughs as the architect, is selling and fulfilling insurance policies that agree to euthanize people if they become terminally ill or if they are in a vegetative state."

"Jesus, Merritt, not something we should be talkin' about on an open line. My end is clear but who knows about yours."

"I just had my office swept and it's clear of surveillance."

"Doesn't matter," said Red matter of factly, "if somebody wants to listen, they'll find a way. So, you know this to be true?"

Merritt reviewed summary pieces of her actuary's model and data they had from clients. She didn't mention her Florida trip and what she found there. Concluding she said, "Nothing yet I can take to the Department of Justice, but in time."

More serious in tone now, Red said, "Ya know, I've always wondered how Delaware General could outbid us by ten percent and still make good money. Hmph. Well, the data you have is all statistics and some client phone calls with notes. Why not just dump it on the police and let them handle it?"

"No hard data. And I'm sure their system is well insulated. A lot of hard work and a little luck have only given us a glimpse of what they're doing."

"Well, then why not leave it alone?"

Common sense prevails in the Midwest. "Too late for that. I'm up to my ass in this already."

Another barrel-chested laugh crackled through the phone. "Well, then, let's see if we can help cover that nice backside of yours."

Merritt decided she had heard enough to trust him. "Red, I'm up for a promotion to Deputy Secretary but Burroughs will stop that if he can because of my meddling in his company." *Dad always said if you need someone's help, tell them both the good and bad of it.* "And now I've had to lie to Secretary Vickers to cover my meddling." Merritt remembered Red's dislike of Vickers. She told Red the cover story about mercy killings. "Tell you what, Red, you help me out here and I'll owe you one." *There it is. All my cards are showing. Will he help? I just gave him an opportunity to beat on a major competitor, discredit the Secretary who he doesn't like, and gain an ally for the future – me.*

Merritt heard what sounded like an intercom.

"Head to Reagan National... Well, then *change* it!" Red returned to the phone, "Okay then, Merritt, I'm going to take a detour to DC and see if I can help you out some. Hang on a minute..."

She could hear him speaking on another phone.

"Yes, maam. Name is Red Johnson, Chairman and CEO of Republic Insurance Company. I'd like to see the President this afternoon... Sure... ...Hi, Norma, this is Red. Can I see the President today for a few minutes?... No, be about hour and a half before I could get there... Yep, that oughta work... See you then. Thanks."

Wow. Guess he knows the President better than he let on. "Thank you so much, Red!"

"Glad to help out, but I'll get somethin' out of this, too. Besides, I haven't stopped in to see the President in quite awhile. Like I told you at the reception, he and I go back a ways. Well, now, since you're going to make me late for dinner tonight, least you can do is talk to me on the phone for a while. Tell me more about what you found and what you got shakin'."

For the next half hour she told him more about Actuary Nichols' work, about the surveillance, and about the Baker and Jensen connection. She even found herself sharing with her new friend how she had been used by Grant to get information.

"I'm real sorry to hear some guy treated you like that. I don't deal with that law firm, but I know a couple guys who could go have a talk with him."

"Thanks, no, I think I've got that covered. A question for you. You never heard anything about a policy like this, nothing about a euthanasia scheme?"

"Nope," said Red, "but they aren't a public company. Less exposure to the outside. We went public because of tax advantages. They obviously found another competitive advantage."

"What do you think of what they are doing?" she asked.

"My business reaction is it's not something I can use against them, publicly anyway. It would just sound outrageous, make me look stupid. And I bet some of my customers wish we had a policy like that."

"Really?"

"I, uh, I don't think I've ever spent time thinking about ending it because I was terminal. But, ya' know, there are a lot of people out there that think tubes, bags, diapers and wasting away is pretty criminal in itself. Modern medicine overstepping nature."

"Yeah, maybe," said Merritt. "Doesn't make it right, though."

"Well now, Merritt, it doesn't for *people*, because we are *so* civilized. But where I live, a big ranch in central Oklahoma – my family has for a couple generations – you get to see life and death daily as nature intended it. Sometimes happy, like when my best filly had her baby. God there's just nothin' cuter than that little foal. All wobbly tryin' to walk, momma nuzzlin' him up. Has a white star right in the middle of his forehead. Named him Magnus 'cause he's a handsome, adventurous boy." He paused. "And then there's the sad times of nature when these critters that you've become so attached to get old and their life spans are just so short that, well, it's hard to see them go down hill like that. I mean, I want to remember them as they were in their prime. All shiny and snortin'. But, the point I was making here is that nature has a way of handling these things. You don't see this often at the ranch but, when I was younger, my Daddy and I were gettin' the horses in when he stopped me and put his hand on my shoulder and pointed to an old horse of his who'd been ailing for some time who didn't come in for feed. It was winter, real cold, late afternoon. We watched as the old horse just kept walkin' real slow, head down, up over that last hill away from the barn toward the far corner of the pasture. I volunteered to go get him but my Daddy said, 'No, son, he's telling us it's his time.' I remember to this day how sad that made Daddy." Red took a second.

"You know, Merritt, on the other side of the issue, my mother, God bless her, taught me important lessons about dying." He laughed quietly while he remembered. "Mom had a horse named Ira. Ira was old and dying and Grandpa had gone to the barn late one night to check on the horse because she was laying down on her side earlier. Well, Grandpa found my mom in the barn with Ira's head in her lap. Grandpa cussed her out 'cause when a horse dies they sometimes thrash around and mother could have been hurt. Well, Mom wouldn't leave. Guess that's where I get bein' so headstrong. She told Grandpa, 'You don't let someone – human or animal – you've grown close to, die alone. Hold their hand, talk to them gently or, in the case of Ira here, hold their head in your lap. Animals have a place in God's heaven. And you need to help give them courage and trust to face the light beyond.' Grandpa never forgot that and he told me that story about my Mom many times."

"No, Merritt, it doesn't make it right, and it's not somethin' I'd do, but there are those who disagree and that judgment is personal. Well, we're heading into Reagan now, coming in from the west down the river. I can see 1600 Pennsylvania Avenue from here. Hope I can help you out, Merritt."

"Red, if my Dad were still alive, I know he would be happy that I have you as a friend."

CHAPTER SIXTY-TWO

Reception desk at Baker and Jensen
H Street, NW, Washington, D.C.
Wednesday, 8:30 am, November 11

"Good morning. I'd like to see Mr. Nathan Jensen." Mike Nichols handed the receptionist his business card. "I don't have an appointment, but he will want to see me."

"May I see your government ID, please?" The receptionist looked suspiciously at the ID and then at Nichols' blond locks. "Elizabeth, the Chief Actuary of the Department of Health and Human Services is here to see Mr. Jensen. He said Mr. Jensen would want to see him." The receptionist waited for a response. "Okay." She turned back to Nichols. "So what does the Chief Actuary do?"

Nichols tugged at the lapels on his suit and leaned forward onto the bar height reception counter. "I chase lawyers who bug my phones."

Her friendly demeanor vanished. "Top floor. He will see you."

Nichols took the elevator to the top floor and then walked up the circular staircase to the penthouse level where Elizabeth greeted him and ushered him into Jensen's office.

"Dr. Nichols, to what do I owe this unscheduled visit?" said Jensen offering Nichols a seat and motioning to his curious loyal assistant to close the door.

Nichols unbuttoned his suit coat and canvassed the office while he sat down. "I came for advice, Mr. Jensen. Should we report your senior partner, Jackie Best, to the Federal Protective Service, the FBI or should we just start with the Inspector General?"

Jensen folded his hands on his lap and studied the young man.

"My vote," said Nichols, "was to turn this whole matter over to the FBI and Criminal Division of the Justice Department, but my boss thinks that may be premature. What do you think, Mr. Jensen?" Nichols stood and went to the large window overlooking the White House grounds to the southeast. "Electronic surveillance of a Federal Building? We have her on video escorting your two wire tap mechanics into the Rockville HHS building." He turned and looked at Jensen. "Sloppy. Certainly not befitting a man of your caliber and distinction."

Jensen took a breath but chose to hear Nichols out.

"Oh, but we both know that's not the reason I'm here." Nichols continued to stroll through Jensen's large elaborately decorated office. "Your client, Delaware General – specifically, the chairman, Mr. Delbert Burroughs – has been euthanizing large numbers of people to lower healthcare costs. My model – you ever heard of the operations research methodology called 'fuzzy logic'? No, I suppose not. My model concludes with actuarial certainty, which, Mr. Jensen, is a log normal step above *lawyer* certainty, that Delaware General is *killing* people. And you and your firm, Mr. Jensen, are helping Burroughs do it – knowingly." Nichols returned to the chair and sat down folding his hands on his lap mimicking Jensen's pose.

"Dr. Nichols, your assertions are preposterous. Obviously you cannot prove any of this. If you could, you and your *model* would be in front of the authorities, not me." Jensen took a deep breath. "So then, what is it you *want?*"

Nichols leaned forward, his forearms on his knees. "Since you asked… One, kick Grant Launder to the curb. He's a dirt bag, and you should be embarrassed. On the streets. No 'of counsel,' no contracts, no severance, nothing. Two, Jackie Best separates from the firm here in DC. Off your rolls and never to return. Help her get a job somewhere else, fine, just not in DC. Three, your dirty tricks department, your snoops and techies, whoever they are. If we get *any* indication they are surveilling us again we will come down on your firm, and you personally, with everything we can muster because you snooping in my shit, that *really* pissed me off." Nichols exhaled loudly through his nose. "And four, disengage from Delaware General – no lobbying, no legal work, no representation of any kind." He stood and handed Jensen his card with scribbled notes on the back:

kick Grant
move Jackie
ixnay snoops
ditch DG

"Just so you remember," Nichols said with a wiry smirk. "And this is an all or nothing deal, Mr. Jensen. We'll know by your actions because we now have eyes in your firm. You have two days to comply. No action means day three – that would be Friday – the IG and FBI are on your doorstep."

Nichols stopped on his way past Elizabeth's desk. "Beautiful flowers. Say, you may want to clear his schedule for the rest of the day. He's going to be pretty busy."

CHAPTER SIXTY-THREE

Office of Assistant Deputy Secretary Merritt Royce
HHS Headquarters, Washington, D.C.
Wednesday 9:20 am, November 11

Merritt hurriedly walked into her suite of offices. "What is it, LaGretta? I was in a meeting downstairs and I get calls from everywhere saying you need me in my office ASAP. Is every -"

"Honey, the Vice President's office is on the phone for you. He wants to talk to you right away. They want you to go to his office, *now*."

"I'm not sure I know where that is," Merritt said, flustered at LaGretta's frenzy.

"They said he's sending over a car, front entrance. It's his office in the Old Executive Office Building, you know, where OMB…"

"A car?" *Geez, Red must have stirred things up big time.* "Okay, let me get my coat."

LaGretta popped out of her chair and led her by the arm to the private restroom. "Freshen up, brush your hair, check your makeup."

Merritt stopped, "Why are you...? I'm not going out on a date. I'm just..." Then it hit her. Her mouth was wide open. "Oh my God, LaGretta! It's him, the beautiful, single, elegant, handsome, A-list, *very* eligible bachelor Vice President of the United States, Bobby Rolls! And he's sending a car?" She was now bouncing in front of LaGretta.

LaGretta's smile lit up the room. "*Now* you know why I've been tracking you down furiously for the past 15 minutes!"

Merritt adjusted her Armani charcoal pin striped suit and her royal blue Dior silk blouse, changed to a pair of black Monolo pumps and headed downstairs. "Wish me luck!" she said to her faithful assistant.

LaGretta crumpled up the phone message note from Grant and threw it in the trash.

"Secretary Royce, come in. Thank you for coming over to see me."

Merritt confidently walked up to the rough-hewn but formidably tailored Bobby Rolls. "Mr. Vice President, a pleasure to meet you." *He's shorter in person, and tanner and more rugged and, wow, what an office...*

An assistant offered coffee or tea with both choosing black coffee with sweetener.

"Let's sit over here," offered the young VP.

"Nice view of the White House. Only a sand wedge from here." She knew his addiction to golf. But then she and every other single woman in the western world knew about Bobby Rolls.

"You play?" They sat in gold brocade armchairs facing toward the east and the White House and were warmed by the morning sun through the twelve-foot windows in the ceremonial office.

"And this would be a perfect day for it. I'm having a little trouble with my driver lately. I usually play a fade but it's been going straight." She looked into the vaunted blue eyes that helped get his boss elected two years earlier. Merritt leaned back, took a sip of the coffee and crossed her legs.

"My drives are all over the place. Maybe we should take a lesson together."

She put down her coffee. "You know, lessons are the only guaranteed way to add strokes to your game. I always shoot terribly after a lesson."

"True, takes a while to sink in. My handicap is sliding up. Can't seem to sneak away from here enough to work on my game."

"I can only imagine your schedule, Mr. Vice President."

"Please call me Bobby."

"Okay, you can call me Secretary Royce," laughed Merritt.

The VP shook his head. "My Dad told me redheads are trouble. He ought to know, he married one."

"Don't your folks live around here?" asked Merritt.

"In Virginia Beach," said the VP. "My Dad's last assignment was as the Admiral at Naval Station Norfolk. They love it down there."

"Then this is the perfect office for you, isn't it?" Merritt looked around and saw what she had only heard about: two large chandeliers, ornamental stenciling and allegorical symbols of the Navy Department in Victorian colors, two black Belgian marble fireplaces, and a wood floor intricately inlaid with mahogany, cherry and white maple. "This office used to be the Office of the Secretary of the Navy. I'm sure your Dad enjoys visiting you here."

"Your first trip to the Eisenhower Executive Office Building?"

"Yes, it's amazing in its detail. Granite, slate and cast iron exterior and the marble floors and bronze balusters I saw on the way in," she commented.

"A student of architecture?" he asked.

"I appreciate the old buildings. I live in one in Georgetown. I'm glad this one was restored rather than torn down. I thought the Vice President's office was in the West Wing?"

"I do have an office there, but it's way too... white. Very light colors. No testosterone." He laughed.

Merritt uncrossed her legs, adjusted her skirt a little and leaned forward. "Bobby, I hope my being here doesn't mean I've caused trouble for you."

"Oh, not me, for my boss." He laughed and stood up taking off his suit coat and throwing it over the back of a chair closer to his desk.

"The President. Uh oh. That's not usually a good step in career management." Merritt looked out the window shaking her head.

"Don't worry about it. I think he was actually entertained that a fourth level – sorry – appointee could jack up a couple of billionaire Republican heavy weights in the same week. He said I should get together with you and see – in his words – 'What in the name of Abe Lincoln is she doing?'"

Merritt's stomach started turning sour. *Keep smiling. Dad said to 'keep smiling.'* I didn't bring paperwork to support what we have found, but I would be glad to share what we have so far."

"We?"

"Me and the Chief Actuary at the department, Mike Nichols."

"Let's start there. Give him a call and have him..." the VP went to his desk and flipped through a binder "...meet with this guy, right now. I'll get someone to pick Nichols up. The VP left his office to make arrangements with his assistant.

Merritt found Nichols at his Washington office and asked him to bring his model, phone logs, interviews and other backup data. She gave him the contact, the Office of Management and Budget research chief.

She reported the conversation to the VP. "Actuary Nichols was pleased both that he would have a chance to share his predictive model and that he was, for once in his life, appropriately attired. Usually he's in jeans and sandals. Brilliant, eccentric, and a very good guy." Nichols had also given her a verbal thumbs up on his meeting with Nathan Jensen.

"We'll take good care of him." The VP brought over a yellow legal pad and sat down. "Red Johnson from Republic Insurance says you have some specifics that we can work on. Del Burroughs from Delaware General says this whole thing is a 'vendetta' – his word – against him and his company."

Merritt grinned, "I thought you were an ace Navy fighter pilot and then a software genius. When did you become insurance company sleuth?"

"Just after junior U.S. Senator from Virginia and youngest Vice President since John Breckinridge in 1857. I hear you're a Libra."

"And my shoe size is…"

The VP looked at Merritt's shoes and the corner of his mouth approved.

"Listen, you have the advantage of being able to make a call and get answers from just about anybody. Me? I have to dig for it."

He leaned back in the big chair and cocked his head with pursed mouth and raised eyebrow. "I'm an Aries and I think you and I better get to work so I can report back to my boss."

Merritt started at the beginning and took the 40-year old VP through a month of digging into how a simple question of 'why is DG so profitable' turned into a cascade of data and novel insurance policies. As each piece of the conundrum presented itself with a specific fact or location, she stopped so he could call yet another part of the Federal Government machine to run down the data and collect yet more. The clock rolled through lunchtime so they took time to go to the White House Mess in the West Wing where they continued their discussion and give and take, not noticing the looks from White House staff around them. Into the afternoon they worked, each becoming more comfortable with the other, the data congealing to a reasonable synopsis of what had transpired, of what Merritt and Mike Nichols had found.

Rolls took calls and spoke with his assistant again while she searched her memory for pieces she may have forgotten to mention.

He threw the now two-thirds filled yellow pad on his expansive desk and walked back over to the chairs and sat heavily. "Merritt, you've convinced me. I need to put this together so I can brief the boss. Your ride should be out front in a few minutes. Nichols will be in the car with you. I'm sure you two won't mind riding together back to the department." They stood and walked together to the door of his office. "Merritt, before you go. You said I can call and get data I want. Well, not *all* the data. So, I'll just ask. Would you like to play golf with me this weekend?"

Merritt blushed, hazel eyes twinkling a message, "Secretary Royce would love to play golf with the rakishly attractive youngest Vice President since what's his name." She offered her hand and hoped he would never let it go.

CHAPTER SIXTY-FOUR

The Oval Office, West Wing, The White House
Thursday, noon, November 12

"So what did you come up with, Bobby?" The President cocked his head and grinned at his Vice President. "Staff tells me you are anxious to discuss this situation. Wouldn't have anything to do with how attractive this young woman is, would it?

"Mr. President, I do have information that…"

The President wagged his finger at the youngish number two executive. "Redheads are dangerous, Bobby, although this one, my sources tell me, is refined, smart and, of course, single."

"I must admit to being taken by her, boss. You should meet her. And I think she's got something here. Red was right. And Delbert Burroughs… may be hiding an explosive truth.

The President pushed an intercom button on his phone. "Want some lunch? Of course you do," he waved off the answer. "Norma, order some lunch for us, please. Bobby looks hungry. Surprise him."

"That means I have 14 minutes if I want to eat without having to brief at the same time."

"Roger that, Mr. Vice President. We have a full agenda today, so not much time to settle this Burroughs flap. Shoot."

"Merritt Royce, Assistant Deputy Secretary, HHS, since Vickers arrived. She was on your transition team. Came over from Senate Staff, Senator Tidwell. Background is clean, stellar, in fact."

The President laughed. "Sounds like you took a liking to this young woman."

"Widely respected at the department and in the industry, according to White House Office of Personnel. She was de facto deputy while Deputy Secretary Houghton was out for a couple months with a heart attack. Chief Actuary Mike Nichols works for her and, together, they have uncovered a covert type of insurance policy, one than will handle terminating the policyholder should the person become terminally ill or comatose. Obviously no paper trail on this. The actuary's model, substantiated by the OMB research director, scores likelihood of this 'contract' at 95 percent probability and spread of between 200 and 400 thousand policies. Likely active over the last decade at least given logistics, growth path, need for secrecy." The VP took a breath.

"Holy crap, no wonder Del was antsy about Fed snooping."

"Hang on, I *am* hungry and I'm just getting started. Royce ran into a sales rep of this policy on a trip to Florida – had to snoop into a private computer system to get the data – so I had a couple agents with the Bureau try to track down this sales rep to question her. Condo empty, repainted, utilities cut off, condo sold yesterday to a shell company in Aruba, no info from neighbors, her Dad in Maryland – a couple more FBI agents sent there – played dumb and said he *thought* she still lived in Florida, no plane or other travel ticket issued to her, no passport use according to Homeland Security, bank account closed, no credit card usage. Also sent agents to visit the policyholder seen on the computer system of the sales rep and this policyholder – totally defensive – said 'leave me alone' and that it was a long-term care, as in nursing home, contract…"

"Hang on, Bobby, that's the second time you've used the word 'contract.' Special meaning?"

"Probably. Policy shorthand is 'TSC' with the 'C' likely 'contract.' My guess there, not theirs. Other research on this by the actuary was with companies who use Delaware General and, through a contractor, with policyholders directly. Agents who talked with the contractor, Bain Mason, last night found him to be uncooperative, citing an employment contract he had with Delaware General preventing him from talking with government agencies without first consulting with the company general counsel. Secretary Vickers believes all this is a set of mercy killings most of whom happened to have Delaware General as the health insurer, although he said his source for this assertion is Royce who told me yesterday she fabricated that story to get him off her back."

The President swayed way back in his padded brown leather desk chair. "Oh, I *like* this girl."

"Vickers does appear in the dark on this, attempting to protect long time friend Burroughs. Secretary Vickers would like to dump Deputy Secretary Houghton and replace him with Merritt Royce as part of a deal he has with her to get off this investigation. Red's motivation here is, as he put it, 'Pigeon hole Del Burroughs for awhile and blast Secretary Vickers for being a useless windbag.'"

"Yeah, Red doesn't mind competition but competing against this…"

"And lastly, Mr. President, Del Burroughs is playing the loyal Republican, big donor card and wants us to look the other way." The VP looked at the grandfather clock. "How about that, two minutes to spare."

"You didn't tell me what the solution is, Bobby."

"Hey, that's why they pay you the big bucks," noted the VP.

"Nice analysis, done quickly, low key, no noise," said the President. "Just what I wanted." He tapped his fingertips together. "Here's how we'll do this. Ask Secretary Vickers to bring Deputy Secretary Houghton and Miss Royce here with him this afternoon to the Cabinet Meeting. Tell Vickers I want thirty minutes with him alone before the meeting. And sit in with me after lunch for a couple calls. I need to talk with State and Communications and then with Del Burroughs. You handle the rest."

The curved door to the Oval Office opened. "Sirs, lunch is served in the Private Dining Room."

The two executives, now alone at the dining table, ate in their shirtsleeves.

"Bobby, what do you think of Del Burroughs' 'contract'?" asked the President.

"I don't think even the Netherlands would give the nod to that approach."

"Because…"

The VP wondered where the chief executive was going with this. "Our justice system calls it murder, even if it is agreed to beforehand."

"I'm quite a bit older than you, so maybe I have a different perspective on this." The President leaned back and locked his fingers behind his head. I remember when I was just a GS numbnuts at State right out of school. My baby brother was on his second tour in Da Nang, along with God knows how many other GIs, bored, feeling unappreciated, wife and baby long since left him, drinking himself stupid, guarding some corrupt Vietnamese general. I talked to him on a Christmas there. Felt pretty helpless." The President exhaled. "Years later he calls me from the hospital at Fort Lewis. Said he wasn't going to make it: liver about gone. They wouldn't put him on a list for a transplant. He told me he had a couple months to live and that he was in a lot of pain but they wouldn't give him pain meds. Told him it would damage his liver." The President sat up straight. "How fucked up is that?" He stood and walked over to the window overlooking the south lawn. "By then I had Hill experience, found out who the commanding general was at the base, and made a call to the three-star at home. I apologized for calling him at home but explained how my tech sergeant little brother in his hospital was in his last couple months and in pain with the doc telling him no meds. The general said guiding physicians was a delicate bit of diplomacy, but he'd give it a shot. The next morning baby brother called me and said, 'I don't know what you said to the general, but they gave me some great shit and I am in *no* pain.' My little brother died in that same bed 34 days later." He turned and looked at the Vice President. "Seems to me this Del Burroughs 'contract' we're talking about would have been a better solution."

"Here's what we're going to do," said the President. "I'm going to call Vickers in here before the Cabinet Meeting and tell him he's going to be Ambassador to – that's why I need to talk to State because I need a good spot for him – and that we're going to let him announce Houghton as the next Secretary and Royce as his Deputy. Get Senator Tidwell in it so he gets some credit and then he can manage Miss Royce's confirmation. I'll call Burroughs. I'm going to tell him he needs to disappear for a while. You talk to Miss Royce and tell her what you found and that we're going to pursue it, but we're going to do it my way, sub rosa."

"So we're not going to prosecute Burroughs?" asked the VP.

"We don't put billionaires in jail in America. Bad for business."

CHAPTER SIXTY-FIVE

Merritt's Townhouse
Georgetown
Thursday, 2 pm, November 12

Merritt paced in her glassed-in bedroom deck high above the Potomac River, still on top of Venus over being invited to the Cabinet meeting this afternoon. She had gone home to change into a svelte and sophisticated black label Armani suit in deep Atlantic blue, an opened collared maroon silk blouse and her navy Jimmy Choo pumps.

LaGretta had called moments before to report the trip to Baker and Jensen with Claudia had done the trick. Merritt clenched her teeth as she tried to force from her mind the malevolence of Grant's betrayal. She shook her head as she recalled the conversation with LaGretta. She had told Merritt they only had to talk to four girls at the law firm to have the office gossip circuit in full trash mode. *Grant's baggage with old girlfriends he'd treated badly. God, I was so stupid.*

The ringing phone broke her away from the past. She sat next to Meatball on her bed and answered, "Hello."

"Hi, Merritt, this is Brett, you know, hulk."

"Hi, hulk. Nice to hear from you." She stroked the purring brown tabby. *Grant probably told him I wasn't returning his calls.*

"I just wanted to tell you personally that I had nothing to do with what Grant did. I had no idea he was reporting back to Jackie on your conversations. I swear…"

"Hulk, it's all right. I know you weren't a part of what Grant did."

"Man, I told him when I found out what a…"

"Hulk, I think you used the term 'certified piece of suck.'"

"God, you must have heard him in the bookstore at the terminal. What a shitty way to find out your boyfriend is ratting on you. Oh man, I can't even feature how that made you feel."

"*Ex.*"

"Yeah, *ex*-friend of mine, too, along with most everybody else over here at the firm. Well, the women anyway. Doesn't matter. I haven't talked to him since we got back, but rumor is he's not only not getting partner, he's out of a job. I haven't seen Jackie either so she could be gone, too. Old man Jensen has some exposure on this, I bet. Anyway, Merritt, I'm really sorry and I hope maybe after some time when you run in to me somewhere you'll still say 'hi' because I think you are a committed public servant, a total babe, and I'm just sorry a friend – ex-friend – of mine could do that. Hope to see you around."

"Thanks for the call, Brett. We're fine. But I'm still going to call you hulk."

CHAPTER SIXTY-SIX

Headquarters of Delaware General
Dover, Delaware
Thursday, 3:45 pm, November 12

"Del, staff tell me we have a secure line. I have a Cabinet Meeting at 4, so we'll have to make this quick."

"Yes, Mr. President, thanks for the call. You must have some news." Burroughs sat stiffly and rubbed his forehead.

"I've been trying to sort through this problem we have."

The Delaware General Chairman didn't like the way this was beginning. "Yes?"

"You have some people after you, Del, and it's because they think they've figured out your contract. Interesting notion, this contract. My young Vice President asked me if we were going to prosecute."

Burroughs throat drew closed as if a noose were tightening. He felt his face redden and the grip on his chair whitened his knuckles. "Your intention, Mr. President?"

"First let me ask you a question about how this works. Your contract covers people who have your insurance. That way you know what their health status is. Your sales reps sell this contract without paper but with, I presume, an enormous amount of security – knowing you. But what happens when the policyholder turns 65? Your health insurance doesn't pay the medical bills. Medicare does. So what do you care then?"

He wouldn't be calling me if he were going to try for indictments. He's trying to rationalize this. "We still cover the contract. It's the deal we have with the policyholder. They want dignity, not overzealous doctors prolonging life beyond what is natural." Burroughs took a deep breath. *It comes down to this. He wants to know what* he *gets.* "It's called The Socratic Contract. I'm covered. I wish my mother had been. Perhaps, Mr. President, you know someone who would have benefited from a more… peaceful death."

"Hmm." The President remembered his conversation with the VP just hours before. "What does this Socratic Contract say?"

Burroughs' grip on his armrest eased slightly. "In the winter of my life, as the drifts swell over my soul, I will not burden my family and friends. I will go with my dignity, cherishing the time I have had and know the grace of God will comfort me."

"You… are a renaissance man, Mr. Burroughs. Tell you what. I'll give you cover on this. My Feds will… lose interest in your 'contract.' But, you need to chill activity on this for some time. And *you*, Del, need to get out of the country. Give it a year or two. You okay with that?"

"Mr. President, I am in agreement with your terms. The company will go quiet on this activity and I will move out of the country for at least a year."

"Back on the Medicare program – people over 65 who are terminally ill. You are cutting costs for Medicare?"

"Of, course, just as it works for Delaware General for those under 65," said Burroughs matter-of-factly.

"One more question, Del. How does your company get inside the Medicare program?"

"I'll tell you in a year or two."

CHAPTER SIXTY-SEVEN

The Cabinet Room, West Wing, The White House
Thursday, 5:15 pm, November 12

Merritt could tell the Cabinet Meeting was winding down and her heart began to beat faster. *Soon. Very soon.* She tried to stay in the moment and not jump ahead. She studied the room. She faced a window overlooking the Rose Garden. Only the office of the President's personal secretary stood between where she was sitting and the Oval Office. She sat against the wall with Deputy Secretary Houghton. Only Cabinet rank officials sat at the long conference table. She noticed brass plates on the back of each chair at the table with the name and station of the Cabinet Secretary.

"Ladies and Gentlemen, thank you, good meeting," said the President. The attendees stood and began to move. "Why don't we head to the Roosevelt Room and have a drink and some appetizers? We have a couple of staff announcements."

The group filed across the hall and south a few yards and entered the Roosevelt Room, an interior room used for staff meetings, as a staging area for those about to enter the Oval Office and, on this occasion, as a room to announce staff changes. A half dozen orderlies in short white jackets and white gloves brought already prepared drinks for the Cabinet and quickly took requests from the others and then served light finger food appetizers with small white linen napkins monogrammed with the White House seal.

Merritt stood alone at the end of the room by the fireplace and not far from the door she had entered. She noticed Secretary Vickers and Deputy Secretary Houghton speaking in a corner of the room. She held a glass of chardonnay though she had not taken a sip. Just then Senator Tidwell and her friend Claudia entered the Roosevelt Room.

"Great news, Merritt," said the Senator, "and I'm sure that business with Del Burroughs is all taken care of now. I'll be happy to sponsor your confirmation." He gave her a short hug and moved into the room to speak with others.

Claudia also gave Merritt a little hug. "I'm so glad the Senator let me come along. This is *so* exciting, honey! Here comes the big guy," she whispered, "talk to you later." Claudia squeezed Merritt's hand.

The President and Vice President came over to talk with Merritt.

The VP spoke first. "Mr. President, allow me to introduce Miss Merritt Royce."

"Nice work finding this 'contract' activity at Delaware General, Merritt," said the President. "We're on it and are slamming it down. Don't think you're going to be seeing Delbert Burroughs anywhere for quite a while. And his operation, thanks to you, is done for. Have to admit, it's a novel idea. Just happens to break every law in the book. So, nicely done."

Merritt brushed her auburn hair away from her face and beamed. "Just trying to do my job, sir."

Turning to face both Merritt and the assembled officials the President said in a bold and serious tone, "Your promotion here today is well deserved. I met your father some years back when he was Chairman of the Federal Trade Commission. A man of great integrity and intellect. I am sure he is looking down on you today and is very proud."

Merritt's eyes glistened, her breathing short and halting.

"Bobby, why don't you show Deputy Secretary Royce around the Roosevelt Room and introduce her to her new colleagues." The President joined several of the Cabinet Secretaries in discussion.

The VP saw her eyes and with one hand on her shoulder pointed behind her on the fireplace mantle. "See this, Merritt? It's the Nobel Peace Prize presented to Teddy Roosevelt in 1906 for his leadership role in mediating the conflict between Russia and Japan. And along this wall over here, flags representing all the military services in the order they were established." They walked along the wall together.

"I'm not usually at a loss for words but… I didn't know he had met my Dad," she said taking a deep breath.

Rolls smiled and surveyed the room. "He's a good man, this President."

"Why does he call the Cabinet Secretaries by the name of their department. In the meeting I heard him say State, HUD, Interior. What's with that?"

Still viewing the group, the VP responded, "It's his way of reminding them they only rent the space. It's not them, it's the department or agency they represent that's important. It's also the reason he allows even his closest friends here to always refer to him as 'Mr. President.' He respects the Office of the President."

Merritt looked at the VP with a grin, "But he calls you 'Bobby.'"

The VP looked at her and, seeing her teasing smile, raised an eyebrow and then looked back toward the President. "Yeah."

The President strode toward the Attorney General. "AG, you had a question for me?"

"Just wanted to know, Mr. President, if the dozen agents your VP pulled into duty yesterday led to something I need to follow up on."

"No. It's handled. We buried that earlier today." The President walked to the front of the room. "Ladies and Gentlemen – Don, please join me here – HHS, soon to be *Ambassador* Vickers representing the United States of America to the Swiss Confederation in Bern Switzerland, has two staff announcements to make. First of all though, Mr. Secretary, thank you for your dedicated and loyal service at HHS and I look forward to your representing America before the Swiss Confederation."

The next few minutes of Vickers' talk telling the officials of his decision to leave the Department of Health and Human Services and his 'supreme' confidence in the team of Secretary Houghton and Deputy Secretary Royce seemed surreal to Merritt. His airy words, heavily doped with the finest of Washington pharmaceutical grade horseshit, wafted through the erudite set of cynical onlookers.

As the group began to leave the Roosevelt Room, the President, with both a photographer and a press corps video man in tow, motioned to the VP and Merritt to join him by the array of service flags. "Okay we have a picture with me and the new HHS, let's have one with the two of you." Merritt walked to his right side, the VP on his left. "Wait, let's switch this around." The President moved Merritt to his left and the VP to his right.

The gathering at an end, Vice President Bobby Rolls walked Merritt to the west entrance of the West Wing. "I'm looking forward to getting together with you Saturday afternoon for golf. I'd also like to have dinner with you, if you don't have plans."

"I'd love it," said Merritt. As she took his hand she felt a warmth, a glow – excitement and yet comfort, a confidence from within. "Good night."

"It sure is," he said.

She walked toward the massive iron gates that led out of the White House compound. Turning around, still walking slowly away backwards, she said, "Why did he change us around for the picture?"

The VP laughed. "He cracks me up. That picture will be in every society page and entertainment clip around the world tomorrow. It'll read something like…" the VP moved his hand across the sky as if showing the headlines, "… 'Telegenic VP with his new, hot Federal flame' and, of course, he'll be there, with us, sandwiched in the middle. Why did he change us around? It's the names: 'Rolls *President* Royce.'"

EPILOGUE

Law Offices of Baker and Jensen
H Street, NW, Washington, D.C.
October, 1 pm, seven years later

"Elizabeth, when she arrives, please show her in. She's young and may not be comfortable with the surroundings, so see if you can put her at ease. We'll need a couple hours. No further appointments today, please."

"Yes, Mr. Jensen, of course. I'll meet her downstairs and bring her up myself. Sir, may I get something else for you to eat." She retrieved an ebony tray with his uneaten lunch.

"No, thank you. I'm sorry, I don't have much of an appetite today." He saw the look on her face. "Perhaps you would wrap the sandwich for me and I'll have it later."

"Yes, sir. How about some hot tea and a couple cookies?" she said cheerily.

"Thanks, no, I'm fine."

Nathan Jensen, cofounder of the firm, sat facing the doorway to his office, shifting side to side in his seat, waiting for his last apprentice. Finally he heard them climb the last of the circular stairs to the upper floor. He braced himself against his desk with both hands and stood, an ache from his innards slowly the ascent. He walked deliberately to the doorway.

"Mr. Jensen, so nice to meet you," said the girl of 21 years. The door closed behind her.

"Please, come in and sit. I have been anxious to see you."

They sat in brocade armchairs facing southeast to the White House. He exhaled deeply as he sat. She took the edge of the chair and looked quickly around the office and then at the gray-maned managing partner.

Jensen began, "I spoke with your father last week. He said your studies to become a physician's assistant are going well."

"You know my father? I thought my advisor from school…"

"No, I don't know your father other than the time we have shared on the phone. But I knew your mother. She was one of my favorite people. I visited your home with others from the firm the day she died. You were such a serious little girl. And so very pretty, as you are now as a young lady."

She bowed her head. "My Mom loved her job here. I didn't know that's why you asked me to come today."

"I have followed your progress in life because I believe your Mom would have wanted me to keep an eye on you." Jensen's eyes twinkled. "Your Mom left work unfinished."

"Mr. Jensen, you know I'm not studying to be a lawyer."

"Other work. You know how sick your Mom was. Yet she passed peacefully, before she was no longer herself. Before she could no longer kiss you goodnight. Before anyone could say, 'It was a blessing.'"

"Yes, Dad talked about that, a lot. That's one of the reasons I'm interested in healthcare."

"So you are familiar with the Hippocratic Oath?"

"Yes, well, generally," she said.

Jensen leaned over to pick up a frayed leather bound volume from the small marble topped table to his left. He grimaced slightly as sat back in the chair. "Let me read just a little from the Greek translation." He put on his reading glasses and smiled at the young woman. "Indulge me, I do so love the Greek philosophers. Yes, here it is: 'I swear by Apollo Physician, by Asclepius, by Health, by Panacea, and by all the gods and goddesses, making them my witness, that I will carry out, according to my ability and judgment, this oath and this indenture.'" He glanced over his glasses. "The oath has been modernized and in many circles is simply 'to cause no harm.' Yet the language is interesting in its specifics." Jensen turned the page. "Later it says, 'I will use treatment to help the sick according to my ability and judgment, but never with a view to injury and wrongdoing. Neither will I administer poison to anybody when asked to do so, nor will I suggest such a course.'" He closed the book and held his glasses with both hands. "Your mother and I didn't believe in those last words."

She looked at him quizzically. "You mean about poison?"

"Our belief in this matter followed more closely the views of Socrates who said, 'Not life, but good life, is to be chiefly valued.' You may remember from your schooling some of his teachings."

"Not really, sir. But you said my Mom..."

"I will explain." He patted her hand and they both eased back in their chairs. "Socrates was a homely little man, some might have called him arrogant, and yet he was by most accounts a social man who loved to be in the company of others. And, of course, he was always asking questions – his pedagogical mainstay." He hummed a laugh. "I have also read that he could consume enormous amounts of wine without becoming drunk. He lived in Athens from 469 BC to 399 BC, a time of classical philosophers in ancient Greece. One would certainly not believe the Greece of present day could have possibly generated such greatness – Athens today is crumbling and dirty, a relic of the past filled with little people who bathe weekly or not at all. But, I digress."

She grinned at Jensen shaking her head.

"Socrates led a life devoted to the search for goodness. One of his students, Plato, would later describe this 'idea of the good' as justice, truth, freedom, simplicity, beauty. Socrates believed that goodness and truth were the fundamental realities and that the search for these realities came from seeking, asking, not lecturing. His constant questioning sometimes irritated those he questioned. You may know someone who always seems to answer a question with a question. Unnerving, isn't it?"

She nodded.

"So Socrates tested men's patience and made some uncomfortable through what has become known as the Socratic Method. Prominent Athenians, many of whom had been made to look foolish or unwise in the face of Socrates' questioning, turned against him. He was accused of corrupting the city's youth, interfering with its religion, as he did not believe in the gods of Homer, and, because he was a mentor to several powerful oligarchs, opposing democracy. In 399 BC he was sentenced to death by an Athenian jury of 500 – considerably larger than our juries of today. Socrates' defense to the jury was defiant, though Xenophon, a young colleague believed Socrates purposely struck out at the jury due to his old age and a belief that he would be better off dead. Seventy years old in the fifth century BC was, after all, extremely old. He may have believed this was the right time. And so he took he own life, dying as a martyr of philosophy. With friends gathered around him in his prison cell, he drank the poison hemlock." Jensen shifted in his chair looking toward the grandfather clock on the wall leading to his private living quarters.

Looking again at the young woman he saw exuberance balanced with caution and patience masked by a veneer of nerves. "Your mother was a partner here at the firm. All of our senior people are covered by extensive insurance policies, including the Socratic Contract. It says: 'In the winter of my life, as the drifts swell over my soul, I will not burden my family and friends. I will go with my dignity, cherishing the time I have had, and know the grace of God will comfort me.'"

"Mr. Jensen, are you saying my Mom committed suicide?"

"No, honey. She chose. She chose the Socratic Contract when she became partner. She and your dad. The contract was fulfilled when she was terminally ill but before…" His train of thought was interrupted by the sound of the elevator opening in his private residence. "…Before she could no longer kiss you goodnight."

Jensen spoke in a louder voice toward the private quarters. "Come in, Elliot, and meet your new employee."

Elliot Weekly entered Jensen's office from the living quarters, introduced himself and pulled up a smaller sitting chair.

"Am I being offered a job?" she asked.

Elliot nodded and Jensen responded, "Yes, your starting salary will be $250 thousand annually and, as you progress, you should be able to increase that by fifty percent within three years."

"Wow," she said. "But how does this relate to my Mom and… you said she *chose*."

Elliot added, "You will work in the Washington, D.C. metro area out of your home. Given your age and the access that provides you, we would also like you to travel occasionally to other cities for assignments. After your training period you will usually work by yourself. Mr. Jensen has arranged for you to be on the employment roster at George Washington University Hospital as a substitute physician's assistant. That will be your cover and your entree to other health facilities or wherever your assignment takes you. Of course we want you to first complete your schooling, but we will reimburse you and your father for your tuition expenses."

She looked at the two men saying nothing. Her eyes asked a thousand questions.

Jensen said to her, "We have told you something, and nothing. The contract is here…" Jensen put his hand to his heart, "…but with full understanding" and then touched his temple. Then, turning, he said, "Elliot, it is my time." Speaking again to the young woman, Jensen said, "I have known for some months of my cancer. I am no longer able to be with my colleagues here at the firm where I have lived and worked these many years, and I have no stomach for withering away, the object of pity."

Jensen put his left hand over the back of his right. Elliot stood, leaned over and touched the black onyx stone on the third finger ring of Jensen's left hand.

"Thank you, my friend," Jensen said to Elliot.

"Is that how…" she asked.

"Elliot will meet with you tomorrow and answer all your questions," Jensen said, bracing himself on the chair arms as he rose. "Thank you for coming to see me, dear. Your mother would be pleased to see you carrying on our work." Jensen slid off the black onyx ring and handed it to Elliot. Elliot quietly left using the private elevator.

Opening the door to his office, Jensen said, "Elizabeth, would you please have my driver meet me downstairs? I'm late for my walk. My friends will be expecting me." Melancholy eyes followed the young woman to the spiral staircase. "Careful, Sarah."

DEDICATION

For Dad, who needed the Socratic Contract, but didn't have it.

For my loyal, Golden friend and constant companion Strut, who told me when it was his time.

For Rocket, my Golden son who died before his time.

AUTHOR'S NOTE

This novel uses actual locations, technology and practices. Characters may be real or combinations of personalities but, in any event, use different names. Government offices and representations are generally accurate, although some creative liberties have been taken. Insurance company names are not actual, but interactions are based on accounts taken from published or interview sources. The covert insurance company division may or may not be fabricated.

An uncomfortable subject to talk about, but in the recesses of nearly everyone's mind... Sixty-eight percent of the American public supports assisted suicide. A handful of states allow 'death with dignity' in one form or another. Yet the vast majority of the American population finds end of life something they just don't want to talk about because they don't want to, and because choice and dignity are not yet part of the equation.

Each of us knows someone, a friend or family member, whose end was described as 'It was a blessing.' The story here may serve as a catalyst for further thought on "the winter of my life."

ABOUT THE AUTHOR

Born in Arlington, Virginia and raised in McLean just outside Washington, D.C., David Colin Russell earned a BS and MBA from Virginia Tech, and made his way through school playing in five rock groups. He started his career in the Federal Government as an auditor and economist and then served on U.S. Senate staff for four years, including two years with the Senate Republican Policy Committee under John Tower of Texas. It was there he met President-Elect Reagan's campaign manager, Senator Paul Laxalt, who asked him to work on the Reagan Transition Team. Staying on for President Reagan's first term, Russell held roles of Deputy Assistant Secretary and deputy bureau chief. Moving to the private sector and Omaha, he changed gears and spent 17 years in technology, not as a coder, but in strategic planning and operations, the last six years of which he was president and chief operating officer of ACI Worldwide, where he traveled to 42 countries and helped take the company public. Taking some time off to enjoy traveling to homes in Aspen and Scottsdale with his beautiful artist wife, Sandra Dee, and their Golden Retrievers, Russell rejoined the corporate mix, this time in healthcare. He now serves as administrator for physician practices for a hospital corporation in Melbourne, Florida – a surfer, dog, and biker friendly beach community that puts a smile on your face. *The Socratic Contract* is Russell's first novel with a spinoff, *Vengeance, Inc.*, planned for next year.

www.DCRussell.com

Made in the USA
Lexington, KY
02 November 2015